SIMON FAIRFAX
A DEAL TOO FAR

This is the second book in the Rupert Brett Deal series.
The current titles are listed below in chronological order:

By Simon Fairfax

A Deadly Deal

A Deal Too Far

A Deal With The Devil

A Deal On Ice

Medieval Series

A Knight and a Spy 1410

A Knight and a Spy 1411

To my son Jamie, my harshest critic!

With lots of love.

Chapter One

England, November 1990

It was eerily still. None of the natural world's creatures were stirring, but after a while the shapes of four men could be made out, moving stealthily, bent at the waist and knees, crouching for concealment and against the cold, cradling their rifles to their chests. It had been a long night, and a damp, cold and miserable one. The mist hovered above the patches of swamp and marsh grass, seeping into the bones like the chill bite of cancer. The dawn light was breaking, bringing with it the promise of a watery winter sun. Trees that a few minutes earlier had been nothing but the suggestions of grey shadows were now taking shape and form. The terrain was undulating heath and woodland, with sandy grey flint and soil paths cutting through the vegetation. Occasionally, the foul smell of boggy mud or marsh gas permeated the air as one of the four men inadvertently left the track. Despite their camouflage clothing, the coming dawn outlined them against the paths, and they were faced with having to abandon the path to seek shelter among the bracken, trees and humps of gorse, or they would be found.

But leaving the path meant delaying their objective. It was a fine balance: press on quickly and risk discovery or retreat and use more stealth under cover of the landscape. The leader of the group motioned to the other three soldiers to follow him. They left the track and squatted down in a natural hollow behind some gorse bushes. The rustle of bracken sounded like shattering ice to the tautly strung group. White eyes blinked out from camouflaged faces, shielded by camouflaged helmets. The leader took out a map and produced a torch which cast a dull red glow that he shrouded beneath his open jacket, ensuring no light was emitted to the surrounding area.

In the quietest of whispers he pointed and said: "There, about 450 metres from the base of that slope. That's where the guard is that we have to take out. The gorse will provide cover, but we go in, and we go slow and silent. No rushing."

The landscape before them rose steeply to a crest before flattening out onto a natural plateau. Behind then a wide rutted track, shining in the ambient light gave vehicular access to the plateau. The leader extinguished his torch and the four men moved off in single file, carefully placing each booted foot on the ground, curling from the outside edge inwards as they had been taught to produce minimum disturbance and sound. They moved stealthily towards their objective, their SA80 automatic rifles tucked into their shoulders ready to secure and fire. Periodically checking through the Susat night sights despite the growing dawn light, they moved as quickly and quietly as they could from one patch of cover to the next, with the tail end Charlie constantly turning to cover their six.

Their senses were raised to breaking point as they strained to pick up any sound that couldn't be attributed to natural sources. Each of them was perspiring despite the cold – more through fear of discovery than exertion. The leader raised a hand in the gloom, signalling them to halt. They stopped dead, motionless, ears straining and eyes alert, each trooper facing outwards to the peripheries, covering the other team members' blind spots. The leader's instinct told him something was wrong, but he didn't know what. It just felt wrong. But the objective was only a hundred yards away. *Get in,* he thought, *do the damage and get out.*

He motioned his team forward by circling his hand slowly and pointing with one finger. Each soldier copied the action, ensuring the man behind had seen it. Each man raised himself into the familiar crouch, maintaining a low profile and moving off as silently as possible, beginning the ascent as the team met the start of the incline. The climb was short, with deeply cushioning heather underfoot now, and only the occasional swish of bracken gave any notice of their passing. They skirted a small group of greyish rocks canopied by a clump of trees and crept forward.

Then their world exploded in a flash of light and noise: a tripwire had detonated a Thunder Flash ambush. The disorientating banshee wail and bright white light temporary blinded them, ruining their night vision. A snap and crackle of gunfire from BFAs split the air, adding to the confusion. Figures appeared immediately, blows were struck and the four turned according to IA drill and began firing, but they were thrown to the ground; rolling over and trying to escape amid cries of "Down! Down!" Rifle barrels appeared in their faces as the four men were covered by another group of camouflaged soldiers and laid into by the attacking force. They lay with on the ground their hands above their heads.

A figure in a high-viz vest and a white armband appeared from behind a rock. "Right, you four. You're dead. Armbands off and give me your tags." The DS commanded, holding out his hand. "OK, back off to the RV point at the top of the hill and report in."

"Hah, we had you!" shouted one of the capturing force, gleefully slapping the leader on the shoulder. "Heard you from miles away, like a herd of fucking elephants!" he said grinning under his camo paint.

"Bollocks," the group leader rubbed his shoulder and arms ruefully where rifle butts and kicks had landed none too gently. "You didn't have a clue until your little toy told you we were here."

The remark was heralded by jeering and good-natured banter from the captors as the four men headed for the RV point and a welcome mug of tea. The team leader removed his camouflaged hat, ran his hand through his wavy brown hair and rubbed his blue eyes to remove the mixture of dust and sweat from them. At thirty, he was in good shape. The daily runs helped, as did the TA training, keeping his six-foot frame lean and muscled. There was no sign of any middle aged paunch, something he'd noticed on many of the other surveyors in the West End after a few too many company lunches and nights on the piss. But he was annoyed with himself and turned to his colleagues as they walked up the hill.

"I am so pissed off. We were so close. Bloody trip wires and flash bangs!" He snorted in disgust.

"Ah don't worry, boss. I reckon we got closer than anyone else, and we did better than the last exercise. Still, we would be dead or captured now I suppose if this were the real thing..." Corporal Dixon said, leaving the comments hanging in the air.

"Cheers Clive, you always make me feel so much better. But it'll be a lot warmer in the Gulf if we ever get there and the rag-heads won't be able to hide the wires under bracken like they can here. There's no cover in the desert," the leader said. The others laughed and moved eagerly up the hill to the waiting brew and maybe a bacon butty.

Sergeant Rupert Brett and his three-man team were all members of The London Regiment of the TA, the only army reserve regiment in the Guards Division. They had been taking part in night exercises at the Longmoor training area and orienteering grounds at Liss in Hampshire. The regiment recruited from all over the Greater London area and all members of the four-man team lived and worked in the Capital. Rupert was a commercial surveyor and the other three members were respectively an accountant, a lawyer and a mechanic

It was nearing the end of September 1990, and the Gulf War was raging in Iraq, hoping to bring down Saddam Hussein and his regime. Operation Desert Storm had started the previous month, but it looked unlikely that any more Territorial Army regiments would be called upon to help before the war had been won. If anything, they'd find themselves part of the mopping up operation. Desert Storm looked like being a brutal but short-lived engagement, with American and British forces driving across the desert with the aim of putting an end to the dictator and his puppet regime. The war and the build up to it had concentrated all military forces in the area, calling for most of the UK's military strength to be deployed. This was the first major conflict the UK had seen since the Falklands in 1982 and it had given the whole country a focus – which according to most political pundits would most likely lead to another landslide khaki election for the Conservatives in a couple of years' time

"How do you feel about it, Rupert?" Clive asked. "I mean, half of me feels like I want to go out there and get stuck in while the other half is scared shitless."

"Don't let the officers hear you talking like that," one of the others commented, "they'll go apeshit on you. That's coward's talk, Corporal!"

The banter continued until they reached the RV point; a NAAFI tent located on the plateau above the scene of their ambush.

Two hours later, the small teams had been debriefed and were heading for the White Fleet that had brought them to the training grounds, the four tonners trundling behind them bringing the NAAFI tent and the heavier ordnance. There was a two hour trip ahead of them, swaying to and fro, dozing in the back of the troop carriers taking them back to the barracks in Clapham. The soldiers would have time enough to consider the possibility of deployment and what it would mean to each of them.

Chapter Two

London

The London office of surveyors where Rupert Brett worked had once been known as Halpern and Beams. It was in Grosvenor Street, set in a large double-fronted Georgian building that had been converted into offices. As a result of a corporate American takeover, the building now housed one of the largest firms in the West End. Although the older members of staff still thought of it as H & B, it was now officially known as HBJ, newly branded after being taken over by Jarvis International. The new owners were happy enough with either title, it gave them some leverage when it came to maintaining H & B's identifiable brand and image.

With the fall of the Berlin wall in 1989 and the opening of the Iron Curtain, the world had become a different place as new international markets opened up. John Major's first move as Prime Minister had been to join the European Exchange Rate Mechanism, effectively pegging the UK's economy to Europe's, with disastrous results. This was felt particularly strongly in the property market, which after the boom of the late 1980s had fallen into decline as the country slid into a deep recession. Residential repossessions were up, markets were falling, house prices were dropping and funds were chasing a falling market. Yields were moving out monthly, meaning that no-one could match the book value of a property unless the circumstances were pretty special. As a net result, agents and surveyors, the deal-hungry characters who had made their mark over the last few years, were suffering badly.

International companies such as Jarvis International had American funds behind them, and had seen the perfect opportunity to buy established UK firms that were only too pleased to allow themselves to be bailed out at discounted prices. After the takeover, Rupert had moved to HBJ following the closure of MAS Investments and the part he had played in the imprisonment of its director, Paul Simions. After the death of a former lover – a murder he had stood accused of for a few nightmare weeks – Rupert had worked under cover for a shady police department tracking fraud in the city. He had helped bring Simions down, risking his life in the process and realising that in the final analysis he was a disposable pawn in a much larger game. Simions was guilty of a lot more than he was charged with, including the murder of the woman Rupert had been growing to love and his own partner, David Shingler, whose body was never found. The memories were still raw, and Rupert could not have gone back to his former employers, Cowell Rubens, where it had all started. With his unique experience and particular talents, he was in demand for agency roles and had been headhunted by HBJ with the promise of a junior partnership in the investment department – or Capital Markets as the Americans referred to it. One of the benefits of his new job was that he had his own glass partitioned office looking out over the dealing floor of the open plan office, which played host to six state-of-the-art workstations for the exclusive use of the investment team

After his chilly weekend on Longmoor training grounds, Rupert was at his desk early on Monday morning, getting a head start before the rest of the team came in. In place of his army fatigues, he was wearing a grey Birdseye suit with a silk paisley handkerchief protruding from the jacket pocket and black brogues which he had propped up on the desk in front of him. With a Dictaphone in one hand, he contemplated the two sales instructions he had won last week and wondered how in the name of God he was going to market them and get them sold for the price his clients expected.

Sales weren't impossible, he considered, but they had to be pitched correctly, and he knew only too well from his own experience that if the price he asked was unrealistically high, no one in this market would attempt to negotiate; they would just file it away in a thick pile of other no hopers.

Who the hell, he thought, *am I going to sell this prime bit of kit to?* The main buyers coming through were foreign funds looking to buy into a solid leasing system provided by UK lettings, but such clients were few and far between. He thought he might need to run an off-market campaign and keep everyone thinking that they had some kind of exclusivity. *If you can't play to their pockets, play to their egos,* he reasoned.

He was dictating the particulars of the sales into his Dictaphone when his phone rang.

"Brett," he answered. The receptionist said told him the caller was Simon Dove, his CO from the TA.

"Dove? Sure, put him through," *What the hell,* he thought, *he never calls me at the office.* "Sir?" he said, removing his feet from the desk as if somehow Dove could see him.

"Rupert, morning to you. How are you feeling after the weekend's exercise? I hear you did pretty well, almost made it. Your CBSA report was excellent."

Rupert thanked him and made some modest remark and the

conversation flowed along these lines for a couple of minutes as Rupert wondered what he wanted. Dove finally came to the point.

"Rupert, we need to meet. Something has come up that I need to discuss with you."

"OK – I mean yes, of course, sir." He hesitated "What's it about, if you don't mind me asking? Is it about the weekend?"

"I'm not going to talk about it over the telephone, but in answer to your question, indirectly yes. Can we meet up tomorrow after work? 7pm, dinner on me? Excellent. No, not at the barracks, let me give you the address, have you got a pen?"

Rupert scribbled down the address, and they said goodbye. Rupert put the phone down. *Bloody hell*, he thought as he looked at his pad: it was an address in Knightsbridge – the location of the Special Forces Club.

Chapter Three

Whitehall

Foreign Secretary Douglas Hurd was shown into Tom King's inner office. The Secretary of State's room was well furnished and deeply carpeted. A chandelier hung from the ceiling and various prints and photographs of battles, soldiers and uniformed men adorned the walls. The room was bathed in an odd reflective light due to the armoured glass panes in the windows, security measures that had been installed after previous IRA attacks and threats.

Hurd, whom the media had started referring to as Mr Whippy because of his shock of wavy white hair, walked across the deep carpet with his customary erect bearing, adjusting his dark-framed spectacles nervously, a little apprehensive about this meeting with his counterpart in defence. The two men had been at Cambridge together and although they were friends – if such a concept could ever pertain for colleagues in the political arena – Hurd was acutely aware of the ramifications of what they were about to discuss. The news he had to impart would not be welcomed.

Tom King rose as Hurd entered. He came around his desk

with a genuine smile of warmth and welcome on his florid face. He did not look well, and his responsibility for Britain's involvement in the Gulf over the last three months was clearly taking its toll. Hurd noticed that behind the horn-rimmed spectacles more lines had appeared, and flashes of grey were showing in the sandy hair at King's temples.

"Douglas, good to see you," King said, shaking hands warmly with Hurd and indicating a circular table surrounded by armchairs to his right. He motioned for him to sit. "Thank you for coming over, it's pretty bloody hectic at the moment. Saddam appears to be fighting on. The bugger's invaded Kuwait and has plans for the Saudi oilfields. I'm sure our American friends will stop him, but you never know…" He left the sentence hanging in the air with a shrug of his shoulders, the slight inflection of his native Devon burr still evident in his speech.

Hurd sat down with a smile and a polite, deprecating wave of his hand. They were both career politicians, they both knew that this was not going to be an easy meeting. Tea that had previously been set out on the circular antique table was offered and accepted, and King poured, each man taking a few moments to enjoy the time-honoured ritual of civilised diplomacy. The ticking of the clock above the beautifully carved ornate fireplace filled the short silence.

"How are things really going out there?" Hurd asked.

"Well enough," King replied succinctly. "If war can ever be said to be going well. But it's the Americans I'm more concerned about." Hurd raised his eyebrows at this news, eager to hear more. "I have a very uncomfortable feeling that they don't want to finish the job," King continued. "The indications I'm getting point to the idea that they'll be happy enough to take back Kuwait just because they can, but when they've put Saddam back in his place they'll stop at the gates of Baghdad and leave him in place as a puppet dictator – with them pulling the strings."

Hurd nodded as though this was no surprise to him. "And that's what we get from the Yanks for helping them, is it?" he replied. "I've heard similar intelligence to that effect from my department. Bloody Americans. It's all down to the oil rights of course, when is it not in the Middle East? The Yanks are the largest consumers of oil in the world, and dear old George needs to keep it cheap to buy himself a few votes to make this whole farce seem more worthwhile. Same old story, I'm afraid. It'll shape the politics and power of the oil-producing countries for the foreseeable future, of course, and we'll say yes to whatever the Americans want no matter who's in charge. Might be good politics to lose an election or two soon. We all know that if the only commodity in the whole Middle Eastern region was sand and a few camels the Americans wouldn't give a flying whatnot about who did what to whom or why."

Both men laughed and King reached out for a Custard Cream.

"Anyway," Hurd continued, "that brings me on to why I wanted to speak with you about. All potentially related in a way, I suppose."

"Go on," King offered, a worrying frown appearing upon his face

"As I'm sure you know, we've been keeping close tabs upon Argentina ever since the Falklands. We have two very good MI6 operatives there, attached to the embassy, and they're picking up information which is starting to worry us a little. Humphrey and Dawcett have raised their own concerns and we don't want a repeat of what happened in 83." Hurd was referring to Humphrey Maud, the British ambassador in Buenos Aires and Squadron Leader Dawcett, senior military attaché. "We've been advised in the strongest terms that we should take the verbal threats being voiced by the Argentinean government seriously. They aren't just rattling sabres, which is what we thought before, and it wasn't until they walked into Georgia that we actually believed the blighters."

King considered the information. He got up from the table and walked back to his desk, where he pulled a file from the top right-hand drawer. Back at the table, he passed the document to Hurd. "This is the latest report from Dawcett. It bears out your suspicions, but you'll see that there's nothing concrete. No military build-up that we can see – and where would they get the funds, never mind the physical armament? Even Margaret's boy would know better than to sell them guns, and there's no way they can afford it anyway, we made sure of that. They're still a broken nation, both militarily and financially.

"The problem we have, of course, is that we only restored diplomatic relations earlier this year, with a token foothold care of the Swiss Embassy keeping the door open for us. Cheese and chocolate, Douglas, that's all the Swiss are good for – that and holding everybody's money when the handbags start swinging. So there's no diplomatic staff, no receptions and every member of HMG out there is looked upon with suspicion and resentment. Not a hope of moving freely, especially near the military bases. If by some miracle the Argies have found the financial wherewithal to re-arm, we've no reasonable excuse to go wandering around the country checking, and the last thing we want is another William Cross on our hands!" he finished, making reference to the British military attaché to Dar es Salaam, who had recently been caught taking photographs of military and nuclear installations before being caught and thrown out of the country for spying.

"Yes, quite," King mused, thinking of the furore and embarrassment the incident had caused. "Well what do you propose to do?"

"The situation is exactly what spies were invented for, Tom. I'm waiting to hear back from Dawcett, who's currently running one of the two Six operatives – chap by the name of Andrew

Waddington. He's following up a lead. In the meantime, I've arranged a meeting of the Security Council where I plan to put forward a proposal based on what we learn from our man in Buenos Aires. We have someone in mind who may be able to move freely and pass information. Someone not directly associated with us, who may be able to pass under the radar. Full deniability, of course."

"Do we keep John in the loop?"

Hurd shook his head. "Best not. Margaret would have been a different matter, of course. Bit more mature in that respect, bless her." He smiled thinly as he outlined his plan in more detail to his colleague. The meeting ended and each wished the other good day. Hurd left the building deep in thought and considered what they had discussed over the last half an hour as he travelled back to King Charles Street in his government Jaguar. *Not good*, he concluded, *not good at all.*

Chapter Four

Buenos Aires

If the weather in England was cold, the opposite was the case in Buenos Aires. The deep-seated heat was omnipresent, a buffer of warm air that insulated the city against any other climatic influences. When the sun finally set, it left a clear starlit night, but little relief from the daytime temperatures. The night was a steady 30 degrees.

The British Embassy in BA was a beautiful Edwardian building set in its own grounds on Dr. Luis Agote Street in the Recoleta area, commanding views across the nearby parks and squares in one of the most elegant districts of the city. The Recoleta housed some of the city's most beautiful and culturally rich buildings. Art galleries and museums bordered the streets that led out in a radial pattern from the central square and the famous Recoleta Cemetery, providing the country's major tourist attraction. It was composed of wide open spaces and streets, and unlike other areas of the City it was safe for tourists day and night. Having been under Swiss control with no direct contact since the Falklands conflict, the newly opened Embassy had just held a reception with a view to fostering better relation-ships within the capital. The British were hoping to encourage an *entente cordiale* with their counterparts in the *Ministerio de Relaciones Exteriores y Culto* – Argentina's Ministry of Foreign Affairs and Worship.

Andrew Waddington and Valentina Perez stepped out of the gates of the British Embassy onto Dr.Luis Agote Street arm in arm, to be embraced by the warm wind blowing from the park opposite. It was mid-evening, and the streets were still busy with tourists and locals out for an evening stroll. The smell of dusty streets, fragrant Jasmine and Plumbago mingled in the air to create a heady cocktail of scents. They had met a few weeks ago at a formal reception when Waddington had visited the newly finished MREC building on Esmeralda 1212 to the east of the City, close to the bay area and the park of the Plaza San Martin. The MREC had recently opened its doors and was deliberately courting the British, giving them immediate cause for suspicion and concern even as they welcomed the overtures of Argentinian government with apparently open political and diplomatic arms. The reception had been a perfunctory affair: a mannered and tightly controlled political evening, carefully and diplomatically sweeping under the carpet both the Conflict of 1982 and the ensuing repercussions. The fact that the MREC was also responsible for the Foreign Office and certain elements of the Argentinian internal secret service had not been entirely lost on the British contingent.

Valentina had been there in a semi-official capacity, adding colour and sparkle to the affair. Like so many well-bred Argentine women, she was tall and slim, with dark blonde hair that bespoke a lineage of foreign ancestry (many Argentines had married Irish Immigrants in the early 1800s), with long legs, a café-au-lait skin and slightly slanting, almost oriental brown eyes. Andrew had been immediately attracted to her, and the feeling was obviously mutual. He felt that she could be useful to him and had therefore decided to combine business with pleasure. He had courted her patiently over the following weeks.

Waddington was slightly taller than Valentina, and as they sauntered down the street away from the British Embassy he demonstrated their growing closeness with a carefully placed arm around her waist

"Well, that was all very tame, formal and safe, wasn't it?" he commented, laughing with her.

"I know," she replied huskily in a strong local accent, accentuating the 's' in her English pronunciation; "let's go somewhere more exciting and real, shall we?"

"I am all yours. You can be my local guide," he replied as she flagged a taxi. During the short journey she described how the real BA could be found in the barrio La Boca and the area's raw tango clubs and bars.

"It is where the real locals go to enjoy themselves." she said. Andrew for his part knew the dangers of this barrio; like so many areas of big cities the world over it was in turn very safe and extremely dangerous, a place where everything changed from one street to the next.

The brightly coloured buildings of the barrio were famous, and by day they were a magnetic tourist attraction, but by night it was a different story. Andrew was no innocent abroad, and his MI6 training left him in no doubts about what to expect and how to deal with it. He need not have worried; the taxi dropped them in the Avenue Don Pedro de Mendoza, close to the waterfront and a thriving club Carminto, where Valentina assured him he would see the best Tango dancing ever.

When they entered through the bright red doors, their senses were assailed by the thick atmosphere of smoke, raunchy music, heavy sickly perfume and sweat, mingling to create an exotic mix. They managed to get a table close to the floorshow, with Valentina exerting some sublime charm and a little flirtatious banter with the manager, where it was evident that she was known. After some good dances, Valentina squeezed his hand and whispered, "watch this now."

The spotlight emerged from the subdued lighting, highlighting an extraordinary performance from a slick, sexy couple timing their every move to the haunting brassy notes of the band. Their interpretation was mesmerising and had everyone entranced: the applause at the end of their display was rapturous and earned them a well-deserved encore.

A couple of hours later they decided to leave. Andrew paid the bill and they moved through the crowd and out onto the street. A combination of the night air and brandy on top of the champagne from the reception seemed to hit Valentina quickly, and she staggered and sighed, leaning into Andrew's arm for balance. As she did so, he momentarily lost his balance himself in an effort to support her, stepping off the kerb and straightening his shoulders to support Valentina's slight weight.

The Mitsubishi Montero that had been cruising slowly and inconspicuously some 50 yards behind them accelerated fast, the wheels spinning in a squeal of rubber despite the four wheel drive and the heavy weight of the car. Alerted by the sound, Andrew just had time to twist his neck and glance over his right shoulder to see the vehicle bearing down upon him. What caused him more alarm and a split second of frozen fear was the partially open door scything across the pavement as the Mitsubishi closed in upon him. The sound of steel against flesh came with a sickening thud as the car caught Waddington on his exposed hip. The force of the blow knocked him from his feet and he was quickly caught a second time by the partially open door, spinning his shoulder and driving his head to the pavement where it bounced viciously up and then back down.

Andrew Waddington lay still. Blood seeped from the crack in his skull and Valentina, who had been caught by the fall was on her knees beside him trying to support his head as the car screamed off and turned down the next street, disappearing from view. For a split second there was silence, and then the night air was torn by the sound of Valentina, screaming at the top of her voice in a manic wail.

Onlookers and pedestrians rushed forward. One or two ran into the nearest bars to demand phones to call an ambulance. Valentina continued screaming in shock, but her screams subsided into a mewing sound as Waddington's blood seeped into the channels between the pavement slabs, running dark red. The ambulance arrived quickly – it was only a short distance from the Hospital Pacifico Assistencia Jose Tiburco Borda to the northwest of the barrio. The medics assessed the situation quickly, then strapped the prostate form of Waddington onto the stretcher, lifted him carefully into the ambulance and sped away, sirens wailing and lights flashing. Valentina was not allowed to accompany him and was left distraught and in tears on the pavement. After a while someone brought her a brandy which she swallowed gratefully, and someone else hailed a cab for her and she was carried away in the wake of the ambulance.

But after they'd disappeared from view of the crowd of spectators, she gave instructions to the driver to take her to her apartment. Bursting into her living room some fifteen minutes later, she ran to the telephone, dialled a number and ranted in staccato Spanish when it was answered.

"You weren't supposed to kill him!" was the gist of what she said.

"He's dead? Ah well, the fortunes of war. Now, listen pull yourself together, do the expected thing and call the embassy. Tell them what has happened. Cry, be upset, just as you are. Do it now before you calm down!" the voice commanded and the call was terminated

She sobbed as the line was cut – a mixture of fear, anger and genuine compassion for Andrew. It was never meant to get this serious. But what should she have expected working for the Government? They were as ruthless and fanatical as they had always been. She dialled a number for the British embassy and burst into tears halfway through telling one of the embassy secretaries on night duty what had happened. Details were taken and the call finished with a promise to keep her informed of any funeral arrangements.

Alarm bells rang in the embassy; night staff were put on alert. Ambassador Humphrey Maud and his attaché, Squadron Leader Dawcett, were notified. Senior staff left their warm beds and rushed in. Waddington's partner and MI6 operative appeared in the briefing room, dishevelled and with an angry and determined look on her face. Sophie Carswell was of medium height and build, athletic but not masculine. Her open looks were neither striking nor plain, but could be made up either way as the situation required. She was a perfect Six operative. She and Andrew had been a good team and she wanted answers and revenge, in that order.

"What do we know?" she demanded, taking a seat opposite the Ambassador.

"We have checked with the Jose Tiburico, and despite what his companion thought, he is not dead. He has a broken hip, a smashed shoulder and bleeding on the brain. They have relieved the pressure on the skull and are keeping him in an induced coma to see how he responds. He could still die – the next 24 hours are critical, so they tell me. The staff are very good at Jose; they see a lot of street violence at the A & E. He's in good hands. We have placed a discreet security presence outside his room and he is being monitored around the clock." Dawcett spoke in clipped, unemotional tones

"Who was with him?" Carswell demanded. "That bloody woman from the MREC? You know he was getting close, and this is how they shut him down. But to kill him – or at least try to – isn't that going just a little too far for a "friendly" nation? I need to report this back to Six" She turned to leave, furious and upset; Andrew was a good friend. As she turned, Dawcett's voice called her back.

"Sophie, we don't know for certain it was a hit. It could just be an accident, an unlucky coincidence; La Boca can be a dangerous place, and they drive like lunatics in this bloody city at the best of times. You of all people know that. We cannot just assume he was a target."

"Don't you think it's a bit too much of a coincidence?" she responded sarcastically, motioning with finger and thumb a fraction of an inch apart, "that this should happen now, just when the intelligence was starting to flow. Surely this proves our suspicions are right. Somehow, he must have had his cover blown. He was due to head up north to Corrientes with her this weekend on a summer trip to see the Ugazu Falls. Just coincidence that they'll happen to pass a major military base on the way. They've figured it out. They know. They are on to us – or at least Andrew. So no more embassy staff, and no more replacements. They're too easily spotted. Make your report, I will make mine. We need to find another solution and quickly." She stormed out as politely as political etiquette permitted.

Dawcett and Maud exchanged glances, both silently agreeing with each other. "She's got a point," Maud said. "And as upset as she is, it's a valid one. I believe that the FO will now take this seriously. But how exactly we proceed given the constraints Sophie outlined so succinctly I am not entirely certain," he finished.

"Oh, I believe that there are already contingency plans in place for this kind of thing," Dawcett replied. "And I for one do not intend to be the second military attaché to wind up with egg on his face for not ensuring that such a stern warning was received and acted upon."

"Leave it with me," Maud said, raising an eyebrow in acknowledgement of the cryptic remark that referred to a previous MA who had been forced to resign over just such an issue. "It'll be mid evening in London. Probably won't even have to get anyone out of bed."

He left to file a report to his superiors in London. The evening operators were in for a bit of action, he thought.

Chapter Five

London

The late afternoon weather had changed to a steady drizzle. The sort of fine rain that's deceptive, as it seeps through clothes and bones quicker than a more persistent downpour. 'Wet rain', Rupert's grandmother had always called it, and as he walked across Whitehall towards King Charles Street he reflected that while he had always smiled indulgently at this description, perhaps his grandmother had the right of it. It did not bode well for the meeting ahead of him, which he was approaching with more than a little apprehension, a little non-plussed at the nature of the subject matter. His thoughts were similar to someone with a guilty conscience being faced with a policeman on the doorstep, whose first conclusion is 'What have I done wrong?'

Rupert thought back to last week's meeting with his CO, Simon Dove, at the Special Forces club. He had found the club in a quiet street in the middle of Knightsbridge, identified by a small brass plaque displaying only the street number. Dove met him at the door and showed him around, and they'd finally walked up to the dining room via a staircase whose walls were lined with photographs of past heroes and heroines from the Second World War to the present day, together with a short tribute to their valour and the deeds they had performed on behalf of their country. Looking at the photos of the brave men and women, he'd felt humbled to be there, aware of the comparatively small part he might be called upon to play in the near future in the Middle East. Over dinner, and despite being in one of the safest and most secure places in the UK, Dove spoke in hushed and cryptic tones about his reasons for wanting to meet with Rupert.

"You're probably wondering what this is all about, and I'm sorry but I still can't tell you too much. We're waiting for an update on events and it could be that your services won't be required after all. If they're not, it's best you don't know too much – but if they were, would you be prepared to help us with a little matter abroad?" Dove said.

Rupert's first response was predictable. "Iraq? Of course, it's what we've been trained for. A lot us in the TA have all been expecting the call, but why me? Why the cloak and dagger stuff?"

"No Rupert," Dove replied. "It won't be Iraq, and it won't be straightforward soldiering. You have certain qualifications and a specific skillset. It might not be obvious to you, but you fit the bill perfectly for what we have in mind."

Rupert raised an eyebrow and motioned for Dove to continue

"So my question is, would you be prepared to help us and travel abroad? It would of course be very important to the security of the nation."

"Well, from what little you have told me, yes, at least in principle," Rupert answered. "But what exactly do you want me to do, and how long would it take? I have a career too, you know, and the last time I got involved in all kinds of skulduggery for Superintendent Webster I was kidnapped and nearly killed. I don't really want to go there again, I'd prefer a bit of God's honest soldiering," he finished.

"Like I said, I can't go into details, but all I need right now is an indication that you are, in principle, prepared to consider our proposition. HM government will be pulling the strings, of course – and I can assure you that what we are looking to do will have no adverse effect upon your career. Quite the opposite, I'd imagine," he finished cryptically.

Rupert sighed, shaking his head in disbelief. "So it's not Iraq, but you won't tell me where it is. And it's not soldiering, but you won't tell me *what* it is. All you'll tell me is that it's for the benefit of my country. Which of course is why I joined the TA. So yes, I'll listen in principle, but I reserve the right to say no. Will that do for you?"

There was a pause. Rupert suspected that Dove was on the brink of saying no, but he wondered how many others would fit the specific criteria Dove was asking for, and he wasn't surprised when the other man nodded abruptly.

They finished their meal and Rupert found himself with an appointment at the Foreign Office in two days' time.

As he passed through the archway off the street that led to the entrance of the FO, he found that his body had gone into fight or flight mode as a surge of adrenalin flew through him. *Come on*, he thought to himself, *I've been shot at, beaten up, kidnapped, threatened and lived on the edge spying for the police undercover. Why should I be afraid now?* He shrugged, and grinned wryly to himself; *I'm an investment surveyor, not some kind of James Bond!* The voice that nagged at the back of his mind would not be entirely silenced.

He closed his umbrella as he approached the metal gates, where he was met by a civilian guard who took his name, checked it against a list on a clipboard and allowed him through to the next gate, where he was passed through by two policemen. He was then confronted by a rather shabby reception area where he was given a visitor's pass and asked to take a seat. Within a short space of time, a severe looking secretary appeared who bore little resemblance to the Miss Moneypenny he was expecting. She confirmed his name and asked him to follow her into the bowels of the building. After negotiating numerous corridors they turned a corner, where Rupert found himself in a large and elegantly proportioned hallway with pictures on the walls of former heads of state and a general feeling of gravitas and hushed power. A wide and magnificent pink marble staircase swept upwards, dividing at a mezzanine landing to form two graceful branches. They ascended, and upon reaching the galleried landing of the upper floor Rupert was shown into a waiting room and offered tea, which he accepted.

The room was completely different to the previous reception area: it was opulent, resplendent with antiques, portraits and a beautiful clock that sat upon an ornate mantelpiece ticking loudly. Rupert was reminded of a bomb, one of those old fashioned ones with an analogue clockface moving backwards, counting down. This room, he was to learn, was used to humble waiting ambassadors who'd had the effrontery to cross Her Majesty's Government and were being kept waiting prior to an audience with the Minister or Home Secretary. The room was open across one entire wall, and large windows offered a panoramic view out onto the square below, where more important visitors were permitted to enter. Rupert stood at the window, watching the activity below through the curtain of drizzle, his mind racing.

The door opened some five minutes after the appointed time and the same secretary appeared, slightly less severe in manner this time and asked him to follow her with what might even be described as a slight smile.

She opened another door for him and showed him into a substantial office. Half panelled walls, deep carpet and a large oval table gave the impression of an old members club – an impression which to a certain extent was quite accurate, he reflected. Simon Dove was there; he rose from his seat and quickly walked across the room to shake Rupert's hand in welcome.

"Rupert, so glad you could join us. Now please allow me to introduce you to these gentlemen"

The company consisted of four other men. They were a disparate group, completely different in most aspects save one: they all carried an aura of power, strength and a firm belief in their ability to wield it. The first to be introduced was Paul Robinson, one of Douglas Hurd's lackeys. He was a junior cabinet minister for the Foreign office; a short compact man of about forty, with a strong handshake, a determined demeanour and the quiet certainty of a civil servant. Next was Richard Johnston, head of MI6, a man of about 50 with the figure of an ageing athlete going slightly to fat, but with the steely eyes of a predator. A man who Rupert recognised came forward, hand extended. Tall and sparse, with greying hair neatly combed, wearing the uniform and rank of rear admiral. James Fisher was a familiar figure; he'd been one of the senior advisors to Margaret Thatcher during the Falklands war.

Finally, the fourth man came forward. About the same height as Rupert at just over 6 feet, he was easily the youngest present. Dark, slightly wavy hair; tanned skin drawn tightly over prominent cheekbones with premature crow's feet around his eyes that spoke of long hours abroad in hot climates squinting against the sun. He appeared to be made of corded sinew rather than bulk and muscle. There was a natural power to his grip, enhanced by unnaturally thick fingers and joints that told of either manual work or work with horses; either that or intense, hard physical training. Rupert suspected that it was the latter, a thought that was confirmed with the introduction.

"This is Sergeant Chris Adams of 22 SAS, he's on secondment

from their RWW section and he'll be joining us for today's briefing," Dove finished.

The introduction made Rupert look at Simon Dove with a deep questioning expression. He knew that the RWW (the Revolutionary Warfare Wing, sometimes called the Increment) was an elite section within the SAS, which was effectively an elite group itself. If Chris Adams was part of such a unit, he was surely at the top of his game. *What does all this have to do with a part-time soldier and a career surveyor?* he asked himself.

Dove gestured for Rupert and the others to sit around the table, then he began.

"As I am responsible for you being here today, I thought it best to explain our situation, and then the others can answer questions and explain the position from their point of view. Obviously you have signed the Official Secrets Act so it goes without saying that everything discussed today comes under that ordnance, but this goes deeper, as you will soon find out. Nothing, not even to loved ones or colleagues, must leave this room unless authorised."

He looked questioningly at Rupert who gave an affirmative nod of his head. "Or you'll have to kill me, no doubt," he said. The quip was met with stony silence.

"Yes, good," Dove continued, "The problem we have concerns Argentina and its ongoing quest to secure the Falklands – or Las Malvinas, as they will insist on calling it." The comment elicited a few tight grins.

Rupert's head shot round. He had not seen this coming at all. *What the hell had this to do with me?* he thought.

"As you will probably be aware, we have only recently been considered *persona grata* in Buenos Aires again and our embassy has re-opened after camping out on the Swiss embassy's floor for the last seven years. Since this re-opening there has been a tacit agreement between our two countries – an *entente cordiale*, if you will. This of course is little more than surface deep, and tensions run a little higher underneath all the well-mannered diplomacy. And now, despite all the canapes and ambassador's receptions, we have strong reasons to believe that Argentina is planning a second Falklands invasion." Dove paused, letting that bombshell of a statement sink in. Rupert strove to keep his face as straight as he could. "This has been confirmed in a rather critical manner over the last 24 hours," he said, looking across the table at Richard Johnston as he spoke.

"MI6 has had two operatives inserted in the embassy as staff since the re-opening. One of them was getting rather close to some vital information, and had a perfectly legitimate reason – through an Argentine connection – to travel up-country within reach of the major military base that launched the last invasion.

"However, his proximity to that information proved his undoing, and he is now in hospital with at best a 50% chance of recovery. In short, his cover was blown and steps were taken – we can only assume by the Argentine government – to negate his efforts permanently. Which brings us to the problem in hand: everyone at the embassy or attached to it is under suspicion from the minute they arrive there. The embassy's just re-opened, so all the staff are new. The Argentinians believe – not without justification, it has to be said – that we're planting spies left, right and centre, so they're watching everyone, and no amount of diplomatic status or titles will change the perception that they are spies or potential agents."

Dove paused, giving Rupert a chance to speak. "I understand, but I still don't see how I fit in. I am certainly no trained spy."

"Which is precisely why you would be of use to us. What we need is a perfect cover, not a manufactured one. Someone with a legitimate history who is not connected with HMG at all; someone who has a legitimate background and a reason to travel to and within Argentina without drawing attention to himself.

"Now, as I'm sure you know, HBJ – or more particularly Jarvis International – is very keen on global expansion into new and emerging capital markets."

The penny was beginning to drop for Rupert with alarming clarity. *Here we go again,* he thought, *another undercover operation in a foreign country – this time one that's ruled by a brutal regime with no love for the British. What could possibly go wrong?*

"Now, what you will not be aware of yet is that HBJ are about to open a new office in BA, and they'll need a European or American property expert, someone who can bring in European and international investors who wish to be exposed to the excitement and risk of the Argentine markets. They will shortly be advertising for two European surveyors and a secretary to complement the existing team they have sourced from within the BA market. They will of course need an investment specialist." Dove stopped and looked directly at Rupert, as did the other men around the table. The trap had been baited and sprung, and he was the quarry trapped in the cage.

"That's all very well," Rupert answered, trying to appear calmer than he felt, "but who is to say that I will get the job? It will need to be advertised to appear legitimate, and others will apply who are equally well-qualified. If, as you say, this is undercover work, no one at HBJ can know of any ulterior motives for me being picked – and who else is going to go as my assistant and the secretary? I can't go charging around the country trying to look authentic and keep the details of whatever it is you wish me to do secret from my colleagues. These are just my initial reservations, but I am sure I can find a few more before you send me off to be sacrificed on the altar of national security. And apart from being an investment surveyor in BA, what the hell do you want me to do exactly and why choose a surveyor? Why not an oil man or something?" He cried in exasperation.

Richard Johnston and one or two of the others had wry grins

upon their faces, but not Robinson, who looked as dour as ever. It was Robinson who replied to Rupert.

"The thing is, Mr Brett, that whilst I…we…appreciate your concerns and reservations, they have been anticipated and dealt with." He said. "Pressure has been placed upon one of the senior partners in your firm. Given certain alternatives, he was…shall we say…more than happy to help as we let him know that we had become aware of some of his…more private preferences." Robinson's pauses were as eloquent as his words. Rupert decided that he didn't like him. "Anyway, his confidence and support can be guaranteed," Robinson continued. "Yes, as you rightly suspect, the posts will be advertised, and prospective candidates will be interviewed alongside yourself…but ultimately you will be successful. You have the right qualifications, you're the right age and have immense experience in the necessary fields – and I understand you gained a respectable grade in A-level Spanish?" The last coming from under interrogative raised eyebrows. He continued after Rupert nodded. *A-level Spanish? My life will be at risk because I got a B in A-level Spanish? Bloody hell,* Rupert thought, *who is this fucking idiot?* "Good…you will in short be a perfect fit. Now as to the other two members of your office. Sergeant Adams here," he nodded in Chris Adams' direction, "will be your junior colleague. Records will show that he qualified as RICS with two years' postgrad experience. Finally, a member of 14 Int who is a qualified secretary will accompany you as the third member of your team." Rupert was amazed; questions rushed through him, and although used to taking in facts and deals quickly, the answers were coming before the questions could be asked. 14 Int? The spooks of the military? These were the people who provided all kinds of clandestine information and backup to colleagues in the field. Trained at their base in Wales, they often worked closely with the SAS, particularly on undercover operations in Northern Ireland. They were extremely well trained, often recruiting from other regular army regiments to go undercover and supply information.

"All right, I accept that the 14 Int would possibly fit in – but no offence, Chris, you are no surveyor. Every breed has it habits, it's mores and attitudes. Other surveyors in other disciplines walk, talk, act and dress differently. This would be like me coming into Stirling Lines and saying: 'Hello chaps, I've just finished Selection. I've spent a fortnight in the Brecons eating fluffy bunnies and heather, let's go out on a mission!' It just wouldn't work," he finished. Chris Adams grinned at this, clearly taking no offence.

Smiling tightly, Johnston spoke up. "Yes, you're quite right," the MI6 boss said. "And this is where you come in. It will be your responsibility to ensure that he does dress appropriately, walk the walk and talk the talk. Just like an army training course, except you can have carte blanche on how you do it. Prepare an idiot's guide on phrases and jargon, and it'll form part of Sergeant Adams' dossier which he will have ample time to study before you both leave. You'll have him speaking like a Sloane Ranger at a Harrod's wine tasting in no time flat, I'm sure." Rupert saw Adams grimace at the idea. "You in turn will be given a dossier on Argentina and the various systems, networks and protocols that are observed out there. Now, how would you proceed if you wanted this to work?"

Rupert considered the point for a few moments. "OK, but we'll need to get him somewhere out of town to at least put a veneer of a surveyor upon him. Fortunately there are quite a few surveyors in the TA, and quite a few qualified army officers go into surveying too. If you're going to lie, keep as close to the truth as possible. So, he's a former Royal Engineer with a background in military surveys. We'll send him off to Birmingham for a few weeks. I have a good mate there who is in the TA as well, and I'm sure that if you paid him he'd take Chris under his wing, show him the ropes away from prying eyes and provide him with a background that would withstand a bit of scrutiny if anyone phoned up to check him out. Yes, it could work, and after a few weeks he'd be a bit better known and he could come down to London to do an induction course at HBJ.

"He would of course need to attend the interviews with the others, even if he just sits in a room twiddling his thumbs behind closed doors for an hour. Then I could take him out on inspections. He would need to look the part though, it's is as much a question of attitude as anything, but I am sure being a part of the Regiment you're trained to blend in."

Chris nodded and spoke, betraying a slight Welsh lilt to his voice which sounded more like an officer than a typical squaddie. "Yeah, I've blended in as an Arab bombmaker and a Slovakian dissident in my time. I'm sure I could manage a taste for fine wines and a bit of 'Okay yah'. I can and will learn fast. Just help me as much as you can and I'll pick up the rest."

Robinson continued, "we'll get him background…qualifications…records and references, don't worry."

"How?" Rupert asked, earning himself a flat stare in response from Robinson.

"Admiral Fisher took up the story. "From a military perspective, the situation is complicated by a number of factors. We currently have a massive military presence in the Middle East. The army and navy are stretched to full capacity as all our carriers and most surface craft are operating in that zone; the Royal Marines aren't fully engaged but we might need them yet. That bugger Hussein is unpredictable at the best of times. Logistics for a swift trip to the Falklands like the last one would be tricky, if not impossible, and costly both to the Iraq conflict and the supply lines which are crucial at the moment. Anyway, the politicians have pulled that let's-send-a-fleet stunt before and they probably wouldn't do it again, so from the Argentinians' perspective it would be an ideal time to launch an invasion.

"The Falklands' defence force currently stands at 800 front line troops, Signals and support staff on rotation from the Royal Marines; 4 Phantom F4Js and two Lynx helicopters. The Islands have full radar capability and well mounted anti-aircraft missile defence emplacements around the island to deal with any air attack with Rapier Missile Systems. In addition there is the usual RAF regiment. out there guarding the two airfields. The original runway at Port Stanley has been extended and improved, as has the second airstrip further inland at RAF Mount Pleasant, offering greater flexibility to all aircraft, especially the Hercules C130 transport planes that can be flown in from Ascension Island. The harbour has been improved and the road systems aren't just tracks anymore, they're fully metalled two-lane roads allowing fast coverage from one side of the island to the other."

"You've been busy," Rupert commented.

"We have indeed, Mr Brett," Fisher grinned. "In short, we are in much better shape to repel any new invasion. We also have two Trafalgar Class nuclear submarines patrolling on standby in the Straits of Magellan and the South Atlantic off the US listening and monitoring, ready to act swiftly if needed. Also in the summer sailing months, which of course is now in the Southern Hemisphere, HMS Endurance patrols the waters as an added deterrent."

"One foot wrong and you'll nuke BA," Rupert said. "That's reassuring to know…"

"I very much doubt it would come to that, Mr Brett. However, given my comments on logistics, we are still potentially vulnerable to attack. If our defences could be breached prior to reinforcements arriving in sufficient numbers to defend the island, the opposite would apply, and all our precious infrastructure would be to the Argentinians' advantage in securing the defence of the island." Admiral Fisher finished his summary and looked around the table to see if he had missed anything. Everyone nodded in affirmation other than Rupert and Chris Adams, who looked directly at Rupert, his eyes boring into him, gauging his reaction.

"So that is what we know and that's the current position. But here's what we don't know: what is the Argentinean's current military capability? If they've increased it, where are they getting the funding? Who is funding them and how? What are their plans to invade and with what troops? Also, what is their motive? Political advantage and revenge are not enough, given the state of the current government and its finances."

Rupert nodded, starting to see where and how he would fit in and beginning to feel a little calmer than he was earlier. Robinson spoke again.

"The Americans have been helping us with satellite imagery through the NGA…"

"NGA?" Rupert queried.

"It's the equivalent of our GCHQ, but so far nothing concrete has shown up. Yes, there has been some activity in the civilian shipyards and a little more troop lorry movement around the base at Corrientes and south towards the River Plate. But nothing to warrant our suspicions to this degree.

"So, all we want you to do is essentially be yourself and do your job. Close property deals, listen and get to know how money changes hands…find out who the main players are and who buys what from where. Property in any country is still the best and cleverest way to move money around legitimately. And you will have a perfectly legitimate reason to travel in-country… We have people who will pose as buyers wanting to buy residential land or for polo ranches for holidays. Your whole position will be legitimate, but sergeant Adams will accompany you at all times. He will be able to see and understand things that you cannot, and he will report back with a military view. And he will act as your…protection in the event of anything going amiss. There is no reason for you to be worried…but better safe than sorry." He finished, holding up a hand in a typical civil servant style as if he wanted Rupert to believe something that was patently untrue. Rupert's distrust for the man grew.

"I was given similar meaningless assurances by superintendent Webster once before. Shortly afterwards I was kidnapped, beaten and shot at. Forgive me if I do not quite believe you."

"But Rupert, unlike last time you will have sergeant Adams with you on the ground," Dove interjected. "So will you consider it? It's a promotion and the salary will be good. The experience would be good for you too. It might just be a few months of harmless fun and it'll do your career no harm at all. Let's face it, the UK market is pretty ropey at the moment. You could come back next year to a different world and be a senior partner."

Rupert looked sideways at Dove, assessing everything he'd heard.

"All right, I'll do it, but I have a partner, Claire. What do I tell her? We share a flat, we have been living together for a year. Can she come out too?"

Johnston, the MI6, man jumped in quickly.

"Sorry Mr Brett, but no. If she was your wife perhaps. Maybe later, but at the moment she must not even be aware of the real reason for you going. Call it a promotion, a temporary post. Tell her she can join you in six months. By that time we can almost certainly make the arrangements if you wish to stay. Anyway, she likes polo does she not? She could come and visit you; a great opportunity to see some of the best polo in the world and provide an even greater degree of cover for you."

"How do you know she enjoys polo?" Rupert was suddenly nervous and angry at the same time. The men looked away, apart from Robinson, who gave him that flat stare again, the one that told him not to be so naïve.

"One or two others were put forward for the position. You were first choice, I won't deny it, but everyone was vetted very carefully…relationships, loyalties, family, this kind of thing." Robertson opened his hands and shrugged. "What did you expect? We aren't playing games here, Mr Brett."

Rupert nodded, still feeling very exposed and vulnerable. "Two thoughts," he said. "I saw from the news that the UN has just denied Argentina's final request for claims on the oil rights around the sea shelf surrounding the Falklands. Which means that we continue to control them, is that correct? And if it is, isn't that a good enough motive for taking the islands?"

Robinson frowned. "Yes, and it's one that we have already considered…it's a very powerful motive indeed. But it's all very well them rattling their bloody sabres and quite another for them to actually take the islands, hold on to them, find the oil and bring it home. It would take years of massive costs and expertise with a very dubious tenure of the islands. Who would back them and how? Bear in mind that for all its pomp, Argentina is virtually bankrupt. However, maybe some light will be shed upon this when you begin working there."

Rupert continued: "Secondly, one of the men I know in the TA is a reservist and was in on the original taking of the islands. His view was that it wasn't hard to take them, the problem was hanging on to the damned place once you'd done so. Surely, even from my limited knowledge, aren't the airfields the key? If you have control of them, particularly in their enhanced state, isn't it just as easy for the Argies to re-arm and entrench using the airfield for their own ends while we struggle to get sufficient troops there to mount a counterattack? It is right on their doorstep. No re-fuelling, just straight in with supply planes like they did before when we tried to knock out the airfield with Harriers, yes?"

Chris Adams and Admiral Fisher exchanged looks with each other, reassessing Rupert, who had just gone up in their estimation. The admiral continued: "There are measures in place in the event of a second invasion for the airfields to be immobilised and the smaller airstrip destroyed. I cannot elaborate any further, suffice it to say that that contingency has been considered. But thanks for pointing it out, the input is very valuable. I am sure that you are going to be a great asset to us in Argentina."

"Right," Robinson said, grimacing as he pushed a file across the table to Rupert with the tips of his fingers, as if the file and Rupert himself were each as distasteful as the other. "Here is your briefing. Everything you will need to know is in there. From now on your only contact will be with another member of the FO team, a Mr Peters. No one else, not even Major Dove… except of course sergeant Adams, whose contact details are also in there. You will see an advertisement in the Estates Gazette this week. Please apply for the position and by all means discuss internally and with your…ah…girlfriend in the usual manner. I am sure that you know the drill." He stood offering his hand, "Good luck!"

Rupert felt as though he were entering the lion's den. He shook hands with all of the men at the table, and Chris Adams promised that they would speak soon. Rupert picked up the file and left the room, his world whirling.

Once the door had closed, the members of the group turned to each other.

"Well," Dove said. "What do you think? I thought that he took it rather well, and I'm sure he will be perfect for the job. A little nervous, which is understandable. But he grasped the position quickly enough; he's a bright boy. Also picked up on the weak spot for the Falklands pretty quickly: the advantages of having someone with basic military training. Can you work with him, Sergeant Adams?"

"Sure, I've worked with much worse. He'll be fine, he just needs to do what he is good at and leave me to do the rest. I need to get started on my background. If you will excuse me, gentlemen," he scanned the room, shook hands with everyone and left.

CHAPTER SIX

Rupert left the Foreign Office with his head spinning. *What the hell had he agreed to now?* he thought. And the biggest question of all: *What am I going to tell Claire?* The rest of the day was a blur. He sat in his office trying to finalise the details for the sale of the two investments he had agreed to sell for his new client. *Hah, at least I won't have to worry about the shitty UK market for a while,* he thought ruefully.

With his day finished, his journey home was the usual packed tube and crowded, jostling pavements. Arriving at Notting Hill tube, he walked slowly down Ladbroke Street into Wilby Mews, a quiet cul-de-sac. He looked longingly at the Ladbroke Arms on the corner, tempted for a moment to enter and have a few before braving Claire. He decided against it. It would only delay the inevitable and probably make things worse. His front door appeared before him and he entered, ascending the flight of stairs to the first floor mews flat.

"Claire?" he called.

Claire's tall and willowy figure appeared, her large, appealing green eyes framed by a full mane of strawberry blond hair and he thought, not for the first time, *she looks more like Rene Russo every day. How can I leave this for 6 months?* He was rewarded with a full kiss and a hug.

"Mmm, where have you been all my life?" she breathed, smiling at him.

She tasted slightly of champagne, just a flavouring on her tongue.

Rupert laughed despite himself. "Drinking already? Have I driven you to ruin?"

"No, you are looking at someone who has just pulled off the Holy Grail of deals," she purred.

"No. Not the swap? You did it? You actually did it?"

"Oh yeah, exchanged today – and we are going to celebrate!" she cried

Claire had moved over to the in-house team at Cowell Rubens, where she and Rupert had started their careers in the mid-1980s. She had helped Rupert after the death of his girl-friend, Liz Carmichael – a killing that had been ordered by Paul Simions – and the kidnapping attempt, and their subsequent love affair had grown into something special. He had left the firm as part of the subterfuge to trap Simions, and had not returned.

Claire had worked her way steadily through the investment team and had gone on to be one of its top stars, a difficult achievement in a male dominated world. This meant that she had risen up the ranks and was now in charge of one of the main in-house funds, being personally responsible for the company's multimillion pound insurance sector. Given the stagnation in the market, many funds were reluctant to buy or sell, as Rupert knew only too well. The best option was to trade: if one fund wanted retail investments and another office space, there was a chance to do a swap. This was notoriously difficult as both parties had to agree an off-market value for both holdings and agree on any shortfall. Such deals could fall through for any number of reasons. But she had done it: agreed the values, covered the valuer's reports and exchanged today. Not only that, it was on three separate properties and represented six months of work.

"Two hundred and twenty-five million! That's going to make the Brucie bonus look good this Christmas!" she exclaimed.

She returned holding two champagne glasses of frothing pink bubbles. Rupert took a glass and clinked with her.

"To you my darling. Great deal!"

They embraced again and exchanged a long, lingering kiss. *Oh my God*, thought Rupert, *I cannot do this tonight, it will have to wait. Maybe I won't get the job. Maybe they won't invade. Maybe they will and it will be a waste of my time and too late*, he thought hopefully.

"Change," she ordered. "We're going out to dinner at Luigi's – on me."

Their favourite special restaurant, he thought, mentally picking up a gear; *she deserves this. I cannot ruin it.* The evening went better than he had hoped, they laughed and flirted their way through the meal, already well on their way with the bottle of Laurent Perrier Rose champagne before they ate, and by the time they staggered home they were completely foxed. Fumbling with the door key they climbed up the stairs, discarding clothes as they went.

One of the things Rupert loved about Claire was that the more inebriated she became, the more uninhibited and sexually voracious it made her. This was one of those moments; the high of the deal fuelled with champagne, and she was on fire. Clothes left a trail to the bedroom. Her teeth, hands and lips were everywhere as they scrambled for the bed. A muted bedside lamp lit the way as Rupert, now clad only in boxers, was pushed back onto the bed

Claire growled at him, her normally cultured voice now low, husky and strained.

"Now, you've been slightly distant from me tonight, surely

you're not jealous of my deal? Either way I'm going to bring you back to life!"

His body was caught in a world of lust, and reacted predictably as he reached for her breasts beneath the teddy covering her body.

"Uh-huh," she muttered, shaking her head. "My turn to give you pleasure." She gripped his wrists, pushing them down, knelt astride him in stocking clad legs and proceeded to kiss him all down his neck and torso, lingering over his nipples, driving him insane. Her mane of hair released from restraint enveloped him in a cloud of Patou's Joy, increasing the eroticism of the moment. She moved steadily downwards, easing him out of his boxers, taking him completely in her mouth and teasing with long nails. Rupert writhed beneath her, getting closer to climax. Then she stopped and slid further up his body, opening the teddy with one hand and placing the heat of her core directly above him, hovering until he came down slightly from the point of climax. Then in one smooth movement she drove down with her pelvis, completely impaling herself upon him.

He cried out and arched his head backwards, tendons standing out like cords, not daring to breathe, and thinking of anything to hold on. Claire clenched her muscles and slowly started to rock as she rode him. He joined her rhythm, as much as she would let him. As the pace increased, she leaned back, releasing his wrists, arching her pelvis forward in strong thrusts until neither of them could bear it any longer. They both cried out in unison, Claire lurching forward gripping his chest, scratching him as her orgasm swept over her in a rising tide. Rupert's hands gripped her hips and pulled as his neck arched backwards, tendons stretched in a paradox of pain and anguish with his own release. Crying out as wave after wave of pleasure shot through him.

"Oh my God! Wow. Can you do deals like this more often? That was incredible."

She laughed and bent down to kiss him on the lips, locking her legs behind his and rolling sideways onto the mattress in a loving embrace. They stayed like that, locked in each other's arms, pulling up the covers and falling asleep. The dawn found them still tangled and they made love again in the morning light of a red sky.

Dozing, Claire rolled over, supported her head on an elbow and stroked his chest

"Rupes, what is it? You're distant. Is it work? Come on, you can't hide it. You were with me last night but not a hundred percent. You were almost trying too hard, if that makes sense. Come on, tell me," she chided poking him. Rupert smiled gently.

"Tea, I need tea." He moved to get up from the bed.

"Oh dear, this sounds serious," she murmured, pulling the duvet up around her knees as she leant back against bedhead. Rupert noted the sombre mood. No temper, no rage, just calm collection as the shutters came down. He had seen it before and it was not a good sign; rage and temper were much better. This had to be dealt with soon or it could break them.

He returned to the bedroom with tea and to find himself facing Claire's clear, stark green eyes. They seemed to look right into his soul. She patted the bed. "Tell me," she commanded.

It was almost a relief for Rupert as he sat down and told her that he was applying for the position in Buenos Aires. He used his thoughts on the market as an excuse; difficulty doing deals at home, short term contract helping his career.

"You could come out and visit, and we'd watch the best polo in the world," he finished a little lamely. She had sat silently for five whole minutes as he related his well-rehearsed speech, her face expressionless – but to anyone who knew her, the eyes told the whole story. From initial concern to chips of ice and, as Rupert finished rather weakly, sadness. The silence hung in the air for a never ending period it seemed to Rupert. Finally she broke it

"So this is your none-too-subtle way of breaking up with me, is it?" Tears welled in her eyes. "I thought that we had something special. No wonder you were distant last night. Why, Rupes? Why? I thought it was going so well." She reached for his hand, grasping it tightly. "Please tell me what's going on. For God's sake say something! We're supposed to be going on holiday in three months' time. If you want it finished, at least have the courage to say so, don't just skulk off and leave me."

Rupert's face was a mask of fear and sadness. "God no, Claire, it's nothing like that, I promise you. It really is just work. Come on, you know how shit it is here. There's deals to be done out there, money to be made and careers to be improved. Six months – a year tops, and maybe you could come out and join me in a few months."

"Join you? No way. I like my life here too much. Why should I up sticks to a far-off place on a whim? And Argentina of all places. For Christ's sake, Rupert, they fucking hate us. Who's to say it will be any better there – and remember I've been there more than once myself. Rupert, if you really loved me, you would stay. There is still something you are not telling me, isn't there? Oh my God, I am so stupid. There is another woman, isn't there? I am such a fool."

"No, For God's sake, Claire, no. It's nothing like that"

"Then what is it? I know there's something. Tell me, damn it!" He moved away towards the window that was letting in a wintery sun, hands on hips gazing into the far distance. He turned slowly and returned to the bed, considering what he was about to do and say.

He made the decision and exhaled slowly.

"OK, the truth – or rather the rest of it: I haven't lied, every-thing I said was true. But there's more, I have just missed out one or two minor details," he confessed.

"Go on."

"Before I say anything more, you must promise me that it stays between us. I'm serious, OK? No parents, friends, not even the dog! You promise?"

"We haven't got a dog, Rupert."

"Just as well."

She nodded in affirmation. Rupert shook his head. "No, that's not good enough. Promise me," he said.

Claire looked serious. Some feminine intuition told her that this was a vital part of the whole thing, and that it was nothing to do with any secret lover or that elusive property deal that he'd been hunting all his working life.

"Alright, I promise. Not a word."

He told her everything. Her face expressed a kaleidoscope of emotions: concern, fear, pleasure at realising it was not their relationship that was at stake, and finally incredulity.

"Well? Say something don't just sit there shaking your head."

"You stupid little shit!"

"Thank you."

"Oh for God's sake, Rupert. You've been played and they are using you. All of them. This is Simions all over again, only twice as dangerous. This time it is the whole Argentine government, not some tinpot crook. Do you realise what you are letting yourself in for? Do you know what they do to enemies of the state in South American countries? Do you know how many people simply disappear out there?"

She flung her hands up in frustration, ranting at him for five minutes, banging him on the chest. Finally, her tear-filled eyes met his as she clung to him.

"You stupid, heroic bastard! Playing soldiers and spies. It's not big and it's not clever. Will you ever grow up?" He grinned wistfully back at her, kissing her gently on the lips. "But at least you still love me. You do don't you? Because if I find out any different, these," she declared, grabbing him none too gently between his naked legs, "Will be coming off with a rusty knife!"

He held up his hands in surrender and declared his undying love in a mock castrato voice.

"But, oh Rupes, what a mess. You know we always say the no deals done 'til it's done'? This, my darling, might just be a deal too far, even for you! Now tell me again in full detail, slowly."

So he did, and with interruptions from Claire he realised that there were still many questions of his own that he didn't know the answers to.

Chapter Seven

Birmingham

Chris Adams had enjoyed his time at Hughes and Jones, a firm of surveyors in the centre of the City near the Bullring. He found the camaraderie of surveyors and their habit of piss-taking, meeting in packs and sharing information similar to the world of a squaddie, and he had adapted accordingly. It had helped that Jeremy Hughes was in the TA, as it gave them a little mutual understanding of military matters. Hughes had been more than delighted to help one of the members of the legendary SAS, and on one or two occasions had been forced to rein himself in so as not to blow Chris's cover with other agents in Birmingham.

With the natural intelligence and detail to attention that had enabled him to rise up within the Regiment, Chris soon assimilated the workings of the surveyor's world, from understanding the different disciplines involved to imitating the attitudes and clarifying the hierarchical structure of the surveying world in his own mind. The newly opened Metro Bar on Cornwall Street had become a second home for him, and in the short time he had worked there his name had become known and established within the city as the Brummies had welcomed him with open arms, as they usually did with strangers. All things considered, he was delighted to be involved in this assignment.

Anyone from the Regiment who is picked for a special mission is always pleased, and Chris was no exception. He had a few mates who had found themselves caught up in the disastrous ex-fil mission inside Chile in the last Argie conflict, and he wanted to even the score if the opportunity presented itself. But he had to keep focused and maintain a strict level of fitness and preparedness. Luckily, Birmingham wasn't that far from Hereford and the Stirling Lines base, so in addition to daily runs he made sure that at every opportunity – especially at weekends – he returned to train and keep in contact with the coordinating officer.

On the last leg of his 6 mile run, he reflected ruefully how in films and novels the hero would always remain fighting fit for long periods of time, but no mention was ever made of constant training, exercise and running, and how this remarkable fitness seems to magically go on with no additional training during the story. *If only that were true in real life,* he thought, sweating as he powered up the last four hundred yards in a flat out sprint. Next, he worked out on the heavy bag set up in his house; running through fast and hard work, following up with a quick shower then an hour on the range at Stirling Lines, using the three types of weapons he would take with him to Argentina – weapons that would be sent through the Diplomatic Bag.

One more week in Birmingham, then on to London with Rupert at HBJ and the real work would start. It had been over three weeks since the assault on the Six operative in BA, and time was moving against them. The inverted seasons in the Southern Hemisphere were approaching a perfect time for an invasion, and if any intel were to be of use, they needed to get themselves in place as soon as possible. However, planning and preparation were the watchwords, especially in this case, and they could not be rushed. The dossier he'd been provided with had been comprehensive, and he was up to speed on all terms and technical information to do with surveying. Already fluent in Spanish (Regiment members were required to speak at least two foreign languages), a refresher course at the language lab in Hereford with the specific stress on Argentinian Spanish had helped tremendously, and he felt well prepared. The interviews for the new office in BA had been advertised and he had applied and had been accepted for an interview in London next week, which he knew would be successful.

London

Rupert had arranged to meet sergeant Adams at one of the usual haunts in London, the Guinea in Bruton Place, a pub that was frequented by surveyors. It was the perfect cover as it was always so noisy in the small bar, and no conversation could be easily overheard. It would also give Chris another insight into the world of surveying and gave him the chance to show his face in the right crowd. Surveyors, Rupert had told him, and particularly agents, rarely forget faces.

The Guinea on a Friday lunchtime was already crowded, and after braving the run of the crowd shouting hellos and exchanging words with what seemed like half the bar, Rupert managed to secure a relatively quiet perch in a far corner where they could speak together reasonably securely.

"So, how is it going? Are you getting to grips with all the terms and property in general? Rupert grinned.

"Sure. The file was a big help and so was your mate Jeremy. The guys up there were really friendly and they'll certainly remember me, so it all adds to the background if anyone ever checks up on us. My guess is that they will at some point or other. Probably when the visas are applied for, they'll do a bit of digging for sure. It's funny, everyone thinks that Argentina is an inefficient and sloppily-run banana republic, but if you are planning a major campaign," Chris said euphemistically, "you need to be careful and the stakes are certainly high. What you should be aware of is that Argentina has a very strong intelligence force within the country but isn't anywhere near as good in foreign countries. This of course makes our job harder. Also because of the accent and mannerisms it is hard even for a Spanish speaker to pass as a native. They also have a hate-hate relationship with Chile – ever since they argued about Patagonia after the signing of the Magellan Treaty back in 1881. But hopefully, with the solid cover that we have, it won't matter. I'm really curious from a military point of view about how this is all going to pan out. I just can't see how they are creating the build-up or where they are getting the funding from. Hell, it's a broken banana republic with crap infrastructure and low morale. Especially after we kicked their arses the last time."

Rupert nodded. "Well hopefully we'll just get out there and do our job. I'm sure that when we start moving around, especially up in Corrientes near the military base, things will start making more sense. But you're right, where the hell are they getting the money from? I mean, I know that every military junta around the world always prioritises arms and the military, that's how it stays in power, after all, but it would cost billions to kick off another Falklands campaign. On that note, when are we seeing Peters at the FO?"

"Next Monday at Whitehall, 15.00 hours. Hopefully, he'll throw more light on the details, but I get the impression that the more planning and preparation we can do ourselves and the less reliance we place on the FO and their intelligence, the better off we will be. I have never placed too much reliance on others, especially intelligence departments," Chris finished, grinning.

"Talking of which, what did you think of Robinson?" Rupert asked.

"I wouldn't trust him as far as I could throw him, and he's a fat little fucker. I see his type far too often. I think he has his own agenda and would sacrifice his mother for whatever it is he's after. Probably a promotion and more power. People like him are dangerous to people like us. He'll wash his hands of us at the drop of a hat, and drop the hat himself," Chris replied.

"How do you feel about being lumbered with a weekend warrior like me for an oppo?"

Rupert had been slightly concerned about this, knowing how the regulars tended to look down their nose at the TA, particularly if they were from the Regiment.

"We all think you're shit," Chris said, then laughed. "No, seriously anyone in the Regiment is always pleased to be asked to go on a mission like this. It is a good career move and it's great experience. We don't all get to do undercover work and it could get quite interesting. Subtle as well, and good for the diplomacy paragraph on the CV. My gut feeling is that it'll turn out to be a lot of groundwork, reconnaissance and sitting around getting bored, with very little action. That's so often the case on missions like this. And I'll probably be relying on your expertise more you'll be relying on mine. We'll spend our time at receptions wearing suits and marking the honeytraps out of ten," he finished.

At this point the door to the crowded pub opened and a woman appeared. The crowd parted like the Red Sea, calls and exchanges from various members of the surveying patrons showed that she was known and it took her a good few minutes to get close to Rupert's table.

"My God, who is that?" Chris murmured, smiling appreciatively.

Rupert grinned. "That, Chris, is my girlfriend, Claire."

He had to admit that Claire looked fantastic. Dressed in high heels, a cream silk blouse and a green tweed business suit that matched her eyes she was a vision, and drew admiring glances from all over the room

"Good job she's not going undercover. Wouldn't stand a snowball's chance in hell."

Rupert stood and kissed Claire, introducing her to Chris as a colleague from the TA who had applied for the secondary position in Argentina and was tipped to get it. Chris said he was pleased to meet her. Pleasantries dealt with, she took the position that Rupert had told her to adopt. "So you're the poor bugger likely to have to work for Rupert in the land of sun, samba and *chiquitas*, are you?"

"Yes, that's the general idea. I can't wait – if I'm successful, of course," Chris added enthusiastically, his faux-gauche attitude making him look younger and far more innocent than he was.

"Mmm, well, just make sure he stays out of trouble. It seems to find him like some heat-seeking guided missile. Especially where women are concerned," she said ambiguously, casting a withering glance at Rupert. The banter continued for a few minutes until Claire made her excuses, saying that she had to get back.

After she had gone, with a parting kiss from Rupert, Chris commented. "And you're leaving that behind? You must love Queen and country, mate. Here's to you," he said raising his glass of Guinness in salute, polishing off the remaining contents in one gulp. "Now I need to be off too. See you next Monday. Hopefully we can be official by then with regard to the appointment. It will make our meeting a lot easier."

Rupert agreed, said his goodbyes and not for the first time

thought; *why exactly am I leaving Claire behind?* Seeing someone else appreciate her so obviously, he wondered if he would have a girlfriend to come back to.

Chapter Eight

Monday saw Rupert and Chris Adams attend a meeting with Mr Peters at the Foreign Office. The meeting took place in one of the low level cubby hole offices in the rabbit warren of corridors at ground floor level within the main building.

This was no tea-and-biscuits affair; it was a succinct and harsh briefing with no sugar coating. Chris had warned Rupert that the FO had its own clandestine section without an official name that never saw the light of day and whose staff as drawn from the services, Special Branch and others who had served their country in a more covert manner in the dirty tricks department. Peters was no exception. He was a compact, sandy-haired, small-eyed and well-dressed man wearing a dark, nondescript suit and tie. His voice was neutral, but there was a hard edge and little humour to it.

His briefing comprised a set of contact details. He told them how communications were to be made and stressed that little or no contact was to be made with the embassy other than seemingly innocent trade meetings. The briefing included an up-to-date summary of the political situation and a set of do's and don'ts when living in Argentina. Rupert and Chris were each given a file with information and a who's who of the players and characters they should be aware of in the political and military spheres. Peters finished with two rather disturbing comments that Rupert found chilling.

"Just remember that within its own country Argentina has one of the most efficient and ruthless intelligence agencies in the world. Outside their own country they are less effective – probably because they have no friends and few allies. Also – and this is very important – the Argentine secret service, SIDE as it is known, is closely modelled on the British system, but with one fundamental difference: it specialises in recruiting female agents following Operation Marilyn in 1973, particularly blondes. So be wary, don't be fooled and consider every chance encounter as suspicious. Waddington wasn't careful enough, and look what happened to him.

"SIDE is all-encompassing, and collaborates with every aspect of law enforcement and intelligence gathering in Argentina. It is extremely well informed and well-operated. It reports directly to and is powered by the President. All detailed information is contained within the dossier in front of you both." He gestured at the two buff folders he'd given them a few minutes earlier.

"Secondly – and I am sure that you, Sergeant Adams, will be familiar with this – we cannot as HM government acknowledge that you are working for us or have anything to do with us in any guise other than as two British citizens working in a foreign country. You will, in short, have no special status, no diplomatic passports and certainly no form of acknowledgement that you're working for us, regardless of the circumstances. Do I make myself perfectly clear? As a matter of fact this will probably work to your advantage, as anyone who is even remotely connected to the embassy is put on a watch list similar to the Cold War days behind the Iron Curtain. So stay away from all contacts or any suspicious interest for your own safety."

Rupert was shocked, having not considered such possibilities, but Chris accepted it with a calm equanimity as though it was an everyday occurrence for him – which of course it was. Peters looked both men in the eye and they nodded acceptance and confirmed that they understood and agreed.

"Right, gentlemen, that's it. I hope to hear from you with regular reports, and I wish you the best of luck." They shook hands perfunctorily, the meeting at an end. Rupert and Chris walked from the room, neither saying a word until they had left the building.

"That went well," Rupert commented sarcastically.

"He's a cold fish. Works with Robinson, and he's another one I wouldn't trust any farther than I could throw them. They're all the same, bunch of prissy pen pushers. Never get their hands dirty and look after their own spooks first. Welcome to my world! But don't worry, I've made contingency plans with my own guys at the Regiment. We won't be totally on our own – and to be honest, I would much rather trust them than that lot," he finished, jerking his thumb back over his shoulder towards the FO buildings they had just left.

"Hey, look on the bright side," he continued, "At least we both got the job." Chris was alluding to the confirmation of their appointments to the BA office. They both laughed and decided to go back to Rupert's flat to go over the dossiers

"Claire's away on inspections, so we won't be disturbed," Rupert said. "You can crash the night and save getting the train back to Hereford. That Paddington line is a nightmare and it'll take two and half hours to get home."

"Tell me about it. I'm not snooping, but how much have you told her? I know what the panel said, but we don't always adhere to that. But I need to know what might be on the line and whether there is a security risk."

Rupert stared him straight in the eye and told him a half-truth. "There were tears, tantrums and recriminations. But no, she thinks I am on some special deal with a secret investor that I can't tell her about. Competition, do you see? Anyway, hopefully she will come out to meet us, especially as the Triple Crown is about to start soon."

"Triple Crown?"

"Sorry, the three main polo tournaments in the world culminate in the final at Palermo in the Argentine open. Claire grew up in Gloucestershire, played at pony club, spent summer on HPA exchanges in Argentina, played at uni. She loves it, and she's desperate to see it played on the hallowed turf in Palermo. Best polo in the world, so she says. Amazing to watch."

"Mmm, hopefully we'll get the chance," Chris conceded, sounding totally unconvinced. Whether about the polo or the explanation Rupert could not decide, but the subject was dropped. They entered Wilby Mews and settled in at Rupert's flat, where they made coffee and started to go over the files provided by Peters.

Rupert started with questions. "OK, I know she's been accepted because the secretarial pool has already notified me of her appointment, but do you know anything about this 14 Int operative? What's her name, Siobhan something-or-other?"

"Siobhan Clifford," Chris said. "I worked with her in Northern Ireland. She was backup to an operation we did over there in the late eighties. I can't say any more than that. She is a straight operator, and a good one. Lost her brother as one of the 'disappeared' to the IRA. Some say it was a punishment killing, others that it was something that just went wrong; he was suspected of being a grass. Who knows, but she is very bitter about it, or she was. She's now dedicated to our side and has been since she joined Royal Signals back in '83."

"Yes, but what is she *like?*"

"Good sense of humour, very focused, pretty – the photo is in there," he nodded to the folder. "Fluent in Spanish and other languages. She'll make the ideal secretary as a cover and she's definitely someone I'd trust watching my back and checking intel in the case of trouble. She's playing the role of secretary out there with us, but do not make the mistake of underestimating her." Chris finished.

Rupert sensed that there was something unsaid, but he did not push any further. "Can't say any better than that," he said. "We're meeting up with her tomorrow, it says here, so hopefully we can get everything straightened out then and we can go over as a team, soon as the visas come through." They went over the documents twice, and much to Rupert's surprise he discovered that the legal system for property was not that different to the UK's. Argentina had a system called Triple Nett, which was equivalent to the UK FRI leases. While Argentina had its own Pesos currency, things were expressed in terms of US dollars. It seemed that the whole country was wedded inexorably to the USA. Everything was registered to a central government-run ledger that recorded prices and deals just like the UK's Land Registry. One interesting point was that every deal had two brokers and that they charged two or three percent according to their position, and that they could act for both purchaser and vendor. When Rupert found this out he was amazed

"Bloody hell, Chris, that's a licence to print money. It leaves everything open to corruption. You could make six percent on the entire deal. Hell, I could retire after a year!"

"Well, it'll beat Regiment pay, that's for sure."

"Do you get to keep it? On top of your own salary, I mean."

"I don't know, but I'm sure that the head shed will not ask too many questions as long as we're successful. I do know that I am on the HBJ payroll, so it can go through the proper channels. So yeah, hopefully I can squirrel some away. Especially as I see we are on an incredible bonus scheme. Thirty percent commission! When I leave the army I am going to be a surveyor, that's for certain."

"I reckon you'd find it very dull. Nothing ever happens apart from deals and making money. Who needs that?" Rupert finished, grinning.

Chris raised a cynical eyebrow, shaking his head in disbelief. He had reached a stage in his career when like most SAS soldiers he was starting to wonder what he was going to do when he got out. Private security for some spoiled celebrity, maybe the Middle East; he could end up on the Circuit, blowing ragheads' faces off and escorting oil plutocrats and arms dealers around the Arab states or doing mercenary work in Africa. It didn't bear thinking about. He shut it from his mind. *Concentrate*, he told himself, *you've got years yet.* They finished the evening with a glass of single malt and headed for bed.

The next day saw them in the Human Resources department of HBJ's offices, where they met Siobhan Clifford. She was introduced by Mary Wellman, the head of HR.

"Siobhan, this is Rupert Brett, the new head of our Buenos Aires office, and his assistant, Chris Adams. Gentlemen, Siobhan Clifford."

Siobhan was of medium height, with a slim but very feminine figure, pale skinned with a sprinkle of freckles and a mane of red hair that fell to her shoulders. Despite the makeup, there was a hardness around her pretty hazel eyes that told of anguish and experience beyond her twenty-eight years. Her voice, when she spoke, was not as hard as Rupert was expecting and some of the harsh Belfast accent had been smoothed off over the years. The 'g's were silent in places, making her voice rather appealing

"Pleased to meet you. Glad we're goin' to be working together, lookin' forward to BA, it should be excitin'."

She shook hands with both men, giving no hint that she was already acquainted with Chris Adams. It was a smooth piece of mental legerdemain on her behalf, and Rupert was impressed.

"Well, I'll leave you to get acquainted," Mary Wellman said.

"Siobhan, I'll see you in the WP for induction training later." Siobhan nodded in agreement and they were left alone. Once they were certain no one was listening, she spoke directly to Adams.

"Hey Chris, it's great to see you again after so long. Should be a good crack, don't you think?" she said, smiling at him.

The two of them fell into an easy banter born of former comradeship as they exchanged reminiscences, before she turned to Rupert.

"Sorry, just catchin' up. So, you are my new boss? Hopefully I can help in more ways than just typing."

"I hope so too. It'll be good to speak openly, although I understand that none of the Argentinian staff in the office are to be trusted."

"No. Don't trust anyone. We're a tight group, so let's keep it that way. From the briefing that sounds fine if we stick to it, but if Ireland taught me one thing, it's that no one can be trusted." Her voice became harder as she referred to the Troubles and home. They talked for a little longer and agreed to meet up after work at an Italian restaurant in St Christopher's place. Siobhan would spend two weeks at HBJ before leaving in WP, attached to the Investment Department as a temp shadowing Rupert's current secretary.

Later, over pasta, they talked more about their upcoming mission in BA. During the course of discussion it became apparent that despite her looks and obvious sexuality Siobhan was very focused, and there was no hint of flirting or eye contact other than directly for the purposes of the mission. Rupert was pleased but also slightly puzzled. While he considered himself no Greek god, he usually got on well with every woman he had met through surveying, and his charm was a legendary aspect of all his dealings. With Siobhan it felt like he was speaking to another man and she held herself aloof, the only outward sign of any light-heartedness had been when she'd met Chris at HBJ. *Still*, he thought, *it means there will be no compromise of position either for me or Chris*

The evening went well and they each came to their own conclusion that the three of them would make a good team. In two weeks' time they'd be in Argentina, so Rupert considered it very important that they gelled as a commercial team if their cover was going to be plausible to their Argentinean counterparts.

Siobhan left the restaurant first, thanking Rupert for holding the door. The three of them walked to Bond Street tube where Chris and Rupert headed west to Rupert's flat while Siobhan took the Jubilee line. Getting off at Kilburn, she walked along Christchurch Avenue until she found a vacant phone box. The accent hardened to pure Belfast as she spoke carefully down the line in cryptic references.

"Hiya darlin'. Yeah, we had a good enough time and everythin' went well. Two weeks and we're off to sunny BA. It'll be a good crack and I'll send you the usual postcard with the names of all the friends I make." She continued for another few minutes and finished with: "Oh and send my love to the wee man on the island. Tell him I'll be in touch soon." She said goodbye and ended the call.

She looked furtively over her shoulder as she left the phone box, a trained reflex from Northern Ireland. All she saw were a few commuters and a couple holding hands as they walked along. Yet, she felt that familiar tingle; that strange feeling of being watched that was born of long hours working dangerous surveillance ops. Stopping to look casually in a shop window, she saw the couple and a few others pass by in the window's reflection. No one seemed interested in her. She shrugged it off, thinking that she must be getting paranoid as she headed for her friend's flat

The couple entered the nearest pub, immediately lost in the smoky atmosphere. Without stopping for a drink, they came out thirty seconds later.

"Call it in now, before anyone else uses that phone," the woman ordered. "Have them trace the number if they can." The man made the call, telling the person on the other end of the line the number of the callbox.

Leaving the box, he commented; "What do you think? Could be innocent – or like we suspect, it could be a whole lot worse."

The woman rolled her eyes and scowled, cursing under her breath. "Come on, let's get back," she said.

Chapter Nine

Buenos Aires

Just over two weeks later Rupert, Chris and Siobhan landed at Ezeiza International airport in BA in the middle of a thunderstorm brought on by the intense heat of the last few weeks. The rain came down like bullets, bouncing off the canopied walkway to the terminal.

Gazing upwards as they made their way towards the taxi rank area to the front of the main terminal, they were awed by the huge galleried arch that reached high above them. The taxi took them to the Belgrano district of the city, where they had arranged accommodation. Belgrano was open and clear with grassy spaces and parks, where the mixture of new high-rise apartments and elegant traditional late nineteenth century baroque housing made for a delightful environment. The storm had cleared and the air smelled fresher than it had been of late. Even in the heat of the summer, the close proximity to the coast made it a perfect place to live, benefiting from the onshore breeze that kept the worst of the city's heat at bay.

They were staying on the Juana Azurduy in a new apartment

block with full air conditioning and a lift servicing all six floors. Siobhan was on the fourth floor directly above them, while Rupert and Chris were sharing an apartment on the third. Their new office was on the Avenida 9 de Julio in Consulado de Colombia, one of the main commercial areas of the city. The double doors of the apartment block led in from the street to a vestibule of tiled floors which clacked under Siobhan's heels. A winding, balustraded staircase spiralled upwards in mock art deco opulence, but they all took the lift. Both apartments were well furnished, more suited to a five star hotel than rudimentary staff accommodation – a point that was echoed by Chris as he entered through the front door.

"Bloody hell, it's better than the barracks, that's for sure!"

"Yeah, HBJ certainly know how to look after their staff. And look at that view," Rupert replied, moving to the balcony and opening the windows onto a panoramic vista of the harbour at Parque de la Memoria across the bay.

"We'll certainly need to stay focused and remember that this is a mission, not a holiday," Chris commented, breaking the spell. "Right, let's get unpacked, and I'll need a run before we meet up with our oppos in the office. God knows how long we were on that plane, but my muscles have tied themselves in knots."

Rupert rolled his eyes but said nothing. He realised why the SAS were so special; the energy levels were just on a different scale to that of a normal human being. All Rupert wanted to do was drink a bottle of something cold and sleep for twelve hours. But he was glad that Chris was along and in the short time they'd known each other he realised that his meticulous planning, preparedness and attention to detail was as much a characteristic of the Regiment than the macho image so often portrayed by the media hype. Chris was always trying to figure out how he could do things better, and for all the planning that the FO had set in place, he had made his own provisions and was always looking at what could go wrong and how to counter it before it did. Rupert reflected that for all Chris's assertion that he would be leaning on Rupert, he had a sneaking suspicion that it might turn out to be the other way around.

For her part, Siobhan settled in straight away, pleased that everything had so far gone according to plan. She too was going to go for a run but with a stop in the park by the Monument Vespucio football stadium.

Some fifteen minutes later, out of breath and pausing to stretch, she stopped by the football stadium at the south entrance to the stand and leant against the wall getting her breath back. Someone who looked like a local, dressed in a linen suit with his face shaded by a wide-brimmed panama hat, casually got up from his bench next to the stand, leaving a bottle of water unopened on the seat beside him. Siobhan stretched on the bench and quickly substituted her water bottle for the one left by the bench's previous occupant. The move was cleverly executed, and she left the shade of the stadium and jogged back to the apartment building. Upon entering her apartment, she peeled off the double label and read the instructions and telephone numbers that had been concealed between the two labels.

Chris was returning from his run and offered a warm smile as he saw Siobhan disappear from view, taking the stairs at a run. *Good to see the girl keeping in shape,* he thought, wiping the sweat from his brow. He too took the stairs, arrived at his landing and dropped to the floor to do a hundred press ups. *Not bad,* he thought, *not bad,* as he checked his pulse, which was still only 165.

He entered the air conditioned apartment to find Rupert poring over the contents of a letter that had been pushed under the door. "This came while I was in the shower," Rupert said. "Instructions to meet, but under no circumstances are we to contact the embassy except for functions receptions etc. Pretty much what Peters said in London, yeah? They're being awfully careful, aren't they?"

"Like I say, you can never be too careful, and you can never make enough contingency plans. Where are we meeting?"

Rupert grinned at this. "Claire is going to go nuts; we're going to Pilar to the Tortugas Country Club for a polo match on Saturday. We will meet – if that's the right word – with a woman called Sophie Carswell, but we aren't allowed to acknowledge her in any way. We just sit next to her and exchange bags. The plot thickens. What's that all about?"

"Normal stuff, Rupert, don't worry. We're going to pick up the contents of the Diplomatic Bag. Most people think it is just that – a bag – but I've seen bags the size of a shipping container. Hopefully ours won't be so unwieldy. Just a few bits and pieces that we will need over here that can't go through customs. You'll see."

Rupert raised an eyebrow at this, but he was learning fast. When Chris adopted that tone and look, nothing more could be gained from questions and it was best to keep quiet and be patient.

"Where is it located?"

"About twenty-five minutes northwest of the city," Chris said, looking at a map. "Should be an easy drive."

"Good, I'll pack a bag."

The office had provided a company car in the form of a Toyota Land Cruiser, much to Chris's approval. He vouched that it was the chosen vehicle of the Regiment: parts were easy to get hold of, and it was heavy, fast and reliable. With the right tyres it could go pretty much anywhere. Rupert asked Chris why he wanted such a heavy vehicle.

"If you get into a problem and need to do some defensive driving, you don't want to be in a Mini. Might have worked in *The Italian Job*, but it won't work here. I told them we'd be going off-road to prospect some of the sites we were interested in. Just for cover, of course."

"Good point," Rupert conceded, hoping it wouldn't come to that. He just wanted to find the money, spot the bad guys and leave.

They went down to the street an hour later and picked up the car from the Toyota dealership on the Avenida Presidente Figueroa Alcorta near the stadium where Siobhan had gone for her run earlier.

The Land Cruiser turned out to be one of the new powerful J80 turbo diesel models; an upgraded version of the older 60 series and much improved. More importantly, it had a very good air conditioning system which coped well with the full heat of the day. "Smooth car!" Rupert grinned as he pulled into the traffic to the howls of horns; he was not quite quick enough for the BA drivers, although he had plenty of experience in driving around Rome, which was quite similar in terms of suicidal tendencies. As they passed a small side-street Chris asked him to pull over. He left the car and came back a few minutes later with some bits and pieces from a hardware store. When Rupert asked him what they were he tapped his nose.

"You can be bloody frustrating, you know that, don't you?" he said.

Chris's response was a thin smile. "Famous for it," he retorted.

Back at the apartment, the purchases proved to be pretty ordinary but very practical. A cordless drill, hinges, a lock and a few other bits of hardware.

"I never trust an apartment like this," Chris commented. "Too many keys, weak hinges, anyone can get in. If we need time this will buy us a few extra minutes – which could save our lives."

"Aren't you being just a tad paranoid?" Rupert asked.

"No," came the emphatic response. "Always try to think how to do it better. Prepare for the worst and hope for the best."

By the time he had finished, the main door had three more robust hinges and a second mortice lock. The fitted wardrobe had a new lock too, together with an almost invisible flap at the base that was deep enough to conceal a briefcase. It could only be opened by a clever angling of screws and a hidden spring catch.

The next day was their first at the office on Avenida 9 de Julio, a street that was reputed to be the widest street in the world, named after the Argentinian Independence Day. It was, Rupert had to admit, a really impressive part of the city. The many lanes of the main street led off into some of the best office space in BA. Acres of new, shiny glass were cleverly mixed with more traditional stuccoed buildings in a vibrant atmosphere. They entered the manned reception and the security guard provided passes before directing them to the 29th floor, where the lift doors opened to a wide and well-lit reception area and a desk. The attractive young receptionist behind the desk wore a smart suit over her trim figure, and beamed a typical thousand kilowatt Latin smile and in a thick but attractively accented English asked how she might help.

Introductions were offered and the girl confirmed that they were expected. A moment on the phone and a fast exchange of Spanish that Rupert's B grade A level couldn't hope to follow and they were shown through to the main office. The double doors opened out into an open plan area with a number of desks, of which only three were occupied. Two small glass offices were partitioned off in each corner, offering a spectacular view of the city. A man of medium height approached them confidently, his full head of hair swept back from his forehead and his smiling brown eyes set in a suave countenance. Dressed in an expensive dark suit he offered a hand to Rupert first.

Encantado de concerte. Raphael Olmos, *la bienvenida a Buenos Aires!*" His smile encompassed them all, taking in Siobhan in particular and admiring her figure that was shown off to good effect in tightly-tailored jacket and trousers. He was all Latin charm, and Rupert smiled inwardly, thinking that he wouldn't trust him an inch. Olmos had trouble pronouncing Siobhan's name. which came out as *Siffvon*, and she was known from that point on by this sobriquet. She took it in good grace and smiled at him in return.

The other two members of the team were Alejandro Cassette, known as Alex; a young and charming surveyor with broad shoulders and a strong handshake; and finally Maria, a secretary to the team, whose looks were strangely androgynous under a short and rather masculine-styled haircut which nonetheless complimented her elfin features.

Siobhan took an immediate liking to her counterpart and they paired off to compare notes and for Siobhan to be shown around the office. Rupert was surprised at the instant rapport, and not for the first time was taken aback by Siobhan's bonding with those whom he would not have considered important. But he shrugged; it was vital that they got along with everyone, and Siobhan was playing her part to the letter.

Rupert turned his attention to Chris and Rafe – as Olmos had asked them to call him – realising just how good Chris's command of the language was. He found it a constant battle to continually juggle the role of boss and second-in-command as Chris was so often in control in other matters. He found it necessary to reclaim his dominance every so often for the sake of cover and to reassert the prescribed position of boss and subordinate. This was one of those occasions, and he chose the familiar territory of property – one at which he excelled. The conversation reverted to English after a few minutes.

"So, how is the market here?" Rupert asked. "I understand that it is hotting up, is that right?"

"*Si, Senor* Brett." Olmos's English was not perfect. "We have seen very much of activity over the last two quarters. Many new development, good interest from, how you say, prospecting tenants and most important of everything, a demand for the new space. But the problem is of no investment. I am sure you know that our economy is…what is the word…fragile? Yes, fragile, we have very little inward investment. So we need foreign to be buying into what is becoming a strong letting market. But still no one will build. So we need money invested to fund local developers or direct development from foreign investors. Which is what we are hoping you can help with."

Over the last two months, FO contacts and staff from within HBJ had been as good as their word, and Rupert had a list of requirements from foreign investors who were more than willing to buy into a potential growth economy; providing the underlying factors were all present and secure in their minds. He realised that he needed a far better understanding of the local market, but that this would come quickly with local help from Rafe and Alex. His response was cautious but encouraging.

"Well, we have the mandates to buy, and while they are not completely discretionary, all we have to do is find the right investments, offer a reasoned approach for buying and satisfy the clients that it is a good deal and they'll follow our advice. The main thing that's attracting them at the moment is the yields; you have Triple A leases, equivalent of our FRI in the UK. The leases, while they aren't as long as ours, are becoming more comparable following our recession at home, where tenants are no longer prepared to sign twenty or twenty-five year leases. Argentina, with its emerging economy, is much more attractive to our home grown investors who need better returns than the stagnant UK market can offer, with little prospect of rental growth.

"So basically this is the whole rationale for us opening the office and buying here. We want to get in on the ground floor now before the rest of the world realises the as yet unexploited opportunities Argentina has to offer. So what I need from you," he continued, warming to his theme and taking command, "is an intro to the players here; a good understanding of the markets – and most importantly, some good deals to put to our clients. Piece of cake, yes?" he finished, smiling.

Rafe, who saw the humour in the final ironic remark, smiled warmly. "Pieces of cake," he echoed. "What we need to do is to get you introduced to the market, perhaps a cocktail party to celebrate opening of office? Then a complete guide to city. OK?"

"Perfect. Let's get going with some dates and perhaps you can begin our education this afternoon with a tour of BA? Oh, one other thing, which is not as important, but it might help oil the wheels..."

"Yes, *senor* Brett?"

"Well, some of the clients have more private interests, and that's where Chris comes in," Rupert said, nodding towards Chris, "Chris has been working on some more specialised aspects which may not be quite as lucrative, but will nonetheless add interest to potential investors. His clients are interested in land and estates outside the City, for polo ranches and country retreats to go dove shooting, which I understand is very popular here."

"Of course," Rafe responded enthusiastically, "I will certainly show you great areas for visiting investors. There is no problem."

"Someone mentioned land up north in the Pampas towards San Miguel. Said it was good country, quiet, away from it all."

"*Si*," Rafe responded with a shrug. "But it is not in real polo country, you know? It is eight or nine hours' drive to that area. Beautiful, but..." he finished with a puzzled shrug.

"What you're saying is that down here it's more expensive so there'll be more commission for us," Rupert conceded, smiling affably. He clapped Rafe on the shoulder. "Spoken like a true agent!" he said, and let the subject drop.

Chris had watched this interchange with much internal amusement and almost winced when Rupert mentioned San Miguel, given its relatively close proximity to Corrientes. In the end he realised that this was Rupert's domain and that they had the makings of an excellent team.

Siobhan had been over at the other side of the office admiring the view with Maria, but returned in time to hear of the proposed trip around the city. Rafe and Alex were surprised to hear that Rupert wanted to include her, especially as Argentina was an even more patriarchal society than the English surveying scene, but conceded with non-committal shrugs. They all piled into Rafe's 7 series BMW, which having been parked in the basement was mercifully cool, giving a chance for the air-con to catch up before they drove out into the dazzling sunlight.

The tour was concise and took in all the main office and commercial areas, finishing at the newly developing waterfront down by the estuary of the River Plate. Offering a sophisticated selection of restaurants and bars opening straight out onto the esplanade and sea, the area provided a calm and refreshing oasis, but as with so many large cities – and Buenos Aires in particular – if you strayed too far off the beaten track the dangers increased very quickly.

They parked up on the rue del Costa under the shade of some trees and walked to the beautiful waterfront Cafe Mendes, which had a large canopied terrace looking out over the river rolling by mixed with a heady aroma of local spices and herbs wafting through the air.

Large private ocean-going yachts glided smoothly by; the playthings of the fabulously rich element that was attached to the city. At times like these, Rupert reflected, it was difficult to imagine the potential danger they were in or the real reason for them being in Argentina at all.

The beers arrived, a tray of Quilmes, the local beer for which they were to develop a real taste.

"*Salud*," Rafe toasted, raising his frosted glass in the air to clink with Chris's. The drink had a clean taste with more flavour than lagers he normally drank. The hoppy taste was more associated with beer. Chris approved, smacking his lips after his first mouthful

"*Muy bien*," he commented to the delight of Rafe and Alex. "Quilmes is my new favourite beer – and this," he said, expanding his arms to take in the new development and the water, "is like paradise. Where else could you go to work and enjoy this on your doorstep?" The others nodded in agreement.

Chris nodded towards an area of the river further upstream, where there was a commercial docking area. A seagoing liner had anchored and seemed to be having a new fit-out, with gantries and derricks dancing attendance upon the ship, which looked like it was nearly ready to start a new voyage.

"Where do the liners travel to from here, or is it just sea cruises for rich tourists?"

"This one, she is the *SS Esmeralda*," Rafe answered. "She goes on a cruise up through the south Atlantic to America, calling at Las Malvinas along the way, then to the Caribbean, Miami, Florida and back."

Chris and Rupert schooled their faces at the reference to the islands and just smiled, nodding like two back-shelf car dogs on a bumpy road.

"Is the Falklands – sorry The Malvinas – a tourist spot now?" Chris asked in a tone of mild curiosity. Rafe smiled at the correction Chris had made in deference to the Argentinian name for the disputed islands. "Yes. After the war your government deepened the harbour in an effort to promote the islands as a tourist spot, and now the tourists flock in. I think, yes, ships go maybe twice a week. Another ship also calls there on the way back from America. They do good trade – but more with foreign tourists than local people," Rafe shrugged. "For me, I don't care. Malvinas, Folk-lands, if it works is great. I would rather forget the problems, promote business," he continued with another shrug. "And, you know, why dig up the past? Let's get on with making money, whatever our governments think."

Rupert smiled. "Surely there's no danger of another invasion happening again, not with the embassy opening and talks starting between your government and ours?" Rupert questioned in disingenuous horror at the thought. "That would be the death for business here."

"Ach, you never know. There are always a few hot heads, given the chance of power." Rafe continued. "But is one thing I say that is true, whoever should get for us back the islands will have power for life." Rupert nodded, remembering Margaret Thatcher's landslide election victory on the back of pretty much the same sense of nationalism. "Pride, you know, victory would be great. Perhaps that is the main attraction for any president. That and the oil everyone says is there. But who knows? If we make money, money will be more important than power. Come, this is getting depressing, let us not dwell on the past. Another Quilmes?"

Everyone nodded, and in that moment Chris caught Rupert's eye discreetly and what passed between them was worth a whole conversation. Siobhan turned the subject again to the liner, but in a different direction.

"You know, it would have been on a boat about that size that many of the Irish emigrated to Argentina in the early eighteen-hundreds. Not as smart as that one, of course, but it was a great adventure to escape the homeland and go exploring in this warm and fertile place." She looked around appreciatively.

"I didn't know that," Rupert commented. "Were there many?"

"Oh yes, we've always loved the land, us Irish. Loads of families came and settled here. You still get lots of blue eyed, blond-haired Argentinians, and there's a lot of Irish names. You love your polo, Rupert?" He nodded. "Well one of the most talented and well known polo dynasties here is of Irish descent."

It always surprised Rupert just how partisan and loyal to their roots the Irish were, no matter how disparate a connection and no matter where in the world they were.

"Really, who?"

Rafe jumped in, "The Pieres family. They produced a whole family team of ten-goalers and now the sons of Gonazalo, the father, are well on the way to being the best in the world, along with the young pretender Cambiaso, of course,."

"Ten-goalers?" Chris queried.

"Yes," Rupert answered. "Polo's like golf, and every player gets a handicap. But in polo it is the other way around. Zero is rubbish and ten is the best. To put it into perspective, there are many hundreds – maybe thousands – of scratch golfers in the world. But there are only seven ten-goalers, and they are all South American," Rupert finished. "Must be something in the water, but either way I shall look forward to my first game on Saturday."

Rafe was impressed with Rupert's knowledge and smiled. "Really, where are you going?"

"Oh, I thought I would take Chris to the Tortugas Club; part of the Triple Crown is being played and a friend of Claire, my girlfriend back in England, has invited us to meet up for a drink and watch the game," Rupert's explanation was at variance to the truth, but it sounded natural enough and nobody batted an eyelid.

"That will be excellent," Rafe said. "It will be good for you to see your first game at such a level, Chris." The conversation moved on and drifted around the Irish immigrants, polo and property.

Finally, the late afternoon sun started to drop a little and the heat began to dissipate as a gentle breeze blew from the river. They left their waterside table and returned to the BMW and drove back to the office to make detailed plans for the reception party.

Chapter Ten

London

Unlike Buenos Aires, the weather in London was cold, wet and depressing. For the couple who had followed Siobhan a few days earlier, it was not the only depressing thing going on in their lives. They sat in MI6 headquarters in front of Richard Johnston, learning very little.

"Well?" queried the man, Davies.

"Nothing concrete, I am afraid. It was just a call to her cousin in Northern Ireland. Nothing really suspicious, just general chat, maybe a slightly cryptic reference to a 'wee man', but that could be a lover, nephew. There's nothing really."

"Look, when you sent us to check, you said that it was just routine and nothing was concrete." Johnston nodded. "But when we were following her, both Chrissy and I felt that she was either evading us, or that she was really on edge. Yes, I know she's trained and that she lived a double life in Northern Ireland, and I know from experience that that always stays with you. But there was *something* else. Something not quite tangible, call it a hunch. It just didn't feel right." he finished lamely.

Chrissy continued, "Is there anything at all in her record or her ability to perform that called this surveillance on? Or is it just routine?"

"You don't know the full story, and I have no intention of telling you it, but I know you are aware of what happened to Andrew Waddington–"

"Any news on that front?" Chrissy interrupted.

"Vital signs are getting stronger, but he's still in an induced coma so we don't know any more about what happened, but to all intents and purposes we're treating it as if it was an accident. Now, as I was saying–"

He frowned and broke off for a moment, realising that he needed to give the two of them some leeway, knowing that everybody felt the potential loss or harm of a close colleague very keenly. MI6, despite its cold blooded attitude, was a tight knit group who all pulled together, and the loss of a teammate was always devastating.

"Everyone on this job is being double vetted, even Sergeant Adams – who has come up clean, you'll be glad to know; the man has an exemplary record and is one of the most decorated soldiers in the Regiment, so I would expect nothing less. But my point is, no one is above suspicion. Now, on an otherwise un-blemished record, Siobhan Clifford had just one small question mark. Nothing could be proved and no action was taken; it was just a 'coincidence too far' in my opinion."

"Go on."

"Four years ago we were tracking two IRA suspects and a third man who we didn't know. But we wanted him badly because he was reputed to be quite high up, a former bomb maker turned quartermaster and more importantly a planner and financier within the IRA. He was apparently well connected and getting the real money in for arms and the cause. Regular trips to America, that sort of thing. Anyway, just before the ambush we'd planned to trap them in a safe house, our mystery man disappeared. He was clearly warned and he wasn't there when we went in. Still don't know how he got out.

"Just before the trap was sprung, Siobhan went AWOL, off the grid for fifteen minutes; comms down, so she claimed. Came back up just before it was sprung. Nothing could be proved and the only thing out of the ordinary was a paperboy making his delivery five minutes before the hit. We couldn't stop him as we reasoned it would alert them. Everything else went as smooth as clockwork. And after that," Johnston gave an expressive shrug and offered them an insincere grin. "Her career and missions, intel, everything else, were all exemplary. And let's face it, she has as good a reason as anybody for hating the IRA." They both nodded.

"So what the hell would the IRA have to do with the Argies? It's a damn long way from Northern Ireland," Chrissy asked.

"Which is exactly why she was chosen, along with her typing skills and excellent Spanish; apparently she went to Chile on a school exchange and excelled. Anyway, there is a good deal riding on this. So, I know it is Five's home turf, but I want you to liaise with a Five contact," he flipped a file across, "In Northern Ireland. Go over there as a couple, see what you can find. But, and this is very important, if you come across any 14 Int, not a word about the operation or Clifford. Make up any cover story you want. Understood?"

They both nodded, got up and left the room. Once they were gone, Johnston steepled his fingers, gazed into the distance and made a decision. He picked up the phone.

"I need the CO of 14 Int, secure line. Thank you."

The call came through and he brought his opposite number up to speed on everything that had occurred, outlining his thoughts and concerns. He also asked that no communications be made with Siobhan Clifford directly, and to advise other members of

14 Int that she was in deep cover and that it could jeopardise her safety if she spoke to anyone in the unit. His request was granted and the call terminated

The next call was to arrange to meet with the other members of the Security Council who had been present at Rupert's briefing, as well as Peters. Things were getting more complicated by the minute, and Johnston didn't like the direction in which it was heading. He reflected that he had nothing concrete either. Like Davies, it was just a hunch. But in his world hunches usually proved correct.

Northern Ireland

The next morning Chrissy Meyers and Adam Davies boarded a flight to Northern Ireland. Landing at Aldergrove airport in Belfast some two hours later, they were met by a Five driver who took them to a secure government building on the outskirts of the city. The briefing with the Five team was precise and informative. An operation was brewing, and while they couldn't be a part of it, the team promised them that they would be kept fully informed.

In contrast to the romantic image of Irish terrorists living in farmhouses and making lighting strikes in a bid for freedom before disappearing over the border by dawn's early light, the reality was much more mundane and boring. The usual haunts were council houses on the many estates that surrounded Belfast, with the inevitable Protestant/Catholic divide. These estates were partly vacant because of the Troubles, and there were always houses to rent in many of the terraces. What was harder to organise was realistic cover for anyone renting a house, but once that had been established, the rest was easy.

The old terraces, like many in London and other UK cities,

had no dividing walls in the attic space. As a result, what the IRA often failed to capitalise upon or secure was the ability to move from one house to the next, often with the possibility of traversing a whole row of a dozen or more houses without being discovered. Many operations had been carried out by the intelligence services by making use of the roof spaces without being discovered. Using details that had been gathered through listening devices, they had often been able to foil IRA plots,

'Det', as 14 Int were known, had become very adept at this sort of intelligence gathering and used women in many roles. It was very easy for Irish operatives to pose as a couple and carry on with normal married life as far as the outside world was concerned. Lying up in a roof void for three or four days was smelly, dirty work, but the operatives could not afford too much movement or unnecessary noise. Meyers and Davies were given the details of the latest operation, which was about to be put into play. A local quartermaster was using a mid-terrace house as his HQ, and they had managed to secure an end terrace to rent. The 'Players' regularly came and went to this house and it was deemed to be a potentially rich source of information.

The MI5 team met with them and showed them the setup, promising them full disclosure of anything relevant, and with the meeting concluded, they suggested that the two of them should now return home as soon as possible. There wasn't much point in them hanging around; two spooks rolling around the city, posing as newlyweds but speaking with crystal clear English accents was asking for trouble, and they would soon be noticed. They left on the afternoon flight, not feeling as if they had really achieved much for their day's travel. But as Meyers said once the wheels were up and they were safely in the air again, intelligence work was all about patience and reliable information.

When they returned, they reported to Johnston, who was surprisingly pleased with the news.

"It's in place then? Good. We shall see what transpires. I just hope that we gain the confirmation – or not – in time to help our team in Argentina."

"They seemed to think that it could take weeks of lying up in some mouldy attic waiting for a nugget of relevant information," Davies said. "I mean we don't even know if this particular quartermaster – who we understand is a member of the IRA army council – is relevant to Siobhan or indeed anything to do with Argentina, do we? The only link I can think of is religion, as they are both staunch Roman Catholic countries. At least the IRA's area is."

"Come on, don't be naive," Johnson said. "We all know that as the power struggle in Belfast has weakened, the real reason for the 'cause', as they will insist on calling it, is money and power. They've become nothing more than a bunch of Irish gangsters masquerading under the banner of ideology. There's only one relevant mutual point of interest – the Provos and the Argies both hate the British. The other point to bear in mind is this: the IRA have long held suspected links with the Revolutionary Armed Forces of Colombia and we know that Niall Connolly, fluent Spanish speaker and a leading member of the PIRA, has been training FARC rebels down there. So there is a link, and the two causes could easily help each other if necessary."

Meyers and Davies looked at each other meaningfully, feeling they had been dismissed with that final remark. They rose from their chairs and left Johnston's office. Johnston spun around on his chair and gazed out over the murky Thames, a worried frown on his face. He still wasn't sure how it all fitted together, and hated the idea that something this important could be riding on a surveyor and a soldier way across on the other side of the world.

CHAPTER ELEVEN

Rupert and Chris had a busy week. For his part, Rupert was in his element, and thoroughly enjoyed learning about a new city from a commercial viewpoint. While he had no intention of forgetting the real reason they were there, he had to admit that he liked Buenos Aires a lot. The vibrancy was palpable; everything a mixture of exotic colours and sights; with old colonial mixing cleverly in with the new shopping centres and high rise office buildings. The basic infrastructure was excellent, but he could not believe how quickly the smart areas degenerated into urban slums as soon as he left a specific zone. The riverside development was a major fascination for him, and clearly played a significant role in the overall focus of development in BA – not dissimilar to the Docklands in London and Canary Wharf, but with a more Latin sense of daring and flair.

Chris could not get over how excited Rupert was at the prospect of doing deals here, and was beginning to realise just how perfect their cover was with Rupert as the front man. It would be impossible to fake the enthusiasm and energy coming off him as far as deals and new markets to conquer were concerned, and it made him smile. In fact the only person who seemed slightly less than completely at ease was young Alex, who while superficially friendly towards them always seemed a little reserved. Chris had the distinct impression of being constantly scrutinised.

The round of lunches with other agents that Rafe organised was perfect cover, allowing them to become quickly recognised as a new force within the city. Although it was still early days, everyone seemed to take them at face value and were keen to benefit from the potential influx of investment capital they had brought with them as ambassadors for HBJ. At the end of the first week, they left on Saturday morning for Pilar and the Tortugas Polo Club. The twenty-five minute drive to Pilar, as predicted, was an easy one, and they soon found themselves at the club itself, which was set in magnificent grounds befitting one of the country's top three polo clubs, and home to one of the Triple Crown tournaments.

A sweeping tree-lined drive led up to a main arched entrance in bright white stucco, granting access to the carparks and the clubhouse. The colonial buildings and the main clubhouse sat in an island of rich green, spawned from a number of polo pitch-es, each of around thirteen acres set against the backdrop of a beautifully manicured golf course. The car parks were starting to fill up with a host of four-wheel drives, Mercedes and shiny black Range Rovers being the transport of choice. As it was an important game, the match was to be held on the Number One pitch, with the magnificent stands leading up from the pitch side.

Chris looked around, shaking his head.

"Never in my wildest dreams did I imagine I'd find myself working in a place like this. It's like I've walked onto the set of *Pretty Woman*," he commented.

The knowledgeable crowd were mostly Argentinians, with quite a few aficionados of British origin, but there was no sign of Julia Roberts in a spotty dress. It was a sea of white linen, capybara belts, ankle boots and flat Gucci loafers. And Chris was surprised to see that so many of the woman were blond or fair haired.

"They certainly are a good looking nation – and the women don't seem to go off with age, which is another bonus." Rupert laughed, grinning at Chris. "You see, life as a surveyor ain't that bad."

"Yeah, when I retire from my other life…" Chris said quietly.

There were hundreds of children running around or riding bicycles, wielding short polo mallets or 'foot sticks' and hoping to be the next ten-goaler. Rupert explained that while English kids would kick a football around from an early age, the Argentinians would be given a small polo stick and every waking moment would be spent with it in their hand, until it became an extension of their own arm.

"It really is a different world," Adams observed, then continued quietly. "Just before we meet our contact I want to have a look at the seats from a distance to get it set in my mind so I can plan exactly what will happen. What seats are we in again? Row one wasn't it?"

Rupert consulted the tickets. "Yep. Row one, seats twenty-three and twenty four. That means that you will be able to use your camera equipment easily. We'll have to get seated at least ten minutes before the game starts and our contact will be in the row directly behind us, right at the end of the seating run. Apparently it should be obvious when we get there.

Chris was carrying his camera bag; a large leather holdall with two hand straps and a shoulder strap, and although it weighed quite a bit, he knew that on the return trip after the exchange it would be considerably heavier. As they made their way to the elegant clubhouse that presided over the grounds, he spied out their designated seats, nodding with silent approval. Not surprisingly, they bumped into various members of the property world along the way, people with whom they had become acquainted over the previous few days. It all made perfect cover and added a strong layer of veracity to their position.

Not for the first time, Chris was pleased with the strength of their cover and the lack of any connection with the embassy or any government agency. They ascended the steps into the cool, porticoed veranda that led to the main entrance hall of the clubhouse. The walls were adorned with pictures of famous players and founding members from the club's inception in 1927. Rupert felt honoured to be there, surrounded by a significant part of Argentinian sporting history – somewhere as important as Lords or Wembley. They made their way to the bar and ordered a couple of bottles of Quilmes before going out onto the raised veranda that looked out over Argentina's own hallowed turf. Gazing out across the crowds, Chris spotted a familiar figure.

"Isn't that Alex there? Look just past that Merc near the end of the stands."

By the time Rupert had looked in the correct spot, Alex, if it was him, had been swallowed up by the rest of the crowd.

"No, you must be imagining it, he would have said, surely?"

Chris shrugged, but he had been pretty certain it was Alejandro. He filed the sighting away in his mind – somewhere where he wouldn't forget it. He didn't believe in coincidences. "OK, but I want to get my camera set up and look legitimate before the game starts. They wandered down to the stands and took up their seats. Directly behind them in seat twenty-four of row two sat a woman. She looked like a native; dark hair hanging loose, tanned skin, layered linen, big sunglasses and her slim waist cinched with a sliver concho belt studded with turquoise stones; very popular amongst the polo-going set over here, Rupert had noted. She ignored them both, concentrating instead on the players warming up on the field, but at her feet was a leather hold-all identical to Chris's.

Chris removed a long bipod camera stand and set up a heavy

camera with a telephoto lens, looking every inch the professional photographer. He tested the motor drive, setting off a series of whirring clicks as the fast shutter responded. If Rupert had noticed, he would have seen Chris taking a series of pictures of the spot where he thought he had spotted Alejandro. Reaching down, Chris pushed the bulky camera bag towards the back of his seat in a seemingly natural move in order give himself more space.

The players came out and lined up to be introduced by the commentator. Having never been to a polo match before, Chris was amazed at the skill and speed with which the game was played. Rupert explained that some of the best players in the world were out there today, and even he had only seen the Coronation Cup at Guards before, which paled into insignificance compared to this. Chris commented on the speed of one player in particular, who appeared to be about 15 years of age.

"That's Adolfo Cambiaso, he is a freak of nature and will probably be one of the best players of all time. He is already an eight-goaler and he's still only fifteen. Unbelievable!" Rupert enthused, watching the boy take an air shot; plucking the ball out of the air and tapping it with his mallet, keeping it from the surface of the field as he rode towards the opposing team's goal. No one was able to touch him. "How the hell does he do that?"

In the excitement of the goal, Chris reached behind to his right and pulled forward the leather holdall by the woman's feet, which was zipped closed.

The game was eventually won by La Dolfina, Cambiaso's side, by a narrow margin of 11-10. It had been a brilliant match by anyone's standards, and Rupert had enjoyed himself thoroughly – although he wished that Claire could have been there with him rather than Chris, whose attention had seemed to wander once he'd picked up the basic idea of the game, and who seemed more interested in scanning the crowd. With the presentations over, the crowd began to dissipate. Rupert and Chris made their way back to the Toyota, with Chris trying hard not to show the true weight of his newly acquired holdall.

Two girls were walking towards them, talking to each other and completely unaware of what was happening around them. The nearest woman almost collided with Chris. He stopped abruptly, just avoiding full collision and the woman arrested her stride by placing both hands forward on Chris's arms, bracing herself for rather longer than necessary. She gasped and apologised in Spanish. Then, making eye contact and laughing gently, she changed to heavily accented English

"I am so sorry."

Chris found himself looking at a pair of beautiful, slightly slanting, almost oriental brown eyes framed in an oval face and set against cafe au lait skin. He smiled winningly and said in fast Spanish that it was no problem and that he was at fault. She and her friend giggled together appealingly and she continued in English.

"Your Spanish is very good. I am sorry. I am Valentina Perez, and my friend is Susannah Ortega, how do you do?"

"Chris Adams, and this is Rupert Brett." He nodded, introducing Rupert.

"Please call me Susie," her pretty companion invited.

Rupert ran his eyes over the shorter woman. She was a typical Argentine in looks; dark, brown wavy hair, slightly bleached by the sun, dark Hispanic eyes and tanned skin, dressed in a white linen dress cinched in with a plain broad, capybara belt. "I am sorry," Chris declared noticing her rubbing her shin. "Did you hurt yourself on my camera equipment? The lenses can be sharp and heavy."

"No, no. I did wonder what was in there though."

"Ah yes, an amateur hobby I am afraid. Would you allow me to buy you a drink to apologise for my aggressive cameras?"

"We can do better than that. We have a picnic set out in the back of our car just there." Valentina pointed at a black Range Rover Vogue with the tailgate down and a white suited waiter setting out crockery and delicacies on a folding table. "Perhaps you could join us instead? It was after all me who bumped into you." She smiled and flirted with no hint of self-consciousness, as though it were a perfect progression from an accidental meeting.

"I am sure we would be delighted to accept."

Chris deferred to Rupert with a look, urging him silently not to refuse despite the clumsily-staged encounter that had taken place. He need not have worried. Despite the almost imperceptible exchange of worried looks, Rupert agreed with a smile.

"But first I need to drop my camera equipment back in the car." Before the women had time to object he departed, leaving Rupert there to keep them company. He returned five minutes later to find all three in a deep and flirtatious conversation, apparently unfazed by his departure. Chris soon learned that despite her heavily accented English, Valentina understood the idioms and subtle humour of the language perfectly, enabling her to spar with all the aplomb of a native. He accepted a glass of champagne and sipped the bubbles appreciatively, smiling with his eyes as Valentina finished an amusing story about her first time in a polo match, which had ended with her horse bolting in the opposite direction of the play, only to have the ball land in front of her and see her pony kick it through the goal. The way in which she told the story was very funny, and her timing immaculate, like someone who had been trained in the nuances of conversation and social behaviour.

After a few minutes, Rupert and Chris became acutely aware that they had valuable merchandise back in the car, which Chris was making sure he never lost sight of in the distance but did not want to leave unattended. "I hate to be boring," Rupert said after a short while, "but I am afraid we do need to get back as we have so much to catch up on. New markets, office stuff, that sort of thing."

"On a Saturday?" Valentina said. "You need to relax and adopt the Argentinean way. Enjoy the sun and balance your life. This is Argentina!"

"I'd love to," Chris said in a resentful tone. "But he's the boss. Times like this you can see why." Chris shrugged, laughing at both Susannah and Valentina's horrified expressions at the idea of working on a Saturday.

They made their apologies and made to leave, but not before Chris had asked if they could meet again. They agreed, and Valentina passed him a scrap of paper with her number on it. Rupert played along, although he really was a one-man woman and he recalled Claire's threat about the action she would take if he was ever unfaithful. They walked quickly back to the Land Cruiser, saying nothing until they were back inside it, at which point they both laughed, shaking their heads.

"Unbelievable," Rupert said. "She's as savvy as they come, that one. The gall of her. I couldn't believe it when I saw her face without the sunglasses. I thought I had made a mistake from the file photograph, then when she told you her name…" he finished shaking his head.

"I know," Chris continued. "But it was a clever move. If we had shown even a hint of recognition at her face or name she would have known instantly that we were connected with the embassy or we were spooks. She had nothing to lose. If we'd shown any recognition, they would have known that we weren't who we were pretending to be – and because we pretended not to recognise her, she carried on digging, thinking she was safe. After all, why should an embassy warn two perfectly legitimate surveyors about the dangers of a secret service agent? Good call about the extra work and pushing the boss/employee button, got us off the hook and out of there quickly. I don't want to lose the contents of this bag. But at least it shows how thorough they are, although I would say we passed with flying colours."

"Brave shout about the date though, she looks as though she'd eat you for breakfast," Rupert said. "Still, if you hadn't followed it up after such a blatant play it would have been another dead giveaway."

"Thank you, were not just thugs with guns, you know," Chris chided. "But you're right, we have to play the game to the hilt. We need to let Siobhan know that a test contact has been made; she'll know what to do with the intel and it'll also give her the heads-up if she gets a test contact of her own. What it does prove though, more than anything, is that something is up and we just need to find out what."

"When I did some work before for DCI Webster over in Italy, he said on more than one occasion 'follow the money'. He was right every time, too. I have a feeling that's what this is all about. It's about power and the clear run to rule the country for ever, and it's about the emotive pull of the Falklands to the Argentinians. But I bet we find that it all boils down to money, and who is getting what from where."

"Maybe so," Chris said. "But you also never really know your enemy until you know what he wants. Maybe it's money, maybe it's some kind of ideological supremacy, like Ireland used to be. 'We both believe in the same God, but your way of believing in him is wrong, so I'm going to kill you.' Once you understand the logic and sense behind a statement like that, you're halfway towards understanding the ideas of revolution. Just replace God with politics. For you it's money because money's all you know. No offence, but you just haven't met as many crazies as I have – yet. But whether it's money or ideology, the rest of the pieces will fall into place when we find out what they want."

Over recent days the three of them had gelled really well, with after-hours debriefs in Rupert and Chris's apartment away from the eyes and ears of the rest of the local HBJ team. Not that any question marks had been raised, apart from a general feeling about Alex, but they adhered to the motto of trusting no one outside their tight little group. Siobhan had arranged for a direct line to be added to the HBJ switchboard in London which automatically transferred to the mysterious Mr Peters. But if anyone traced the call or the background number it would show as a line registered to HBJ. It could still be tapped, so they needed to be careful what they said, but things could be worded cryptically, and Siobhan was an expert in the art of deception. This would change to some extent with the secure comms equipment that Chris had picked up today.

"Come on, let's get back as soon as we can and see what's in the magic bag you're guarding so closely," he joked.

Back at the apartment block, they secured the door after letting Siobhan know they'd arrived and giving her a few minutes to join them. She had spent the Saturday shopping with Maria, getting to know her and getting a feel for the mood of the country, trying to sense if anything was amiss.

Chris opened the large bag, and Rupert immediately felt a lot more respect for the female MI6 operative who'd had to carry it to the drop off point with all the contents inside. Chris pulled out a Browning high-power 9mm in a Price Weston pancake holster, a second generation Glock 19 9mm with a standard 15 round and an extended 19 round magazine together with another pancake holster and a Diemaco C8 SFW with extending stock, night sight and suppressor. There were three additional magazines together with two spare boxes of 5.56 x 45mm cartridges. The C8 had the longer sixteen-inch barrel for greater accuracy and was also fitted with a laser sight and sliding top rail.

Chris finally took out a Smith & Wesson 10-10 revolver with a three-inch barrel and a box of 9mm cartridges. The last piece of equipment was the most intriguing; a small silver metal box about two and a half inches deep and nine inches square with two metal clips holding it shut. Chris opened the lid, and inside the padded case was an electronic device comprising a keypad, a small screen and a cable to what looked like a normal telephone handset.

Argentina's government run telecoms industry had been sold to two operators a month or so previously: the southern corporation was ENTEL (soon to become Telecom Argentina), which had a mandate to set up the first mobile communications system in the country. In reality this was proving very inefficient due to the lack of infrastructure and masts to support the system; for many months it would only work sporadically around BA. It was also monitored by MREC, who picked up on any calls that sounded suspicious. Rupert and Chris's mobiles would undoubtedly fall into that category.

The encrypted satellite phone that Chris was now holding was an essential part of their equipment, as it would enable them to speak freely with Peters at the FO and report back without being overheard. It could also be connected to the private fax machine that had been put into the apartment so their Argentinian counterparts would not know everything that was being reported to their legitimate clients from UK and worldwide

"Wow, I have heard about these but I've never seen one before," Rupert said.

"Actually, you will have. You know when you see the Queen on trips and her assistant walks close by with a tan briefcase? Well, that carries her own personal encrypted phone, we can't have the press finding out that the corgis have got the shits, can we?" he chuckled. "I'll need to show you how to use this. Siobhan already knows, of course," Chris said, nodding in her direction and smiling. "But you will need to get up to speed, just in case."

"It's not that hard. It's a straightforward bit of kit really,"

Siobhan said. "Codes are the hardest things to deal with if it is locked," she looked at Chris.

"Yes, but we'll deal with all that in a minute. This is yours, Siobhan," he said, passing her the Browning, the magazine and the spare cartridges.

She took the automatic and stripped it down into its component parts in a matter of seconds, inspecting them. After re-assembling them, she checked the action, racking back the slider and letting it return with a metallic click. Her actions clearly showed that she had done this many times before – which she had, sleeping with a pistol under her pillow in Northern Ireland on many occasions. She picked up one of the pancake holsters and checked the fit for the Browning against her lower back and side

"I prefer the side, but without a heavy jacket or a Barbour it's a bit of a giveaway," she commented, her accent thickening unconsciously as she handled the Browning, as though the gun took her back to her native land and the Troubles

"The only thing I don't like is that the safety is on the left, which makes it awkward for a southpaw like me." Chris nodded, picking up the Glock 19 and stripping it down. "I prefer the Sig Sauer. It's more reliable, but the 19 is smaller, better for undercover work. He looked around in the bottom of the holdall and found one or two more items, including a wicked looking Sig Sauer Tactical folding knife. He depressed the button with his thumb and the straight three-inch blade sprang out. He smiled without any humour whatsoever and made a couple of passes with it in the air

"Mmm. They say that if you need a knife you've fucked up, but as a last resort I would rather have it than not."

Finally, he checked the Smith and Wesson, flicking out the chamber and filling it with cartridges, slipping it into the small ankle holster.

Rupert looked from the weapons to Chris and Siobhan. The guns and the knife seemed to turn them into different people and he wasn't sure he liked what he saw. "Don't I get one?" he asked.

"No, if you needed a gun it means we'd be dead, and so would you. Don't worry, we will look after you in the unlikely event that we get into trouble. This is for security, and revolvers hardly ever fail and never jam. They're a lot less accurate than an automatic, but they've saved my life on more than one occasion." Chris nodded, feeling more comfortable with the real tools of his trade around him. He turned his attention to the C8. It was of light-weight construction and he held it like it was a part of himself.

"Now, there are a couple of gun clubs on Avenido del Libertador about ten minutes north of here, and the Tiro Federal Argentino looks good. I've checked, and apparently we can just rock up, pay a fee and test whatever we like. I love this country – no restrictions, not like the UK. I have a permit here with a false name and we are good to go."

He waved some false papers he'd taken from the bag. Before they left, he secured the satellite phone in the false bottom of the wardrobe along with the rest of the contents of the bag and put the rifle and handguns back into the holdall together with the ammunition.

They arrived at the club, showed Chris's false paperwork and booked some time on the traps to show good cover and also to get their collective eye in before moving on to try their personal weapons in a private booth on the indoor range. Rupert surprised them both with his ability, although it came as no surprise to him. He had grown up shooting with his father and had handled a gun as soon as he could safely use one, regularly sharing a half gun on the shoot his father attended. Eventually they moved to the private range and tried all their different weapons. Chris stripped his three and Siobhan demonstrated her considerable skill on the range and in her fast draw from the pancake holster. Her first try was slower to Rupert's eye, but as she practiced she became quicker and quicker, until she was finally able to produce the pistol in one smooth, fast motion, cocked and ready to fire.

An hour on the range proved sufficient, and they went through two boxes of cartridges for each weapon. Predictably the Browning jammed once, much to Siobhan's frustration. She stripped it down, oiled it and put it back together, testing it until she was happy with the action. Chris, for his part, showed great dexterity and fine-tuned the sights on the C8 until he was happy with the set up. Rupert tried all the guns even though he had not been assigned a weapon, just to get some familiarity with them. He confessed to liking the Smith & Wesson best for its simplicity and feeling of natural alignment, even though its accuracy over greater distances was less than either of the automatics.

They left the gun club and returned to their separate apartments, with Siobhan saying that she needed to go for a run to loosen the stress of concentrating. Rupert said he'd go with her. In the short time they had been there, he had run every day, and while he wasn't up to Chris's stamina and speed, his overall fitness had improved to a good level. Chris had also set up a medium weight punch bag in the spare bedroom and had taught Rupert the rudiments of chi sau: the 'sticky hands' training system of Wing Chun. He had told Rupert that while the Regiment's training for unarmed combat was second to none, he and others had gone on to hone their skills and find more traditional fighting systems to complement their arsenal. Chris discovered that Wing Chun suited his physique, and found it very effective, especially for close quarter fighting. Chi sau was perfect, as it speeded up the reaction times of blocks and strikes

While Rupert and Siobhan ran, Chris reported back to Peters at the FO, giving a full briefing of their findings and insinuation into Argentinian society, including his meeting with Valentina

Perez. The report was copied to Johnston at MI6 and the whole chain of command would soon be aware of everything.

Chapter Twelve

Monday saw a new start to the week, and following a formal report on the market to HBJ in London, a raft of hard and specific requirements had been confirmed from European and UK investors keen to buy into the buoyant, rising markets of South America. Rupert was genuinely excited at the prospect of acquiring investments in the burgeoning market.

They had been offered three office blocks by local agents in the central office area of Buenos Aires, and there were two major developments on the river estuary area by the dockland developments up for grabs. One was nearing completion and almost fully pre-let to multiple tenants; the second was at ground level and needed forward funding to kick-start the stagnant development.

Local banks did not want to open themselves up to the financial risks associated with more development; they felt overexposed in the property market anyway. The situation was not dissimilar to periods of the boom-and-bust economic cycle in the UK, and Rupert was only too familiar with the situation. However, there was one major difference here, which had come as a great surprise to him: mortgages, especially commercial ones, were non-existent. All lending was arranged through short term finance and loans. The few mortgages that did exist were so prohibitively leveraged and had so many penalty clauses that they had proved disastrous and had stifled growth.

Rupert felt a certain frisson of excitement at the prospect these opportunities offered. Not just because of the deals themselves, but because he would effectively be 'unlocking' them, making himself a leader in the local BA market. Any agent worth his salt had an ego – it went with the job, almost – and Rupert was no exception.

He stood before the mirror in the bathroom making a final adjustment to his diamond weave tie. The face that looked back at him had not changed that much since his naïve debut on to the London markets six years ago. His jawline at thirty was still strong; his clear blue eyes noticed a few new lines of crow's feet and there was a slight bluish tinge under the sockets. His wavy brown hair was as always immaculately styled. But his life experience was there now, reflecting his past adventures in the hard deals of the surveying world and the brutal, criminal hinterland in which he had fought; a scene that was fraught with murder, corruption and kidnapping. There was a steel there that was gradually replacing the laughing, ingenuous young man he had once been. He shrugged off his maudlin thoughts with a cavalier grin. "To battle," he said to himself. He felt like he had in the London of the mid-eighties. There were fortunes to be won for any self-respecting deal junkie

They had made arrangements to visit all of the properties over the next two days. The office buildings were, to all intents and purposes, not dissimilar: shiny, towering edifices of glass, steel and marble, glittering in the hot BA sunshine. The specification was amazing.

"This is at least as good as top London office buildings, if not better. And you get the added bonus of not being hammered by local authorities on car parking ratios and the Motor City rules," he laughed. The main agents, Ravos Eire Imb, had led the viewings of the offices and Rupert and Chris had been impressed with their smooth operation. Garcia Imb were next; they were the firm involved with the riverside developments. Rupert and Chris arrived at the entrance to the development site, where they found themselves looking at a sign at the guarded gates which read *O'Gorman Developments.* They exchanged clandestine glances.

"Si," Rafe explained. "In the 1800s we have many of Irish emigrating to our country, more so in 1845 with your *ambruna de la patata,* how do you say?

"Potato famine?" Chris offered.

"Si, potato famine. They all came over and many did very well: construction, farming, property, especially in Rio del Plata, Punta Arenas, BA and of course in the Malvinas: big Irish population lived there. Although many left, I think there are now about between half and one million Irish families in Argentina today. Many have kept their names through the generations, together with their traditions and loyalties. After all, we are two strong Catholic countries. So this company are two brothers doing well, but they need finance to get the deals off balance sheet and produce more," Rafe concluded.

They went up to the marketing suite, where any one of the charming Argentinian beauties could have sold snow to Eskimos, provided said Eskimos were red-blooded males. They kept their flirtations just within the bounds of professionalism, mixing business with persuasion. Eventually one of the O'Gorman brothers arrived, a chunky, middle-aged man whose Irish ancestry showed in his angular features and twinkling eyes. He had grey showing at the temples and in the sideburns of his crinkly hair. The face showed threaded lines of red veins on his chin and nose from too much whiskey; he looked a hard, tough man.

"Pablo O'Gorman," he offered. "Good to meet you."

The accent was a mix of Latin and Irish, and he had clearly

learned his English back in the old country. The handshake was firm and dry; and the eyes searched each of the two surveyors with a direct scrutiny.

"So, what do you think of our developments? Pretty fine, eh?" he continued, spreading an all-encompassing arm around across the bay area. They nodded in acquiescence, commenting on the strategic prominence of the scheme.

"Well, if everything goes right this is just Phase One, but I am sure that you know about Phase Two. That's what we need finance for, it'll allow us to expand into the commercial docks up-river."

"Ah, yes," Chris commented. "That is where they are fitting out the liner we saw last week. Great to see ship building surviving. Not like back home."

"Indeed, and where is *home* for you Chris?" O'Gorman asked.

"Wales. Cowbridge to be precise."

"Ah, a fellow Celt, good man. Our family are originally from Wexford. Came over on the infamous *SS Dresden* in 1889, but that is a story that's best saved for another time," he finished smoothly before anyone could ask him to elaborate. He showed them up to his office, which was at mezzanine level with views across the marketing suite to the harbour beyond.

In the office, O'Gorman, the agent from Garcia, Rafe, a leggy beauty from the marketing suite and the two English surveyors sat down to discuss the project and, most importantly, the price. The plans were examined and the cashflows considered in detail. The bottom line was a quoted price that seemed a tad full to Rupert's experienced estimation: One hundred and fifty million dollars. Chris had trouble keeping a straight face; this was a different kind of stress for him. *Give me the battlefield any day,* he thought

To Rupert, it was just another day at the office.

They discussed business and the prospects for the site for a few minutes before Rupert concluded the meeting. "All right, we'll think about it. There are one or two other projects we have to consider and we'll add it to our report back to London in due course."

As a parting shot O'Gorman threw in: "Of course if you'd like to do both projects I am sure we could come to a price to reflect some kind of scale discount. It is after all in both our interests to progress matters and I am sure the agency terms would reflect favourably with Rafe here."

Which was about as subtle a fee bribe as Rupert would have expected from the Argies. "Oh, I'm sure it would," he replied amicably. "But you know the client is king and he has the final say. Let me see what I can do. Perhaps we can speak in the next couple of days."

With that, a final handshake and wave to the others, the party left

"Fuck me, Rupert," Chris admonished him in the car back to the office. "Remind me never to play poker with you. What gives? Was that a good price or not?"

"No, it didn't feel right. I think we will get him below a hundred and forty without the second Phase. We'll see. He needs us more than we need him, and I don't like the Blarney even if it is sugar-coated with Latin charm." He chuckled as he thought of the negotiations that were to come. "Don't worry, we'll get there. You'll get a supplement to your army pension yet."

The confidence was fizzing palpably from Rupert. This is what he lived for, he nodded in concession to his own ego: the chase and the kill of the deal. Chris knew instinctively that this sort of cover could not be learnt or manufactured. Rafe or Alex would know straight away if Rupert was not what he seemed to be. But now they would find the whole process completely credible without question, although apart from Alex's slightly hostile, diffident attitude nothing had led them to believe that anything was untoward. The figures were analysed again over the next twenty-four hours, and despite Rupert's misgivings the yield was up in the double figures for what was not only the biggest, but also the best deal in town. The price they eventually settled on was a shade under one hundred and forty million. With a major UK pension fund and a venture fund as the buyers, UK Panoramic had set up capital for just this sort of opportunistic high risk, high yield purchase, and they loved it. Two days later, after the deal was agreed, an exchange of documents was arranged, leading to the *intercambio de contratos*

"This," Rafe explained. "As I am sure you know, is the equivalent of your exchange of contracts, and the process is very similar. A deposit is paid, there is no going back without loss of deposit and they could, in theory, sue you to complete the deal. But I don't think this will happen here, no?" he finished, laughing.

"Now there is one more thing you need to know," Rafe continued, "which I think will be of relevance to you and your financial partners. The money, when we exchange and pay over the final amount in Argentina, the deal is certified and registered by the *escribano, notario publico,* for you I think the Notary Public? Yes, well when the deal is completed and the money is handed over, a minimum of ten percent is paid in cash, and—"

"What? You mean I have to turn up with a briefcase containing one point four million US dollars?! You're kidding me!" said Rupert.

"I know that seems strange, but here in BA it is how things are done."

"And I suppose the *notario* just records the price that is transferred in wire transfer or in cheque amounts, and the bag of money becomes some kind of commission on the deal, is that right?" *My god, this is just like Italy, only worse,* thought Rupert.

A nod from Rafe confirmed this. A simultaneous thought occurred to Rupert and Chris at this moment. They had to free up some money to start the trail. Once they had done that, they would do what Rupert had suggested – follow the money.

Chapter Thirteen

London

Later that day, Chris reported everything back to Peters at the FO on the encrypted satellite phone. He included in his report the details about the money for the deposit; the Irish connection of the developer (which he considered pretty tenuous) and the possibility of a very large briefcase full of money 'disappearing', to be used as an untraceable funding source. If it wasn't just a matter of personal greed, funding was clearly the intention; but the question remained as to who was sitting in line for this particular windfall.

How did it tie in with a possible second Falklands invasion? A few million was nothing compared to the cost of funding a major military operation, and in any event the government could just ensure a stricter tax system if it wanted to and fund the invasion itself. No, this was just another piece of a more complex puzzle, along with the potential interest from the Argentinian secret service in the form of Valentina Perez – if indeed it was any more than a casual check-up on a newly arrived group of foreigners. After reading Chris's report, Peters called Johnston at MI6 to inform him of all that he'd been told. Johnston was receptive and very grateful for the update on the situation. He reciprocated, offering Peters some information that had been passed on by the MI5 and 14 Int forces in Northern Ireland. He explained to Peters about the surveillance operation in the housing estate and their suspicions of an IRA tie-in, however tenuous.

"Interestingly I had a call from Major Simon Dove. Apparently the agency chap in Birmingham…" he refreshed his memory from his notes. "…Jeremy Hughes, who Adams worked for in the first two weeks, reported someone asking for him. No, not English, they had a slight Spanish accent and wanted to know how they could reach him. Hughes gave all the correct answers – gone to London, worked for him for a year, sad to lose him, so on and so forth. So the Argies are definitely checking up on them; they did the same for Brett and Clifford at HBJ apparently. Which I take as good sign, given that it is all watertight and essentially in place.

"Now what is interesting is that the latest reports coming in, apart from the usual boring stuff about bomb preparation and NorAid, is this; there was a definite reference to *the island.* Remember that was exactly the same phrase as Siobhan Clifford used at the end of her conversation with her cousin in Belfast. Now looking at the transcription she said the *"wee man on the island"* He read out loud. "Now what if it is a homophone and they have the same reference? Ireland/Island, you see? This expression was used in reference to a main quartermaster of a number of cells who the players clearly look up to, and they mentioned a contact in the America. The sums of money they alluded to seem far more than the usual boyos in the pub passing the buckets round for a few grenade launchers and M16 carbines, this is serious stuff."

Johnston could hear the cogs turning at the other end of the phone and waited for the response.

"You think that *the island* or *Ireland* might refer to the Falklands? That is a bit of a stretch isn't it? And how do you know about the details of Clifford's conversation with her cousin?"

"If I have the slightest suspicion of anyone who goes off on a mission, they get my special attention. She has few relatives and this is one of her main contacts – who is of course Roman Catholic. I felt it prudent to tap this and one or two more of their family's lines. God alone knows how much it cost me in favours and arm twisting, but there we are."

"Mmm, how very prescient of you," Peters responded drily. Johnston ignored the sly jibe and continued, "What if this is connected in some way? If it is, think on this: it is now November, we are approaching summer in the Southern Hemisphere – sailing season. And the war in the Middle East is hotting up and coming to a crucial point with a very high percentage of our armed forces committed there. If the second invasion is going to happen, it has to be now or in the very near future."

"You could be right. Can you copy a note to all concerned? I'd be grateful – and by the way, I appreciate you sharing everything. Very grateful."

"Not at all, will do."

My God, whatever next, Peters thought, *a word of praise and thanks from the FO, wonders will never cease!* They finished the call and Peters put through a transcript warning Adams about the checking and to stay on high alert.

Meanwhile Johnston turned his mind to the facts and began writing a list in his own inimitable hand:

Falkland's – IRA? Reason?
  Siobhan Clifford – connection? Why?
  Argies – financial wherewithal? Why hurt Waddington, what did he know? Was it coincidence?

Money – where does it go? Is it relevant? Invasion – How is it to be achieved?
Timescale – next 6 months

He began with these points, and expanded them, dictating a memo to all members of the security briefing council and various relevant Ministers concerned. He would have been very interested to hear a conversation that was taking place on the other side of the Atlantic at that moment.

Boston, USA.

Boston was five hours behind the UK and it was mid-morning at the offices of the USE Oil Corporation. The company's palatial offices, which gave amazing views over the beautiful city, were home to one of the most successful oil companies in America. They had drilling rights in the US, the Middle East and interests relating to Russia and the Balkans. What they did not have was a good relationship with Venezuela and other south American oil producing countries – with the exception of Argentina.

The CEO, as he referred to himself – a new phrase not yet in common usage in the UK – was a tough, tanned street fighter of a man, who was as broad as he was tall and had a compressed strength to his powerful frame. Michael Kelly had come up from the streets of South Boston: first as a rigger on the oil rigs and then working his way up to become head of a medium-sized but highly profitable oil company. They may not be the size of Mobil or BP, he had mused many times, but they sure as hell punched above their weight and pro-rata to capital they were far more profitable than the bigger players. He was proud of his Irish heritage and had on more than one occasion clandestinely donated to the cause.

He also privately admitted that the whole thing was screwed unless it changed direction. There were too many leaks and moles within the IRA and its associated groups. It was a leaky sieve, and it was getting worse as time went on, with their power slowly seeping away. He also knew that for the moment, with the war in the Middle East carrying on, their dual fates were closely intertwined.

His secretary buzzed through to say Phillips was on his way in. The rough Southie accent that gave away his Boston origins had been smoothed, and only traces of his original neighbourhood still shone through.

"David, hi. How's things? I hope that you have some good news for me."

Phillips, a tall and ascetic man, was not a soldier or a fighter in the accepted sense, but he was highly intelligent, especially where numbers, accounting and strategy were concerned. He had been recruited by Kelly a long time ago, and while Phillips was a Yale graduate and on the face of it was very different to Kelly, the two men had found something in common, and a friendship of sorts had developed between them.

Phillips's diction was precise and to the point.

"Good, thank you. In answer to your question, I believe I do have good news. We have agreed terms through O'Gorman to sell Phase One and potentially Phase Two of the Rio de la Plata schemes…"

"Who to?" Kelly interrupted.

Phillips permitted himself an indulgent smile, savouring the moment. "You are aware that one of our major US real estate firms took over a British agency earlier this year? Well, they are expanding still further and doing rather well it seems, in Buenos Aires, amongst other cities, bringing much needed capital to a city that's desperate for any kind of financial input to get business rolling."

"No," Kelly interrupted again, chuckling at the irony. "You don't mean we've got the Brits funding our war? Oh man, that is fuckin' priceless. Tell me more."

"It will be just shy of 1.3 million dollars after arrangement fees and a few local bribes, but it's in cash and will be paid into the usual account where it can be passed through the normal channels to the Quartermaster's service. This will of course be the final payment, and secures us the necessary services for the last part of the operation."

"Good. And are we sure everything is secure down there? You know what these dumb fuckin' dagos are like. We only have a small window of opportunity here, as you well know. Once the Middle East is sorted and the Brits are operational again we will not be able to do this. It can't happen at any other time; it has to happen in the next six months. The fuckin' towel-heads set their own fuckin' wells on fire. I mean what a goddamn stupid thing to do. But it helps us, it sure does."

"I realise that," Phillips nodded, "but the UN resolution to exclude Argentina and deny their rights to the Falklands' oilfields have helped us more, although it did cost us a pretty penny."

"Yeah, don't I know it. Everyone's got a price, it just gets higher the further up the shitty stick you get. But we need to move fast, the sailing season's on and so is the exploration season. We need to take control by next year so we can start operations. With Iraq and the Middle East cut off it's a perfect opportunity for us to move in and put ourselves in among the big boys."

"As to security, yes, we have our own people on patrol and looking after things, although we have identified no threats at present. The only potential issue was the embassy man, Waddington, but nothing was certain so we took precautions – or rather we told the MREC to hit him, so we still have complete deniability in the country. A little heavy handed, I felt, but it was made to look like an accident and I don't think the man will be talking for a long time."

"Was he SIS or Secret Service, or whatever the Brits call it?"

"Almost certainly, but every embassy has at least a couple of spooks masquerading as attachés. Don't worry, it is all clear and we've got an eye on the other potential spook, a woman, Sophie Carswell. As yet she's met with no suspicious players at all, so we are clear."

"What about the Brits in the agency, are they clean?"

"Oh yes, the Argentinians have had them checked out; all the backgrounds are exactly as they say – but more importantly, you can't fake what they are doing. It would take years of training to look the part of true agents – or surveyors as they call themselves. And they definitely have the right connections, no self-respecting UK pension fund is going to let a spook invest a hundred and forty million dollars on their behalf."

"Looking good then. So, let's grab the dough and pass it on to the quartermaster. Make sure he's ready to give us the IRA's end of the bargain."

Further details of the plan and its timing were discussed, then Phillips left the office to implement the next stage of the operation.

Chapter Fourteen

Rupert ran steadily around the park in the intense heat, letting his mind drift. He always did his best problem solving when he was running, and today was no exception. The pieces, as far as he was concerned, were starting to fall into place, but there were still huge gaps.

He was convinced that the Irish connection had something to do with it; everywhere he turned there was an Irish influence – even from a century and a half ago, during a time of mass immigration from Ireland. If Siobhan was not on the level, he would have suspected her involvement too, in some way or other, although she must have been vetted thoroughly for this mission and many others. But time was running out if the second invasion was going to happen, and they had all agreed it had to coincide with the Iraq War and the sailing season.

The legals went ahead as the week progressed, and Chris – either despite the warnings or because of them – proceeded with his third date with Valentina Perez. He wanted to know more, and was working on the old adage of keeping his enemies closer. On previous occasions, Rupert and Susannah had been there as a double date, but it became clear that Rupert, although he appreciated Susannah's charms, was going to stay faithful to his relationship with Claire, and this only confirmed what Chris already knew – that Rupert was a one-woman man. The thought of cheating on Claire for no reason other than lust was not in his repertoire. Claire was due to visit in two weeks' time for Christmas, and Rupert obviously wanted to keep his balls exactly where they were. His attitude reassured Chris. At least he wasn't going to be blackmailed through some south American honey-trap and be forced into giving up secrets under the threat of losing Claire.

So tonight was Chris's first single date with Valentina. He knew that it would be interesting and he was not about to let his guard down. So far, the perfunctory question and answer session had been dealt with, everyone now knew who was what, and even the village idiot, he decided, would see that they were the real thing.

So why was she still keen?

He was determined to turn it to his advantage. They agreed to meet at her apartment, and she had a suite in a new development at Puerto Madero overlooking the river. It was a beautiful spot and she suggested a small restaurant around the corner that he noticed was reassuringly expensive. The meal passed amicably and he learned that she came from an old and well-established, almost aristocratic BA family with estates in the country. Her father had been a Colonel in the Argentine army. Chris admitted that he too had been a soldier a long time ago.

"Really? Were you in the Malvinas War?" She looked almost startled, like a rabbit in the headlights. *Score one to me*, Chris thought.

"No, I was just a boy soldier then, serving in Northern Ireland on my first and second tours. The Falklands was all over before my first tour finished. None of my regiment served, it was mostly Paras and RMC."

She seemed to relax at this point, although she had been decidedly discomposed when he told her of his military background. For his part, Chris had wanted to see her reaction to reassure himself that their cover was as airtight as he hoped. He doubted she could access military records that might say anything different, but better safe than sorry. He had actually been in the Paras before passing Selection, and had been in Chile as part of the Falklands conflict on clandestine inland missions.

"So what was your regiment. then?" she asked.

"Lieutenant Adams, Royal Green Jackets, ma'am, at your service. Yes, it was fun for a while and the camaraderie was good, but in the end I became disillusioned, as so many soldiers do, and left for a career in property – also as many surveyors do," he joked, lightening the mood and moving on quickly, interested to see if she would bite further. She did not and the banter of a romantic evening continued as the clouds over her forehead lifted.

They finished their meal and wandered along the street slowly, heading back to her riverside apartment and finally arriving at the waterside just down from the complex, arm in arm. She stopped walking, relaxed in his embrace and looked out over the river.

"I love the water, you know. It is so peaceful and I always wonder where it is going and what stories it can tell," she gave an embarrassed laugh. "Oh, listen to me. I must sound very foolish."

"Foolish, no, enigmatic, yes."

Most of the evening they had talked in a mix of Spanish and English, each slipping easily between the two languages.

"*Enigmatico?* How lovely," she purred, smiling gently at him. "I will take that as a compliment."

The open lips set in a half-smile were too much for Chris, and he took it as the invitation it was. He kissed her gently, parting her teeth with his tongue, deciding to take this as far as it would go and see what happened. She was very good and pretended to be slightly surprised before responding as the full blooded Latina she was, engaging his tongue and probing deeply and lasciviously back into his mouth. His hands moved over her body and she strained against him, closing the gap between their bodies, moulding them into one. She moaned slightly as his left hand twined her thick hair in his fingers, luxuriating in the thick coils. They broke away, their eyes meeting, each recognising the mirrored lust in the other. He rubbed her full lips with the ball of his thumb, sending shivers through her.

"*Aqui no, vamos a mi apartamento.*" He kissed her again and they walked towards the riverside entrance, moving a little faster now. They managed to get to the lift before they succumbed to each other again, stealing a deep kiss and embrace. "*Che boludo,*" Valentina whispered.

They virtually fell into her apartment, her shoulder bag dropping to the floor with a clunk as she braced herself against Chris, grasping his shoulders and feeling the bunched muscles there. She kissed him with passion as his hands left her face and hair to slip the linen dress from her shoulders. In the half-light her skin had a wonderful dark sheen with a dewy film reflecting between naked breasts that were crowned with dark, erect nipples.

Valentina smelled of some exotic perfume that reminded him of mint and herbs and cassis. The scent was wonderful, and he moved his mouth down to her breasts, inhaling the smell of her. She flung her head back in ecstasy, thrusting her breasts forward for him. Reaching down he grabbed her around her bottom and lifted her easily to him as she entwined her legs around his waist. He carried her through the open bedroom door to a beautiful canopied bed and fell forward with her legs still in place. He gently broke free and slipped out of his clothes to stand naked before her. She reached up and by some clever, practised, manoeuvre pulled him forward, twisting as she did so and ending up on top of him. She gazed down, her eyes slits of lust as she sensuously slid off her tiny thong, swaying her hips as she moved and dropping the undergarment provocatively from between her finger and thumb.

She turned her attention to Chris, exploring his body slowly with her lips and fingers, curious at the scars and battle wounds she found. She wound him up as tight as a drum, making him gasp and strain but refusing to let him gain control. When he could stand it no longer he rolled her over and landed between her splayed legs. Supporting himself, he entered her swiftly, causing her to cry out and wrap her long legs around him again, this time more tightly than before.

They soon found their rhythm, rocking gently at first, her hips moving in harmony with his deep thrusts. Their pace increased to a frenetic ride, on which they were both carried away by lust and obsession until she arched, bracing herself and crying out loudly. Her cries reached a high pitched crescendo and she raked his back savagely with her nails as she climaxed. He finished seconds later, drawn into a quivering embrace as her internal muscles clenched hard around him.

When he could finally move he fell forward gently, completely spent, and lay beside her.

"*Madre die Dios,* if they say the first time is never the best, then I can't wait for the second," she proclaimed. He laughed, softly caressing her skin with the backs of his fingers as he ran them up and down her thigh and over her flat stomach. She rolled over, stroking his body in return.

"Look at all these scars, what happened?" She asked. "Did you have to fight your way out of a brothel? A lot for a boy soldier in Northern Ireland."

"Ah, rugby is a tough game," he joked. "Much tougher than polo."

"Yes, but do they use bullets and knives? Look at this, that is a bullet hole, no?" she said, pointing to a puckered scar on his pectoral muscle, which had been an entry wound from a narco raid during the drug wars in Columbia when the SAS were drafted in to help the local forces.

"Oh that, it was a jealous boyfriend who didn't like the attention I was paying to his woman."

She smacked him on his chest

"My father is the same, always making a joke and never admitting the realities of war. Tell me really, what happened?"

He chose a story based on the reality of an ambush on the border in Northern Ireland that went live; although he had escaped scot free, a mate hadn't and still bore the scars. He had survived, and still served in the Regiment.

She shook her head, "You soldiers, all the same."

"Ex-soldier," he chided. "That's why I left. I got fed up with being cannon fodder for someone else's ideals and wars." This was a popular retort amongst disillusioned squaddies, and always went down well with anyone who was against the cause.

"I know. My father, he too was fed up, as you say, but against the government and the Junta. Politics, you know, it gets everywhere."

"I understand, politicians are a soldier's worst enemy. They say the first casualty of war is the truth, but I find that a loss of innocence comes before that. The first casualty of war is innocence."

"That is very sad and profound, it is a famous quote?"

"Yes, from every soldier's favourite film, *Platoon*. Now, enough of this kind of talk, I believe we have a theory of yours to test," he laughed and rolled over to face her.

They made love again, slowly this time but just as passionately, and afterwards he asked her what the perfume was that smelled so wonderful.

"It is *Alguien Suena* by Fueguia. Do you like it?"

"It's amazing," he sighed. They settled into a warm embrace. Later, sometime in the middle of the night, he stole from the room, leaving her sleeping deeply. He held a glass of water with him as an alibi for his nocturnal ramblings just in case she woke.

He searched her apartment as carefully as he could, finally nearly tripping over her bag in the moonlight. In it he found an MREC pass which went above the usual clearance levels and a small two-toned Beretta Pico .38 semi-automatic. At eleven and a half ounces it was one of the best concealable pistols; it was very reliable and had good stopping power. A great ladies' gun, in Chris's opinon. *Well, well, you're not so innocent after all,* he thought. Replacing the gun, he crept back to bed with the glass of water.

He left early, leaving Valentina snoozing with a half-hearted protest. He crept out again and was gone, leaving a note on the main table.

The following morning at the apartment Rupert went in for some ribbing at Chris's expense.

"Yeah, well when you have finished taking the piss, let me tell you what I found during my sacrifices for Queen and country. A high pay grade secure pass to their secret service and a Beretta in the handbag. She is a bit more than window dressing, I can tell you that much, and my money says she was definitely in on the set up for Waddington. In all seriousness, you can tell a lot about someone when you sleep with them and she knows all the tricks, believe me and I don't just mean physical!"

Minus certain details, Chris relayed the information to Peters in London, who offered a non-committal grunt and rang off – but not before warning him to be careful.

Chapter Fifteen

The day of the exchange came and Rafe organised a guard for the money from the Banco di Argentina's central branch in BA. It came as no surprise to Rupert that they considered it a normal request to transport over a million dollars around in cash.

Rupert had asked what would happen to the money. "If it is not going to be recorded, do they just stuff it under the mattress or what?"

He was answered rather cryptically by Rafe. "You know we have a saying here in Argentine: *Don't open the door unless you know what is on the other side.* However, in this case I will explain. You see, we are stifled. The government taxes us so highly and we cannot get any money, so we have to be inventive. Everyone hears about Cayman Islands offshore accounts, but we are also are very fond of Miami as a place for our funds. The banks in Miami, I am told, are very amenable and ask no questions for a fee. It is then very easy to transfer to anonymous accounts around the world or turn it straight back into cash." He shrugged.

Rupert sighed; it was Italy all over again. He and Chris exchanged knowing glances as the mantra reappeared in his head: *follow the money, follow the money.* The deal was to exchange contracts in the late afternoon at O'Gorman's behest. Rupert had had a quiet word with Siobhan and told her about the money and how it was to be paid. She raised her eyebrows and tilted her head, eventually nodding an acceptance. "What the hell. When in Rome..."

Rupert chuckled inwardly at the coincidental reference to Italy.

"Ah, Siobhan, you have no idea..." he said, shrugging at her enquiring look. "Anyway, there's more, and this is what I want you to do. The briefcase will be easily identifiable, and so will the man carrying it. Here is the *notario*'s address. You will get a headache soon; please take the afternoon off and follow the man to the airport on that crazy bike of yours. I want to know which flight he gets on and where it's going. I know you do this for a living, so I don't need to tell you: but be careful, OK?"

Since her arrival Siobhan had declared her love for motorbikes, and had had one in Northern Ireland since she was seventeen. She had bought a hot Yamaha RZ 350 and drove as crazily as the Argentinians around the streets of BA.

"Sure an' I will," she affirmed, turning up her accent with a smile.

They went over the details again to ensure that everything was clear. Twenty minutes later she complained to Maria she was not feeling well. She made her excuses and left for the day. Rupert closed his office door and thought about his next action. In his previous brush with the forces of law and order he had been recruited by DCI Webster, who worked for a special taskforce that dealt exclusively with crimes that fell between two stools; in Rupert's case this had been murder and money laundering.

After the successful conclusion of the operation, Webster had wanted to recruit him as a special agent, getting on the inside of white collar crime, given his obvious talent and credentials. Rupert had refused, having had – quite ironically, he now thought – enough dangerous work and wanting to return to the safer life of surveying and making deals. He had, however, stayed in touch with Webster sporadically, tipping him off if he thought there was something particularly nefarious or dangerous taking place within the property world. They had become nodding acquaintances and Rupert had learnt just how far Webster and his department's authority stretched. It was with this in mind that he called Webster's private and untraceable line and hoped that he would catch on fast, as the call would almost certainly be taped and listened to in due course.

He spoke in the vernacular of a typical surveyor, in nothing like the usual sombre tones he used with DCI Webster

The phone was answered. "Webster?"

"Webster, dear boy, Rupert Brett. How the devil? How's it going in Blighty? Sorry if the line's bad, I'm working way out in the boonies in Argentina, believe it or not." There was a pause, then Webster caught on fast, asking sensible questions, knowing that by the nature of the conversation this was no ordinary call.

"Rupes? How are you? Long time no speak. You sound miles away. Argentina? What the devil, aren't the London deals good enough for you anymore? You'll be looking like a Dago with your skin." Webster laughed, adding a bit of depth to the conversation.

"Bugger off! How are your own deals going there? Still putting them away, I hope. Anyway, I was thinking of you just this morning. Remember the fun we had in Italy? Well I know you have relatives in Miami, and it is just a short flight from here, so I wondered if you were coming over in the near future. I know you fly over to get some winter sun at this time of year. It would be great to catch up; it would be good to meet that niece of yours who is so pretty. Banker wasn't she? Maybe she could lay on a reception? It would be just like Italy all over again, that was some party. Looks like the same sort of fun and games all over again. Different day, different hemisphere, that's the only bloody difference, I swear."

"Hah, I wouldn't let any female family member near you, Brett, but yes, she is a banker. As it happens I was planning to arrange to meet her and I'll be speaking with her later today. I could be out soon, when did you have in mind? It would be great if we could have the same sort of fun as before? Sounds fabulous, old chap."

"Flights to Miami tend to be late afternoon from BA, I'll send you some arrival times. I was checking today, and we can plan from there. Miami is a hotbed of fun, just like Viterbo. Do you remember Rico? Well, we have a similar guy here, a whole suitcase full of tricks. Look, the line's cracking up a bit, can I fax you? We have a secure line here, always goes through." Webster gave him the number, made a few more jocular, mundane comments and rang off.

Well done, Rupert, Webster thought, *well done.* He realised that Rupert was telling him about money laundering in Miami and a courier landing this afternoon who needed to be traced. He waited for the faxed confirmation – which Rupert, unless he missed his guess, would send via a secure satellite phone.

On the other side of the world Rupert was thinking the same thing; he was hoping that Webster had caught all of it, but he hadn't dared to spell it out. Despite the privatisation of the telecoms industry, he was almost certain that any specific conversations – especially international ones to the UK – would be listened to in detail

In the afternoon, they arrived at the plush offices of the *notario.* Agents and lawyers crowded the room on both sides, waiting like vultures at the kill. Rupert, by his own admission, was one of them. He enjoyed the chase more than the climax, and the signing was, as ever, almost perfunctory. As the contracts were signed, the suitcase containing the money was handed over and checked by the *notario*. O'Gorman was pleased, Rupert could see a vulpine smile on his face.

"As a bonus for the deal, you get to keep the case: it was given to us by the bank as extra security and it has a dye release in case of theft," he handed over the handcuff bracelet key and combination numbers

"Thanks," Rupert said. "That is good of you. I don't think anyone would tackle Sean here in a hurry, but you can't be too careful."

"The criminals over here would'nt bother to start a fight with him. They'd just shoot him dead and lop his hand off with bolt cutters. People would do a lot for the sort of money that's in there," O'Gorman nodded to the case.

The *notario* handed the case to a hard looking man, whose suit appeared to have been made one size too small for him. Chris noticed the slight bulge under his arm, confirming that the man was no ordinary guard.

The formalities completed, the *notario* registered the 'official purchase price' as $137,610,000 – the full amount less the cash deposit. Rupert mentally shook his head and exchanged a brief, almost imperceptible look at Chris, who barely responded.

O'Gorman, however, caught the exchange. "Hell, Rupert, it's only money you know, better we have it than the government, eh? Why pay tax? Money makes the world go round, and when we have concluded the deal we can go out to my ranch and celebrate in style – on the government!" He chuckled at his own witticism.

As they left the building, he noticed Siobhan parked discreetly on the Yamaha at the end of a side-street opposite the offices. She normally eschewed a helmet, loving the feeling of freedom and wind in her hair, but this time she wore a full face visor and Rupert thought she looked sexy as hell in her red leathers. She ignored him, but he saw her head turn as she recognised the briefcase held by the big man in the small suit. She put on her helmet and started the bike, pulling out smoothly and following the taxi the courier had taken.

Up in his office O'Gorman placed a call to USE Oil in Boston. "Phillips," the respondent answered.

"All done. Exchanged today and the package is on its way to you now. What? No, no problem, a couple of raised eyebrows at the cash but hey, the Brits are a bunch of stuffed shirts at the best of times. If he checks – as I'm sure he has with Rafe – he'll find that it is perfectly normal practice down here. Relax, it's all going well, you know. *Si, bueno,* we'll wait to hear confirmation from the wee man in due course."

The call ended and Phillips gave the information his undivided attention. He reached a decision and called into Kelly's office, entering through the habitually open door.

"Hi, all go off well?" Kelly queried.

"Mmm, yes, at least as far as the transaction goes, it's all paid. However, we had a call this morning from our friends in Argentina. They've learned that one of the surveyors, Chris Adams, used to be in the British Army. Might be nothing, many ex-soldiers enter the surveying world, especially officers, I just thought that you ought to be aware." Phillips finished.

"What was he? Not the fuckin' Paras, I hope," Kelly almost spat the words.

"No apparently not. Royal Green Jackets: and he did not serve in the Falklands, before you ask, but he did serve in Northern Ireland..." Phillips let the words hang in the air.

The explosion from Kelly was not as bad as he had anticipated given his partisan views, but it was vociferous enough. He swore viciously, but when he calmed down he asked; "So what the hell are we gonna do about it?"

Phillips responded with his usual cautious approach: "I don't know. MREC are nervous, they do not want another Waddington on their hands and we might best be advised to just monitor it. I'll give it some thought and cover all possibilities if necessary. But at the moment no one seems too alarmed and the fact that he was so open about it indicates that he's harmless. All the same, I don't like loose ends or coincidences."

"Take him out. You're best at all this covert bullshit, and you can always be relied upon to take a more dispassionate view than me." Kelly said.

Siobhan weaved her way through the BA traffic, following the courier. They arrived at the airport, where she parked and followed him in. She saw him check in for 16.40 flight to Miami, a journey that would take him just under nine hours. As instructed she made the call to Rupert back in the office.

"Yes, Mr Brett, it's all done. I popped her on the plane and she should arrive in Miami in about 10 hours' time. Yes, no problem."

The next call she made was from a public call box, and was a good deal less cryptic.

"It's Siobhan. We need to speed this up, they're gettin' suspicious. If what I know about Brett is true, he'll be startin' to put the pieces together: he's no spook but he's used to corporate intrigue and he's not stupid. All we need is Adams to get sight of things he shouldn't and we could all be in trouble.

"Yes, I know it is a long shot but they asked me to check where the courier was going as soon as they knew about the cash, and I had no chance to use the Satcom. So no way could Sean be traced or followed by the time they get back and things are put in place. It will be too late, and I gave them a later flight time anyway. It was all I could do without drawin' suspicion. I am tryin' to get a bug there, but he changed the locks and we never get long enough before one of them gets back. No I don't know the encryption code for the sat link; he's kept it to himself. Listen I must go, we'll keep in touch in the usual way. Ok, fine."

She put down the receiver with her mind whirling. She knew she must calm down or it would be obvious, especially to Adams. She picked up her helmet and made her way back to the Yamaha. She checked no one had followed her just by instinct, all her training in play, but still felt that itch at the back of her neck.

After the call from Siobhan, Rupert put the phone down and told everyone that she was still not feeling well. She had a migraine and was lying down in her room. Privately to Chris, he passed on what Siobhan had told him. Chris was concerned at the timing and the possible loss of contact at Miami

"We'll never get our guys on course in time to intercept him or follow him."

"Don't worry, I've made contingency plans. Should all go well. I have a cunning plan, my lord," Rupert smiled.

He explained what he had set in place with Webster, and Chris was impressed. "Friends in high places, indeed. Let's hope he sorts it in time. Can I report all this back using his name?"

"Sure. I'd be very surprised if Johnston or Peters don't already know, but be my guest. You know there's still a gap here – what are we missing? I mean, if the IRA are involved, what are they going to do, invade the Falklands with a little over a million dollars? And then what? Hold it for the Provos as an independent state?" he finished sarcastically. "No, I don't think so."

"I don't know either, but let's go over it tonight back at the apartment, away from prying ears."

As they moved out into the general office area, Rafe approached them, wanting to celebrate the exchange of contracts, but Rupert admonished him with the old agency adage, "No deal's done 'til it's done."

"What does that mean?"

"It means, Rafe old boy, that until the fat lady sings and the ink is dry, and all monies are paid, no cigar!"

"You English, you are crazy"

"Hey, leave me out," Chris said. "I'm Welsh!"

"English, Welsh, all the same, British the lot of you!" Rafe waved his hands in that particular Latin way that spoke volumes, shaking his head in mock disgust as he walked off. The two surveyors smiled at each other while Alex looked at them quizzically.

"Oh come on," Alex said. "At least have a bottle of Quilmes with me after work. It is supper at my parents' later and I don't want to turn up too soon. Uncles, aunts…" He rolled his eyes.

"No honestly, I've got a report to write. Chris might join you, and I'll think of you sipping cold beers whilst I'm slaving away."

Chris agreed with a smile, wondering what was behind this sudden outbreak of bonhomie on Alex's behalf. They left an hour later and drove separately, Chris in the Land Cruiser and Alex in his BMW 3 series, to a waterfront bar. It was off the tourist route and situated in a quiet side street to the north of their offices. Chris was the only non-Argentinian there, but the atmosphere was friendly enough and Latin music played out of the wall speakers at an exciting tempo. Chris suspected the third degree, however subtle, and he was not disappointed.

"Now, this is real Argentina, you know, not some tourist bar. Is great, yes?"

Chris agreed and the talk moved back and forth, finally settling on backgrounds and how they came to be surveyors. Alejandro had joined after his military service, and in an effort to find common ground, Chris admitted that he'd also been a soldier, but in the regulars of the Royal Green Jackets.

"Really, where did you serve? Northern Ireland perhaps?"

"Now why do you say that?" Christ asked, thinking, *you've slipped up there, matey. Who's been feeding you information?* and was immediately on his guard. Alex recovered quickly, realising his possible mistake and smoothed it over

"Well, you are like me; too young for the Malvinas and everyone knows the British are at war in Ireland so I assumed all soldiers go there…" he shrugged

"We are not at war with them, we're just peacekeeping, but yes, I was there. Two tours and then out."

"What was it like?" Only another soldier would dare to ask that question, and Chris knew he was being tested. Normally, if someone asked, he would tell them to fuck off and mind their own business. Questions like that made him remember things he'd sooner forget. "Hours of strained boredom; living in constant fear of being shot or blown up, followed by a few minutes of action that left you tired and afraid."

Alex must have realised this was a soldier's response, and he offered his sympathies. "I can imagine. I never fought, but my brother, he was in the Malvinas war. Taken prisoner, luckily for him. Many died there."

Dangerous ground here, Chris thought, *Let's move it along.* They talked in more general terms about the army and life, sharing a few more beers amicably, and then Alex looked at his watch.

"*Mierda*, I'm in trouble; my mother is cooking for the family tonight, big get together as I said. I am sorry, but I must go. We must do this again, it was fun."

He downed the last of his Quilmes and left the bar, patting Chris on the shoulder before departing. *Well, score one to the good guys,* Chris thought. Valentina was clearly a setup, although no damage had been done. He'd kept his story the same with Alex. He finished his own beer, got off the bar stool and walked out into the into the evening air. It was dusk, and the noise of the traffic had abated. He walked down past some closed shops and another couple of bars, heading towards the Toyota, which was parked a street away.

It was then that he heard the soft footfall behind him, moving out of a doorway. He did not turn around; he looked in a shop window at the dim reflection of a man; hefty, above average height, wearing a leather jacket. Before him two more men appeared, cutting off his path to the car. He reached inside his jacket pretending to fumble for his keys, seemingly unaware of the threat from both directions, his adrenalin levels shooting up.

So, a set-up. Thank you Alex, I will repay you for this, he thought. The three assailants were expecting an office worker, a former officer and a gentleman in the Royal Green Jackets. Maybe the odd bit of fisticuffs in the bars, but nothing serious. They were not expecting a former Para and SAS veteran sergeant, trained in unarmed combat. Chris had been taught in the Regiment that when the time came, if no other option presented itself, to explode with maximum surprise and extreme violence, no questions asked. Questions could be asked afterwards if anyone was still alive. He planned it out in his mind: first the guy on the left, take the other with whatever came in handy and use him to deflect the man behind.

As the distance closed, he went through an opening gambit.

He looked up at the two men with an innocent smile. *"Buenos tardes, sig–"*

He never finished the sentence. As his left foot landed on the ground, he appeared to take another step forward with his right. Still smiling, he drove forward with the stamping forward wing chun kick. It was usually aimed at waist height or below and was really just that, a stamping snap.

But Chris was very flexible and had perfected the move to a higher level. It was a perfect opener and took the man totally by surprise. The hard heel of his shoe landed in the man's sternum and made a satisfying crack. The man's sternum plate broke and he collapsed in agony, barely able to utter a sound.

The second man started to recover from the surprise attack, closing the distance in the best way: he spun on his left foot, launching a lethal roundhouse kick to Chris's head, which had it landed could have been fatal. Chris dropped a double *fook sau* with his forearms, twisting into the arc of the kick and meeting it at the shin. Catching the leg with his left hand, Chris twisted a *tan sau* block with his right arm to the second attack from a left punch and responded with a snapping a side-kick to the assailant's knee cap. The leg bent sideways at an unnatural angle, breaking and dislocating the knee. But the man was game and tried to cling on.

Chris knew he was in trouble now as the third assailant closed the distance. He heard the whirr of displaced air as a cosh exploded onto his shoulder. He narrowly avoided taking the blow to his head and received a hefty a kick to his thigh. Off balance, he fell sideways, avoiding the sweeping follow up kick which caught the second fallen colleague who Chris used as a shield. Rolling away, he felt inside his jacket pocket. Still on the ground he caught the next vicious, incoming stamp and swung with the nasty little three-inch blade of the Sig Sauer folding knife; the blade glinted an arc catching the Achilles tendon of the kicker, just above the heel. He was rewarded with an inhuman scream as the pain from the severed tendon shot through the attacker's nervous system.

Spinning again on his hips, Chris kicked the man's good leg behind the knee and the attacker fell. Rolling onto his hands, Chris pushed himself upright, feeling the deep bruise in his shoulder where the cosh had hit him; realising he would be dead or unconscious if it had been his head, as had no doubt been intended.

Shaken but in control, he surveyed his work: one dead or dying, one permanently crippled and the third out for a good three months. They had asked for it and would have left him in the same condition: he had been lucky, and as his wing chun instructor had said 'better to be judged by twelve than carried by six!

He walked quickly over to the one whose leg was broken. "Who sent you?" he demanded in Spanish.

"Fuck you!" came the response.

American! What the hell? he thought. He stood on the man's broken leg at the knee and twisted with his foot, repeating the question. The thug shouted and passed out with the pain. People had turned at the sound of the second assailant's scream, and Chris didn't want to be caught. He decided not to push his luck, ran to the Land Cruiser and drove off.

He did not see the shadow of Alex appearing around the corner of the street, shocked at the sudden violence and destruction of the team in such a short a space of time. It had been over in a matter of seconds. He shook his head and ran to the bar to call an ambulance. Shaking, he dialled, thinking that he had never witnessed anything so cold, calculating and brutal, and that if Chris was an ex-soldier from a normal military background, he would be very surprised.

Chapter Sixteen

Fifteen minutes later, Chris arrived back at the apartment to find Rupert had returned some time earlier.

"Hi, how did the – what the hell happened to you?" Rupert exclaimed, looking at Chris's torn trousers and scuffed shoes.

"This is nothing, you should see the other guys," Chris quipped. "I had a discussion with three men about a dog, you know how it is. But the most interesting thing was that they were American, would you believe?" Pouring himself a shot of whisky, Chris explained in detail what had happened, and that he believed he had been set up by Alejandro.

"And you are convinced, after your assignation with Valentina last night, that he was told you were an ex-soldier," Rupert said. "And they did this because of that? No, it goes deeper. And why are the Americans involved? Also why pick on you? Yes, an ex-soldier but so what, you weren't in the Falklands."

"I agree, but I think we've maybe turned a few stones too many and 'they' don't like where we're looking. All they have on us is that we are legitimate surveyors, we've proved that and they picked on an ex-soldier who can handle himself in a fight. But what I don't get is why show their hand and why me, with respect, when you'd have made an easier target?"

Rupert shrugged. "Look, let's write this down and mull it over before reporting back. Should we have Siobhan down to get another head in on this?"

Chris nodded, "Yes, why not." He ran up and fetched her.

When she saw the bruises she exclaimed, "Been picking on the big boys again, have you? What happened?"

She was much more matter of fact about it than Rupert when she heard the full story. Rupert guessed that growing up in Belfast would do that to a girl.

"How did you leave them?" She asked. She'd seen Chris and other Regiment boys in action before, and she knew how deadly they could be

"One probably dead, one crippled and third OOA for three months, maybe." The nonchalant way in which he said this shook Rupert. He knew Chris as a nice guy, good company and had the makings of a good agent. But the cold, clinical way he described the events unnerved him a little. Rupert reflected that he'd rather have Chris onside than against him.

"So, what do we have? Let's write this down." Rupert took a pen and his daybook and headed it *Facts:*

Falklands – invasion, when and how?

Irish involvement – IRA, but how and why?

Irish companies and transporting cash – who to and why?

Americans – how do they fit in? What do they gain?
Why pick on Chris?

Valentina – sent to spy or check up and connection with Alex,

Alex also in MREC?

They checked the list out loud. Chris thought hard. "Put 'Docks' on there – query fitting out *Esmeralda*." Rupert and Siobhan frowned.

"I don't know why, but something triggered my memory, and something didn't fit right. Often the subconscious is your best friend, tells you things you didn't know when they're staring you in the face."

They talked it through some more and drew up a full report for Chris to send through later that evening.

"Oh, and thanks for the confirmation today, Siobhan," Rupert said. "That was good work. Hopefully we should get a result in a couple of hours when he lands."

"No problem, but how will you get a trace on him that quickly? They'll never get someone there in time, will they?"

Rupert tapped his nose conspiratorially. "Friends in high places. I have a contact and I just needed to have confirmed it was Miami not the Caymans, so the trail could be followed. The Argies always go to one or the other."

Siobhan silently cursed, she could have sent them on a wild goose chase. "Right, I'm for bed," she said. "Too much excitement for one day."

She left the room for her own apartment and once the door closed, half clenched her fists in frustration.

"Shite. They can't even get that right, I warned them he was good," she muttered under her breath.

She considered her options and realised that nothing could be done until the following morning. It was too late to make contact now, and she hoped that the money would arrive without mishap.

In the apartment below, Chris was sending a detailed message to Peters, recording everything that had occurred, including their list.

London

The message was picked up in Whitehall, despite the fact that the UK was four hours ahead and it was the middle of the night. Peters was woken at home, as he had asked to be if anything urgent came in from BA.

"Read it to me again, slowly, and send a copy to my private fax here straight away. Send a copy to Johnston: I don't care if it's the middle of the bloody night," he snapped. "Page him, call him, send a driver, do what you have to do, but get hold of him *now*. Idiot," he said to himself, replacing the receiver

He went through to his study and read the two page fax that had come in from Adams, then waited for the call from Johnston. It was not long in coming.

"Peters? Yes, so you've received it, what are your thoughts?"

"I think we have a leak, and that on balance Adams did the right thing in pursuing the woman, they have clearly shown their hand. But where does the PIRA fit into all this? What are they doing with the Argies, and what's the American connection all about? I cannot believe this is official. They're our allies, for God's sake. They're in the Gulf and providing detailed satellite imaging. I've heard of friendly fire, but this is beyond stupid."

"I just can't reconcile that either," Johnston replied, scrubbing a hand down his face to chase away the last cobwebs of sleep. "Anyway, I'll tell Fisher to get one of our subs to put a listening device on the telephone cables like the Yanks did in the Cold War. The technology has improved since then and it is nowhere near as dangerous as sneaking into a major Russian harbour was. But it'll take time and we have to siphon off and filter all calls with various trigger words. If only this was Hollywood film, I'd have the information on your desk before the sun came up." He'd recently seen *The Hunt for Red October* and had smiled at the speed of intelligence gathering in the film.

The Americans had, with amazing gall and courage, launched a daring, clandestine submarine operation in 1975, sailing the hybrid submarine USS *Halibut* right into the heart of Russia's Petropavlovsk harbour. They'd planted listening and recording devices, as technology at the time did not exist to transmit to the waiting submarine some miles way. Then when enough time had passed, they sneaked back into the harbour three months later, retrieved the device and got clean away, the espionage operation a complete success. They did it three times and it had been the toast of the espionage world when news spread through the secret service. A similar but less hazardous operation had now been put in place by the British on the North American cables from Argentina.

Peters snorted in response to the film reference. "Good. Highly illegal of course, but only if we get caught," he said. "What about a rogue Washington government department? Hell, they have more acronyms for spies and black ops than anyone I know, even the Israelis. But I agree, it doesn't fit and what do they have to gain by it? Indeed, the Yanks came to us in the last Falklands conflict offering to intercede with their military, and we turned them down – or Maggie did; said we needed to be seen to do it ourselves."

"Yes, well, I'm sure she thought we'd had enough of the Americans winning our wars for us. But if we're not careful we'll find ourselves shooting at shadows. Anyway, how did Brett manage to get a tail so soon on this courier? Sean, that was his name, wasn't it? Irish name. Funny, that. My belief is that he is meeting this high level Quartermaster we've heard about from surveillance in Belfast; but that begs further questions: who is he? Where is he flying in from? Where is he going with the money? And finally the million dollar question – no pun intended – who is really paying him and why?"

"I believe I can answer the first question," Peters replied. He told Johnston about Rupert's first experience of helping the government, and gave him the name of the officer in charge; DCI Webster of the special police unit. "Brett would have known that we couldn't have reacted fast enough, and he wouldn't have had time to return to the apartment with Adams, send the message and then get back to the office without creating suspicion. Especially if this Alejandro chap is informing on them to MREC or SIND. It was a resourceful and clever move on Brett's behalf."

"Yes, that's partly why we chose him, Brett is not stupid, nor does he lack courage. And clearly they have gained credibility in the market – otherwise they would not be doing so well. But someone, somewhere, has put a fly in the ointment: their cover was too good and deep to be blown by an indiscretion. I wonder if it was just Alex telling MREC or something more. Look at what happened to Waddington. But the set up for Adams' hit was planned in haste by the sound of it – and thank God it wasn't successful. Serves the bastards right."

"Careful," Peters said. "If they're American agents they're supposed to be the good guys. I just don't know what they were doing trying to whack one of us."

They went on to discuss flights and passengers from both the Irish Republic and Northern Ireland. To date, reports of passenger manifests hadn't shown anyone who might remotely be a suspected IRA quartermaster or any of the usual suspects travelling under suspicious circumstances. They had also checked Columbia for any of the known Provos there, but to no avail. They often sniffed around the drug industry; there was good money to be made. But everything seemed quiet on that front.

"We're running out of time, and the stakes are getting higher," Johnston said. "Clearly they could all be in danger. We still don't have confirmation of any planned invasion or how it is proposed to take place. Any news on Waddington?"

"Interludes of consciousness with minor moments of

lucidity," Peters sounded as if he was reading a hospital chart, and Johnston shivered at the impersonality of the man. "They are confident that he will recover to a certain degree, but his memory is completely blank, apparently. So he's not going to be a lot of use to us, I'm afraid."

"Look, it is coming up to Christmas, everything will shut down and I understand that Brett's girlfriend is going out to join him over the holiday period. Is that wise? I mean what if things turn nasty? Do you think we should pull the plug and get them all back?"

"Well, we could hardly stop her," Peters observed. "He's supposed to be on an innocent surveying job. It'll add more credibility to the scene if Brett has his girlfriend over for Christmas, I am sure she'll be safe enough," Peters concluded. "And if we pull them now we've lost it all. Next thing we know the Argies will be flying their bloody flag and dancing the samba on the runway at Port Stanley. Anyway, we need them to go up country to check out the military base at Corrientes; all we have is a few vague satellite images that look a bit suspicious. Get Adams to invent some requirements for ranches in that district. Send them an open fax so that the others in the office will see. Brett could take his girlfriend with them for colour."

They agreed to think more on the information and to speak later in the morning.

Chapter Seventeen

Buenos Aires

While Johnston and Peters made their plans, one of the attackers, a former Delta Force mercenary, was making a call to Boston, speaking to Philips, Kelly's right-hand man.

"Yeah, we set him up as planned by that dickhead Alex. It was last minute but there were three of us. Hell, if that guy's an ex-officer faggot from some regular unit, I'm Nancy fucking Regan! He went down through us like he was expecting it. Roberts is dead with a smashed sternum, Craig will never walk properly again and I'm in hospital for three goddamn months."

He relayed the full blow-by-blow account, to which Phillips listened in silence. When the man had finished he said, "We'll get you back up here as soon as possible, into a US hospital and away from prying eyes. You were mugged. Stick to that story, you were set upon by a gang. Got it? Good. Stay where you are, we'll come to you." He rang off without wishing the man a speedy recovery.

The mercenary, whose name was Mitch, knew only too well what kind of care he was likely to get. He decided to release himself before any representative from Philips or USE Oil turned up and get away somewhere safe, like the other side of the world. He had contacts down here and would rather trust them than fall victim to Kelly's infamous reputation.

Phillips moved through the top floor to Kelly's office and told him what had happened.

"We cannot let this go any further, understand" Kelly said. "I think it was a mistake to attack Adams.

What the hell did he know anyway? Nothing. He was just an ex-soldier who didn't even fight in the Falklands. Did Mitch say anything more about it? Did they know he was American?"

"Apparently not, so he says. Reckons Adams, left the scene quickly and drove off, probably assumed it was just a mugging. They were dressed to blend in. Dark hair, leather jackets, like pretty much all Latinos. I don't see how it hurts us really, they are no closer to connecting us to the military build-up or indeed to anything. The money went off as planned, no hitches," Phillips finished, unaware of the full damage caused by Mitch's outburst at Chris.

"Good to hear. Hopefully, that will finance our side of the operation and we can just sit tight until the Argie side is in place and ready to roll. I saw on the news today that we are winning in the Middle East and they reckon we could be in downtown Baghdad in three months or so. The window is closing."

"OK. Anything else?" Phillips asked.

Kelly sighed and looked out across the Boston streetscape. "Best we clear up the mess," he said. "Get a couple of tame locals on it. Take what's his name from the hospital, find the other guy and whack him wherever he is. Make it look like a gang hit. Put it down to drugs or some bullshit."

Phillips nodded wordlessly and left the room to make some calls. Kelly walked to his desk and fetched a fifth of Bourbon from a top drawer. He took a slug straight from the bottle and mulled over the facts. The money had been deposited at the Bank of Miami by the courier and no one was any the wiser, unaware they had been followed by an undercover officer. The money was sitting in an untraceable overnight escrow account; it could be shifted very easily by anyone with the password and correct identification. It could then be bounced around until the trail was pretty much impossible to follow, especially if the transfers were activated quickly. The Miami banks were like the Swiss. Money talked and the staff didn't. The BoM was no exception. By the time warrants had been served and footage of any CCTV obtained, the courier would have disappeared, his false identity and bogus passport shredded and never used again. But Michael Kelly knew that the required legwork would be done and the long process of detection would start soon. He'd need to stay ahead of it. He wondered about the courier but decided it would be a bit too heavy-handed. Nobody wanted a logjam of corpses turning up or floating face down in various harbours. He wasn't the Goddamn Mafia, for Christ's sake.

The following morning, Siobhan took her early morning run, stopping by the memorial bench to take a glug from her water bottle and stretch her tendons. She finished and set off again at a good pace in an effort to get back to her apartment before the sun got too high. She was without the bottle of water, which she had abandoned on the bench. A minute after she'd gone, a man appeared, sat on the bench and began reading his paper, smoking a cigarette in the low early morning sunlight. Finishing his cigarette, he stretched, read a couple more headlines and made to leave. He walked away from the bench with the bottle of water wrapped carefully in the rolled up newspaper.

It took the man a while to get back to his own apartment. He retraced his steps a few times to ensure he wasn't be followed, sticking with the training he'd been given by the IRA members working for FARC. These were guys who had grown up on the streets of terror-torn Belfast. Blending in and avoiding tails were as important as shooting people in different-coloured balaclavas. As Siobhan had done, he peeled back the label and read: *They know the hit was set up. Let the wee man and the Argies know. Keep US out of loop, we don't want trouble there. I'll get more and let you know.* The man memorised the note and then burned it, scattering the ashes from the apartment window and watching as the wind took them away.

Two days passed, and Chris was still showing signs of stiffness. He had a rainbow of bruises on his right shoulder, his lower back and hips.

Coming from a run, Chris stripped to the waist and began to stretch in the hope of easing some of the stiffness.

"You were lucky," Rupert commented. "If that cosh had caught you on the temple or the side of the head, you'd be in the hospital now."

"Or on a slab," Chris conceded, grunting with exertion. "But in any combat, you need an element of luck. They were well trained, and that's what concerns me. They weren't just bruisers or gang muscle. I'd say they were ex-military, probably special forces, Delta, Seals or Rangers. Not in top shape, but still very dangerous and quick to react when I suckered them with the first move. I was pretty lucky – and if there's one thing an SAS man can't do, it's rely on luck."

"Interesting, the American connection. I'm sure London will make something of it. Claire gets here in three days, so cover up or she'll think we're in a war zone. She's seen me in states like that and she knows it doesn't come from walking into doors. Anyway, we should be just in time to get the completion documented and registered before the start of the holidays."

"Yes – talking of which, what are you going to do while she's here?" he responded, a twinkle in his eye, "apart from that, of course."

"None of your bloody business! Actually, given the situation it probably is – apart from that, of course," Rupert threw Chris's words back at him and the two men laughed. "It'll probably involve a lot of shopping and watching polo. Maybe some time on the beach. Why?"

"Well, like I mentioned, the communiqué last night said that they are going to send an open fax from various clients to the office looking for land in and around BA, Pilar and wherever, but more specifically further up north toward the Paraguay border around Corrientes. Which means we'll be travelling about and it would be good to have some realistic cover. I can't take Valentina up to Corrientes for obvious reasons, but then I'm not sure you can take Claire there either. She's going to want to know what we are doing creeping around military bases, don't you think?"

"Don't worry about Claire. She's going up to see an old friend in San Miguel. He's got an estancia there and she is going to play some polo. In fact we have all been invited to go up for Christmas. As to Valentina, are you still going to follow up with that duplicitous bitch? She tried to have you killed, for God's sake."

"Yeah, maybe, or it could have been Alex. Either way, better the devil you know, and I'll just play it cool, claim it was a mugging and I got the better of them like I told Alex in the office. 'Keep your friends close and enemies closer', that's what they say, isn't it?" Chris said "I also want to go to the Mar del Plata beach and walk along there, so I can get a good look at the dockyards without raising suspicion. That's where their submarine pens are, and their frigate fit-out docks. If there is going to be any military enhancement it is going to be happening there."

"Hmm. You had better not let her catch on; maybe I'd better come and look after you next time you go drinking."

Chris's response was succinct and to the point as he stuck two fingers up at Rupert. They had developed a good working relationship, although it was sometimes difficult to separate work as boss and junior from the mission, where the roles were reversed

He continued, "Didn't know the Argies had submarines; surely that must have caused problems in the Falklands. Sometimes I'm surprised that we didn't lose."

"Well they did. Two German made diesel-electric class subs. Although only one, the *San Luis*, saw active service in the war. It did cause us huge problems as we couldn't rescue the crews from two Sea King helicopters that were shot down by enemy fire, some of which had my mates on board." his face clouded at the memory. "I still owe them big time, and if I can stop another war I'll do anything to achieve that." The conversation was clearly at an end on that topic.

"Listen, the other thing I want to do – and maybe we do this from Paraguay – is go and see the Iguazu Falls as a cover. Maybe slip across and fly from there to the Falklands. We could be back in Paraguay within twenty-four to forty-eight hours, with no one any the wiser."

"What, visit the Falklands? Isn't that a risk?"

"Not really. Like we saw when we first got here, it's a tourist destination now, they send cruise ships there. Perfect cover, your girlfriend's here, do the tourist bits, mix business with pleasure." he shrugged, grinning. "Don't suppose Claire has a friend to bring along, make up a foursome?"

Rupert's doubtful expression said it all. But then he made a suggestion. "Don't shoot me down in flames here," he hesitated. "But what about taking the MI6 contact who dropped the weapons off? If she can evade the scrutiny for that, why not make it look like a clandestine holiday, there must be loads of places she can meet us outside BA."

Chris raised his eyebrows in surprise but said nothing.

Chapter Eighteen

London

Things were being taken out of their hands in London at that very moment, as Johnston of MI6 demanded a second pair of trained eyes on the possible military build-up after receiving the intel from Miami about the deposit of the money and further evidence from Northern Ireland that things were going to plan as far as the IRA were concerned. He dialled a secure line for the embassy in Buenos Aires and asked to speak with Sophie Carswell

"Carswell," she answered.

"Johnston, how are you?"

"Well sir, thank you." She waited, knowing Johnston well enough to realise that he didn't make social calls to pass the time of day.

"I have a job for you – which you will probably relish, given that it will involve indirectly getting back at those responsible for hurting Andrew. What are you doing for the holidays?"

She listened carefully, glad to finally be seeing some action rather than sitting on her hands as the embassy's resident spook.

"I'll contact Adams and Brett and you can join them. Meet up with them as planned on the island, come back overland through the Paraguay border: no one will know or suspect. Carry on as a party of four posing as Adams' girlfriend when you meet up back in Argentina. Got it?"

"Yes, sir." *Finally*, she thought, *a chance to get some action*

"Good. We'll make the arrangements from here through incognito travel agents. Just one final thing; Brett's girlfriend is not aware of the real reason they are there; so play along. It may be necessary to break cover if we get to the endgame, but stay in character until the absolute last moment, understood?"

"Of course, sir." The phone line clicked off and she awaited further orders once a liaison could be made with Adams and Brett. Johnston told Peters his plan, which was relayed to Adams.

Buenos Aires

When Chris received the message from Peters over the encrypted Sat phone he grinned, shaking his head.

"Well, Rupert it seems that your idea has been considered by the top brass and we're on. I have a new girlfriend – Sophie Carswell!"

"Hah, see? This spook stuff is easy for a surveyor. We're a clever bunch, us chaps," Rupert said.

Chris raised an eyebrow and declared that he was going out to meet a man about a dog. He had been mysteriously absent for long periods since the street attack, and as usual when pushed, he had been even more elusive. Rupert had decided to clear his head and went for a walk, heading for a local bar that they had started to frequent. It was Friday night after all, and any surveyor worth his salt would be out having a beer or six.

It was a typical BA watering hole; colourful, loud music and a series of tables and booths packed with a mixture of suits, *chiquitas* and locals letting go after a hard week. It was as always a good opportunity to practice his Spanish with some of the local agents and lawyers. He enjoyed his new-found camaraderie with the local agents. In many ways it was very similar to London: the gossip, the latest rumours of deals and who was sleeping with whom. At and at times like these he forgot the real reason for being in BA.

The others had gone on to a club, and had tried to persuade Rupert to join them, but he had declined. He wasn't in the mood for all night drinking and the attendant hangover. He left the bar and made his way back to the apartment about half a mile away through a series of well-lit streets. Constantly aware of the previous attack on Chris, he was very wary, jumping when a dustbin lid was slammed in a basement somewhere off in the darkness.

When he entered the foyer of the apartment block it was not without a small sense of relief, and he realised that he was getting ridiculously paranoid. Shaking his head in disgust, he went to take the stairs as part of his intensified fitness regime. He made it to the first half landing and nearly bumped into Siobhan coming down. She was dressed in a short skirt and silk turquoise top with a superb cleavage on display that he'd somehow managed not to notice before. High heels clacked on the tiles as she walked towards him, hips swaying.

"Rupert," she murmured huskily. "I've been waiting for you. I thought you'd be in your apartment, but there was no reply."

As she moved closer he noticed that her eyes were beautifully made up and that she looked incredible. "Wow! You look pretty," he said. "Off out on the town?"

Siobhan was now very close to him and he could smell a thick, heavy perfume enveloping his senses. He found it quite intoxicating as she invaded his space and looked up into his eyes.

"I was, but I was wondering if you would like to come out for a drink with me."

She managed a shy smile that managed to look artless and sexy at the same time: it was, Rupert found, quite beguiling. To add to the allure, she had moved her hand to place it lightly on his chest and the contact felt like an electric shock. It was totally unexpected, slightly embarrassing and confusing: he had thought she did not find him attractive – and she was also a work colleague.

"I, um, well I was heading for bed. Long week, you know how it is…" he mumbled through a throat that was suddenly very dry.

"That's a shame," she almost whispered, her accent accentuated and very sexy. The heat coming off her palm made Rupert think he was going to melt, "We could have had some fun? It is Friday after all. Are you sure?"

"Siobhan, I am flattered, but…" he got no further. Somehow her lips connected with his, her other hand reaching behind his head to pull him closer into a full, deep kiss. Her mouth tasted of sweet peppermint and he responded initially by instinct, surprised. With some difficulty he gently pushed her away to arms-length, caught up in the intoxication of the moment.

"Siobhan, I am really sorry, and…" He was interrupted by another gentle kiss on his lips, this one soft and without passion. She smiled sadly and placed a single finger across his lips

"Shh. Not another word. Sorry, I misread everything," she smiled whimsically. "Are we OK?"

He nodded, and without another word she was past him, heels gently clacking down the stairs, hips swaying over beautiful tanned legs. At the bottom she turned and almost imperceptibly winked at him over her shoulder. It was one of the sexist moves Rupert had ever seen. He shook his head, wondering if he was going to wake up from a dream, glad that Claire was arriving soon, as he doubted he could withstand another invitation like that and behave himself.

He walked up the next two flights and fumbled with his keys to the apartment, opening first one, then the second set of locks Chris had installed. He opened the door to a quiet room, the gentle noise of the city below coming through the open balcony windows. Chris chided him for leaving them open, but he loved the fresh air more than the air conditioning. After all, they were three stories up, he reasoned. He stood still, overlooking the city, sipping at a whisky he had poured himself, and jumped when Chris returned dressed in a pair of boots, old jeans and a T-shirt. He smelled odd, and Rupert couldn't quite put a finger on it.

"Hi, you look like you've seen a ghost," Chris said. "What's the matter?"

"You are not going to believe this."

"Try me." So Rupert told him the whole story, and his response was not what Rupert was expecting. He was suddenly alert, all lethargy and casualness leaving him.

"What? When did this happen? Just now when we were both out, yeah? And you were back – what, just before me, say 10.00?" Rupert nodded. "Tell me again exactly what she said and importantly how long she kept you talking."

So he recounted word for word the events of the last few minutes

"So, she delayed you coming into the apartment by about two or three minutes? When you got back to the apartment, was the balcony window open? You left it open didn't you?" Chris accused.

Rupert looked a bit sheepish as he nodded. Chris went straight to the secure wardrobe. The door was unlocked and he checked the base. He smiled at his own security work, which had foiled the attempt to prise it open and then went around the room methodically, looking for listening devices. He found one in the telephone receiver.

"Hah," he said, producing the small device and carefully replaced it.

"What the hell?" Rupert said, sotto voce. "How did you know?"

"Well, when you told me she came on to you it had to be a setup – a distraction to delay you entering the apartment to give her accomplice time to get out. My guess is she was on watch, ready to either make a play for you or me, whoever came back first. And you don't need to whisper. It's voice activated, but only when you're on the phone."

"Why are you so suspicious?"

"Well, don't go broadcasting this, but she bats for the other side. There is no way that, despite your undeniable charms, she is suddenly going to want to bonk you, matey."

"What? Wait a minute, you mean she's a lesbian? You are joking." But it all started to fall into place with him; the lack of flirting, the looks and palling up with Maria.

"Hey, no flies on you, you catch on fast, don't you? But what worries me is what or who was here, and luckily you returned just in time or we would have had no warning. My guess is that they wanted access to the satphone, which would have been disastrous. Now for fuck's sake, keep the bloody windows closed when we are not in from now on. I'll secure them with a better locking system."

Rupert nodded. "But I thought she was on our side? What the hell is she doing spying for them?"

"That I don't know. All I know is that some of the boys in Belfast tried it on with her and she was rumoured to prefer the girls back then. I was out one night and saw her with another woman, and they were definitely more than just friends. Didn't think it's anyone else's business what her preferences are, but it rang alarm bells when you said what happened. She never comes on like that, not to anybody – well maybe another woman," he finished lamely. "Anyway not a word. We act like it hasn't happened."

Rupert shook his head. "Tell me, is there anyone we can trust on this job? Or is it just you and me against the rest of the world."

"Hopefully Sophie Carswell's on our side for real, or we are well and truly fucked! One thing though, if it is true and Siobhan is against us, news will definitely have filtered back to Valentina of who we are, don't you think? I think that the game is up there and I had better finish it. Too many games and loose ends, saves excuses for the holidays. She's invited me to her father's estancia over Christmas, by the way; talk about walking on eggshells," Chris concluded.

They agreed not to report the incident to Peters as it was inconclusive. After all. Siobhan had only tried to kiss him. What they did report in was that someone had tried to tamper with their room and gain access to the secure satphone. They were also told of the deposit and that the money had been traced onto a 'bounce account' which pinged it around, before arriving at its final destination. It would take time, but they would trace it in the end.

CHAPTER NINETEEN

London

Johnston received the report on the potential bugging and room break in. It would have meant a good deal more to him had he known of Siobhan's involvement, but even without that knowledge the pieces were falling into place for him. The news from the attic in Belfast had confirmed that the 'wee man' had picked up the money, so he knew it was heading into the IRA coffers for some reason. He just didn't know why, or who the 'wee man' was.

The FARC connection was being looked into, and the two particular IRA contacts there were being monitored. Against this background, the war in the Gulf was now in full swing, and the ground war was being actively progressed with the insertion of SAS troops to bring in intelligence on missile launch sites and other vital tactical information. All of this was coming across his desk, and it was an impossible task to evaluate it in full. Johnston's feeling was that the Gulf War would be over by the summer, and if he could arrive at that conclusion, then so could the Argentinians. If they were going to move, it had to be by the end of February or March at the latest, before the bad weather started again and the sailing season finished.

The liaison with DCI Webster had been profitable and they promised to keep each other abreast of developments – especially as Rupert would now only be able to make contact using the encrypted satellite phone.

Buenos Aires

The fax detailing property requirements for clients who were interested in buying land in the countryside was deliberately sent at a time when Adams and Brett would not be there. It was picked up by Maria, who passed it on to Alex and then finally to Rafe. They were all mildly perplexed, and compared to the recent deal to buy the docklands development it was much smaller – probably only in lots of two to three million dollars. However, it was still money and it therefore meant commission to the office. As Rupert was at pains to point out, these sorts of clients started off buying homes and ranches, then brought guests over – very wealthy guests who then invested in commercial property. In short, it was all part of the game, he said. They thought it strange, but if it kept the money coming in, so be it. It also added colour and credibility to Chris and Rupert's roles, whatever suspicions the MREC might be harbouring.

Chris and Rupert planned a road trip, one that was elaborately detailed for the benefit of Maria, Alex and indeed now Siobhan. They told the office staff that Claire would be arriving tomorrow and would be joining them, and asked Maria to book two hotel rooms at each stop. Claire, he told them, had a friend with an estancia near San Miguel, and typically with all Argentinian farms it had been divided upon the death of the father, resulting in the potential sale of half. Claire's friend was a former High Goal polo player who now ran coaching holidays, and Claire wanted to play there. Amazingly, Alex knew the man – Kieko Gomez, a former six-goaler and international player. This added further credence to the cover of property and polo – you couldn't really fake that that sort of background. Most importantly, San Miguel was only an hour from the Paraguay border and Corrientes.

Siobhan commented snidely, "So you'll be goin' on a trip with your girlfriend – all very romantic, except for Chris taggin' along."

"Oh, we'll get time by ourselves; he'll probably be going off dove shooting while Claire and I get some time alone at San Miguel," he said dismissively, still embarrassed about the previous Friday night. Siobhan just smiled secretively, and he felt relieved that he hadn't let it go any further.

The next day, Rupert was at the airport, eager to see Claire again. It seemed an age since he'd last seen her, and all the contact he'd had was through occasional calls and letters. He waited a little nervously at the arrivals gate, and then she appeared, sashaying through with a cart full of luggage and a long kit bag containing her polo sticks. She looked amazing, Rupert thought, especially considering the way most people looked after a nine hour flight. Her hair was a fabulous blond mane, which she tossed as she saw him and closed the distance with Rupert, who breathed in the familiar scent of Joy.

"Wow, you look incredible," he said. "How did you come out of an English winter looking like a film star?"

"You know how to flatter a girl," she laughed, kissing him. "Come on, lead me to the sun, I haven't seen any for months."

They walked arm in arm to the Land Cruiser, which he'd left in short term parking. They were both delighted to be reunited. It showed in their body language and Rupert was pleased that he hadn't succumbed to the charms of Susannah or Siobhan. *I'll leave that to Chris,* he thought. On the way in, he had to break the spell and bring Claire quickly up to date with a brief synopsis what had occurred, who to trust and not to give anything away to anyone – especially Siobhan – or offer any hint as to knowing their ulterior motive for being there. Claire grasped everything quickly and was furious with Siobhan, but had the grace to find it amusing that he had almost been seduced by a lesbian. Then she laughed out loud.

"But isn't that every man's fantasy? To convert a lesbian, especially a pretty one? That's what they tell me, Rupes," she mocked. "Mind you, I think Chris is wise to think about dumping Valentina. He's playing with fire there, and she's more likely to get him killed than anything."

"Yeah, you may be right – about Chris I mean…" he caught a thump on his shoulder for that one.

They fought the traffic from the airport, with Rupert displaying a wonderful adaptation to the Argentine driving style, much to Claire's concern – but to her credit she said not a word; just a couple of flinches and raised eyebrows when it seemed certain they were about to be rammed by an irate driver. They arrived at the apartment block, and Rupert parked the Toyota in the underground car park. Then, leading the way up from the basement, they entered the building from the front entrance, and waving towards the apartment he said, "A humble thing but mine own."

"You boys know how to live the high life, don't you? Beach, polo, wine, women and s… oh, sun. Sorry, slipped my mind for a moment there," she remarked.

They took Claire's heavy bags up to the apartment in the lift, and he opened the balcony windows that looked out across the marvellous vista. She joined him on the balcony, and like many close couples who'd spent some time apart she felt the distance between them and strove to enjoy immediate intimacy, to bridge the time gap that always led to initial awkwardness until normality was restored. Rupert, sensing this as much as Claire, put his arm around her and hugged her tightly.

"What do you think of the view? It really is an amazing city, and notwithstanding the real reason we are here I am actually enjoying myself. I hesitate to say this, but I could really live here, certainly for a few years. It gets under your skin, you know."

Claire looked at him sideways, locked in his embrace.

"What's got into you, my Latin lover? Is it the danger, the deals or just a genuine love for the place, hmm? Or the girls?" she finished with a slight edge of jealousy to her voice.

"I don't know, if I'm honest. Certainly not just the girls, although they are very attractive. Argentinians, I mean, they're a handsome race. Everything has a touch of the exotic. I don't know, but despite everything – the corruption, the danger – I feel very happy here. How would you like to be an agent here?" he whispered.

"Oh God no! Great place for a holiday, and great people I grant you, but I reckon I'd get fed up with it. Which reminds me, is there anything else I need to know? Are you any closer to finding out who, where and why?"

"No. Well yes, in a way, but there are still elements we don't know or don't fully understand."

He began to explain it all in full. The complete story since their arrival beginning with the Diplomatic bag; Valentina and the amazing coincidence; the cash involved in the exchange of contracts, ("Just like Italy" she declared), Sean the courier; Webster and the feedback on the IRA, finishing again with Siobhan's odd behaviour.

She didn't say anything straight away, but considered everything.

"I don't trust Siobhan. Call it women's intuition, but something is motivating her above and beyond money, and do you know I think the same might be true for Valentina. I'd like to meet both of them. As for the espionage, you know what we always said? Follow the money. The Yanks will be up to their ears in this with the Mafia or something, you wait and see. I can't wait to meet Sophie Carswell; as a spook she seems to be the most normal person in this bizarre deal – and that says it all."

Rupert kissed her with a grin and a gleam appeared in his eyes that she recognised only too well.

"Oh no, Mister Brett. I've been on a plane for hours. I reek like a polecat, I need a shower, a cold alcoholic drink and maybe, just maybe, something to follow." She winked at him suggestively over her shoulder and disappeared into the bathroom. Reappearing after twenty minutes, she went straight into the bedroom. Two minutes later she called out:

"Girl getting thirsty in here."

Rupert smiled and walked in with a freezing bottle of Quilmes in each hand. He and Chris had taken to it so much that they now always had some in the fridge. She was dressed in a towelling robe and had just finished her makeup. She looked amazing, Rupert thought. She accepted the beer and took a swig, the ice cold liquid making her eyes water.

"Wow, that's good," she gasped.

Rupert advanced and undid her towelling robe, exposing her full breasts.

"So are these." She made a half-hearted attempt to swat him away and ended up in his arms in a full kiss. He gently lifted her up, and her legs seemed to wrap themselves around him as he carried her to the bed. He muttered through her kisses that they would not have long as Chris would be back soon

"After this amount of time away from you, it's not going to take me long!" she said. They proceeded to make love quickly and passionately, sex that was born of desperation and abstinence, culminating in a noisy climax from both of them. They lay laughing in each other's arms, savouring their renewed union.

"Oh wow, that was worth waiting for," Rupert laughed.

"If you think that was good, wait 'til tonight!" she retorted.

"Do you think…?" he started, reaching for her shoulder and trying to roll her towards him.

"No. I would be so embarrassed if Chris walked in on us. Get dressed. I need to put some clothes on before he arrives."

They both dressed, and when Chris arrived ten minutes later they looked a picture of innocence except for the glow in Claire's cheeks

"Claire, so you came for me after all," he declared, his Welsh charm on full throttle, walking towards her and embracing her in a bear hug.

"I know, but just don't tell him," she angled her head at Rupert, laughing.

He asked after the flight and how things were in London generally, swapping small talk.

"So, I see you've got to the important things first," he said, nodding at her empty beer bottle, "What next, lunch?"

She nodded her agreement and the three of them headed for a little place that Rupert and Chris had found just down from the office in a new complex. Over a lunch of huge Argentinian steaks and a strong bottle of Malbec, Claire caught up on the news.

"Oh god, I've missed these steaks!" she declared, rolling her eyes in delight. Rupert shook his head.

"What is it about women and steak? They go on about men, but I think women are worse."

She laughed, taking another sip of the rich, velvety Malbec. They talked about the attack on Chris, and Claire expressed her concern.

"It was just a typical street mugging and they picked on the wrong guy – or maybe I got lucky. Either way, all's well and no harm done."

He laughed it off, but as they looked at each other they in-stinctively realised that neither of them had been fooled and they smiled knowingly. Not for the first time, Chris wondered just how much Rupert had told Claire. Lunch finished with some strong coffee, then it was on to the office to meet the others, including Siobhan.

The state of the art building did not fail to impress Claire, but she found it odd when she finally met all the people she had heard about; putting names to faces and knowing more about them than they did about her.

"So, you're going to see the final in Palermo?" Rafe asked.

"Yes. I can't wait, I've been close so many times but never actually seen it. Luckily I will now, as it's been delayed this year. I am so excited." No one could fake that sort of enthusiasm, and Rafe and Alex smiled indulgently.

Siobhan raised a smile but said, "Frankly I find the whole thing boring, I just don't get polo," she said. "But hey, each to their own."

There were howls of derision from the others – even Chris, who was beginning to appreciate the game.

"Then after that, I understand you are up the country for some sightseeing?" Rafe continued.

"Yeah. The boys are dragging me around, but then I get to see Kieko and play some polo myself. But first the beach, I need to get a suntan. Look how pale I am compared to all of you." The banter continued and they were in no doubt that she was excited to be here and genuine in her love for the game.

The next day they headed for the beach at Mar del Plata, and this was to prove Chris's last date with Valentina before they left. But Chris still needed her for cover and was not disappointed to see her. The beach was a playground for the citizens of BA:

a place to pose, be seen and flirt while getting a tan. The sand was packed with the bronzed and the beautiful. For her part, Claire was slightly out of her depth. She had bought what she considered to be a skimpy bikini before leaving the UK and had winced at its miniscule proportions. But arriving on the beach she felt as though she'd been dressed for the opera and taken to a barbecue. Every woman there wore only bikini bottoms and the tiniest thongs or micro bikinis in the south American style, leaving little or nothing to the imagination. Despite her bravura she was slightly abashed and a little disconcerted

"Don't you have any ugly people in Argentina?" Claire asked.

Valentina smiled, catching on quickly to the English humour. "Sure we do. We just don't let them out until after dark," she joked.

Claire thought it was a shame. She took to Valentina immediately, but she could see how the unwary would be trapped and slain. After a lunchtime drink, Chris suggested a walk up towards the dock area to enjoy the breeze and get away from the crowds.

"Oh you English," Valentina replied. "You always want to exercise. Come on then but will *ambladura, si?*"

"Yes we will walk slowly. We will amble, no problem."

They walked hand in hand, Chris with a linen shirt on to hide the last of his embarrassing bruises.

"How are you feeling?" She said. "I am sorry once again for my countrymen who treated you so badly."

"Oh no, don't worry, it could happen anywhere, and they didn't get my money, I lived to tell the tale and I am a big boy. I had worse in the army." He smiled and looked ahead towards the quayside, where the *Esmeralda* was moored next to a frigate downriver from the docks. The cruise ship was having plates fitted, and what seemed to be large scale modifications to the side. They looked strange to Chris's eyes and he couldn't see what the purpose was. He looked puzzled for a second and Valentina followed his gaze.

"What is the matter? Stop frowning," she said, reaching up and smoothing his brow with her fingers.

"What? Oh, sorry," he answered with deliberate vagueness. "Just strange to see a civilian ship in a military dockyard. I saw it down in the dock area when we first came here and I was just trying to figure out what they were doing to her – but hey, you do things differently here."

He laughed and turned away to go back. But he'd spotted the large gantry that was still there, and the modification to the bulkhead didn't look permanent. He had seen enough, and an idea was forming in his mind that was starting to alarm him.

The stroll back was slightly stilted between them, despite efforts by Valentina to lighten the conversation. "So, when are you coming to my parents' estancia?" she asked him. "They would love to meet you over the holidays; you can talk over old war stories with my father, he'd like that."

Chris stopped and turned, taking Valentina's hands in his own. "Listen, something has come up. I am really sorry Valentina, but I am going to have to go on a road trip to sort out some urgent requirements for a new client. I can't put it off, I'm afraid. New office, new clients. You know how it is, we have to make a success of it."

She looked deeply into his eyes, and Chris saw anger, hurt – and strangely, fear. Before he could analyse it, the walls came down and she immediately went into strident Latin mode, with the high spirited accusations and a good deal of shouting.

"What work? Why don't you want to come? Are you finishing with me, Chris? Tell me, I need to know." Her rant continued until they started to attract glances from the crowded beach, but Valentina didn't seem to care. "Oh to hell with you, then. Go to your stupid deals; go adventuring or whatever you do, if it means more to you than me, *jodete*"

She ran off to her car, tears welling in her eyes. It was a good performance, Chris thought, wondering just how real it was. She had jumped to conclusions a little too quickly, and the taps had turned on a little too fast as well. It was as good a time as any to call it quits, he considered. He'd probably be a lot safer for it, he reflected. Claire, along with a good deal of the beach, had witnessed the altercation, and as Rupert re-joined them he commented, "So, that went well, didn't it?"

"Hah, you know how it is, I'm just misunderstood." Chris shrugged, grinning. He stripped off his shirt, no longer caring about the bruises, and declared that he was going for a run along the beach and a swim.

Claire, who had remained silent throughout, said: "You know, in a funny kind of way I quite liked her. Yes, I know she's a two-faced murdering spy who was using her feminine wiles to get by, but we all do that. But there was a human side to her that I found vaguely appealing. There was a sense of frailty about her… yes that was exactly it. I would love to know her real story and background," she finished, clearly intrigued. "Having said that, I think that Chris was right to get out. She was trouble and he will be a lot safer without her presence

While Chris sought to expunge the incident with a hard run and swim, Rupert and Claire took refuge in the heat of the sun, with Claire demanding regular applications of sun cream from Rupert to ensure she did not burn. Breathing hard from his exertions, Chris returned from his final swim half an hour or so later. Towelling himself off, he commented privately to Rupert; "Right, that part is sorted; now we move on. We need to be very aware that even without Siobhan's possible involvement we must be extra vigilant against any retribution from Valentina. But I think she knows better. Anything they do would just confirm to us that she's a spy."

They decided that Claire had had enough of the hot Argentinian sun for her first day, despite her protestations, and moved to leave the beach. Back at the apartment, Chris was pleased to find everything as he had left it, with nothing disturbed. Claire was wise enough to leave well alone and withhold any comments on the apparent demise of his relationship, and went to shower all the sun cream off, leaving the two men together.

"Did Claire say anything about the scene at the beach?" Chris asked.

"No, not really. She just sympathised, but she did say that underneath it all Valentina seemed like a nice girl." Rupert shrugged. "She doesn't know the whole story, obviously, so she can't comment on the fact that Valentina might have been responsible for nearly having you beaten up and killed. That sort of detail could well alter her opinion," he finished drily.

Chris winced, "You know when I told her I wasn't going with her, it wasn't obvious we were splitting up until she said it was. She showed *fear*, amongst other emotions. Now what do you suppose caused that? Do you think it's like with the Russians in the Cold War? Move forward and defend your country because the enemy's bullet may miss, but if you fail the government's forces will definitely kill you for your failure?"

"I don't know, but this country is to all intents and purposes ruled by a military junta, with a puppet president, and by your own admission it's got one of the most powerful and omnipotent secret services in the world. So it wouldn't surprise me that they might have some other hold upon her. Her family perhaps?"

"Could be." Chris shrugged. "Anyway, we need to move on, and it's the final at Palermo tomorrow, is it not? Be good to take my mind off it all and enjoy the game."

Chapter Twenty

The famous final took place at the hallowed ground known affectionately by all polo aficionados as the Cathedral. Its vast vaulted stands rose up from the pitch side in the form of a huge bowl that seated 30,000 spectators. Today's events were effectively the culmination of the world series. Only the best players in the world attended and it was the only time that anyone ever got to see forty-goal polo – when four ten-goalers played on each side. The skill level was out of this world and Rupert, Chris and Claire were looking forward to it. Rupert had invited some clients along to attend as a grand gesture; these investors were already in Argentina with their wives or less official companions, and were only too delighted to receive such an invitation, as the tickets for good seats were hard to come by. It was a great social event and it had added more veracity to their cover as surveyors working in the country.

They had arranged to meet up with clients at a local bar, and had laid on a chauffeured car to take them to the Alveare Hotel near the stadium. The grounds had no restaurants; just a few champagne bars open for the event, where it would be standing room only. So everyone ate beforehand and drove to the event or took taxis – or if they were locals simply walked to the stadium which was about ten minutes outside central BA.

The hotel was one of the oldest and finest in the city. Today it would be packed with an eclectic mix of all nationalities with one thing in common – a love of polo. The hotel was magnificent: its high-arched windows were all cast in marble and it had an old world feeling of opulence. The clients loved every minute of it, as did their wives, most of whom were inappropriately dressed for polo. They felt spoiled and privileged, which of course only encouraged their husbands to spend more time and money in the country.

Arriving at the grounds in a limousine, they disembarked and were ushered into the champagne bar and then on into the stadium. Conspicuous consumption was everywhere, from the fake straw fedoras given out by the Chandon stand to the beautiful girls from the Argentinian Polo Association offering gift packs to all. It was an all-round assault on the senses, crowned by the sheer size of the grounds and the unrivalled excitement in anticipation of the eight gladiators who were coming out to do battle.

As they took their seats, Rupert realised that this was a time and place that he would probably never see again. The event held a sense of fragility for him, a *carpe diem* moment. The colonels and the hangers-on would come back year after year, the polo set oohing and aahing. But Rupert sensed that for him this could never quite be the same a second time around. His instincts told him that he would not return, or that if he did the circumstances would be completely different. Different feel, different company, a different world. How he knew this was beyond him – it was instinctive and he embraced it, enjoying the seduction of the atmosphere, the smells and senses for the first time, like a virgin with a first love. He loved polo in its simplest form, yet at the same time was sad in the knowledge that he would never again experience the raw passion of the game as a spectator quite like this, and sample these sensations imbued by the thousands around him.

They were treated to a master class of polo; with stunning moves that were so fast they were hard to follow. The final score was 14 - 16 and the arguments then began in a good natured way amongst the locals about who had been the best team, who should have scored; why a penalty had been awarded, the usual post-match analysis. Claire was ecstatic and the clients were thrilled to experience their special day out; promising to buy more property in Buenos Aires and in the countryside beyond for their personal use.

The next day was the start of the holidays and the day that Rupert, Chris and Claire would begin their trip into the area around BA and up to San Miguel for Christmas before heading further north to Corrientes. The final plans were finalised in the office, omitting the fact (even to Siobhan) that the trip would extend up beyond San Miguel to Corrientes and the proposed flight to the Falklands from Montevideo airport.

"So, Siobhan, what are you up to for the holidays? Back to Blighty or staying here?" Chris asked.

"Hah, Belfast in the winter with the family arguing over Christmas pud; freezing rain and the chance of a bomb or two for company or sun, sea and great company here? That's a hard one, but I think I'll stick with the hot climate. Anyway, Maria's asked me to come to her family for Christmas by the beach. It's a tough decision, but I had to make the sacrifice," she finished, rewarding Maria with a warm smile in case the sarcasm was lost in translation.

"Now there I agree with you, Wales in the winter: what a bloody awful thought!" Chris said.

"I guess we're all settled then. Let us have a number where we can contact you just in case we need anything sent back on client's requirements," Rupert asked.

"Rupert, do you ever stop working? Jeez, that girl of yours is goin' to be very pissed off."

"Not a bit. She is a surveyor too, remember?" he replied, smiling at Siobhan and forgetting for the moment the deadly game of cat and mouse they were playing against all sides. She laughed at him, shaking her head.

"Here," she said. "A little something for under the tree; but don't open it until then, you promise?" she demanded with mock seriousness. She had produced two small and identical packages for Chris and Rupert.

"Siobhan, that is really kind of you. To my eternal shame I have nothing for you," Rupert said, looking guilty and giving her a peck on the cheek.

"Hah, but that's just typical of a man. Now be off with you and have a great time, send me a card." Chris too looked a little shamefaced. He'd never thought of such a gesture, particularly on a mission.

"Siobhan, what can I say..." he finished lamely.

"Nothin', just buy me a big present for when you get back," she replied archly.

He kissed her, then turned to wish Rafe and Alex the compliments of the season, which given the intense summer heat felt rather foolish.

They bade the office farewell and left to pick up Claire from the apartment and start the first part of the journey to Pilar and the surrounding area. This was very much polo country, especially popular with ex-pats and wealthy Brits wanting to buy into the country. At the apartment, Claire was almost ready, and just doing some final packing in the bedroom, so Chris took the opportunity to re-pack all the items from the bottom of the secure compartment in the wardrobe, including the Satellite phone in its case. He re-loaded them all into the leather holdall. It was still imperative to Chris that Claire remain ignorant of the real reason for their being in BA, although the time would come in the near future when she would have to be made aware of their mission, at least to some extent.

Claire felt a great sense of adventure as they all piled into the Land Cruiser. Although completely aware of what was going on in the investigation, she still had that feeling of excitement, with a little whiff of danger and intrigue and no real thoughts as to the possibility that it could all go horribly wrong.

The first leg was to the northwest of Pilar on Route 8, out in the wide open spaces so characteristic of this part of Argentina. The rich, dark red soil showed through in vast swathes of cultivation amidst the grasslands of the pampas and beyond, stretching as far as the distant horizon. The heat swirled in bouncing waves, setting off mirages along the distant strip of tarmac. It was a new experience, especially for Rupert. It was very alien to someone who had been used to the relatively confined spaces of Europe.

There were in all about ten properties for sale in this region and they had arranged to inspect them all for the various clients. They comprised of anything from 20 hectares up- wards. They were big enough for an estancia, private polo field and the ground for a pool. All of them were within an hour's drive of BA. They'd stay relatively local today, and head further out after that, away from the comfort and safety of the city, out into the broad spaces of Argentina's interior.

CHAPTER TWENTY-ONE

As the group left BA, another British citizen was making her own plans for a holiday getaway. Sophie Carswell was heading back to the UK for an extended break, to spend Christmas with her parents and friends. The move was well documented and all above board. The flights were booked, and MREC made sure she was carefully followed to the airport and seen onto her flight. The Americans, MREC, the FARC contact and even Siobhan all breathed a sigh of relief once Sophie had departed. There were no spooks and no meddlers, and the Brits were safely out of harm's way – or so the Argentinian authorities thought.

A call was placed from MREC headquarters to Boston

"Philips," came the dry reply.

"We have just had confirmation that Sophie Carswell has left the country. She, as I'm sure you will recall, was the other suspected agent at the embassy. She left on a flight for the UK and her return journey is set for the first week in January. So she is either being pulled out or they suspect nothing. We're pretty sure she's just going home for a couple of weeks for Christmas. In any event, we will monitor all passenger manifests on all flights in and out and check them for suspect British personnel entering the country. It looks as though we are clear to progress our plans with the others up country and away from BA."

"Good," Phillips replied. "How do you know the others are where they are supposed to be?"

"They have a present waiting for them, and they are heading for San Miguel as planned. They have also visited every place on their itinerary so far. Don't worry, everything's in order."

"I always worry; it's part of my job. I don't need to tell you exactly what is riding on the success of this operation – without putting too fine a point on it, it's your country's future."

The tone changed on the other end of the phone; "You do not need to tell me that, and we have a lot more to lose than you."

With that, the receiver was replaced. Phillips swore; something he rarely did. "Fucking dagos," he muttered, and went through to Kelly to report the news.

"Why the long face? It's good news. Relax, everything's going to plan; the soldier-surveyor is out of our hair, Carswell is going home at a crucial moment, and Brett has his girlfriend along, so there won't be any trouble. Come on, it doesn't get much better," Kelly said.

"Well, like I just explained to our Latino friends, I am paid to worry and something is going on that we're missing. I am going to put some men down at the base at Corrientes, working the perimeter, just in case," Phillips finished, holding up a hand to stall any remonstrations at his caution.

London

Sophie did indeed catch the flight back to London Heathrow, and in case anyone was still watching, she caught a cab from there into central London and on to her parents' home in Highgate. To hell with the expense she thought, it's on HMG. She stayed with her parents over the Christmas break and for New Year, eating turkey, sipping sherry with her mother and twiddling her thumbs. She did all the normal things, going to the sales on Boxing Day, shouldering her way through the crowds in Oxford Street. Any Argentinian tail would have been bored stupid. God knows, she was. But during the interceding period between the two holidays she went to see Johnston at MI6 headquarters, being a lot more careful about any possible surveillance. There she was briefed on all that had taken place so far, including the almost certain double agent threat posed by Siobhan Clifford

"So, that's how they knew, and that's why they ambushed sergeant Adams?"

"Well, not quite. They needed confirmation that he was possibly something more from one of their own – if indeed Valentina Perez is working for MREC or SIND."

Sophie snorted in disgust. "If you saw the state of Andrew you wouldn't need much persuasion. So somebody sacrificed three agents to prove a point, yeah?"

"The Yanks, evidently. Christ knows why. Anyway there's no point in getting emotional, it gets in the way," Johnston said. "There are a lot of moving parts here and we need to be sure of each piece of this puzzle or we will get burned. Pawns are getting sacrificed all over the damn place, which means it's big. As I was saying, the attack made them show their hand, and it looks like the Yanks are not all on our side this time. God knows why, but you can never tell with them. Soon we'll have the telephone recordings from HMS Spartan and they will hopefully confirm the identity of the US side of the operation. Once we know that, another piece will be in place. So far we know for certain that FARC are working with the PIRA and that Siobhan is involved – but as to why, that remains a mystery.

"We also know that the Argentinian government is liaising and operating with someone or some organisation within the

US through MREC. We suspect that it has to do with the Falklands and that Waddington was on to something – hence the rather draconian move to prevent him from visiting the base at Corrientes. We also have an IRA involvement in what I assume is money laundering for some nefarious purposes which will benefit the Argies, the US entity and the IRA. It's the IRA that will benefit from the cash, that much is obvious. But what are they doing in return, who is doing the running, from where and to what end? And who is the 'wee man'? That is what we need to know. Clear?"

"Yes sir." She nodded.

"Good. You'll head out on the first transport after New Year. Good luck," he added. "Thank you, sir. I'll keep in touch via the smartphone with Adams, and hopefully we'll have some answers soon."

Sophie Carswell left the office, her mind exploring all angles, analysing and rejecting each thought as she considered it. Home was comforting and familiar, she realised as she walked back into the familiar smells of her mother's cooking and her father's pipe tobacco. Canned laughter came from a seasonal chat show on the living room television, and the central heating was cranked up a couple of degrees on the uncomfortable side. She kissed her mother on the cheek and went through to sit with her father. The atmosphere was a little stifling, and the chat show wasn't funny despite her father's chuckles. The thought of getting back into the action was compelling – and she had a score to settle for Andrew.

The next day she headed out from her parent's house, driving to stay with friends in Oxfordshire for a day or two. If anyone had been following her, which she doubted, she would to all intents and purposes be following a normal routine: home with family and a couple of nights out with friends.

But there were more ways back into Argentina than through the usual channels.

After New Year, she drove her mother's car to RAF Brize Norton, passing through the gates on her government security pass. Someone took a note of the registration number, and the car would be returned to her mother in the next couple of days. The base was on high alert because of the Gulf War, and security was strict. RAF Brize enjoyed one unique quality amongst RAF bases in the UK: it flew twice weekly to the Ascension Islands and on to the Falklands. Run by 216 Squadron, the plane took civilians as well as military personnel and supplies, and was in fact the only way to reach the island by air.

A note was handed to her by the communications commander prior to boarding her flight. She called Johnston on a secure line from the communications office.

"Sir?"

"Listen carefully. We now have confirmation that the calls are being placed to the headquarters of USE Oil in Boston."

"Boston? The home of Noraid, where every second citizen speaks the Blarney and longs for the auld country. This gets better and better."

"Exactly. Now, the recordings show a number of calls placed there, including a call to a hospital in BA. It was the hospital where one of Sergeant Adams' victims was recovering from his ordeal. From the conversation recorded, it was USE Oil who put the hit on him and they thought he was supposedly a former Royal Green Jacket like his cover made him out to be. That information can only have come from Valentina Perez and/or Alejandro. But he would have had to have prior knowledge in order to set it up in time, which means it was Perez who reported back. They've also picked up on the fact that you have left BA and are retuning in January: it's all been reported back to Boston and they are very pleased with themselves.

"So, among all this bad news, at least they have underestimated your role and your clandestine return. However, this is getting difficult and dangerous for innocent people: Brett's girlfriend is over there and while it legitimatises their cover, she's another civilian who is not in the loop, who might get hurt.

"We've also heard back from Five. They've got more intel on the Quartermaster. They reported a trip to the US, a pickup of funds and a return to Ireland. It is now almost certain that the 'wee man', the Quartermaster and the courier are one and the same."

"So, more pieces of the puzzle in place," Sophie said. "But we still don't know the connection between the IRA and USE Oil. And more importantly, why they should be paying them a hundred and forty million dollars? Can this DCI Webster track the money route? It is clearly headed for Dublin as payment to buy something else."

"It is being tracked and we will find it. Getting proof it is dirty and stopping it becoming legitimate is another matter. It does, however, get us closer to the answer and clearly if an oil company is involved, then maybe they want a share of the action for oil rights. But on the Falklands? There are many variables that have to be in place, not least of which is possession of the islands. Good luck with your trip. I will brief Adams via Peters at the FO and he will be fully up to speed when you meet up."

"Can we get to the agents that ambushed Adams?" Sophie asked.

"Funny you should ask. That's exactly what we tried. Adams killed one of them, the others have disappeared off the face of the earth."

"Disappeared?"

"The Yanks are cleaning up after themselves. Getting rid of any weak points, anything that can be compromised. They'll be Piranha food by now."

"Piranhas are Brazil, sir. Argentina has caimans. Probably even more effective."

"Either way, you should know the stakes, Carswell."

"Thank you, sir." The line disconnected and she was lost in a world of thoughts.

The flight to Ascension Island took eighteen hours in a RAF Tri Star transport fitted out for passengers. At this time of year she was the only civilian travelling the long haul to the island and beyond to the Falklands. Sophie passed through customs, boarded the plane and took her seat, making ready for the long flight and the final hop to re-enter Argentina by the back door. By the time she was noticed she would be well ensconced in the embassy back in BA, hopefully with a good deal more information to report than they had at the moment.

The flight was long and tiring and she was looking forward to a hot bath and a good night's sleep before she met up with Adams and Brett on the Falkland Islands. The journey had given her time to reflect and consider all the information that Johnston had passed on to her. Making notes had always been her way, and her notebook showed a diagram with arrows pointing and linking all the elements concerned in the conundrum. It always came down to two key questions no matter how she drew the diagram: what advantage could the IRA or FARC give to Argentina and/or the US oil company, and how was the invasion to take place? Who was directing it, and who was funding it?

Added to this was of course, how did it benefit all parties? Hopefully some of these questions would be answered over the course of the next few days.

Arriving on the Ascension Island was a transformation. Only eighteen hours ago she'd walked across the runway in a freezing cold Britain, the wind tugging at her coat and her hair. Now she was enveloped by the warm sub-tropical breezes of this small, virtually unknown and distinctly uncommercial paradise. As a tourist destination it was unheard of, but she reflected she would visit it again just for the sheer bliss of the silence and the calm and relaxed way of life. Like so many island populations, the Ascension Islanders could not do enough for their guests. Despite the rather rustic choices for accommodation, Sophie considered it a paradise – with hardly any traffic, long and unspoiled sandy beaches and rocky inlets. Like Cornwall only warmer and without the people, she thought.

She was booked into one of the small bed-and-breakfasts on the island and was due to leave the following morning on the last flight to the Falklands. The meal was adequate but rather unspectacular, and she learned from the waitress that a lot of the food was imported frozen – including the vegetables, which Sophie considered strange, given the fertile nature of the island's soil. However, the service more than made up for the lack of culinary expertise, and she enjoyed a relaxed night in the B & B and spent the following morning exploring the coast before her flight.

The smell of the salt breezes and the gentle crash of the waves against the rocky coast were a balm to the soul. If she hadn't been working, she thought, a week here with a pile of books would be the most perfect antidote to life. But the reality of her situation came back to her as she made her way to the airfield and the flight to the Falkland Islands. Like Johnston said, pawns were being sacrificed, and she didn't want to be one of them.

Chapter Twenty-Two

Argentina

The trip so far had been successful. Over the last few days, Rupert had sent faxes back to the UK with initial reports to various clients on the properties inspected and brief comments on suitability and recommendations as to price. The tour was taking them ever further north on the main A9 freeway, where they would end up in San Miguel in the northern province. In reality, this was pure indulgence on their part, as very few clients were going to want to be this far from BA.

Chris had enjoyed the last few days; it had been calming, with no hint of danger, and he had actually found himself able to relax. However, he continued with his punishing exercise regime of runs and training routines, including *chi sau*, at which Rupert was now also becoming quite proficient. He especially enjoyed Claire's company; she had not behaved like a typical girlfriend on a holiday and had done everything to include Chris in their company without making him feel like a gooseberry. Her natural charm was infectious and she flirted harmlessly with him.

For her part, Claire enjoyed spending time in the beautiful

countryside and travelling with them both. However, it was becoming increasingly apparent that at some point she was going to have to disclose her thoughts or suspicions as to what was really going on.

The long ribbon of road seemed to go on forever and it took them nearly eight hours to get to San Miguel. The roads were virtually traffic free, except for the large coaches that regularly travelled the long trips north and south. The coaches were rumoured to be fantastically comfortable, and in other circumstances they'd have been a perfect way to travel the long distances.

They finally reached San Miguel, a rural town in the middle of nowhere. The mainly single storey buildings were a significant feature of the town and it felt as though nothing had changed there for the last hundred years except for the few 7/11 corner stores, which displayed advertisements for modern sweets and fizzy drinks. To Rupert, it looked like a set from a Spaghetti Western.

They were met in a car park by Kieko, who pulled up in a dusty Pajero jeep. Getting out of the vehicle, the first thing that struck Chris was that Kieko was short for a polo player. He had become a six-goaler through hard work rather than having a natural physique designed for the sport. He was very tanned and had a smooth-skinned face and soft brown eyes. His charm was legendary, and it had led to an early divorce and a string of lovers thereafter – most of whom were at least ten years younger than him. He always declared that it was his lovers what kept him young and fit in the years before he finally settled down once again.

"Claire, ciao," he exclaimed delightedly, coming forward and giving her a big hug and a kiss on both cheeks. "It is so good to see you." His face seemed to wear a permanent smile, which he bestowed on the others as Claire introduced them.

"This is Rupert, who you may remember from the Longdole Polo Club. And this is his colleague, Chris Adams."

"Of course, of course, Rupert. It is good to see you, no? And Chris, great you could make it too. Good trip I hope?"

His grip when he shook hands made even Chris wince slightly, which was not surprising given that Kieko practiced with a heavy 53-inch mallet every day, which was a little like a latter day knight in armour wielding a sword.

"Yeah, we have seen some beautiful country, so vast and flat, but I love the spaces and the sky," Rupert said.

"*Si*, the Pampas is beautiful, especially at this time of year. Now come, let us make a move, we still have an hour's drive before we reach the ranch."

They went back to the cars and set off into the deepening gloom. After driving down various side roads, they finally arrived at a rustic five bar gate with a branded wooden sign which read *Estancia Gomez*. Kieko got out, opened the gate wide, drove through and then waited as Rupert drove through, jumped out and closed it.

If they thought they were nearly at their journey's end they were wrong. The road was left behind, and the farm track upon which they now travelled was rough aggregate, winding its way into the distance in complete darkness. No light was visible beyond the beams of their headlights, and they saw no living thing. The vast emptiness gave them a feeling of complete isolation, which to Claire and Rupert was a new and unnerving experience.

Five miles later they saw an array of lights in the distance, outlining an L-shaped layout of buildings. As they came closer they saw rows of twinkling oil lights hanging from a veranda that ran the length of the single storey estancia. The buildings were shadowed by huge trees they could only see in greyish outline. It all looked very welcoming, and it came as a relief after the dark journey across country to get there. The two cars swung down towards the building and the gravel crunched as they pulled to a halt in front of the main house. Close up, the oil lights gave a mellow, comforting glow, pooling around the base of each pillar that supported the roof.

"Oh wow, what a great place to spend Christmas!" Claire exclaimed, opening the car door and inhaling the unique smell of the pampas: a mix of sweet grass, horses, cattle, dry soil and unknown herbs that wafted in on the night breeze. The cicadas, crickets and other less identifiable insects all fought for prominence, their night calls chirping all around them.

"Welcome to my home," Kieko offered, waving an expansive hand at the property.

As he did so the glass French windows to the main house opened, throwing more yellow light onto the drive and the raised veranda. Two figures appeared, silhouetted against the light, throwing long shadows across the ground. The taller of the two was a slim, blonde woman with straight hair to her shoulders, framing a pretty, heart shaped face that was just starting to lose its youthful beauty, but was enhanced by exquisite high cheekbones. She approached Claire with raised arms, hugging her in an embrace.

"You finally came. I am so pleased to see you in our home, welcome, welcome," she exclaimed.

"Oh it's so good to be here, Silvia. I've heard so much about it and now I am finally here, I can't believe it. Franky!" she cried turning to the second figure.

The girl was about seventeen; her features a pretty mix of both her parents. She was just losing her puppy fat to the promise of a real beauty in the making. Her dark, honeyed hair flew out behind her as she ran forward to squeeze Claire in a hug. She talked in fast Spanish, which Claire had trouble following.

"Slowly, slowly: so you're not pleased to see me then?" Claire laughed, finally holding Franky at arm's length.

"Sorry," she said, turning to Rupert and Chris as Claire introduced them.

"Rupert you know, and this is his colleague, Chris Adams, another surveyor working with him in BA. Chris, this is Silvia and Franky," she finished the introductions. Rupert received a kiss on both cheeks from the two women and Chris shook hands with them.

"It is a lovely spot you have here, Silvia," Chris said. "I can't wait to see it in the daylight tomorrow – and it will be all the more auspicious as it is Christmas Eve."

"I know, it is so lovely to have the house full. But I am afraid no roast turkey, does that matter? But we will have a wonderful *Noche Buena* tomorrow with *Vitel Toné*, so I hope you like it. Now I am keeping you out here and you must be tired after your journey. Come in, come in."

They unloaded the car and entered the hacienda onto tiled floors, surrounded by whitewashed walls, and a wonderfully cool atmosphere after the outdoor heat. Kieko's home was comfortably rustic with memorabilia on the walls and deep leather sofas and chairs, all set off by the soft oil lamps which added a lovely, comforting smell of lamp oil mingling with the aroma of fresh coffee.

"Now let me show you to your rooms, and I then will have coffee for you and a little bite to eat."

Her time in England had left Silvia with a smattering of charming English colloquialisms that peppered her speech. They followed her through the corridors to their bedrooms, all romantically set out with period mosquito nets around the beds, looking like a scene from *Out of Africa* with charming colonial furniture from a bygone era. Claire sighed and clasped her hands in joy.

"Oh Rupes, this better than I ever imagined. All this and polo too. Wow!" He laughed at her childlike appreciation. "It is really amazing and I think we may even have trouble levering Chris away from here. He is so at home already, much more than he was in the city. He seems almost relaxed, and he's lost that perpetual wariness he has all the time."

"Well it goes with the job, like we cannot ever switch off in a city full of property: always trying to work out where Prime is wherever we are." He grinned knowingly. They quickly unpacked, washing the dust of travel from themselves and re-emerging into the large sitting room.

Fresh coffee was brought for them by one of the live-in maids, together with a selection of small sweet and savoury pastries. They talked of all that they had done since arriving in BA, about the Open in Palermo, and caught up on news of old friends in the UK. Finally exhausted, Rupert, Claire and Chris bade their hosts goodnight and headed for their rooms.

Alone in his room, Chris opened his French doors and breathed in the scent of the Pampas like an old friend, inhaling deeply and feeling, as Rupert had commented, very much at home in the wilderness. He sighed wistfully and returned to work, opening up the travelling holdall containing amongst other things, the secure satphone, which he opened up and turned on.

A message was waiting for him from Peters at the FO, updating him on the current brief from Johnston at MI6. It basically brought him up to date with all the information that had been given to Sophie Carswell prior to her departure for the Falklands. It also gave details of the date she would arrive and confirmed that their tickets from Montevideo to the Falklands had been pre-booked and paid for through an English travel agent and were ready to be picked up from the airport upon their arrival. *It was all starting to come together,* Chris thought, but like Sophie Carswell he hoped that the Falklands trip would somehow miraculously provide a Eureka moment, when the scales fell from their eyes and all would be revealed – but he wasn't holding his breath.

The next morning was heralded with a dawn chorus of mooing cattle, birdsong and the shuffle of horses' hooves on sandy soil. There was a faint whisper of a breeze, blowing the mighty eucalyptus trees that shaded the main building, making them sway and rustle. At 8am it was already hot, and promised to be another scorching day. Claire had risen early and had nearly finished breakfast when Rupert and Chris put in an appearance. It was to be her first day of polo and she intended to make the most of every minute of it.

"Come on you two, we have horses to ride and chukkas to play. Chris, can you ride?"

"Well, if I am honest, horses and me don't really get on that well. I have a story of a girl who got me on a horse and it didn't end well. I'll leave it at that," he laughed, grimacing at the memory.

"I have this really quiet mare, she is quite old, very calm, she will be perfect for you," Kieko said. "I will get Tinto, my groom, to take you out for a quiet hack into the Pampas, you will love it. No surprises, I promise," he offered, more as a fait accompli than a choice

Rupert slipped past him and whispered in his ear sotto voce, "Come on Chris, 'who dares wins', eh? He was rewarded with a thump on the shoulder and a scowl.

Claire frowned. "What was that?"

"Oh nothing. Just an in-joke, boys talk, you know."

Breakfast finished, they ventured outside into the bright sunshine and were surprised at the scope of the setup. The house was a single storey L-shape as the oil lamps the previous evening had suggested, but it extended further than they had thought, providing living quarters for the staff. To the front, across from the yard and the drive were two large American style barns, some corrals, a feed store and a workshop for mending tack, shoeing and storing farm machinery. The long drive down which they had driven the night before was lined with rustic post and rail fencing as far as the eye could see, and cattle lowed, dawdled and grazed on the other side of the fence, in the huge paddocks or grass areas that extended out of sight in every direction. There were occasional small clumps of thorny shrubs and scrub oaks. The main house was framed by large, towering, eucalyptus trees with peeling red and cream bark. The setting was perfect. The sheer size of open spaces was awe inspiring, and even Chris, who had operated in most areas of the world, was impressed with its raw beauty. To the rear of the house was a large shaded area framed by more trees protecting a swimming pool set in the rear garden of the estancia. It was, Claire thought to herself, a sublime place to spend a few days.

Kieko led them to the stable block, which was constructed from rough-hewn timber, faded to a mellow grey-brown in the hot sun. Kieko's *Segundo*, Tinto, was introduced. He was a solid man of indefinable age with brown, seamed skin that crinkled into a thousand lines when he smiled. He could have been a weathered forty or an ageless sixty, nobody knew, and probably nobody cared. He knew no English and spoke an incomprehensible version of Spanish that sounded like the mutterings of the horses he loved so well. Chris liked quiet people, and felt he could spend a relaxing day with Tinto, not needing to say very much. It would be a good break before they set off on their journey to the border and the Falklands beyond to meet up with Sophie Carswell.

They were introduced to their mounts and Rupert was assigned a gentle gelding who would no doubt take care of him on the field. He had ridden as a child in the local pony club, but had given up as a teenager when he discovered girls.

"So what to do?" Kieko asked.

Kieko had played polo around the world, and one of his main patrons was Sheik Al Farouk from the UAE, whose wife had picked up English idioms and was forever saying *What to do?* whenever a problem presented itself. Kieko and his family had picked up on the phrase, and it had become an in-joke amongst them.

"I think today we just play farm chukkas. Very steady, very casual, very relaxed with no hard ride offs," Kieko finished looking pointedly at Claire.

"Who, me?" she replied looking all coy.

They all knew – with the exception of Chris – that polo was one of the most dangerous sports in the world; so much so that holiday accident insurance specifically excludes it and the only way to get insured at all is to say that you are 'just playing practice chukkas'. The main chukka field lay off to the left of the main house, and the two teams made up of Kieko, Rupert, Claire and assorted grooms and friends of Kieko's went out to play a fun game for the next two hours before it became too hot. Chris, for his part, was taken on a grand tour of a small part of the estancia with Tinto as his guide. With a soldier's eye he absorbed all manner of details about the landscape; what grew where; how to find water; looking at animal trails and landscape details. In that sense, he never switched off; in case one day his life might depend upon it. But it was so second nature to him that it was not an effort, just something that he did as naturally as other people breathed or spoke.

The day flew past, and as the sun began to lower itself towards the western horizon they all settled in woven wicker chairs to enjoy a beer. They were worn out but relaxed from a hard day's riding behind them. Chris, however, was not satisfied and set off at dusk for a five mile run with Kieko's dog; a cross between a Labrador and some local mutt of indeterminate origin. He returned looking hot, sweaty and happy, with the dog panting at his side – a friend for life. Chris settled on to the veranda sipping an ice-cold Quilmes, joining in with the conversation.

Chris remarked that he had seen a small crocodile and ostrich, which much to his amusement he and Tinto had tried to round up for the sheer hell of it.

The evening came with a speciality veal dish traditional to Argentinian Christmas Eve. The conversation and the warm feeling of inclusion extended by Kieko and his family made the occasion feel very special. After the meal, half intoxicated by a strong local Malbec, an exchange of presents was orchestrated by Franky, who handed them out from beneath the tree. Chris and Rupert turned to the two identically sized boxes given to them by Siobhan. They were cubes of about three inches on each side, and were surprisingly heavy in a solid sort of way. They scrabbled with the wrapping paper having read the cryptic note attached to each present:

Happy Christmas, just in case you fall off! Si. xxx

"Heavy boxes, I wonder what they can be? A jar of *dulce de leche?*" Rupert laughed.

"Just open them and find out," Claire ordered.

The boxes opened on a cardboard hinge and revealed, in each case, a modern, rubberised, shock resistant wristwatch, with all the usual dials and buttons associated with the genre. They both looked at each other slightly surprised; especially as Chris habitually wore his Breitling diver's watch, which was good for 200m and very robust. They were a fun present and Rupert proclaimed; "Well, that is very sweet of her. The girl has a good sense of humour."

"Yes indeed. We will have to thank her when we get back. It's good of her, especially as we got her nothing in return."

Claire caught the look that passed between them, but said

nothing. The meal over, they departed to bed and Chris called Rupert into his room for a brief chat.

"Read this latest note from Peters," he said offering the screen to Rupert.

"Good God, an American oil company?" Rupert said. "But how will they profit from all this? I mean it will take full ownership of the islands and time to keep them while they get their act together. I suppose if they stalled; prevented military action and kept up diplomatic pressure while the Argies had possession it could work – especially if the government worked hand in hand with the corporations. They're probably getting some practice at doing just that in the Middle East."

"It begs at least two questions," Chris replied. "What are they doing for the Argies, and how does the IRA fit into it? I mean, every way we turn, from property to espionage, we come across an Irish connection. The money laundering makes sense as far as the IRA need funds, given that their cause is floundering; they need to appear legitimate and earn proper, traceable, income from legitimate sources, as Peters has made very clear. But what are they doing in return? Finally, and most importantly, if an invasion is being planned how and with what means?"

"I'd say that the oil company is funding or helping the Argies in return for a piece of the action," Rupert replied. "But like you say: how? I mean, no huge new task force of ships and subs is evident: that would have been picked up by US spy satellite imagery, surely. So, what are they going to do? Beam across to the Falklands like something out of *Star Trek*? And the bloody Yanks are supposed to be on our side. Why can't they just deal directly with the British for the oil rights?"

"We wouldn't let them dig for oil even if there was any. It's sovereign territory and the islanders don't want all the upheaval. They're happier with sheep, and even if we had the oil we wouldn't let the Yanks just share it. In fact we'd probably sell it to them. The Argies will give them better rates. And meanwhile the invasion's being coordinated through some dodgy corporation with an Irish connection. It's perfect cover, and perfect deniability at government level. They've got cover, motive and opportunity. The Yanks will help Argentina to invade again, then stall any repossession talks while they siphon billions of dollars' worth of oil out from under our noses. Then when the fields run dry they'll pretend to help us get our Islands back and look like fucking heroes in the process. And I bet there are people in our government, right at the very top, who know exactly what's going on and who will retire to castles in Scotland or villas in Spain with a few more noughts on their bank balances when it's all over. Money talks, Rupert. Meanwhile, I can tell you that the Regiment is very heavily committed in the Middle East. I am hoping that some of these questions will be answered in the next few days… and talking of timing, look at this."

He had broken open the stiff cardboard box that had encased one of the watches Siobhan had given them. In the recessed bottom, which was about three quarters of an inch thick, was a large, silver metal battery, together with a casement containing an electronic device. Rupert was amazed.

"What the hell is that?"

"That, Rupert, is the electronic tracking device that they have been tracking us with for the past few days."

"What do you mean 'they'? And have they been tracking us since we left BA? Can they hear us now?" Rupert said, dropping his voice. Chris grunted a humourless laugh.

"No. It is just a tracker, but this is interesting. The problem with trackers is that it's not like James Bond or the movies when you put a tracker on and hey presto off you go. It's all about power and signal strength. In other words, to reach BA from here you'd need a much larger battery and a fucking great aerial. Also, battery life for something like this is limited, not just in range but also in time. So the more you ask it to do, the quicker it goes down. No, someone who is watching for this is no more than five or six miles away. Any further and the signal would be too weak and it would drain too quickly. You know when we track the IRA, the 'Boyos' come across on the ferry and we lump them up–"

"Lump them up?"

"Sorry. Yes, we call it lumping up. We put a tracker on their car, generally much smaller than this. Then we can track them all across the UK using existing signal or radio masts. That's impossible here. We can also power down the transmitter when not needed to save battery life. No way can this be done here. But you remember when I kept feeling we were being watched?" Rupert nodded. "Well, I think we were being followed to make sure we were doing what we said we would be doing. After all, our itinerary was deliberately not kept a secret. So they have been checking and by using this, they don't need to be in sight. My guess is that they are at the end of the drive somewhere or discreetly within range. They could even have a car here ready to pick up a signal as a form of relay. It's not that hard."

And suddenly it seemed to both of them – especially Rupert – that the holiday was over. They were back to the job in hand and the real reason for them being here.

"We need another way out of here, heading north. Then we can leave the devices here and get away unnoticed. I think it's also time that you and I levelled with each other, don't you?"

"What do you mean?" Rupert responded, putting forward a brave and hurt expression.

"Claire," was all Chris said.

"Mm, yes. We should put her in the picture, I think, especially if we're in danger. It's past the time for secrecy and she'll have to be involved now."

Chris raised an inquiring and cynical eyebrow. "Now?" As if

by unspoken agreement they both left the room and, knocking, entered Claire and Rupert's room. Chris opened the conversation, seeing Claire's concerned expression at the seriousness of their expressions.

"Claire, I am sorry about this on Christmas Eve and all, but we need to talk and I think it's time we put our cards on the table," Chris said. "I know or at least suspect you have more than an inkling about what we are going to tell you. I also suspect that Rupert has perhaps at the very least hinted at things."

Chris looked questioningly at Rupert, and Claire smiled slightly quizzically as Chris proceeded to explain in much more detail the reason for their presence in Argentina. She sat silently while he spoke, neither interrupting nor changing her expression.

"Well, it is hardly surprising, you know – although I wouldn't say it was obvious," she said, covering Rupert's back. "But there were just too many unanswered questions and anomalies. As for Rupert, he may be good in the outside world but he can't lie convincingly to me." She then described the clues that led to her knowledge.

"You should be a spook, not a surveyor," Chris observed.

"Well, in a funny kind of way all agency surveyors are. We deal in information, secrets; we pass information, reading people and trying to outguess the others in seeing or looking for angles. It is not that far removed from secret agent stuff, I'm sure. Our armour is our suits, dressed to hide our real thoughts and present a picture that we want the outside world to see. Our weapons are words and covert knowledge. I always remember a mentor telling me: 'We are wordsmiths, pure and simple.'"

Chris smiled, shaking his head but finished seriously.

"I'm glad you're on our side. But not a word, you hear? Not to Kieko, not to anyone. It could get us all killed."

"I understand, and I'm good at keeping secrets. It is part of my job."

They headed out to church on Christmas morning to San Miguel, and it was strange to see the extent of the 'driveway' to Kieko's ranch. Halfway along, the white road split into a V-shape with the other road apparently heading north. Chris asked where it went

"It heads to the northeast and it will be the best way for you to leave the ranch when you head up north to Corrientes to see the other estates you're looking at. Though why anyone would want to buy land that far up is anyone's guess," Kieko finished a little resentfully, probably at the prospect of not selling any of his own land to the foreign investors that they all saw as the panacea to Argentina's national ills.

Rupert tried to lighten the mood, "Oh you know clients," he said. "They're a rule unto themselves and they want land near the Paraguay border where they have other interests. This is just the start; we'll see where it goes from here."

Chris and Rupert exchanged glances, looking at the alternative route out. It would give them a chance to slip past the watchers waiting with the tracker and get out of range. They had both started wearing their new watches and were keenly aware that with this amount of travel they would be tracked for the journey into San Miguel; they would then, as planned, leave them with Claire to move around a little on horseback to create the illusion that they were still there on the ranch. The day went as planned with no sign of their trackers on the route in or out of the ranch

Two days later, they said goodbye to Kieko and his family at the ranch with Rupert and Chris heading off north in the Land Cruiser. Claire took Rupert aside for a final private goodbye before he left.

"No heroics ok? And don't give me that look, I mean it. I want you back in one piece with no holes, scars or broken bones. And you can tell sergeant Adams that the special forces of Argentina will be the least of his worries if you don't come back the way you left," she finished vehemently.

Rupert looked suspiciously innocent. "I know, but look, it will be a long and boring road trip to the border. We'll go across into Paraguay, wait overnight for the plane, then head on to the Falklands – which is very safe, there's lots of our soldiers, a return trip back down the road. Maybe a quick scout around at Corrientes – although we might do that later with you and Sophie Carswell– and we'll be back here before you know we're gone. Where's the harm in that?" he finished disingenuously.

She raised an eyebrow, tilted her head to one side, speaking a thousand words in a single glance. They held each other very tight and shared a long kiss. There were tears in Claire's eyes when they pulled apart.

"Don't worry, it will be fine, just a look around. What can go wrong?"

Goodbyes were said at the car and the two men set off along the white road, heading for the fork they had spotted previously, where they turned north, bypassing Corrientes and driving on up to Asuncion and the border crossing into Paraguay.

Chapter Twenty-Three

The road was long, straight and boring. With Christmas behind them, they just wanted to get on with things now, aware that time was potentially running out and they needed answers as soon as possible.

Rupert and Chris had reported the implications of Siobhan's wristwatches via the encrypted phone back to Peters, confirming – if any further confirmation was needed – that Siobhan was definitely working for the other side for reasons that were as yet unclear. She could not be watched at the moment as they had no personnel to cover the task in what was still a hostile country: that would have to wait until Sophie Carswell returned or new appointments were made at the Embassy.

They found themselves on the last straight road down to the border crossing, and decided to opt for the ferry. Kieko had said it was easier as the main bridge across the river was popular with motorbikes and there would be fewer holdups on the ferry. The security at the border was notoriously slack, as so many people commuted across it every day.

Chris and Rupert had never seen so many motorbikes. It seemed as though all the world's bikes were kept in and around the border. Hardly a car was visible as swarms of motorcycles of all shapes and sizes buzzed across the bridge in both directions.

They headed down to get an *alsa* – a large, flat, open-topped ferry that looked more like a large punt than a cargo ferry. It had a ramp at both ends that hardly moved at all and could just about take two large articulated lorries or about eight cars as a total payload. Just before what was laughingly called the ferry terminal, they saw a large, double-sided blue sign with a white map of two islands and the words: *Las Malvinas son Argentinas!*

Rupert laughed: "They never give up, do they? This is one pissed off country, they just hate it that we won."

"We'd better make sure we win the second time around, too." Chris answered.

There was no ticket office, just a group of stevedores hanging around the dock platform looking suntanned, bored and rather dangerous. They were dressed in scruffy outfits, with old

bombachos trousers and *alparagatas,* shoes like Tinto wore, apparently the uniform of choice. Chris went up to buy the tickets for the crossing and was about to get ripped off when he gave them a hard stare and a menacing look which said: 'don't fuck with me, I am not a normal tourist'. They settled on a price of thirty dollars, and he returned to the car just as the ferry had finished unloading.

The stevedores directed Rupert forward onto the rickety loading dock, and he drove carefully onto the ramp, gaining pole position for unloading at the other side. They left the car and climbed the blue painted metal steps at the side to the passenger area, which offered them a good view across the river and down to the muddy waters of the River Plate that flowed beneath them. Even this far from the estuary the river was vast, and could get quite choppy sometimes, but today it was still and hot, and the tiny breeze coming off the water was a welcome relief.

Arriving at the other side, they were passed up to customs amid the posturing soldiers in full combat gear. Their passports were given a cursory glance, stamped and returned to them as they seemed to be just another boring pair of tourists off on a jaunt to Asuncion to see the sights. Most importantly to them both, there were no computers to record their passing. They were through, anonymous and free to do as they wished.

The scenery this side of the river was pretty much the same as the Argentinian side, and the same applied to the architecture of Asuncion at first glance. But on closer inspection as they drove through the outskirts of the capital it took on a different perspective. The city was very green; the large squares and piazzas were fringed with tropical date and palm trees. The architecture was an eclectic mix of Italianate, Arabic and modern swirling concrete towers, all seemingly colour washed in various shades of pink.

They were booked into a standard tourist hotel not far from the city centre as their flight was not until New Year's Eve, which was the day after. The room was comfortable, modern and clean, opening out onto a balcony with views across to the Palacio de Lopez, the president's palace.

Chris turned on the television, and they watched the latest reports from the Gulf. Saddam Hussein had refused to withdraw from Kuwait City and a massive land and air strike was about to get underway. "I hope the boys are tucked well out of sight in some goat hole or they're going to get their heads blown off," he commentated wryly.

"Do you wish you were there with them?" Rupert asked.

"In a way yes, but if this comes off and we genuinely stop an invasion, I will have saved lives as much as if I was out there doing my bit to keep the Middle East free," he finished whimsically.

"What will your lot be doing out there, or can't you say?"

"Covert work, mostly; finding and disabling the rocket launchers. The media have picked up on that, but no doubt they'll be up to all sorts of other things. But one thing I do know, it won't last more than a few months, and that tightens not only our window but the window for the Argies and the oil company. But even if the Gulf War ended tomorrow, it would still be weeks before they could get everyone back, send a carrier down here and reinforce the Falklands enough to repel an invasion or worse, re-take the islands again. The cost would be horrific in human lives and it would be a mixed force battle, the likes of which we haven't seen since the last Falklands War."

Chris's words gave Rupert pause for thought, and he realised just how serious their position was. They needed answers soon. Chris wanted to go for a run, but decided against it. He didn't want to draw attention to himself, and a foreigner running about the city was bound to attract someone's eye. Instead, he persuaded Rupert to practice some Wing Chun with him. They went over some of the more complicated moves and finished with a session of Gor Sau followed by the first form of Su Lim Tao. Dripping with sweat, they both finished, satisfied with their performance.

"You're getting better, smoother; you're reacting instinctively, rather than just thinking. Keep it up, I hope you're going to carry on with it when we finish here?"

"Do you know, I think I might," Rupert said. "The way my life is going it seems to be coming in handy more than I ever bargained for in my boring surveyor's job!"

They showered and changed and went for a quiet meal in a local restaurant, pretending that they could hardly speak any Spanish and that they were on a tour finishing at the Igazu falls before going back to BA.

The next morning they drove to the northeast of the city and the Silvio Pettirossi International Airport. The tree-lined main access road led to a bizarre building that looked like the terraces of a football stand with creepers growing out of it. In the main concourse was a large scale model of an antique monoplane in flight. The two men smiled.

"South America, you've got to love it," Rupert commented.

Although the airport was Paraguay's largest transport hub, their plane was a small turbo-prop Saab 340 with fewer than normal seats, as it had an extended tank to make the journey to the Falklands. It still stopped at Montevideo airport in Uruguay to refuel, but as neither Chris nor Rupert intended to get off for the half hour layover, no record of the flight manifest was logged there.

They were on their way again soon, heading towards the Falklands. With a flying time of around four hours, it was just about bearable in the small plane, and as he did whenever the opportunity presented itself Chris ate and then slept like any well-trained soldier. Rupert shook his head in disbelief that Chris was able to switch on and off like that, and wished he had the same ability. Chris awoke refreshed just before landing and they were grateful for the chance to stretch their legs. Thanking the stewardess, they walked down the steps onto the runway to be rudely awakened by the weather.

They had just left a sub-tropical climate of gentle breezes blowing through palm trees and bright hot sunshine, so it was the wind that hit them first, both literally and metaphorically. Gone were the calm, gentle, balmy zephyrs of Argentina and Paraguay; This was more like a summer's day in the north of Scotland. The sun was out, but clouds scudded across the sky. Having left thirty-five degree heat with a high humidity, they now found themselves on an exposed tarmac runway that was twenty degrees cooler, leaning into a wind that threatened to blow them from their feet. Chris had insisted that they buy warm Puffa jackets from the Ralph Lauren store in central BA – about the only place they could find to buy them in the height of summer – together with woolly hats. Rupert had mocked him at the time, but was now very pleased with Chris's forethought, and Chris raised his eyebrows in an 'I told you so' expression as they pulled them on against the biting wind.

They passed through the small array of buildings containing the customs house and air traffic control and headed straight out into the car park at the front of the airfield. Two taxis were parked there, no doubt awaiting their twice-weekly supply of business. The chatty taxi driver wanted to know why they were here, and asked the usual questions. They had agreed to keep it simple and tell something close to the truth, using their jobs as their cover. Chris said they were working in BA and had come over for the holidays. Everywhere was closed for the holidays in Catholic Argentina, so they thought they would do a bit of touring in the festive break and see the islands. It seemed to satisfy the driver, and the conversation turned to places to go and what to see, the best pubs and the usual touristy information. They were booked into the Malvina House Hotel, one of the smartest on the island, which was ideally placed right in the centre on Ross Road close to the sea front. They saw that the hotel had been converted from the original two story house, which had then been extended with additional rooms and a quality reception area that spoke of somewhere much larger. The rooms were very well appointed, and most importantly for them they were warm.

"God, I never thought I'd be warm again before we went back to Paraguay," Rupert commented, returning to the reception area after a hot bath and a change of clothes.

"Aren't you pleased that I forced you to buy that coat and a new hat?"

They went outside and faced the weather, which had calmed down a little from two hours earlier. They decided to take a walk around the town before going to one of the local bars for supper, so they began walking down to the quay and the main port area. The area was predominantly flat with a slight hill going up from Ross Road leading inland.

As they strolled down to the pier, Chris tried to imagine what it would be like trying to take the island from a military standpoint. There were no cliffs, no ridges to impede a straight-forward transition from sea to land. But with that came a lack of natural cover: the infantryman's bane. Anyone coming onshore would find themselves in a clear field of fire, he thought. The only other way would be by airborne invasion, or from the sea via the South Georgia route that had been used last time to prevent an all-out assault being obvious. But he also knew there had been far less than the current contingent of 850 marines and ancillary staff when the Argentinians first invaded.

Looking across the water of the bay he saw two huge gas or oil tanks the reminded him of the old gasworks tanks he used to see in the UK that appeared to move up and down on rails. They were off in the distance and difficult to assess as a possible threat: he needed to see more.

"You know there is one slight problem with our plan," Chris said. "We need to be mobile. Despite the small size of the island we need to see a lot and get a good idea of how it all fits together. And we need to do it without some nosey cabbie asking questions. I wonder if you can hire a car or a 4x4 here? Do you think the hotel would hire us one?"

"There are hardly any cars here, so there's not much chance of having a smash. Maybe if we offered a deposit they'd lend us one," Rupert said.

They watched a huge trawler come into dock to unload the day's catch. The vessel had a long deck extending rearwards from the bridge and two huge overhead gantries with platforms and cranes attached. It sidled right up to the quay, dropped anchor and proceeded to unload using a large extendable crane that had driven up to the side of the ship. The boat bore a Spanish Name: *Costa del Diabolo*

"Interesting; a Spanish ship, presumably Argentinian," Chris said. "They must share the fishing rights, unless the boat has been transferred from Argentinian to Falklands ownership."

"Yeah, but you wouldn't get an army on that now, would you?" Rupert joked.

"No, but those raised areas on top of the gantries would make great gun or mortar platforms."

"Now you're clutching at straws. You'd need a hundred of them, all armed in full view. You said it yourself – the only way to invade is like last time: have a sufficiently large force on land, dug in and ready to demolish the occupying force, giving them no option but to surrender – oh, and then there's the small matter of four fighter planes and a number of helicopters that can be brought into play to mobilise the troops sooner than the half an hour it takes to get here by road," Chris said.

"I know, I know, I'm just thinking out loud."

They walked along the front, and after a few hundred yards, Ross Road became Crozier Place which was where they came across a sign proudly proclaiming "Falklands 4x4".

"Hah, this is what we want. Now, get ready to flash that company credit card," Chris said.

The car hire company was more than happy to lease them a vehicle for the few days they were here. Much to Chris's delight they were given a short wheelbase Land Rover Defender turbo diesel with a manual gearbox and all the toys, including a winch. They were warned that the bogs and even some of the roads could sometimes be treacherous, even at this time of year. In effect they were warned not to be a pair of numpty tourists and get it stuck. With the deposit paid they drove off, the proud owners of a Land Rover for three days.

"Just like on the farm back home," Chris chortled. "Now we really can go anywhere. Sophie will be here tomorrow, and assuming her body clock has re-adjusted we can get cracking on a recce."

They drove back along the sea front to the hotel, parking the Land Rover and leaving to explore more of the town and surroundings on foot. Before an hour had passed, Chris had spotted a dozen places where it would be possible to land a task force, but all had logistical problems and none was perfect. He talked as they walked toward the pub they had passed earlier.

"The problem is this: there are obviously many inlets and bays to land men, but only in small quantities; then you have the problem with kit, radar spotting, getting close enough and mustering a force sufficient in numbers to take command quickly so that you don't have a massive fire fight lasting days or weeks while the boys back home get another fleet together or fly in reinforcements to defend land that's already held by the existing Brit forces – particularly as I'm sure they could hold the main airfield at RAF Mount Pleasant, which we haven't had the chance to look at yet."

Rupert agreed, but had no additional helpful thoughts to bring to the discussion and they tossed it back and forth, stopping the conversation just short of the pub. The building in front of them was aptly called the Victory Bar. The white coloured walls reflected the glow of the setting sun at just after 7.15 pm. The door opened into a warm fug generated by the open fire, which they were to learn was kept going all year round. The brown wooden bar had all the hangings and trappings of an old English pub, with beer mugs hanging by their handles from hooks above the polished bar. Some locals were already gathered at the bar, halfway through their pints. One raised a glass and bade Chris and Rupert welcome as they entered, and they were both relieved that it was not like the 'Last Chance Saloon' where everything went silent and everyone scowled at them when they entered. They both mustered a cheery response and ordered two pints of bitter from the landlord. He returned offering them a food menu which they accepted.

"So, you'll be the two gents on tour from BA then?" he questioned good humouredly. The looks Rupert and Chris exchanged it all. The barman shrugged apologetically. "Small town, small island, no secrets."

They laughed together, trying to project an aura of bluff affability. "Yes," Chris replied. "We had Christmas up north near San Miguel, but everything closed up tighter than a duck's arse so we thought we'd take the opportunity to do a little sightseeing before the Catholics realise they've had enough God to last them till Easter and everything kicks off again."

"Well, it's the best time of year to see the islands before it starts to get cold in April."

"Blimey we've come from thirty-five degree heat to this, and it feels like a bloody fridge!" Rupert joked. There were a few chuckles and the landlord asked about their line of work. The bar seemed to collectively prick up its ears at the answer about to be given, so Rupert was cautious. Surveyors and particularly agents never liked to give away the whole story and it was inbred in him: information is king.

"Polo holidays for schools and a few rich patrons in the UK. Dying to get out here now that the moratorium has been lifted, and we're also going to start exporting polo equipment and ponies back to the UK."

It was a good spur of the moment cover and it would hold up well. They had both learned a lot about the polo world in the last few days, especially from conversations between Claire and Kieko. Before the ban, Kieko sent up to a dozen or more ponies a year to the UK for sale to British buyers. As homebreds with little cost to him it was a lucrative business, and one that could start again now that the embassy was re-opened and diplomatic relations had been resumed. "Yeah, we heard that the embassy was open again," the barman said. "Should be better trade for us, the cruise ships can come in easily now in both directions. Good business for us and the tourists will bring a bit of money to the islands."

"Are the cruise ships new then?" Chris asked. "I thought they'd always called here?"

"Well they have, but the ports and harbour have been dredged for deep berthing and now that we are all on speaking terms again they have started coming from both directions up and down to the States. This is our prime season; a ship's coming in tomorrow, I think. Isn't it, boys?" he finished, turning to the crowd of locals. The cluster of men at the bar opened up, turning to face them in a vague horseshoe shape, showing for the first time the faces of all those present. They were the usual mix found in any rural pub in the UK. Only one man stood out by virtue of his red hair and a sprinkling of freckles across his face. To Rupert's eyes he looked familiar, but he couldn't place him. The others at the bar agreed, their voices an unusual mix of accents, almost neutral but with a country burr. The red-haired man drained his glass and left, waving a thanks to Al, the landlord. His accent was different and hard to identify from his brief farewell. The lean figure nodded to all upon his departure and headed out into the night.

"Did we say something to offend him?" Rupert asked.

"Michael? No, it's just his way. He doesn't spend much time down here; he has a place away to the north of the island, actually on Keppel Island. It's very remote and he keeps himself to himself. Runs a few sheep on the farm and helps out with odd jobs when he comes down into town. Travels a bit to Colombia from time to time on business selling odds and ends he makes. Exports it from there to the US, so he says."

Rupert pushed a little – maybe unwisely, but he had a feeling somewhere in his memory. "No, it's just that he looked familiar. Has he been here long? Is his surname O'Donnell, maybe?"

"No, close though. O'Driscoll. Like quite a few islanders, he comes from Ireland."

"Ah that will be it. I have a lot of family over there, I thought he had the Irish looks. Be good to have a chat with him if he comes in again, discuss the old country," he finished passively.

"Good luck with that, he's not the best talker, that's for certain."

"Ah well, we'll look forward to seeing the cruise ship tomorrow," Chris interjected, changing the subject.

"Yes, she'll be in late morning."

"Good, I'll have time to meet my girlfriend off the plane. She'll be tired though, from the flight."

"On the early bird from Asencion is she? She'll find it cold coming from there. It's a hot place up there," he finished. They ordered their food from the bar menu and sat down with their pints.

"You do push your luck. Irish family indeed," Chris mocked. "What the hell was all that about? I mean I know he's Irish but come on, we can check him out and, as the man said, there's quite a few of them here."

Rupert turned, keeping a blank expression as he spoke very quietly, "You didn't see his face clearly did you? Well, surveyors are good at numbers, names and faces. We have to remember everything. There's this one guy at a firm in London – Clive Lewis, his name is. He's a senior partner now; he gets everyone in at prayer meetings on Monday morning and he will pick on anyone at random asking for the telephone number of a firm, or the senior partner or any partner's name and you have to have it, from memory, just like that." he said, snapping his fingers.

"And your point is?"

"It took me a minute, but it finally came to me who he reminded me of – Siobhan Clifford."

Chris was stunned, but quickly made the connection. "What? Are you sure? Do you think he might be her brother or something?" he exclaimed.

"Well, he could be a cousin but the resemblance was strong.

But look, it could all fit; remember that report we had on the sat-phone screen? And," Rupert realised that he was getting excited, so he took a deep breath and lowered his voice. "The spooks in the attic in Belfast; the constant reference to the *wee man on the island*. What if that island wasn't Ireland but *this* island? It would all make sense. Also the landlord said about trips on business to Colombia, the briefing said about IRA links to the terrorist group...what's it called?"

"FARC."

"Yes, FARC, because if he went from here to Montevideo like we did, he could head off to Colombia and fly to wherever he wanted. O'Driscoll, or whatever he calls himself, couldn't be traced. The Home Office, Johnston and his lot, were looking for trips from BA, Belfast or even within the US. But O'Driscoll could bank the money, get it bounced around and boom; disappear."

Chris reflected for a minute, thinking it through. "You might just be on to something there. And if you're right, we could really be in the shit. Shame I left the satphone back at San Miguel, we could get a photo of him before he disappeared. He will have changed a bit, but this makes so much sense. It explains how he wasn't traced back to Ireland or on to Miami as you say. It explains the reason Siobhan is working for them. The bitch has been stringing us along all this time. But it begs one question: what is he doing here? Is he just hiding out or is he up to something? And if so what?"

"Let's get our food and then head back. I want to use the phone at the hotel."

"But it's an open line," Adams cautioned. "I mean, I know it's not Argentina, but anyone could be listening."

"I know, I'll be careful. We need info and we need it fast."

They finished their meal and had another pint at the bar for form's sake before feigning tiredness and returning to the hotel.

"Right, they are three hours in front," Chris said. "He won't be at the FO, but they'll transfer us to him at home. Let's wake him up and see how bright he really is. I hope to God that he's quick on the uptake or this will be a waste of time."

The direct line that had been installed at the HBJ office diverted on the second ring to Peters' home number. It took him a few rings to answer, but his voice was nonetheless crisp and alert "Peters?"

"Peters, how the devil? Its Rupes here. Oh bugger, wait, Have I got the time wrong again? Sorry, old chap, I know I always do it. Just wanted to wish you a Happy New Year. couldn't get through the other day. We're on the bloody Falklands, would you believe? Sightseeing the touristy bits. It's really exciting to be here, and I did promise I'd call."

There was a slight pause and Rupert could almost hear the cogs turning at the other end of the phone. They finally clunked into place.

"Rupert? Sorry, distortion, and yes, I was asleep. Phoning me at this time, do you realise its bloody midnight?" Peters caught on, changing his usual circumspect tone to a chattier one. They both thought fast, wanting to get the information out. They were safer here than in Argentina, but it was still risky.

"Oh bollocks, sorry. Anyway, just wanted to wish you well. How was the office party this year, you old dog?" Rupert continued, trying to find a natural way into what he needed to impart.

"Not quite the same without you and the others, of course, but still good fun. Hope you and the other two celebrated in style: you were missed here."

"Oh we did – and talking of absent friends, we bumped into our secretary's wee brother. Such a coincidence, but you did say that the was on the island, didn't you? Didn't recognise him at first as it had been such a long time, but the resemblance to the sister is remarkable."

Please catch on, Rupert thought, *please.* There was almost a choke on the other end of the line

"Sorry the line went funny there for a minute. Long distance, you know. I think I heard you right, and if I did, give him my best if you bump into him again. Now bugger off, you mad bastard. I'm off back to my bed. Happy New Year to you too," Peters finished in a grumpy tone. Rupert laughed down the phone.

"Good night, old chap, good night." He put the phone down, grinning wryly. "Do you know, he'd make quite a good agent with a bit of work."

Chris punched him on the shoulder. "Idiot. Did he get all that, do you think?"

"I am sure of it," Rupert replied.

Chapter Twenty-Four

London

Peters put the receiver down, his mind reeling at what he had been told. He placed a call to Johnston, who was also raised from his bed, and relayed the contents of the call from Rupert, explaining that it had been an open line and that they had to be careful.

"Yes," Johnston mused, buying time whilst his mind raced. "He is very good at that, I think I might start recruiting from the surveying profession in future; they seem to have a particularly appropriate skillset. Michael Clifford, after all this time. My God, it would fit, wouldn't it? The sympathisers, the two IRA members that are already training in Colombia, the connection with Kelly as a gun for hire: why wouldn't the Argies use him as their hitman?"

"I see all that," Peters agreed. "And I understand what the IRA or Clifford, O'Driscoll or whatever he's calling himself gets out of it, but what is he doing for them? He can hardly hold off more than eight hundred royal marines, sabotage 4 fighter planes and open the doors for an invasion all by himself. Even if a few were there on the island in sympathy, it could achieve very little."

A thought struck Johnston at the mention of sabotage. "I think I know why he is there and what he is going to do. I just wonder how bright Adams and Brett are, and how laterally they can think, because I believe I know what is going to happen. But it won't happen yet, thank God. I wish we could contact them now. Clearly they couldn't take the satphone through customs; it would be too risky."

"We could call the base and ask someone to contact them quietly. Isn't Carswell meeting up with them at RAF Mt. Pleasant tomorrow morning? Now what do you think is planned and what should they know about the threat?" Peters asked.

The Falkland Islands

Johnston's faith in the two men was about to be vindicated. The following morning Chris and Rupert woke early to prepare for a trip around the island and to meet Sophie Carswell from the plane at RAF Mt. Pleasant. After breakfast they left in the Defender, heading away from the town on tarmac roads in the general direction of the RAF base. They passed a flat concrete area just outside Stanley covered with what appeared to huge, collapsed polythene cubes.

"What are they?" Rupert asked.

"They are Air Portable Fuel Containers – APC's for short."

As they trundled along in the Land Rover, Rupert asked him about the SAS involvement in the original conflict.

"We had D & G squadrons here, just over hundred men. Then there were the SBS, but I don't know which sections, maybe similar numbers, probably a few less. It was by all accounts tough fighting and of course we lost men when the helicopter went down into the sea," he commented quietly.

"So, what happens here now? Is it an RAF regiment that guards the base?"

"No it varies. It's usually a Resident Infantry Company and at the moment I understand the current RIC force is the 3rd Regiment Royal Fusiliers, and we are going to see how good they are. I hear their guard dogs are very well trained."

"What? You mean you are going to pit yourself against a hungry Alsatian? You're mad. What if you get caught – or worse still, eaten?"

Chris laughed. "Well, first of all I too am well trained. Secondly they are not Alsatians. They use Belgian Malinois, although they are equally dedicated attack and protect dogs, if not more so. They even look like Alsatians. I just want to see how close to the runway I can get before being stopped, and then if I'm in trouble I will flash my identity card. Call it extra-curricular training," he grinned humourlessly.

"Come on, seriously, what are you thinking? What is O'Driscoll going to do on the island that can be so vital that he and his chums get paid over a million dollars? We have already discounted Horatius at the bridge. What can he do against a regiment guarding the airfield? He can't take it single-handed?"

"I gave this a lot of thought last night, and came to some interesting conclusions – or at least theories. First, cast your mind back to the briefing we had originally at the FO. Correct me if I am wrong, but you raised a very good question. Could they re-arm using the airfields as before? You were told by Admiral Fisher that there were 'measures in place'. Well, those are explosive charges designed to immobilise the runway in the short term, while we mount – God forbid that we have to – a counterattack preventing them from re-supplying in exactly the way you envisaged. Now think about this: what if O'Driscoll and a few boyos from across the water were here first and sabotaged the sabotage? He doesn't need to take the airfield, he just needs to ensure that it remains intact. The second point is this; you may or may not know it, but the protecting regiments have a different brief to other units. They don't defend the base if attacked, they leave and re-take it. Much better, minimal damage to the base, little destruction and everything immobilised by various means until they re-take control."

Rupert caught on quickly. "So, an invasion is somehow coordinated by forces as yet unknown involving the IRA and matey-boy. The airfield is intact, probably the missile systems too – even if the mobile Blind Fire Rapier launch is knocked out. I mean they're a bit out on a limb here and they could be got at with sufficient secrecy or force. They would also need to take out the radar posts at Alice, Byron and Kent that you mentioned, but again it could be done."

"Easily," Chris agreed. "They've refuelling from down at 40K. The Chinooks load up the APC's and take them up when they get low on fuel. Perfect time to strike."

Rupert continued his thought process: "Even the patrol dogs can be dealt with in the final moment if everything else is ready to go. Wow, I see what you mean, that would make sense. But – and this is a *huge* but – how the bloody hell are they going to get the main invasion force here? That is what I want to know. They could still be attacked by our fighters; tracked by our subs before they even landed. I mean, four fighters will do a lot of damage even with surface to air missiles against them."

"I know, and that's the last piece of the jigsaw and the biggest piece that we need to find. But for the moment I want to test a theory. The civilian field that we flew into is easily made safe and they could do a lot with that on the re-supplying side before we can even mount a task force. The fighters, yes, but maybe if someone was up here with SAM launchers or other hand-held weapons, we could be in deep shit."

Rupert shook his head, worried. He watched through the

Land Rover's windscreen as the terrain became more inhospitable – and this, he reflected, was summer. Rocky grey and silver crags appeared, surrounded by coarse bushes and rough grass that seemed only capable of supporting hardy sheep or goats. Herds of wild Longhorn cattle roamed at will, huge flocks of Upland Geese spread out, monopolising large areas of the scrub. Mountains and rocky summits rose up, providing an eerie atmosphere. It looked like something out of *Lord of the Rings* on the final leg of the journey to Mordor, Rupert thought. And as if to confirm the evil atmosphere, huge signs appeared on either side of the road warning against minefields that had been laid down by the Argentinians the last time they invaded.

The base was about thirty kilometres southwest of Stanley and the winding route along Darwin Road roughly followed the coast, twisting around inlets, pools and coves, finally arriving at a headland by Long Pond, giving a view down to the RAF base and airfield. They parked up, looking for all the world like tourists, just out of sight of the base. They were about a thousand metres from the end of the runway that was just visible behind the collection of pods and buildings comprising the infrastructure to the southeast of the airfield. Chris looked through the field glasses he had brought along, bringing the perimeter sharply into focus. He took out a spray and once outside the vehicle doused himself liberally with it. It stank: an acrid smell, wafting in through the open window of the Land Rover, making Rupert's nose wrinkle. Chris laughed.

"You like it? 'Splash it on all over'! Not as good as the real thing at grabbing the ladies, but it will do. I'll be gone about an hour or so. Amuse yourself while I go and attract some real bitches," he joked.

Rupert watched him disappear; melting into the scenery very cleverly and using every bit of natural cover as he proceeded to slide towards the fencing some way in the distance. After about three hundred metres he was invisible: his dark green puffa jacket merging with the vegetation. Only because he was looking and knew Adams was there could Rupert spot the occasional tell-tale sign. And he's not even wearing proper camo gear or paint, Rupert thought. He got out into the colder air and smelt the crisp tang of the sea blowing in from the South Atlantic. He zipped up his coat and pulled on a woolly hat. For appearances' sake, he opened the Defender's bonnet in a pretence of overheating or some other engine problem, should any military patrol happen along. He then strode off for a walk around Long Pond, looking for all the world like the perennial tourist.

Just over an hour later he returned to the vehicle, and was just about to close the bonnet when an army Land Rover bearing the pennant of the Royal Fusiliers appeared along Darwin Road. The Defender stopped and two soldiers got out wearing 3rd Royal Fusiliers insignia. They were armed with Browning Hi-Power side arms and SA80's similar to that with which he had trained himself.

"Morning sir," one of the soldiers said. "We saw your vehicle and wondered if everything was all right."

"Ah, well, the answer is that I don't know. It was making a funny noise," Rupert said vaguely. "And it was overheating a little, so we stopped to give it a rest. Might be all right now."

"We, sir?"

"Yes. My friend Chris went for help. Surprised you didn't pass him on the road; he went towards the base."

The two soldiers looked at each other, exchanging a meaningful glance. The first of the two, a sergeant, spoke again with a little more seriousness.

"No we didn't, sir. Tell me, do you have any ID on you and could you tell me what you are doing up here."

"Well, actually we are on the way to the base to pick up a

passenger arriving on the flight from Ascension Island due in at ten o'clock. As for ID, will my UK driving licence do?"

Rupert put his hand into his coat pocket and saw both soldiers' hands tense on their rifles as he did so, and he continued very slowly and carefully. The sergeant moved out of the line of fire of his comrade and carefully took the licence from Rupert to inspect it.

"I am still concerned about your colleague…"

"Well you needn't be," came a voice from behind them. Chris seemed to materialise out of thin air at the roadside. The result was almost comical as the two soldiers spun around bringing the rifles to bear.

Chris raised his hands.

"Whoa, don't shoot. You passed me on the road, or rather off it; I tried to take a short cut, saw you leaving the base and couldn't get there in time. I fell over," he finished lamely, motioning down at the grass stains on his clothes, and here I am," he finished, smiling harmlessly. The trouble was, as Rupert had found, that although Chris blended in really well and could appear really innocuous, other military men could see through the charade. Just the same as one surveyor could always spot another. Chris had a certain look about him, something that couldn't be entirely faked or hidden from a comrade in arms. They were still suspicious, especially as Chris had manage to conceal his approach until he was right on top of them.

"Do you have any ID, sir?" The sergeant asked.

Chris pondered on whether to bring out his driver's licence or military ID. One might not work, while the other could involve more questions long term, but would save the situation now. He opted for his military ID, with a story about being on holiday. After all, he reasoned, even the Regiment's soldiers get annual leave. He produced his army identity card and waited for the response from the soldiers. It did not of course show his rank or regiment. It just showed a photograph, his name and an expiry date.

"Do I salute you or not?" the sergeant asked, grinning at him.

"Nah, mate. Just a lowly sergeant, same as you," Chris responded.

"Didn't take you for a Rupert. Good one. What are you here for?"

"Come to pick up my girlfriend."

Chris smiled at the reference to officers as Ruperts and caught Rupert curling his lip in a sneer, shaking his head at him ironically. "She's on the next flight in from Ascension, should be here in about twenty minutes."

"Yeah, that's right. We always do a tour round before any flight arrives just as a security check."

"You don't get any trouble from terrorists, Argie or otherwise here, do you?"

"Not as yet, but we keep alert and we often get suspicious people about, particularly when the cruise ships come in. They come up here for a gander and you don't know what they might be up to. Sometimes it's just a Benny looking around."

"What's a Benny?" Rupert asked.

The Sergeant answered straight-faced: "Well as you will have seen, all the locals wear those woolly hats, like Benny in *Crossroads*. Hence the name." he shrugged, smiling at the army humour.

"I thought we weren't allowed to call them Bennies anymore," His oppo chimed in.

"No I forgot, you're right. Now they're Stills."

Rupert was still laughing at the first quip and decided he'd bite. "Ok I will regret this, but why 'Still'?"

Both soldiers answered, laughing. "Because they're still Bennies!" Chris and Rupert roared with laughter. When they calmed down, the Sergeant continued more seriously.

"Now they're getting all the trouble in the Middle East they might send a towel-head down to blow us all to hell," he joked. "Bit too fucking cold for them, though, I should think."

"Huh don't you believe it, the desert gets bloody freezing at night." The banter continued for a few minutes with Chris using his Royal Green Jackets cover. Rupert felt a bit left out of the soldiers' talk but was happy to let them continue, tucking away the information about possible danger from visitors. Finally, Chris introduced them and caused the sergeant to wince slightly in embarrassment when he was introduced as Rupert.

"No offence meant with the joke earlier," he commented.

"None taken, I'm in the TA, and I get it all the time," he laughed it off good naturedly.

"Right, let's get you in for your missus, should be here in the next 10 minutes."

They turned and headed for their Land Rovers, at which point Rupert commented to Chris; "I suppose you think that's really funny, you can't wipe that grin off your face."

"Who me? I didn't say a word," he laughed, trying to look innocent. "Bennies. Jesus…"

Meanwhile, in the other Land Rover, a different conversation was taking place.

"If he's just a sergeant in the RGJ's, I am the Queen of fucking Sheba! No one sneaks up on me like that. The dog was in the back and he didn't let out a peep. He is either a wrong 'un who has served or he is one of the special guys, and I'm betting it's the latter. We'll do a bit of checking into Sergeant Adams later, I think," he said to his oppo, who nodded knowingly.

Chris and Rupert drove onto the base, stopping for ID checks at the gates, where the barrier was lifted for them to pass. The twin pillared sign constructed from local rock announced that they were entering the British Forces South Atlantic Islands Mt Pleasant Complex. Banks of bunding surrounded the site, topped by roles of razor wire. The internal base was surrounded by a criss-cross of internal roads, and the buildings were set out in a series of square pods. They housed the military units stationed on the island, including the RAF regiment, the Royal Fusiliers, Royal Signals, 33 Engineer Regiment and the squadron of Royal Marines making up the full complement of services stationed to protect the islands.

It was a huge operation, more like a small town than a base, with many different facilities incorporated into the complex. Away to the east was the main runway and the huge taxi square and hangars for military jets and helicopters.

"This place is amazing, better than some of the operating bases I've been stationed at," Chris commented.

They parked the Land Rover and waited outside the terminal building and hangars. As they left the vehicle, they heard the whine of engines as the Tri Star jet came into view, banking for its final descent onto the main runway. It touched down with a squeal of rubber, bouncing once, then settling to a smooth landing before turning and heading for the main tarmac apron. The jet engines howled down to silence, the steps were pushed up and the door opened.

A figure familiar from the polo match in Pilar appeared at the doorway. Still suntanned from BA, Sophie Carswell was wrapped up in a worn Barbour, jeans and sunglasses. Her sun-streaked hair was pulled back in a ponytail. Carrying a small walk-on suitcase, she descended the steps and walked straight towards Chris, a big smile on her face at the anticipated romantic reunion with him. As she got within two yards, Sophie raised her arms for a hug, looking to kiss him on the lips. Chris was slightly nonplussed.

"Kiss me, you idiot, we're a couple," she mouthed quietly without breaking her smile, then louder. "Hello darling!"

To his credit Chris caught on quickly, planting a kiss on her lips, picking her up in an embrace and swinging her around in a circle. She played along, breathing in his ear; "Better."

To the casual observer – and there were a few lovesick soldiers who had watched her descent from the plane – it was a picture perfect reunion between a loving couple. When they finally broke apart, they still held hands. Chris gave her a closer look, taking in her light brown eyes and full lips in a face that took well to makeup. He reflected on the hard muscles he had felt in the embrace and knew that some serious gym time had been put in to achieve a toned body. The charade continued as Chris introduced her.

"Sorry, darling. This is Rupert Brett, my boss from the office."

"How do you do? I've heard a lot about you," Sophie said, shaking hands with him.

"Hello? Not all bad I hope?"

The smiles and banter carried on, all perfectly in place as they passed towards customs. The formalities over, they all piled into the Defender. Once the doors were closed Chris offered an apology.

"Don't be sorry, you're a soldier, not a Spook. It comes as second nature to us, always has to look right. Now, where are we up to?" Sophie said, brusque and straight to business.

They drove slowly around the roads of the base, coming to halt near the gate with Rupert and Chris filling her in on all that had happened, including the discovery of O'Driscoll and the fact that he may well be Siobhan's brother. She took it all in quietly, asking careful questions at each point.

She in turn brought them up to speed on her final conversation with Johnston before leaving the UK. This of course had been superseded by the latest information on the IRA connection and the potential threat from O'Driscoll. Turning to Chris, she asked him what he thought they planned to do from a military point of view.

"Well as I said, I crawled up to the fence and sat there quite happily in broad daylight for about twenty minutes to half an hour. That is despite the dogs, and I have to say a very vigilant guard patrol. I was nearly caught when I moved off. However, from that vantage point, the invaders have a number of options depending on what the invasion plan is.

"They could take the planes out with SAMs or similar and disable the sabotage explosives, leaving at least one of the two runways intact for an airborne landing by Argie fighters. Or they may wish to sabotage this strip and take out the missile defence systems around the island: not difficult with a small band of well-trained men. That's pretty much what the Regiment guys would do, then they'd just use the Stanley field for landing like they did last time. So many options, and they could cause chaos if they get a small foothold and are then backed up by a substantial invasion force," he finished.

"But from what we now know," Sophie continued, "this would all make sense if Clifford or O'Driscoll or whoever he is has a small group of FARC or IRA up to the north ready to deploy at any given time. A fifth column ready to strike and cause immense damage: The IRA get the money and do the damage, the Argies get the island and the oil and the oil companies get the oil rights and cough up for the financial or physical cost of the invasion. Everyone's a winner – except us, of course."

"But that would mean putting in a few hundred million at least," Chris said.

Rupert's response was pragmatic and given his experience of multi-million pound deals quite feasible. "Huh, a few hundred million to a massive oil company? Nothing but small change, and look at the upside. Huge, given that it would be a legitimate project, I bet every oil corporation in the world would be interested. A guaranteed exclusive bite at a South Atlantic oil field? Yes please!" he exclaimed.

Sophie re-examined her opinion of him, as most people did after a short while. This was, after all, his territory. They noticed one of the guards walking towards the Defender. He gave the universal sign for winding down the window, motioning a circular movement with his hand

"Are you Miss Sophie Carswell?" She nodded in affirmation. "Ah good, glad I caught you. Can you report back to the main SHQ on that road." He pointed. "There is an urgent message for you from the UK."

They all looked at each other, thanked the guard and turned the Defender around, heading for the main complex. Sophie left the vehicle and headed for the main building that housed a number of offices off a main central waiting area. She was ushered through to the office of the Station Commander: a uniformed man in his late thirties; tall, sparse and bearing the insignia of a Group Captain.

He extended his hand. "Miss Carswell?"

She nodded and produced her official MI6 identity card, which he inspected closely.

"Ah, I have secure comms in here." He gestured to a sectioned office. "A Mr Johnston for you."

Sophie Carswell followed him in and picked up the receiver. "Sir?"

The conversation that followed confirmed details of all that had occurred from both sides, and Johnston grunted his approval of Chris's efforts to test and penetrate the base's security. He asked for confirmation of one final point. "I'm faxing you a mock-up of what we think Siobhan's brother would look like now. Please pass onto Brett and see if this is the man he saw. Go back to the base and get him to confirm by telephone on the secure number you usually use. Any oblique conversation will do, just get him to use the word 'confirm' and that will be sufficient. Got it?"

"Yes sir, will do. Anything else I need to be aware of?"

"Just report on anything, and I stress *anything*, that may be untoward on the island, however fragile a lead. Secondly, we are getting strange reports from Five in Belfast; the chatter seems to be that they are expecting something big to happen soon, and we need to know what. Time is of the essence. Please keep me informed, and tell the other two well done on their efforts so far. Speak when you return to BA."

"Will do. I'll pass that on." She waited ten minutes for the fax to arrive then left the office, thanking the Station Commander as she stepped out towards the waiting Defender.

"Damn, it's cold here, whatever they say about it being Summer – and I've just left the UK in the Winter," she declared.

The other two laughed, agreeing that they could not wait to get back to the balmy weather in BA. Chris thought he might be getting soft, but he also admitted that he enjoyed the hot, sticky, humid part of Selection more than the freezing cold of the Brecon Beacons. She pushed forward the faxed image asking: "Is this him?"

Rupert scrutinised it. "Yes, definitely, even allowing for any vagaries in the artist's impression." It was all there and the face reminded Rupert and Chris of Siobhan.

They agreed that they would head up to the north of the islands, scout out O'Driscoll's farm then get back in time to see that docking of the cruise ship, which Rupert seemed to have a special interest in; given the nugget of a thought put in his mind by the sergeant he'd talked to earlier. They stopped at the gate before leaving the airfield to speak with the guard house about directions on how to get to Kepple's Island, which coupled with the complimentary map in the glove compartment of the Defender proved easy to find. As they travelled the deserted roads, they passed the now infamous landmarks of Tumbledown, Wireless Ridge and Sapper Hill from the previous engagement.

All the time, the landscape reminded Rupert of what an inhospitable environment this could be, even in the summer.

When they finally arrived at the Kepple's Island farmhouse, they parked some distance away and walked the remaining half mile, squatting down below a ridge above a gentle slope to the shoreline. The position gave them a perfect vantage. They saw a number of inlets curving into the mass of the main headland, offering numerous concealed coves and bays which would, in the eyes of a covert operative, offer a perfect opportunity to effect a small landing of men and small arms sufficient to carry out a sabotage operation along the lines they'd already discussed. The only problem for any incursion would be the close proximity of Saunders Island, but they felt this could be overcome. As Chris had said on many occasions, the problem wasn't landing and remaining undetected, it was being able to do so undetected in sufficient numbers and quickly.

Around O'Driscoll's farmhouse they saw a number of large outbuildings and sheds that could easily house equipment or men for a military operation.

"It would be so easy for a fishing trawler or two to get within a mile or so of the shore; hell, even a passing tanker could drop a number of RIBs over the side, under the radar, full of men and equipment. They'd easily make it in undetected and they could lay low here for weeks in relative comfort, just waiting for the green light. They could be in across country to all points and sabotage all the missile sites. Nothing like having friendlies on site to help you, makes invasion so much easier," Chris commented with an edge of bitterness.

Rupert too, saw the military advantages to be had from an FOB like this; it would be perfect.

"It would just be so easy and as you say, they could lay up here in perfect comfort."

"I really want to know what is in those outbuildings," Sophie said. "But it is too open, we can't risk it. There's just no cover all the way down and we're bound to be seen; particularly if they are up to no good."

As if on cue, the farmhouse door opened and a familiar figure appeared. Red hair, freckles, and the same prominent cheek bones as Siobhan. It bore a striking resemblance to the faxed image they had received Johnston.

"Now do you believe me?" Rupert muttered. "The likeness is remarkable."

The other two nodded, especially Chris, who had known and worked with Siobhan for so long.

O'Driscoll looked around furtively, as though sensing their presence. He scanned the horizons carefully in each direction. He was like a wild animal, sniffing for the potential hunter. Their presence could not be detected with the human eye, they were too well hidden, but it looked to Chris as though O'Driscoll had that sixth sense, the one developed by all those who live on the edge in circumstances of extreme danger or threat. Those who didn't develop the ability were dead. Satisfied, but still wary, he moved on towards the largest barn and knocked twice in a distinctive manner. The door was opened from the inside and O'Driscoll disappeared through it.

Chris, Rupert and Sophie looked at each other meaningfully. "I would love to hear that conversation and see who is in that barn," Sophie muttered.

"You wouldn't get near it. No windows low down to see in, and you'd be in full view of the house where someone else is sure to be watching. That's how they work," Chris whispered. "You saw his reaction when he came outside, he knows someone's here but he just can't quite figure out who or where. Also, the closer we get to the big day for them, the more nervous and security conscious they will become. What I'd really like to have now is a direction finding mic. Come on, we've seen enough, I don't want to risk being discovered and put it all to waste."

They shuffled back from the lip of the ridge, and when they were beyond the line of sight from the farmhouse they walked quickly down the slope, retracing their steps the half mile to where they had parked the Defender.

As the car started up, Rupert checked his wristwatch. "Right, we should just have enough time to get back and see the cruise liner come in," he said.

Chris added; "Yeah, I'd be interested to see how such a bloody big ship gets into what I think is a pretty tight harbour. I'd also like to look at the disembarkation process."

In the short time that Rupert had been with him, he had come to realise that Chris always did things with a reason or an idea in mind. He never fully switched off. A bit like he himself was with property, he reasoned: so if Chris wanted to see the ship passengers disembark it had to be more than a whim.

They travelled the half hour journey south to Stanley and were in time to see the massive behemoth enter the harbour. It was a sight to behold; the huge liner was gently tugged up to the waiting pontoons and quays that gave the massive ship access to the shore.

A new and innovative FIPASS system had been built here, enabling a temporary but very substantial docking system to boom out into the bay and along the frontage. This gave a broad off-loading space for the cruise liners and the massive Hansa Heavy Lift transporter ships.

One such ship was docked beside the liner, looking like a mini oil tanker with a high prow and stern. The low and middle decks had two huge integral gantries for off-loading containers and re-loading wool and other exports from the islands. The huge liner was moored at the dock, towering over it, proudly bearing the name *Princess of the Caribbean.*

At intervals along the dockside of the temporary floating harbour were the harbour master and other port officials, customs officers in hi-viz coats and a number of official guides to the islands, waiting for the tourists to disembark. Rupert, Chris and Sophie some distance away on the quayside, looking with interest and viewing the operation from a completely different perspective to the others who were watching.

Six different sea doors opened and ramps were run up to them by staff on the dock. Once in place the passengers began trooping down each gangplank, leading to the wide, wooden piers that characterised the island's waterfronts. The passengers were warmly dressed, with coats and scarves, having left the hot sun of Miami and the Caribbean. Each had an assortment of bags and holdalls for cameras or souvenirs from the island. They were mostly couples of various ages, along with a few children in family groups.

"And all the animals came two by two…" Sophie muttered. "It would drive me mad being cooped up with all those people on a boat for days on end."

"Hah, it beats falling out over who has to have Great Aunt Ethel round for Christmas; fighting over the TV remote and all the arguments," Chris laughed. "Not as many kids as I thought, given that it is the holidays. Probably couldn't get all the presents on board," he observed.

"There's a lot of people, though, and I don't think this is one of the biggest ships either. Mind you, it dwarfs those two fishing boats we saw yesterday," Rupert commented, as two much smaller vessels came up alongside and docked. "Look at all that space, you could fit an army of tourists in here. How many does the ship hold, I wonder?" he asked rhetorically and dawdled off to speak with one of the guides waiting for his customers.

"Morning. Busy day?" he began nonchalantly.

"Aye," the guide answered. "Though not as busy as when the

huge liners come in; sometimes we get two at once and that makes things really fun."

"How many in this one then? I thought this was large."

"No…well it is, about two and a half thousand today. Which isn't bad, good for the islands of course. But a big one will drop off three and a half thousand or more. Then it does get busy. Sometimes they have to pull up out there." He pointed out into the bay. "And the tender boats come off and drop them in relays. It all depends how busy we are. Sorry mate, but I have to go."

"No not all, it was very interesting. Thank you," Rupert said.

The guide walked off with a sign for the people in his party and started motioning them towards a large London Double Decker bus used for the tours of the island. The tourists loved it, of course, as part of the experience. Rupert started to walk back to Chris and Sophie, and as he did so, he saw a military Land Rover with four marines inside parked discreetly away on the hard standing of the docks. He looked surprised. and then smiled to himself. It was a good precaution, and they could radio back if anything untoward were to happen, he thought.

Rupert jerked his finger over his shoulder; "That's in case any Argentine grannies decide to take over the island. They can lock 'em up *toute suite*," he joked.

"Yeah it's pretty tight," Chris replied, "And like we said, you'd need a lot of fishing trawlers to start a military invasion, and those patrol boats over there might have a thing or two to say about it," he pointed at a groups of large red and white Fishing Patrol boats employed by the Islands to monitor and enforce their fishing waters.

They looked for a little longer as crowds of tourists began to wander up the main esplanade, strolling around, visiting shops and pubs before going inland, sightseeing.

"The islanders certainly have the tourism bit

organised. Although of course, only from October to April," Sophie commented.

"And we still haven't found anything conclusive, even with what we suspect about O'Driscoll and his mates. They can blow up or disable all the airfields they like, but they need troops on the ground. Maybe we'll learn more after we have seen the base at Corrientes," Chris surmised.

"Come on, let's go do some more exploring before it gets dark. I can't be doing with all these tourists," Sophie said, pulling her coat tighter around her despite the summer sunshine.

They walked back to the Defender and drove around, touring the main inlets, particularly Port Louis to the northeast of the main island. The sweeping coast road gave way to an open bay with a long, wooden pier offering deep water docking for ships up to the size of small cruisers or very large trawlers. It was a beautiful spot, they all agreed, and more importantly it gave very easy access to the road infrastructure leading to the rest of the island.

"You know, not for the first time, I wonder how the hell we won the war," Rupert commented. "There are so many inlets and proper areas to disembark, giving great access to the whole island. The opportunities for a strategic strike are everywhere. I mean, if you landed, say, an armoured force here and it met with the infantry, you could be in real trouble."

"Yes, but the first time around the Argies were ill-prepared, and these roads and infrastructure weren't here. Which in a funny kind of way is ironic, in that they have been put in to help the incumbent defensive force – but in the wrong hands it would be counter-productive, offering excellent transport links for any invading force," Chris said.

"You know," Sophie commented, squinting against the sunlight with a hand to her forehead. "I am not soldier like you two, but I understand tactics and it seems to me that for every positive we find a negative and vice versa; and it all seems to hinge upon one thing; how could they get men on the island in sufficient numbers to swing it?"

Chris smiled at her, nodding in agreement; liking more and more of what he saw in Sophie Carswell. He had assumed at first that she would just be some Oxbridge Sloane with romantic ideas about saving her country in some tropical paradise, but he was revising his opinion the more time he spent in her company. There was, he decided, a steel core and a tough woman under that cut-glass accent and immaculate exterior.

They returned to the base on the airfield and reported back to London on a secure encrypted line. Sophie reported directly to her boss, Johnston, rather than taking the usual route via Peters at the FO. Johnston's response was predictable and re-assuring, in that he thought it entirely plausible that O'Driscoll probably was Siobhan Clifford's long lost brother. He also approved the cautious approach to inspecting the barns.

They then checked out Mare harbour and the large oil pipe that ran from it to the 40k refuelling area they had seen earlier. "That," Chris commented, "would be a good point to create some diversionary sabotage." The pipeline represented a lifeline for all military facilities. The other two nodded sagely, adding it to the list of weak points they had found.

The conversation ended abruptly when they returned to Stanley for supper and a bed for the night, to find that Chris and Sophie were to share a room to keep up appearances. Rupert looked on with amusement seeing that Chris was far more em-barrassed than Sophie, who took it well and smiled, increasing Chris's discomfort. Rupert could not resist. Here was this tough SAS sergeant who had been made to look foolish by an admit-tedly attractive woman because of sleeping arrangements.

"Hey Chris, just remember, who dares wins," he said, grinning.

For his efforts he was rewarded with a joint "Fuck off" from Chris and a very un-ladylike Sophie. He went off laughing.

They went back to the Victory for supper, but O'Driscoll did not put in an appearance. Supper was a casual affair: a chat with the locals, banter with the landlord and to all the world they looked like a couple and a friend on vacation for a few days. They left early, Sophie holding hands with Chris for form's sake. To Rupert's eyes, Chris did not seem to object at all.

They did not see a figure lurking in the shadows who had been watching the area since the early evening from the vantage point of his battered old Land Rover. He saw the two men from yesterday, this time with a woman who was holding hands with the younger one, casually leaving the pub in an innocent way, making their way to the hotel.

The watcher entered the bar.

"Michael," the landlord called. "Twice in one week? You're coming close to being sociable. To what do we owe this honour?"

"Oh, I had some stuff for the farm comin' off the Heavy Lift. Machinery for the tractor. Saw some mates and thought I'd drop in for a pint," his accent was a strong Belfast compared to the other island tones. "Nearly bumped into those visitors from BA. They stayin' long?" he continued, seeking a place at the bar,

"What, the young couple and the other chap? No, they're back away to BA tomorrow and she is off home to the UK afterwards, so they said. Why? Strange for you to take an interest."

"Just idle curiosity. Funny time to come after New Year, don't you think?"

"They both work in import/export in BA, doing polo gear and holidays; came over for a break while everything's closed up."

Michael nodded his understanding and moved the conversation on, changing the subject. He left after a pint, deciding that he needed to get back and place a phone call. Something to his mind didn't feel right. He could smell a soldier or a copper a mile off, and the smell was a familiar one. And he remembered that familiar prickly feeling on the back of his neck earlier, when he went to the barn. When he returned to Kepple he called his contact in Colombia and asked them to send whatever they could find on Siobhan's colleagues.

Chapter Twenty-Five

London

It was early morning when Johnston telephoned Peters. He told him everything that had happened and relayed the information passed on by Sophie from the Islands.

"So your hunch was right. How do you think this will play out?" Peters asked. "I mean we know who and we know why – money, power and opportunity. But we don't know how, or at least not all of it. On that basis, I can't see a full military scramble happening based on a lot of coincidences, can you?"

"Trifles light as air are to the jealous confirmations strong as proofs of holy writ," Johnson quoted in response. "Now, the Argies are still jealous. They're jealous that we won, jealous of our oil and jealous of the power we hold. If I ask for a scramble of troops, can I have your backing?"

There was a brief silence as Peters weighed the pros and cons, considering his political career. If he was the man who cried wolf it would destroy him, put him back in the shadows. If he was the man who foresaw the danger, it would make him a legend in the service. His instinct said that the latter choice was the right one; there were, as Johnston said, just too many coincidences.

"I will, but on one condition. We wait until after they have been to Corrientes and reported back. By all means get things in place and ask for a date for another defence committee meeting with the same members present. I'll tee it up from the FO side and make sure someone is available – almost certainly Paul Robinson again. Make the calls, I will find out who is available and we will plan a concerted strategy. You will have my backing, but only when we are ready to win."

"All right. I'm not happy; it could be too late by then, but OK. We wait and I will put as many pieces on the board in place as I can. And um…thank you." Johnston realised that with those words, he now owed a favour to the FO, but it was worth it for the safety of the islands.

He ended the call and immediately called an old friend from university and school, Brigadier Coombs of the Royal Marines Commando. Coombs picked up the telephone on the third ring and after catching up, Johnston told him all that he knew. Twenty minutes later, after the concise briefing, Coombs agreed to quietly start setting up measures under the guise of a new training initiative in the Falklands. Three, Forty and Four Two commando would be attending with full equipment – including, he decided, a joint operation with 29th Royal Artillery Regiment. This would bring troop numbers to over three thousand, along with light armour and howitzers.

After he finished the call, Johnston leant back and stared out over the Thames, his mind considering all angles, sorting every eventuality and selecting each option to counter it like a computer. He turned suddenly and made one final call to the Director of Special Forces, who would pass on orders as he saw fit. Johnston decided that his mandate was clear: he had conclusive proof that a known terrorist was at large on the Falklands. This was, he reasoned, pretty much the truth, and it fell within the auspices of the SAS and therefore came under his authority. He explained in detail to his military opposite number, a Major General Hughes, with full disclosure of all that occurred had so far.

It was a long conversation. They considered all possible tactics, and as sergeant Adams was already involved, Hughes agreed to send two Boat troops from A & B Squadrons to watch O'Driscoll's farmhouse, protect the airfield and guard the mobile missile launchers. Johnston finished the call knowing that he had done all he could, and may even have overstepped the mark. It couldn't be helped; he'd made his decision and all he could do now was wait for developments and the next news in two or three days' time.

The Falklands

Rupert woke early, keen to move back to the sunny climes of Argentina and to Claire, who he was missing more than ever following their recent reunion. In the next room, Sophie awoke first. She was still on English time, and found that in the night she had rolled over and put her arm across Chris, embracing him. She smiled gently to herself, releasing the arm and looking down at his features. They were hard, even in repose: his dark wavy hair was spiked on the pillow, and without the glint of humour in his eyes the strong, almost harsh lines of his face bespoke the depth of his character. He was quite the enigma, she decided, and in another situation she probably would have enjoyed herself a little more with him, she thought to herself. *Lord, the things I sacrifice for Queen and country and the chance of a night of passion*, she sighed to herself. They met at breakfast and Rupert made no allusion to her sleeping arrangements. All of them wanted to return as quickly as possible so as to scout the military base in Corrientes. The charter flight was due in at ten o'clock to the Stanley commercial airfield, and it arrived on time.

"Wow," Sophie commented as they boarded. "Luxury after the Tri Star that brought me here."

Chris agreed; "I know it is not the best, but after a while you just get used to it. Just switch off and sleep."

The small plane was the same Saab they had originally travelled in, and was now fully occupied by islanders and a couple more visitors from before the holidays. No one looked suspicious to Sophie and they all relaxed for the return journey. The long flight was again broken by a refuel in Montevideo and they finally landed in Asuncion late in the day. They were relieved to be away from the wind on the Falklands and back in the sub-tropical heat of Paraguay. They returned to the hotel they had previously stayed in, this time with three rooms, and Sophie looked a little wistfully at Chris as she entered her room. Chris caught the look and wasn't sure what it had meant. He too had been awake that morning as she removed her arm, but he was hesitant to start anything, unsure of his position.

That evening they ate at the same restaurant and chatted about normal things such as Christmas, views on BA and the polo final. The restaurant was crowded and they couldn't risk being overheard. However, they all felt a false sense of security and a stiltedness to the conversation. Chris had experienced it before and likened it to pre-battle nerves and preparation: no one wanted to say too much or appear too jolly, each coping with nerves in their own way. Back at the hotel, they went over what they knew again in detail. Deciding what plans could be made, together with whatever they might find at the Corrientes base, if anything.

The next morning, they reversed Chris and Rupert's outward journey, crossing with the crowds of the morning rush hour. Everyone was trying to cross the bridge from Paraguay to Argentina and vice versa. It was a perfect time to cross. The guards were bored and overworked; passports were barely glanced at and no electronic recording was registered at all. This time they went all the way by car, avoiding the ferry and dodging the kamikaze motorcyclists, swarms of bicycles and pedestrians. They vowed never again to try the bridge crossing, but it was the perfect cover. Their passports received only a cursory glance and they were waved back into Argentina with impunity. Chris and Rupert breathed a sigh of relief to have Sophie safely and securely under the radar and back on Argentine soil, considering that they were all now moving potentially into more danger. The return journey to San Miguel proved uneventful and all three enjoyed the fast road that stretched out forever under the stunning Argentine sunshine. Rupert wondered, not for the first time, that if that was the Falklands in the summer, what the hell was it like in winter? They finally arrived at Kieko's ranch in the late afternoon; tired after the travelling and ready for the estancia to work its magic and embrace them in an oasis of tranquillity and peace. Sophie, who had by the nature of her job travelled a good deal, could not believe how beautiful it was.

"Damn work, can we stay here forever?" she asked as the Land Cruiser came to a halt in front of the Estancia's main house. Kieko was off riding some young horses, but the doors burst open and Claire, Silvia and Franky came into view.

In the four days that he had been gone, Rupert swore that Claire had gone at least three shades darker, and a bronzed vision came to meet him, hugging and kissing him in front of the others. Sophie gave them a tolerant, wistful smile. They had all agreed that they would keep up their role as a couple at San Miguel, and Chris put his arm around Sophie's waist, came forward and introduced her to Silvia, Franky and finally Claire. It was always a slightly tense moment when two strong-minded women met. Each summed up the other in a quick glance, and both women seemed to like what they saw – which was lucky, especially as they would be spending some considerable time together over the next few days, in the close confines of the ranch and the car. Claire broke the moment first, coming forward to shake Sophie's hand with a smile.

"It's good to meet you, I have heard a lot about you already," Sophie said.

Claire responded with a warm smile, robbing the words of any ambiguous meaning or intent. For her part, despite the obvious charms of the other woman, Claire warmed to her straightaway and knew that they would get on well together.

"I need to hear what that man of mine has been up to behind my back," she laughed gently, taking Sophie by the arm and leading her into the house. Rupert stuck his tongue out in a childish display, playing to the crowd.

Silvia walked Rupert in and asked, "Now, did you like the Malvinas? What is it like there? I have never been."

"Not much," he answered. "It was bloody freezing. I can't think of one reason to live there – and this was their summer. I'm glad to be back in the warmth again."

They both laughed, agreeing about the bleak nature of the islands. Franky, who had developed a slight teenage crush on Chris, brought up the rear, helping him to carry the bags from the car. Chris reflected that he was pleased that Sophie was here for more than one reason; gently fighting off a lovesick teenager was not in the job description.

Sometime later, Kieko returned from the horses and made Sophie feel at home. "Welcome to my home, it is such a shame you cannot stay longer you know, ride some horses, sunbathe by the pool. Are you sure you can't?"

"I'm seriously tempted, but we have to be back for work and I want to see Corrientes. I will probably never get up this way again and it is supposed to be beautiful."

"*Si*, I understand and it is a magnificent city; the capital of the province and the second largest city in Argentina. It has wonderful old squares, museums and it sits in a beautiful position right on the Paraña River, with sandy beaches and…well, it is lovely, you will see." He opened the palms of his hands wide in a shrug of explanation.

"It sounds wonderful. But beaches? Up here?"

"*Si*, the river is huge and carries many exports. It has a large container port and docking bay, all the way down from the famous General Belgrano Dam further upriver, amazing construction. It is also where they launched the invasion for the last war," he finished artlessly, as though it was just another piece of tourist information. Like many Argentinians, he simply did not care about the politics of it all.

"It is a shame you are not going straight back down. Franky wants to be back in BA to see her friends and go to the beach. She could have driven with you. Ah well, what to do? I suppose her old father will have to take her," he said smiling at his daughter.

Sophie was shown to Chris's room under the natural assumption that as his girlfriend, they would be sharing a room. She smiled to herself as they entered and found two single beds side by side, both with mosquito nets. She turned to him and said archly. "Do you have a preference?"

Chris turned to her, smiling. "Yeah, I'd prefer a double."

They dumped their bags on the floor and looked at each other: chemistry sizzling between them, neither sure what they should do about it, given the mission and the dangers ahead. Sophie broke the tension.

"I know we've driven a long way but I need to run. Being cooped up doesn't suit me."

"Can I join you?"

"Sure. See you out front in ten minutes." She turned, pulled her long hair up into a ponytail and left to get changed in the bathroom, the tension in the air still palpable.

In their own room, Claire and Rupert were making good

on their reunion. After a long kiss, Claire came up for air. "You know, I am glad Chris is along. I am not sure I'd trust you with Sophie around."

"What? Not my type. And why her over all these dusky, sultry senoritas?" he teased

"There is just something about her. Apart from her stunning figure, there's a certain something. She could be the girl next door one minute and a beauty at a cocktail party the next: she's a bit of a chameleon. It is a rare quality and I suppose one to be prized in her line of work. There is also a certain…I don't know, underlying sexiness about her. Once you light the fuse I think that you might be in for a real surprise, but I am not sure Chris is brave enough," she laughed wickedly.

"He was with Valentina."

"Different thing altogether. He was in control; knew what he was doing, all very obvious. I don't think he has met anyone quite like Sophie before. We'll see." Claire winked at him conspiratorially.

They embraced again and Rupert slid his hands up to release the bow holding her white linen shift dress up. It slid to the floor exposing her body, which was naked apart from a very brief pair of bikini thong bottoms. In the time he had been away, she had bronzed all over to a golden honey colour. She smelt delicious, he thought; sun-kissed skin, suntan oil and soap. It was an intoxicating combination. Claire pushed gently and he fell onto the bed, totally mesmerised by the golden vision in front of him. Her eyes slitted half shut and she slowly slid the thong down her legs, dropping it at her feet. He saw a tiny, pale, bare triangle in the Brazilian style; defined by the three short tan lines. Rupert's mouth was suddenly very dry, his throat constricted.

"Wow…" came his strangled response. Claire said not a word and slowly undressed him, forbidding him to help and then, achingly slowly it seemed to Rupert, made love to him. He was taken to a place of blonde, streaked hair, burnished skin and heavenly movements. He could not resist the onslaught and screamed silently into her shoulder, as she seduced him. Sated, they fell into each other's embrace and dozed in the late afternoon heat

Outside, another kind of attraction was being played out as Sophie and Chris ran together on a steady four mile run. Chris soon realised that she was very fit and good for a competitive pace with a graceful mile-eating stride. They flirted on the way, each able to talk easily and speak while running. No other woman had ever done this before, he reflected: it was a novel and enjoyable experience. They completed the run with a fast final mile, showered and went to supper with the whole family.

"So you're going back to return to BA tomorrow, Franky?" Rupert asked, twisting the new watch he had received from Siobhan. She confirmed that she would be and Rupert asked if she would deliver a small package to their office, as she would be passing.

"It has some papers and files which I want to ensure arrive safely, and most importantly on time. I would be very grateful and will definitely take you out to lunch at a restaurant of your choice as a reward," he finished

Franky's eyes lit up at the thought of lunch with Rupert and especially Chris.

"Yes of course. I will do it tomorrow, Mama is dropping me off now, so it will be prefect, just before we hit the beach," she finished, smiling.

"Great. I will go and put things together now." He left the table, with Chris throwing him a puzzled look. They all retired soon afterwards and prepared for the long day ahead of them.

The following morning they all rose early and said their sad goodbyes to the family, with both Claire and Sophie vowing to return soon. Rupert left the package with Franky and Silvia to deliver. The four of them left via the secondary exit, where the road forked and they set off on the hour journey to Corrientes, where they hoped that the final part of the riddle would be solved.

"What was all that bollocks about with the whole urgent package thing?" Chris demanded as they bumped off up the rough white road from the hacienda. Rupert smiled indulgently.

"I put some papers together with the watches from Siobhan, laid them flat in a file, and hey presto: for all the world we're on our way back to BA." He laughed. "Let the watchers follow them, they will all be feeling safe and secure." Chris and Sophie laughed.

"But what happens if Siobhan opens the package? She'll put it all together."

"Come on. Like we've said previously, it is a just a question of game playing. And if she speaks with her contacts, who I assume are in league with the Colombian FARC, who are all playing nicely with the Argies and the US oil company, so be it. If we can't find out how they propose to start the invasion, maybe we can just get them started and see what happens. Bit of a risk maybe, but what the hell. As we keep saying; time is getting very tight for us – and more importantly for them."

The others shrugged in agreement, seeing his point. "I'll say this for you Rupert, you do like to mix it up a bit!" said Chris.

"Well, it's make or break time really, isn't it? How did you get on with the satphone last night?"

"Johnston has gone out on a limb following our intel and put wheels in motion," said Sophie. "He has put in a request for a second security meeting while we get more intel. But in the meantime he's put the Marines on standby for a 'training operation' and," here she nodded at Chris, "two boatloads of his boys will be arriving to protect the airfield; missile stations and keep an eye on O'Driscoll and his merry men – or take them out as soon as we give the word."

"I got a communiqué to the same effect early this morning from the Head Shed," Chris confirmed.

They discussed the tactics involved and what the likely outcome would be. Sophie confirmed what they were all feeling. "All we want to ensure is that O'Driscoll does not get away again to plot more murders of innocent civilians and fund the PIRA coffers. Period."

They travelled on in silence, re-tracing their steps along the A12 to Corrientes, but this time with Claire and Sophie in tow. There had been some debate about returning with Claire as a civilian; but it would have seemed odd in Kieko's eyes to change their plans, and Claire wanted to see the city anyway. It would, they had decided, seem more natural to be two sightseeing couples viewing the city and its environs. Their journey crossed the arid countryside, punctuated with oases of wild trees, gorse and endless acres of grey and olive grass; steadily munched by thousands of slow moving cattle and occasional herds of horses.

An hour and half later they arrived at the city. It was a sprawling mass in a country where land was a well-supplied commodity and housing spread outwards rather than upwards. It was developed on the grid system that had been adopted by the USA and many countries on the American continent. Old multi-pillared colonial architecture in pale pastel colours sat side by side with new in the city centre, and like Asuncion there were many green piazzas and squares bounded by trees and manicured lawns. But as with so many South American cities, the suburbs were marked by pitted roads, run down housing and a generally seedy feel.

The centre was a bustling hive of activity; sweet smells of scented plants, aromatic tobacco from roadside cafes and a cool breeze that brought with it the smell of the river with an almost salty tang. They headed for the riverbank and the port area. Chris wanted to see the setting, and he was not disappointed. To say it was vast was an understatement: the river appeared to be nearly half a mile across and the huge suspension bridge reminded him of the Golden Gate in San Francisco. The riverbank was lined, as Kieko had explained, with beaches of sand, palm trees and shallow water bathing areas for swimmers. It was really a freshwater resort, and it was currently crowded with bathers and sun worshippers, parading up and down in micro bikinis and posing for each other. "Wow," Sophie declared. "Why did Franky want to go to the beach in BA when this is virtually on her doorstep? It's lovely."

"Yeah, but probably not quite the same buzz as BA; and of course all her friends are there. These things are very important to a teenager," Claire said.

They then moved down the riverside road on the Avenida Costanera Gral. St. Martin as it followed the bank of the river to the commercial area on the Avenida Juan Torres dey Vera di Aragon. Here was the commercial area of the port, with large shipping containers stacked like wooden building blocks waiting to be loaded onto the mighty container ships which used the river like a massive inland ship canal. Huge, seagoing container ships were docked at the quayside where they were being loaded by fixed derricks, dancing in attendance on the large orange and blue containers, ready to be loaded for the river trip down to the estuary and beyond. It was a hive of activity and as they watched, another large silhouette appeared on the distant horizon, much further down the river, as yet unidentifiable; its huge, sleek decks and bulkhead looking magnificent against the skyline.

Chris showed a particular interest in the containers and wanted to walk to take a closer look

"Sophie, will you walk with me closer to the port area, I would like to take a better look?"

She obliged him, playing the part and taking his hand – none too reluctantly, it seemed to Rupert and Claire – and they walked on down to the port area, just two more tourists seeing the sights. Whatever Chris had in mind was a mystery to Rupert, but they watched from a distance, looking out over the bay area, enjoying the view and the sunshine.

While the stevedores swarmed over the dock area, perpetually busy, there appeared to be no officials, security or boundaries in evidence, so Chris and Sophie wandered to the waterside and looked up at the stacked containers. Many were marked for the country of destination; a couple were marked for the Falklands, Chris noted, nudging Sophie and nodding in the direction of the containers.

"Machine parts, food, building materials. Who knows? It is hardly going to be a Trojan horse is it?" she said. Though she did note that one of the ships, the SS *Cochrane*, was registered to Miami and made a mental note to find out who it belonged to.

At that point, a pair of container lorries arrived, wheeling into the yard and halting with a wheezing and whistle of air brakes adjacent to the existing pile of containers to be loaded onto the American ship. They rocked to a halt, evidencing their heavy load, and the cabs moved as the drivers stepped down from their elevated position. From the other side of each cab the driver's mates got down and came around: both of them were soldiers. One un-slung his rifle and began aggressively shouting at Chris and Sophie, asking what they were doing here.

"*De donde eres? De donde eres?*" he shouted, demanding an answer.

"*Nous sommes Francais. Touristes Francais. Qu'est que c'est la probleme?*" Sophie responded in perfectly accented French before Chris could speak.

The soldier modified his tone when he thought they were French, clearly relieved that they were not English. He responded in halting French; telling them that this was a restricted zone and that they had to leave. It was, he said, dangerous; things could fall on them. They could be crushed by lorries: it was a very dangerous place.

Chris just had time to see the labelling for the crates confirming they too were for the Falklands. At this point, two port officials sauntered up, clearly disturbed from their siestas, and again Sophie told them in fluent French that no, they didn't have papers as they had to leave their passports at the hotel. The officials seemed satisfied with the explanation and they were ushered off the docks, back to their waiting friends.

"Well, that was interesting," Sophie declared. "I thought that we got out of it rather well."

"Good call on your behalf to use the French angle," Chris said. "I got the distinct impression that if we had been English it would have been a lot worse for us. But what the fuck have they got in those containers?"

"That's what we need to find out. Let's get out to the base and see if we can find out more."

They all returned to the Toyota and drove quietly away in the direction of the military base. It was only a fifteen minute drive from the city. The base was set in a basin of land surrounded on three sides by a natural crater, providing cover from prying eyes and making it difficult to approach by road without being seen. They parked about a quarter of a mile below the ridge in some trees. They left Claire there, with the bonnet up and just far enough off the road to be inconspicuous, but not sufficiently far into the brush to look like they were hiding.

"If anyone comes, say you have run out of fuel, we will take a spare fuel can and hide it back there just in case. Your friends have gone to look for help. Don't under any circumstances let on that you can speak Spanish. Just act the poor lost tourist." Chris told her.

"Smile and undo a top button, just like the good old days," Rupert said, earning himself an unladylike gesture. "I don't think that there will be any problems, but you never know, best to be prepared with a story."

The three left her looking suitably pathetic in the shade of a large thorny tree, with the bonnet of the Toyota up ready for attention. They walked quietly up to the foothills for about half a mile, stopping at a crest just above the military camp. The entrance to the base was clearly visible from the road: white stuccoed walls with a small grassed triangle, supporting a military statue and a pyramid-like structure made of cannon balls. A tall flagpole held the Argentine national flag, which fluttered listlessly in the faint breeze. The two guards at the gate seemed very alert, well-armed and watchful. Two jeeps full of troops drove around the perimeter in opposite directions, patrolling the barbed wire fences.

"A tight operation," Chris commented, peering carefully through the field glasses, lying just under a scrubby bush close to the crested ridge. "Either they are a different calibre to the other guys or they're on high alert for some reason."

He scanned the whole base, seeing a sprawling mass of well-ordered buildings. They were set out in pods and separated by linear arrangements of roads, demarcation zones and training areas. There were also a series of rough buildings that were clearly used for realistic exercises; similar to those of the 'killing house' used by the SAS at Stirling Lines. To the left hand side a troop of soldiers were drilling with very light packs, running forward from a standstill, lying among typical urban obstacles, running from block to block of cover. It was well done and clearly well-rehearsed to Chris's trained eyes.

"These guys are good, it must be their 4th Commando division. Their elite troops and the 3rd Infantry Brigade. Practicing for some form of urban situation."

Then he re-aligned the field glasses, bringing them into focus on another group of soldiers practicing below. They were moving along a wide, wooden platform having exited from a form of transport pod. There were eight pods in total, each housing a group of soldiers – about a hundred per pod at a push if they were packed in tightly, Chris estimated. An inaudible command had clearly been given; the soldiers exited from each pod ran up two steps and along the wooden platform until it divided into a T-shape. Here they split suddenly, moving quickly to the vantage points that the first team had reached. Until that point, no weapons had been visible, but upon reaching the points of cover, each soldier produced a weapon from a bag they had been carrying; either a shoulder strap bag or what looked like day bags or small rucksacks

"I've never seen a drill like that before. What the hell are they doing? It's bloody odd."

"Pass me the glasses," Sophie said, taking them from Chris' hands. She too focused and a gasp escaped her lips. "I know why it looks odd. Shit, I know what they are planning. Look again, see anything odd?" She passed the field glasses back to Chris and he looked again.

"No, just a rather strange way of...shit! There are women. For every male soldier there is a female soldier. No…no way…but it could work. We have to report this." Chris ordered.

Rupert was perplexed.

"Pass me the glasses," Rupert demanded. "What's happening? Whoa, look at that wooden area; remind you of anything? That's a mock-up of the Stanley docks. They're going to invade right under the noses of the port authority."

"What on a container ship? It won't carry enough men or women, and as soon as they start coming off in hundreds or thousands calls will be made and they'll be stopped. Troops will arrive, it will be a bloodbath I grant you. But the Argies can't afford that. They need surrender, not a battle. They need overwhelming odds to stop it escalating, which means sufficient numbers to take the town and storm the base. Then to support O'Driscoll and his mates, keeping the airfield intact, which would be good enough for re-supply until they either repair or take the RAF base whole. No, there is more to it than that," Chris finished.

Rupert flicked the binoculars back to him, catching the sun with the lens.

"Careful," Chris snapped. "They are dulled, but just a flash can get us killed. Come on, I've had another thought. We need to get back to the port; I've just remembered something."

At that point, two low-loader flatbed articulated trucks entered the base and stopped by a large, hangar shaped building. They watched the far side of the base, at full range for the field glasses, as the hanger doors slid back: a distinctive noise could be heard, even from that distance. Chris knew what he was going to see before it appeared. Two vehicles rumbled into view: AMX-13 light battle tanks. Two more vehicles could be heard, and then they saw them: two M1 Abrams tanks; the prized American medium battle tank. Chris shook his head in disgust.

"Well, now we know how the Americans are involved. Guns for oil: same old story. Fuck, we are in trouble if they land those on the Falklands."

They watched in awe as the tanks were loaded onto the low loaders and covered in stiff tarps and the lorries moved out through the base gateway in the direction of the city. The sun was beginning to set as the evening light stretched ahead of them.

They shuffled back from the crest and almost ran back to the Land Cruiser, nearly running into Claire in full flow, following Sophie's earlier lead and trying to explain in best A-level French that the car had broken down and her friend would be back soon and no she had no documents with her as they were always held by the hotel

Sophie and Chris hid, circling around so that they could be

picked up further down the road. Meanwhile Rupert hove into view carrying the previously stashed petrol can, waving it like some demented idiot. He spoke in terrible French to Claire and then deliberately badly accented Spanish to the two soldiers, who were returning to their Jeep, satisfied that they were just a couple of stupid tourists.

For form's sake Rupert went through the motions of filling the tank, started the engine and revved it thoroughly before setting off, with Claire waving and grinning at the two soldiers, who followed them half-heartedly for a little while just to make sure that they were headed back to Corrientes. Before long they peeled off in the direction of the base. As soon as they had gone out of sight, Rupert u-turned on the road and travelled the two miles to retrieve Sophie and Chris. They appeared out of the bushes by a small dirt lay-by, jumped in the Toyota and Rupert drove off again in the direction of Corrientes.

"Shit, that was close," Sophie exclaimed. "We nearly walked right into them. It would have looked just a tad awkward if it took three people to get one container of diesel!"

"Why did they come?" Chris asked.

"I was bloody scared, they screamed around the bend as if they were looking for someone." Claire explained, "From what I could tell they were patrolling the base. Seemed like they were on high alert. What happened back there? You were clearly in a hurry."

They explained in detail to Claire what they had seen and Chris started to open the large holdall containing the satellite phone and the other equipment that he had brought with him from the apartment

"Pull in near the city at the first quiet space you see," he said to Rupert. "Preferably in the shade near some trees so it looks like we've stopped for a rest. I have to phone this in as soon as possible."

Ten minutes later they stopped by one of the municipal parks not far from the waterfront which was visible in the distance. Chris got through to Peters, who was still at his desk. His response was curt, succinct and positive. He agreed with Chris and asked to be kept informed as soon as they had any more information.

Chapter Twenty-Six

London

Peters put the receiver down and immediately called Johnston. He proceeded without preamble: "Just had a very interesting call from Adams; it seems he was correct in most of his assumptions. We need to get mobilised straightaway."

Johnston listened and swore softly when he heard about the tanks; "Where are they going now? Back to BA?"

"No, apparently not. They have a final theory to try to prove – how the actual landing, which now seems inevitable, will be effected. They're not convinced that it will be just one or two container ships."

"I am inclined to agree with them. You know, out of all the soldiers they landed at the Falklands last time, they only lost 194 men, together with a hell of a lot of equipment."

"What is your point?"

"That they still have a huge military resource in terms of men who are experienced and good soldiers. The main reason they lost last time was poor supply, bad timing climate wise and poor equipment. For God's sake, the islanders were actually feeding the poor bastards at their doors because they were starving to death. Can you believe it?

"So my point is that if they have tanks, well supplied men with modern equipment in favourable areas using missile emplacements that they had captured along with at least one if not two airfields, we could be in a lot of trouble. If the British troops surrender before our reinforcements arrive and the Argies dig in with armour they didn't have last time, it would be carnage. We simply could not mount a task force like last time, and we probably only know the tip of the armament iceberg.

"If USE Oil are arming them, they will have SAMs, anti-aircraft missiles and God knows what else. This has been a well-planned operation and we need troops there now as a prevention, not a cure, in sufficient force to make it impractical for them to stage an invasion. I need an emergency meeting now: tomorrow at the latest."

Corrientes

The military jeep patrol that had found Claire reported back to base, and the sergeant in charge filled out his observation reports. The report was passed to the orderly of the day, a Captain Marques, who read it with interest. Every little detail was to be reported, he had told his patrols, no detail was too small to omit. He knew just how much was at stake here.

He put down the report and flicked back two pages to an earlier sighting of a flash on the southwest hills that could have come from binoculars. *Too much of a coincidence?* he thought. *No.* He telephoned through to the special American patrols within the base. The Advisors, as they were known, were always alert, desperate for some action. Anything to break the boredom. The call was answered by one of the mercenaries, who took the report very seriously.

Putting down the phone, he motioned to three others. "Come on," he ordered.

They gathered a mixture of Heckler and Koch MP5s and G3 Battle rifles to supplement their Sig Sauer side arms.

"We've got something to check out. Let me just call it in to Phillips, he was very particular in his orders."

Boston

Phillips picked up the phone and listened to his operative's report. "You say a girl and one man only? Did you follow them back to town? No, fine, go straight away. Anything – and I mean anything – unusual, report back immediately. Got it? Good, now what was the Captain's name?" he wrote *Marques* on a piece of paper and immediately dialled the base directly, asking to speak with the Captain. The call went through and the Captain repeated the reports word for word.

"Your sergeant, is he absolutely sure that this girl was French? Is he there, can I speak with him? Good, get him please." The line was left open for two minutes before it was picked up by the sergeant.

"Tell me exactly what took place and how it occurred," Phillips ordered. The soldier proceeded to repeat the explanation in his report word for word.

"And you're certain that the woman was French?" The sergeant confirmed that she spoke French, but that he had seen no documents to that effect as she had left her passport at her hotel, which was normal practice in Argentina.

He asked for a detailed description of the woman and her husband or boyfriend who had returned carrying the can. He did not like the answer and confirmed that no one else had been in sight at the time. He put the phone down, concerned.

It didn't feel right at all. Too many moving parts remained unaccounted for. He picked up the phone to call Siobhan Clifford directly, in HBJ's BA office, bypassing all protocol in Colombia and the Argentine government. He needed answers quickly and there was no time to go through the appropriate channels. Maria answered the telephone and put him straight through to Siobhan.

"You know who this is, Miss Clifford? I apologise for calling at work, but we need to speak about certain matters including the wee man. Do you understand?

"Ah yes, I think I can help you, let me just go through to Mr Brett's office where I can look at the papers." Despite Alex being onside, Siobhan wasn't sure about Rafe and didn't want to take any chances, even in a friendly environment.

"I am in his office now. Why the direct call, is everything all right? Is the wee man safe?" Concern rose in her voice.

"Yes, as far as we know. But I need to be brief for all our sakes. Everything is loading up well, but there has been an incident with the cargo. Possibly nothing, but I need some answers from you. Is your boss back yet? If not, where is he?

"He went away before Christmas up to San Miguel as agreed. He was tracked and stayed there over Christmas. Latest reports came in this morning that he was on his way back: both of them were. And they visited everywhere they should have with no problems. Why? What's the matter?"

"Did they go to Corrientes? Because we had a sighting yesterday of a supposedly French couple matching their description being seen around the base. Just two, no more, but the other person could have been *off sightseeing*, do you understand?"

"I do. Alex will co-ordinate with MREC later today and I will do my usual pick up on my run. Do you want me to call back directly on this number as soon as I hear?"

Phillips confirmed that he did and that anything unusual was to be reported. Replacing the receiver he went through to Kelly's office to discuss what had occurred

"It seems you were right to be careful," Kelly said. "But it could be nothing, there's a lot of French touring around there, and they did help the Argies is the last war with Exocets. Relax, we have a good team down there. If anything is wrong Brad will find it, he is very good, you know that." Phillips nodded, still feeling that something was amiss.

Corrientes

At that moment the Land Cruiser was heading along the coastal road parallel to the river and the docks. The road swept round a rugged headland facing down river and the evening sun threw the last of its heat and long shadows across the orange tinted water of the river. As they rounded the headland they saw it. Moored out from the quay, approached via sliding pontoons and orange landing pods, was the ship they had seen in the distance earlier in the day. The vast superstructure of the cruise ship SS *Esmeralda*. The same ship Chris had seen in dock at BA now loomed before them, a leviathan that dwarfed everything around it. Rupert nearly broke their necks as he slammed on the brakes, pulling in sharply to the side parking bays that were virtually empty at this time of day.

"What the fuck, Rupes..." Chris started and then he too saw it from the back seat of the car.

"What is it, Rupert?" Claire asked him. But then she too saw the ship as well as the fenced and walled compound adjacent to the embarkation area. It was swarming with passengers, all waiting to board. The trouble was that they were many more men than women, who even so numbered in the hundreds. There were no elderly passengers and no children. There were thousands of them still waiting to board, and each one carried a kit bag loaded with gear as well as a day bag or small rucksack. A second container transport and two deep sea fishing boats were moored nearby, and none of the vessels carried any military markings whatsoever. Two bore the insignia of the USA, and the cargo boat had a Swedish registration. In isolation, they would all look very innocent. But together…

Chris broke the horrified silence

"There we have the Falklands' second invasion force. They are just going to sail in and drop anchor unchallenged. They will disembark; couples first dressed as tourists, landing in their thousands, completely innocent and unopposed. I guess the container ships are carrying the armour, the heavy guns and transport, whatever, and the whole kit and caboodle is funded and supplied by USE Oil. The Swedish ships, if that is what they are, will also appear innocent. The crates will come off first, I can see it now. They'll rip open the doors and bang, they will have armour and they'll outnumber us by eight or ten to one."

"It is brilliant in its simplicity, and very audacious," Sophie said. "The airfields will be taken and held by O'Driscoll's crew. The missile points ditto. Who knows how many small groups they have up at Keppel island? I bet the smaller boats will drop off at Port Howard or Johnson's harbour."

"Hell, any number of places. They could easily drop RIBs off bigger boats to any number of inlets. Like everyone says, taking it is easy: holding it is the problem. But we're all stretched in the Middle East; we've no spare carriers, and if they dig in now with armour, well provisioned troops and air cover…" Chris finished, shaking his head. "Look at the hull. That's what was worrying me."

He pointed, indicating new panels that appeared hinged and could be lowered. "I bet they're gun ports. And look, they've cleared the upper decks and I see two or three helicopters strapped up there. They'll be camouflaged, no doubt. It won't be a battle, it'll be a walkover. Our marines will have to surrender just like last time, and if they don't they will be massacred long before reinforcements arrive."

Rupert commented. "That's the thought I had on the dock at Port Stanley, but I never imagined anything on this scale. What does a normal cruise ship take? three, three and half thousand? Bloody hell, they could pack five or six thousand on that, easily. And that's without the armour and other boat crews." He shook his head in disbelief. "And using the women soldiers, that is sheer genius. Evil, but genius."

"Well, if the MREC is fifty percent staffed by women, I bet a lot of them would love to get into this. All their military and secret service crossover, anyway," Sophie commented. "Come on, we need to get out of here, report this and get back to the Embassy. Claire, I need you on a plane out of harm's way as soon as possible."

They all nodded in agreement. Rupert engaged first and pulled off rather too quickly, attracting attention from those around him. "We'll not stay the night as planned; we'll get something to eat and head off as soon as possible. We have to get back to BA as soon as we can, we'll take turns with the driving, Chris, it's a long way," he finished. Chris nodded and for the first time on the trip, reached over and took out the guns from the holdall that he had stashed in the boot area, following Regiment protocol of always having weapons ready and able to use and never hidden away. Claire looked over her shoulder, seeing Chris's move.

"You're not going to start shooting here, are you?" She asked in alarm.

"If they're here and we don't need them, no problem. If we need them and I can't get to them in time because they're stashed away, we will be in big shit and you will be very upset, trust me." It sounded harsh, but Claire saw the wisdom of the words and smiled in agreement. Sophie just shrugged as though it were the most natural thing in world to travel with a loaded rifle for company by her side

They moved off swiftly, driving out to a restaurant further down the coast on the outskirts of the city. On reaching the restaurant Chris phoned the news back to Peters in London. The meeting was already set for the next day and now it became even more imperative to organise troops and reinforcements for the islands. The harsh reality was that the Argentinians could be there in just under two days.

Johnston, upon hearing what Chris and Rupert had seen, brought the emergency meeting forward to that night. Home secretary Douglas Hurd and Minister for Defence Martin King were informed and were both waiting for the outcome of the emergency meeting. The Commando units were already waiting at RAF Brize Norton, extra armour was loaded into a C130 ready for wheels up at a moment's notice. HMS Endeavour and one of the subs were steaming on a new course. The problem, as they all knew, was that they could not attack first, it had to be dissuasion rather than aggression: that was the biggest problem, because it meant that they needed to get there in time.

Buenos Aires

While arrangements were being made in London, Siobhan was returning from her run with a new water bottle. She was very perplexed. Alex had reported that the trackers were showing Rupert and Chris back in BA or nearly home, but the message from the FARC contact said her brother had reported two British men on the Falklands; one of whom had a girlfriend arrive from the UK. The Falklands, for fuck's sake! She ran to the office as it was closer, ignoring the stares from Rafe and Alex. She ran in, picked up the phone and called Phillips, passing the message from FARC. He swore harshly down the phone. Before he could say anything more, Siobhan saw a pretty young Argentinian girl walking into the main office, carrying a package.

"Wait one moment," she said.

She put the phone down on the desk and moved swiftly to intercept the girl, who was giving the parcel to Maria. True to her word, Franky had dropped the parcel off on the way into the city, before going to the family's city apartment.

"Oh, is this for Rupert?" Siobhan queried, all smiles and charm.

"Yes. He asked me to drop it off for him. It has some papers he wanted for when he gets back later today. Are you Siobhan? Rupert and Chris both loved the watches, they said it was very kind of you."

"Oh it was nothing. Did they have a good time up there with you?" Franky chatted about the holiday, about playing polo and about how they would be back tomorrow after paying a quick visit to Corrientes

"Ah, how lovely. Thank you so much. Tell me," she fished, "Did they have a good time in the Malvinas?"

"Yes, they picked up Chris's girlfriend there and she came back with them. Seemed a strange place to go for a holiday, but..." she gave a Latin shrug.

With that Franky left, waving goodbye. Siobhan's face instantly changed to a frown and she grabbed the package from Maria's desk and ran back into the private office, ripping it open. She picked the receiver up and cradled it to her neck, pulling open the padded envelope. The watches dropped out, disguised by padding and she ground her teeth in a grimace.

"Fuck, they know. The watches are back, that's why we didn't trace them there."

"Are you talking to me again? What have you found?" asked Phillips.

Siobhan explained as quickly as possible what she had found, as well as the message from FARC and the conversation with Franky. The silence at the other end of the line was menacing; the ill-concealed fury and tension was palpable, despite the distance.

"I would be very careful now. That was sent as a message to upset our balance and to warn you. You need to lay low. Get somewhere safe; as a UK citizen you are very exposed. Disappear for a few days and we will keep you posted. If necessary we'll get you out of there like we did the last group we sent for Adams." The line cut off.

Siobhan stared at the dead phone in her hand, her mind racing to comprehend what she had just heard. She knew she would be extremely vulnerable if she was to be arrested and deported back to the UK, where she would face trial for treason: if it ever got that far and she didn't end up in a dark hole somewhere – or worse. The British weren't as fond of 'disappearing' people as the Argies, but there were always exceptions.

She realised that she had to get out, or at least move away from the city. Siobhan wondered if she could trust Maria to hide her or if she should skip across the border and hide with her friends from FARC. She also wondered about her brother: was he safe?

She decided on Maria first; their relationship over the Christmas period had blossomed and they were firm friends now, as well as lovers. Signalling for Maria to enter the office, she confided in her about the current events. Maria was also a partisan Argentinean, whose values and loyalties lay with her country, and that included the Malvinas. She already knew a good deal about Siobhan's involvement in the espionage activities of her country through the confidences Siobhan had shared, and had actively helped her as much as she could. Maria was more than keen to help further and conceal Siobhan from the British authorities.

Boston

In the USE Oil offices, Phillips hung up the phone and stared into space, his usually razor sharp mind stunned into inactivity as he mentally collected himself; analysing, sifting and placing actions in order of priority. He knew it was going to be a fine line, but all might not be lost. Everything depended on timing. How much did the Brits know? How much had they told their UK masters? How long would it take the UK government to take the threat seriously and if they did, send sufficient troops to counter the mounted invasion force preparing to leave for the Falklands?

He knew that the British government could not, without extreme and unequivocal proof, open hostilities. That had always been part of the beauty of the scheme. They were of course aware of the British subs, but knew that they could not just open fire on an unsuspecting cruiser and commercial shipping, especially when the ships are sailing under an American flag. They were also being joined and secretly escorted by one of Argentina's new subs that had been supplied by the US. She would trail them out of sight beneath the waves. It all depended on the extent of the information they had and how much they had done with it. At that moment his phone rang: it was Brad from Corrientes

"Phillips."

"Brad, sir. We've found some evidence of surveillance up on the ridge above the base. Recent scuff marks on the ground at least two, possibly three unknown sets of recent prints. Whoever was watching had a good view of all that was taking place; including I would say, given the timings, the armour being loaded."

There was a pause as Phillips assimilated the information, cursing under his breath, knowing that it would avail him nothing. Phillips made a quick decision.

"Find them. I don't care what it takes, find them and stop them. Your sergeant has the details of the car in his report: I believe you said it was a Toyota Land Cruiser. They were heading into Corrientes. Start there, but have someone watch the road back to BA. They must return. They will almost certainly have followed the tank convoy to the loading area; but their itinerary will depend upon how serious and exposed they feel their position is. It may mean that they set out tonight or early tomorrow morning."

"Yes, sir. One final question sir, how do you want them stopped?" the ambiguity of the question was not lost on Phillips. He knew exactly what the former Delta soldier meant and the implications of the question.

"Preferably alive and able to answer questions. But if all else fails, stop them at all costs. Make it look like an accident, clear?"

"Understood." The call finished. Phillips went through to Kelly's office to make his final report. The response from Kelly was mixed.

"The invasion force is on its way; we have representation in Congress, oil rights about to be registered. Now it all hinges on timing. Hell, they could be on the islands in two days. Supply planes en route from our private field in Miami marked as Argies. There is no way that the Brits can mount a force in that time and defend the island against 5,000 troops and armour. No way.

"But in the event that this does get fucked up, I want someone to pay. This is personal; nothing will stop me having revenge and I will use any means possible to get back at those fucking surveyors." Kelly slammed his palm down on the desk.

CHAPTER TWENTY-SEVEN

Argentina

The four occupants of the Land Cruiser were tense, wary and becoming exhausted, especially Claire and Rupert, who were not as inured to these situations as Chris and Sophie. They were driving south on the main A12 on the long journey towards Buenos Aires, and they were making good time despite having driven all night. The roads were nearly empty; just the odd car and long distance coach, which they passed at speed, leaving in a trail of lights in the distance. They were all aware that they needed to reach the comparative safety of BA as soon as possible and get Claire out of danger and onto a plane to the UK.

"Rupert, I swear I would like just one trip abroad where one of us is not in danger, or being chased and shot at. How about a trip to Cornwall this summer?" she finished sarcastically. He grinned at her, admiring her bravado and loving her all the more for it

"What do you mean? This is just a lovely road trip with the dawn light breaking across the horizon," he commented at the spectacular red sunrise coming from their left throwing long shadows across the road. "Anyway, I don't know what you mean, no one has shot—"

The rear window shattered as a bullet ricocheted off the thick rear roof pillar of the Land Cruiser. The wind howled in, whining through the cracked edges of the crazed glass. Rupert fought for control of the car as he had swerved and instinctively ducked as the impact echoed through the Toyota.

"Fuck!" Claire cried. "You were saying?"

In the back, Sophie and Chris grabbed for the weapons he had earlier uncased from the holdall. They both swivelled, instinctively ducking and offering a poor target to whoever was firing at them. Chris raised the Diemaco C8, breaking the crazed glass of the rear window with the stock. Some thousand meters away he saw the outline of a dark coloured Jeep, gaining on them. They must, he considered, have a night sight to risk a shot at that distance without confirmation of the occupants of the car. Or maybe they just didn't care about collateral damage.

He set up his own night sight and received a full picture of the Jeep in the spectral green haze it provided. He estimated four occupants. Fair odds, but not if they all had long guns.

Rupert floored the Toyota, which responded as the turbo-charger wailed, pushing the large vehicle close to its top speed, with the needle nudging 110mph.

"Keep it steady and drop the speed a little." Chris said.

"What? Are you mad?"

"It's always easier to shoot backwards than at something you're pursuing, and I need a good shot," Chris answered calmly.

"What will you do, shoot the tyres?"

Chris offered a dry laugh, "That is for Hollywood and the movies. No, at this speed, distance and light, I'll go for the engine or any other nice big target."

He rested the barrel of the Diemaco on the rear parcel shelf and before taking aim, looked across at Sophie, who was holding her Glock19, looking cool and detached as she concentrated. She was mentally calculating distances, odds, and possible scenarios; he knew that much. She was far too professional to even consider raising the Glock. He smiled, liking her composure: she was his kind of girl, he thought. Moving the selector switch to single action he took aim at the windscreen and loosed off a shot.

He was sure that he had scored a hit, but there was no reaction: no shattering glass, no veering. No alteration of speed or course. He looked again.

"What the fuck?" he muttered. "Armoured glass?"

He considered the possibilities, and was taken back to the attempted mugging in BA: professional soldiers, probably American mercenaries, he thought. This could be interesting. Taking aim again, he gently squeezed the trigger a few times, the smell of cordite acrid in the car, the concussion of successive shots reverberating loudly within the vehicle. Nothing: no result and no sign of faltering. The Jeep kept closing and the shots from the men within it were ripping chunks off the Land Cruiser. Chris knew it would just be a matter of time before one scored a lucky and possibly fatal hit.

"Get Claire down," He snapped at Rupert, who told Claire to get as much of herself as she could into the footwell in front of the front passenger seat.

Chris changed magazines in a fast, practiced swap, working by instinct and feel rather than sight. The new magazine had intermittent tracer rounds, which meant he could see where they were landing. He changed the selector to three round bursts and squeezed the trigger. An arcing burst showed against the breaking dawn. Chris adjusted his aim and tried again: he was rewarded with a hit on one of the gunmen hanging out of the windows. He wasn't sure but he swore that the gunman had dropped his weapon. *One down, three to go,* he thought.

In the growing, light a shadowy form appeared in the distance;

grey and large, lumbering ahead on their side of the road: one of the ubiquitous long distance overnight coaches.

"Chris, there is a coach ahead," Rupert called back to him. "What should I do?"

"Accelerate. Overtake it, then pull sharply in front of it, maintaining speed with the coach," he ordered.

Rupert floored the accelerator and gained on the coach in the distance. Bullets continued to ricochet off the body of the Land Cruiser and occasionally sent splinters of glass flying into the cabin of the car. They could now hardly hear each other speak over the howl of the wind through the shattered windows and the assault on the ears from rifle rounds. Gradually Rupert gained on the coach, crawling – or so it seemed to him – inexorably closer. Finally they edged in front, relieved that they were no longer exposed to the fire from the gaining Jeep. Adams shouted above the noise

"Now slow down in front of the coach, keeping as close as possible to the front and tuck right in to the side of the road, keeping as tight in as you can."

Rupert let the Toyota slow down to a steady 70 mph just feet from the front of the coach. The driver blared his horn in annoyance at the close cut in and proximity of the Land Cruiser. To make himself even less popular Rupert let the car drift to the right, off the tarmac surface, throwing up dust and billows of grit as the offside wheels caught the gravel siding the road. Now the four awaited the arrival of the following Jeep and its lethal occupants.

"As soon as we see the front of the Jeep, pull over to the right onto the gravel and Pampas, but try and keep it as steady as you can and pray we don't hit a rock and roll over!"

Rupert nodded in acknowledgement awaiting the call and constantly twitching over his left shoulder hoping to catch a glimpse of its front bumper. And there it was: suddenly flying into view a good 20mph faster than the coach. Rupert swung the Toyota as quickly as possible over to the right, leaving two wheels on the tarmac. The big 4x4 whipped, lashed and twitched on the gravel, its thick chunky tyres fighting for grip and finally winning.

In that brief moment, Chris, who had switched the Diemaco to automatic, sprayed the Jeep with a withering pattern of fire. Now that the Jeep was in useful range for the Glock, Sophie squeezed off fast, careful, single shots trying to take out the occupants. The open windows offered limited accessibility but some rounds hit home and Sophie caught the driver with a ricochet, pinging off the inside of the armoured glass. It was only a wound but it had the required effect.

The driver pulled on the wheel, flinching in reaction to the burn across his tricep. The Jeep weaved from side to side, losing speed, catching the gravel off the side of the road and careering in front of the coach as it made contact with its bumper. It was enough and the result was spectacular; the jeep lurched over, hitting the gravel and a rock and pinwheeling on its front axle. It seemed to hesitate in the air, almost frozen in time; then it rolled violently onto its roof, desperate to scrub off the kinetic energy of its forward motion. The sound of tortured metal came from it as it skidded on its roof for about fifty yards before hitting a ditch and bouncing onto its side to a dead stop.

Rupert was having his own problems fighting for control of the Land Cruiser, as it finally gained steady traction, leaving the pampas and gravel behind. Some two hundred yards later both the coach and the Toyota came to a halt. Chris and Sophie got out leaving the doors open.

"Keep the doors open and the engine running and be ready to go even if we are not in the car. No arguments, got it?" he ordered aggressively and motioned for the coach driver and passengers to stay inside and then to move on. The driver started to argue and stepped down onto the road, obviously wanting a word with whoever was driving the Land Cruiser. A stream of tracer and .7625 rounds fired by one of the occupants from the upside down Jeep raised dust and shale from the tarmac in front of the coach and the driver abruptly changed his mind and ran back to his coach.

Chris and Sophie immediately split, dropping to the ground. The coach driver needed no extra bidding, and the doors closed with a hiss. Gunning the engine he pulled off, narrowly missing the pair of them but giving them enough cover to return to the Toyota, which was already moving off at a slow pace. They leapt up, Sophie slightly lagging, running for the car and as soon as they were half inside Adams shouted "Go, go!" They slammed the doors shut, Rupert floored the accelerator, snapping gears as he redlined the engine. The Land Cruiser kept pace with the coach for about fifty yards then Chris ordered Rupert to pull back, secure in the knowledge that the coach and its occupants were safe.

Chris told Rupert to double back and park a hundred yards or so from the now silent jeep. Leaning out, he raked it with round after round of rapid fire, before getting out to check the Jeep's occupants. Three shredded bodies lay on the dusty roadside. A fourth man, amazingly still alive, clutched his rifle and raised it towards Chris, who put a bullet through his forehead and blew the back of his head clean off. Chris checked the vehicle and the bodies for any form of communications equipment, and stamped on four mobile phones before snapping the vehicle's aerial and pulling some wires from the dash.

"Are they OK? I thought they would all be hurt," Claire demanded as Chris returned to the Land Cruiser.

"They're not in any pain now," Chris replied through clenched teeth. "I didn't ask them to shoot at us. Perfect start to the day. Them out of action, us safe and no way they can communicate with base and tell anyone else where we are. No deal's done 'til it's done, as we say in the surveying world, and that's one fucking deal that's done now." he finished. He turned towards Sophie. "You did well, great–"

It was then that he noticed a spreading stain of blood seeping across Sophie's chest. "You're hit. Where?"

Her voice rasped in reply, stricken by pain, "Shoulder I think, through and through, but hurts like hell. Didn't feel a thing until we got back inside." Rupert was alarmed and suggested stopping. Claire raised herself from the footwell and asked if there was anything she could do.

"No, I've got her. Rupert, keep going, fast as you can. We have to get her to a hospital." Chris kneeled on the seat and reached over to the back luggage area, feeling into the side panel for the First Aid kit. He broke it open, splitting open sterile dressings, and reaching for his case, pulled out a new bottle of duty free scotch.

"Sorry, Sophie, this is going to hurt," he warned. Pulling out his Sig Sauer knife he flicked it open and carefully cut away her shirt, snipping through her bra strap and exposing the wound.

"Ready? Here, have a slug of this first." She did so, then nodded and he poured the golden liquid over the wound. She inhaled quickly.

"Oh fuck…"

"Good girl. Let me see." He inspected the wound carefully, gently probing with a clean scotch-soaked gauze as Sophie moaned through clenched teeth.

"It is through and through, but it's an ugly wound and you're losing blood; we need to get you to a hospital fast."

He was silent for a while, working with his medical training as all Regiment soldiers are taught to. The first aid kit was a full field kit: much more comprehensive than the usual car equipment. Chris had seen to that, purchasing extra items to supplement the basic components. After cleaning the wound, he was very glad of his foresight. Breaking open the pack he pulled out two sterile field dressings and carefully pressed one to each side of the wound. He worked quickly and efficiently, bandaging the two pads tightly, getting Sophie to apply pressure as he strapped them in place with a taut bandage, padding and strapping it securely. Sophie's face was creased in pain and drained of colour, and she had started to shiver.

"She's going into shock. How far to the next major town? Claire, have a look on the map in the glove compartment. Come on Sophie, stay with me. Stay awake."

Chris knew that it wasn't the wound that was the most dangerous, but the shock: that was the killer and he had to get her stabilised as soon as possible. Chris reached into the bag again and produced what looked like a thick marker pen. Rupert glanced over in the rear view mirror.

"Shit, is that what I think it is?"

Chris ignored him and moved his hand down the outside of Sophie's lower thigh where there were fewer nerve endings. He found the muscle and plunged the morphine pen into Sophie's leg. She gasped at the stab of the needle.

"Good girl," he said as she immediately started to relax, the morphine doing its work. He covered her in a blanket and coats despite the high ambient temperature, ensuring she was as well protected from the drafts as anyone in a speeding vehicle with most of the windows shot out could be, and pulled a woolly hat over her head. He noticed that the bleeding had stopped, and reached into Sophie's overnight holdall, pulling out her makeup bag. He fumbled around and produced a stick of bright red lipstick. He undid it, moved her woolly hat up her forehead and wrote a large 'M' on her forehead.

"OK?" he asked. She smiled faintly back at him. The shivering had ceased and she was still conscious

"Best a man has ever treated me," she joked, squeezing his hand weakly.

"That was a morphine pen," Rupert said in answer to Claire's unspoken question about the M written on Sophie's forehead. "How the hell did you get hold of one of those? They guard them like gold dust, even on dangerous training exercises."

"V and A, mate. The second motto of the Regiment is "if you're not cheating, you're not trying!"

Claire raised an enquiring eyebrow. "V and A?" she said.

Rupert answered loudly above the din of the wind howling through the broken side screens: "He means valuable and attractive. All the SF guys love gadgets and modifications to anything."

She smiled in acknowledgement and over her shoulder shouted: "It is about an hour and a half to Rosario; a big town, bound to be a good emergency hospital there." Claire offered.

"Good. Let's head there. I'll get a message to London and on to the Embassy for back up and protection for Sophie. She has Diplomatic Immunity and we don't, so we need to move as soon as we know she's safe. I want you on a plane out of here ASAP, Claire, this is getting all rather serious, and it's no place for a civilian."

"Master of the understatement," she joked, trying to play down the tension of what had just happened. She looked at Chris, and wisely refrained from asking what he had done back at the jeep. She admitted to herself that she was scared and wanted to be safe as soon as she could. She was also worried for Rupert. It was one thing to be a TA soldier, quite another to be messing with the big boys, in the form of a seasoned SAS sergeant able to cope with, it appeared, pretty much anything.

CHAPTER TWENTY-EIGHT

London

The telephone had been ringing all day. Johnston had a headache and he knew it was going to get worse. His third cup of coffee wasn't helping, but he drank it anyway. Three Hercules130C transport planes were already on their way to Ascension Island and three more were being loaded with more troops and light armour. SAS troops were already on the island and dug in, observing. But as good as they were, they weren't going to be able to hold off five thousand Argentinean commandos. It was going to be close, very close indeed.

HMS Endeavour was steaming at full speed to the island but it couldn't just open fire on a cruise ship in international waters. Johnston had been made aware of Adams' report of further activity from the rogue freighters, together with support from the US. The telephone rang again: Peters this time, with a report he'd received from Adams as they were travelling down to BA.

"Sophie? Bloody hell, how badly is she hurt?" Johnston asked.

"Apparently only a shoulder wound, through-and-through, but she lost a lot of blood. They're taking her to a hospital in

Rosario. I have scrambled Embassy security from BA and they are on their way now. She'll have diplomatic immunity and she'll be safe with a guard around her. The others, of course, don't have that, and they'll get Claire Sewell back on a flight to the UK as soon as possible. At this stage the Argentine government are not involved: at least not officially, so there is no need to worry. A 'misunderstanding between feuding foreigners' I believe is the official line. Or the bloody Yanks and their friendly fire again.

"The only fly in the ointment as far as I can see is the 14int operative, Siobhan Clifford. Brett was a bit cavalier there; she's had an oblique warning and my guess is she will run to ground if she's as guilty as they think she is. But my instinct is to leave her for now and see what happens. She can't do any more damage..." Peters hesitated.

"Go on." Johnston urged.

"Well, if we frustrate their plans, which we might yet be able to do, they will want revenge. They being not just the Argentinians but EU Oil, American mercenaries and more importantly the IRA. They will be informed by Clifford and you know how they love a soft target. I think that you might want to keep tabs on Miss Sewell when she returns to the UK. Probably for a couple of weeks until all this is over. Just a thought..."

"I'll bear it in mind. Thank you. Please keep me posted on developments over there," Johnston finished.

Argentina

The Argentinian security forces had noted the rapid departure of some of the British embassy staff. They had tracked them to the airport and quickly discovered their destination. Alerts were put out and enquiries made. A short while later, they found an admission record for a British female patient suffering from gunshot wounds at Rosario Hospital. Senior security had no idea of the extent of the exposure, but were happy in the knowledge that the convoy was on its way, and at most some thirty-six hours away from its destination. A muted sense of excitement prevailed. The Malvinas and their oilfields were within their grasp once again. All they needed was a little time and good luck.

Rupert, Claire and Chris pulled away from the hospital in the Toyota. Chris felt guilty at the idea of abandoning Sophie, but the embassy had promised support and protection within the hour.

"Get out of here," Sophie had urged him, finally comfortable in a hospital bed, being fed morphine through a drip. Chris took a damp cloth to the M on her forehead, and leaned down and kissed her brow where it had been.

"I'll be back," he said.

"Yeah, you and Arnold Schwarzenegger both. Now fuck off and save the world, there's a good chap." She managed a weak laugh.

Outside the hospital, the town was beginning to wake up. The ambush had taken place in the first light of dawn, and the road into Rosario had been quiet. Now it was getting busy with the morning rush hour.

"This car's going to stand out like a pork pie at a bar mitzvah," Chris said. The Toyota's windows were mostly gone, there were stars of bullet holes in the windscreen, smashed lights and holes in the bodywork alongside streaks of paint that had been removed by glancing shots. The back seat was covered with Sophie's blood. "You two, get a taxi to the nearest car hire place. Play the gawping tourists one last time and rent something similar. Big, tough and capable. Come back and get me. I'll be parked in the farthest corner of the hospital car park."

Rupert nodded, jumped from the car and headed towards the taxi rank at the hospital's main entrance. Just over an hour later he was back with a sparkling new Range Rover. He found the Toyota under a stand of trees, with Chris watching alertly.

They transferred their luggage and the bags of guns into the back of the Range Rover and abandoned the Toyota where it stood.

They finally arrived at the outskirts of Buenos Aires in the late afternoon. Tired and emotionally wrung out; strained from watching their backs against a possible recurring threat of further retribution from an unknown enemy.

"Right, straight to the Embassy for you, Claire," Chris said. We'll pick up your things from the flat and drop them off. I want you under protection as a UK citizen as soon as possible."

"I am sorry Claire, we rather ruined your holiday – but at least you got to see Kieko and play polo," Rupert finished lamely. Claire started to laugh almost hysterically; she was on the edge, the events of the last twelve hours catching up with her.

"Oh my God, I don't know what you mean. Chased, shot at, driven off the road, poor Sophie in hospital and a fast and rather dubious exit to the plane like some kind of international fugitive. The perfect end to the perfect holiday." Claire shook her head in a mixture of anger and sadness. "Rupes, I'm sorry but I just want to go home. I know it sounds pathetic but I've had enough. What started as an adventure has turned into a nightmare."

"I know darling, soon we will have you on a plane and back to cold, miserable England, with snow, slush and freezing weather," he joked.

"Bastard!" She said, slapping him on the shoulder.

Chris looked on with concern. He had seen the signs before and knew how stressed Claire was. The trip to the Embassy was without incident and they left Claire there, in one of the assistants' care. Her flight was booked for 10pm that evening; straight back to the Falklands by private charter and on to Ascension, the way Sophie had arrived. She would be taken in a car with CD plates to the airport and escorted onto the plane by the embassy staff in case of any threat of retribution.

Rupert returned to the embassy just before 8pm with Claire's things for a tearful farewell. It had not been easy on either of them, and they were both worried about each other. London, mindful of Peters' warning, had arranged the private transport and onward military carrier. No one underestimated the stakes that were involved or the possibility of retribution. Dark forces could slip in and out of BA very easily, and harm could be done in a number of clandestine ways. It was the hardest goodbye the couple had ever made.

"I'm going to miss you terribly," Claire whispered, aware that they were in the reception area of a busy embassy. "And I'm worried about you. Promise me you'll come home as soon as you can? And no more heroics, please?" she begged, hugging him tightly, sobs coming from her chest.

"Just make sure that you make that connection to Ascension. I don't want you hanging around the Falklands if there's another invasion on its way," he ordered.

"I promise," she murmured softly. With a long kiss and an extended embrace, they finally parted with a call from one of the staff that the transport to the airport was ready. She took one final look over her shoulder. "Stay safe, my darling," she whispered.

A group of three men came from a door marked *private*, unsmiling and wearing dark suits. One man opened the main door to the embassy, another walked to the Jaguar that was waiting outside and opened a rear door, watching his surroundings constantly. The third man ushered Claire from the embassy and into the car, squeezing her into the middle of the rear seat as he and his colleague took seats each side of her. Flanked by two unmarked saloon cars, The Jaguar left the embassy grounds as unobtrusively as possible and took the road towards the airport.

Exhausted, Rupert and Chris finally returned to their apartment, discussing the day's events as they relaxed over a cold bottle of Quilmes.

"I'd better report to Peters and keep him up to speed on what has happened here."

He had contacted Peters earlier to give him a brief update, but now he moved towards the secure wardrobe, lifted the secret panel out and sent a longer and more detailed report to London on the Sat Phone. Once he had finished, he concentrated on the job in hand.

"So what do we do tomorrow, report in to the office as normal?"

"It is the only thing we can do," Rupert answered. "I particularly want to see what reaction we get from Siobhan when we waltz in."

"Yeah and that little shit Alex. I can't wait to see the look on his face when we walk in unharmed," he finished, grinning. "I've got a score to settle with him. What do you think HBJ head office in London will say?"

"Well, despite the Home Office putting us in here, HBJ are still in it for the money, so I suppose, providing it is safe for us, we'll stay on until they find replacements. We're out of the main story now, and our job is done. Of course our security guys might take a different view, but as you are effectively my bodyguard." He smiled. "I guess you'll have to stay too."

At this, Chris raised his bottle in salute and declared that he was off to bed. It had been a long day after a sleepless night, and the action and tension had exhausted them both. But before Chris let himself fully relax, he called the hospital in Rosario to see if there was any news on Sophie's condition. He was told that she was stable and comfortable, sleeping after the operation to clean and stitch the wound.

"Don't worry, there are guards on the door from the embassy. She is in good hands and I expect they'll airlift her home as soon as she's fit to travel," Rupert reassured him.

Boston

In the offices of USE Oil, Kelly was being briefed by Phillips on the latest developments for the invasion force.

"Well, what news? Let it be good," Kelly rasped.

"It is; they cleared the estuary some hours ago and they're steaming at full speed across the southern Atlantic. Calm waters and clear conditions are making it easy for them. The two cargo ships are running a parallel course some way in front, ready to dock ahead of the cruise liner. The Argies have launched their two subs, which are heading in on another innocent-looking course, so it's all going to plan."

"What about our boats?"

"A tanker is headed there, well underway, fully stocked with men and hardware. Two more fishing boats will hit the islands near O'Driscoll's farmhouse to reinforce the FARC force there. It is all coming together."

"What about Brad and his guys? Did they catch our snooping friends? We should have heard by now if they had found 'em. Claimed to be French, didn't they?"

"They did, but no news. But you know it is a long way; no radio works down there and MREC have not reported a sighting of Brett or Adams at the offices of HBJ. But most importantly, no signals of displeasure or concern from the Brits towards the Argie government. And what can they do now, anyway? They can't stop an invasion on a whim, and they've got eight hundred or so men against five and a half thousand trained soldiers with armour and field guns. Also our contacts in the UK have reported no unusual dock movement of troops. The usual flights from Brize Norton to the Ascensions, bunch of Herculeses flying in frozen pizzas and video games for the troops. No, they can't get there in time."

"Good. We'll take the islands, share the drilling rights. The Brits will be fucked. A fresh and invigorated IRA, a war in the Middle East and the loss of their precious territory. The Tories will be out on their ass in the next election and they'll be back to a Labour government dicking around with the People's Republic and fucked up industrial relations all over again. Political winter. Happy days."

At that point there was a knock at the office door and a secretary brought in a fax. Phillips took it, frowning.

"Well, tell me," Kelly demanded.

"I think... I think it's good news," Phillips hesitated. "There was a commotion at the British embassy and some staff flew up country to a provincial hospital to attend a victim of a road accident. Someone was shot up pretty bad, apparently."

"Good. Well done Brad. Anyone else involved? No doubt we will hear from him in due course."

"Yeah. Listen, I am just going to check out a few more details. I'll be back as soon as I hear anything, OK?"

Phillips left the office. Kelly grinned, span round in his chair and looked out over the river, chuckling to himself.

The Ascension Islands

Three massive C130s were circling RAF Ascension waiting for clearance to land, the runway clearly delineated against the surrounding red rocky landscape. The planes gradually descended, coming into land one after the other. They disgorged troops through the rear loading ramp, before being turned and refuelled for immediate take off as soon as the tanks had been replenished.

The troops stretched their legs, headed for the NAAFI and enjoyed the tropical sun after the miserable British winter. Some two hours later the aircraft were ready for take-off and the troops re-embarked for the final leg of their journey. The remaining flight time to the Falklands was approximately ten hours, which would give them time to settle in, arm themselves and set up defensive positions both in and around Stanley and other strategic points throughout the islands. Each plane could carry a hundred troops and forty five thousand pounds of hardware. More planes carrying light armour and artillery were already wheels up from RAF Brize Norton, with more to follow.

Buenos Aires

Chris had one last task to perform before he retired to bed. He checked to see if any movement or light could be detected from Siobhan's apartment, and found none. He and Rupert had looked up from their balcony to the floor above but with no success.

Eventually, needing a conclusive answer, Chris had stood on the railings of their balcony, reached up to grasp the base of the railings above and hauled himself onto Siobhan's balcony. Again silence reigned, and there was no glimmer of light. He peered in through the open window blinds and saw no movement and no sign of occupation. He played with the lock, and found it to be the same as the one securing their apartment below. It would be easy enough to pick. Satisfied, Chris returned to their apartment below, over-handing himself down to the railings and jumping forward onto the balcony. Rupert grinned at him, shaking his head.

"Friendly neighbourhood Spiderman. Well? Nothing I take it?"

"Nada. Just as you say. Which rather proves all our theories. Of course, she could be totally innocent and just staying away for the night with Maria or some other friend. But my money is on the traitorous, little bitch having done a bunk. She's probably in Colombia by now, or holed up somewhere safe with Maria's family."

Chapter Twenty-Nine

Buenos Aires

Rupert and Chris arrived at the offices of HBJ early the following morning. They wanted to understand what, if anything, had occurred or changed in their absence. They wanted to catch up on post – and more importantly catch up on post in other people's inboxes before they arrived. As they'd hoped, the office was deserted when they let themselves in through the outer doors. They went to their respective desks, and among other things Rupert saw the opened package containing the transmitter watches.

"Huh, looks like she got the message then. She'll be long gone. Doubt if we'll see her again. I wonder where she'll end up?"

"My money's on Colombia," Chris said.

They continued searching through the mail, seeing confirmation of the waterfront deal and some other major transactions in the offing. In short, the office was proving a success, and whatever else happened HBJ would not be disappointed with its fledgling enterprise in BA, Rupert surmised. The last desk they looked at belonged to Alex. Everything seemed to be in order until they tried to open a drawer to the desk which appeared locked. It took Chris about thirty seconds to pick it, and they were rewarded with a notebook containing a few interesting names and telephone numbers. Searching through, Chris found a name that he knew.

"Well, well, Valentina. So, my little beauty, you two do know each other," he grinned humourlessly.

"It appears that all our suspicions were well founded," Rupert observed. "Talking of which, I wonder how the Falklands are being prepared? Do you think a force will arrive in time to dissuade the Argies from landing?"

"Word is that troops are on the way and should be there soon," Chris answered. "The big problem is trying to let the Argies know that they're outnumbered or at least outgunned, and defeat is inevitable. They've worked up a head of steam, and getting over it is going to be their problem," he finished emphatically.

They heard the double doors opening from the outer reception area. Quickly, Chris closed the desk drawer but did not have time to lock it again. *Oh well,* he considered, *Alex will just have to think he was careless*

The two of them moved away quickly to the photocopier room and remained just out of sight to see who it was and what their actions would be. It turned out to be Maria. Unusually early, the reason soon became apparent. Dropping her handbag at the reception desk she moved straight to Siobhan's desk and unlocked a desk drawer, removing certain items that appeared to be of a personal nature including a notebook or diary. She flicked through it quickly before gathering all the items together, returning to her handbag and dropping the items inside. At that point Rupert deliberately started the photocopier whilst Chris kept Maria in sight. He smiled as she jumped, hearing his voice, loud over the machinery of the copier.

"Yeah, sure Rupert, will do, and…oh *buenos dias Maria, que pasa?*"

She jumped like a startled rabbit, turned at the sound of his voice and the photocopier, blushing with embarrassment under her tan. She put her hand to her chest in a gesture of shock.

"*Dios!* You made me jump! Did you have a good time over Christmas and at San Miguel?" she replied in Spanish.

Rupert then made an appearance, enjoying the show.

"Hi Maria, good to see you," he declared in his now excellent Spanish. The conversation followed the usual post-holiday banalities as Maria struggled to regain her composure and shock at seeing the two men so well, and clearly on good form. She was just back in balance when Rupert threw in an off putting question. "How is Siobhan? We called at her apartment last night when we got back, but no joy. Is she all right? Staying with you, we thought, mmm?

"No…er, she was, but I haven't seen her since yesterday when I left for home," she finished lamely.

"Ah, she's probably out on the town. A game girl, that one, burns the candle at both ends," Rupert responded, full of false bonhomie and switching to English idioms, confusing Maria still further.

"Yes, but burning the candle at both ends? What is this?" She struggled with the idiomatic expression.

"*Quemando la vela por ambos estremos,*" Chris translated for her. She nodded in understanding and excused herself to visit the toilet.

"Like a rabbit in the headlights! Today is going to be a lot of fun," Rupert said to Chris, who nodded and grinned in response. They both returned to their respective desks and pre- pared to catch up on their work. As the morning progressed, the best reaction of all came from Alex, whose facial expressions were a picture. Rupert brought him up to date, concluding with a final summary.

"So, all four of us travelled back together, but Sophie, Chris's girlfriend, had a spot of travel sickness so we stopped off at the hospital in Rosario."

"Chris's girlfriend? I didn't know you had a girlfriend or that she was going to be travelling with you," Alex said as the pieces started to fall into place from the intelligence he had been provided with by his colleagues in FARC.

"I'm a dark horse, mate," Chris responded suavely. "Picked her up along the way and charmed her into coming on holiday with us. You'd be dead jealous: brunette, about so high, great figure." He motioned curving his hands in an hourglass shape for the benefit of the audience.

"Is she British?" Alex asked.

Chris savoured his response, watching Alex very closely. As he spoke he could almost see the cogs turning in his brain. "Yes. Didn't I say? She works at the embassy as a junior attaché". Chris could not suppress a grin at the effect his words had on Alex, who struggled to master his emotions. Shortly afterwards Alex made an excuse to leave the office for a packet of cigarettes, and seemed to be gone for quite a while. Maria kept looking furtively at the door, as though expecting a dramatic entrance from some unexpected visitor any moment.

The telephone rang; she answered and put the call through to Rupert, informing him that it was Claire.

"Darling where are you?" he asked.

"Falklands. Bloody hell it's cold after BA!"

"I know, and it is summer there too. Still, it will prepare you for Blighty when you get back. When are you leaving?" he shouted, as the line was bad either from static or someone listening in.

"In about ten minutes. The transport has arrived and just

finished refuelling. Biggest bloody pane I've ever seen in my life. It dropped a whole bunch of Chris's mates off, too," she finished cryptically.

"Oh good, did they bring their own transport?"

"Yes, tons of the stuff, and more heavy vehicles to come soon, apparently."

Rupert knew that if they were being listened to it would certainly put the cat among the pigeons. "Good, take care and let me know when you get to the Ascensions; it will be a lot better there I am sure. Love you," he finished.

"Me too. I'll call, I have a stop over there and it is supposed to beautiful – and warm!"

The line cut off, and Rupert replaced the receiver and stared into space for a few seconds, thinking about Claire and his future with her. They had come a long way since they were reunited only a week or so ago. Rupert cursed to himself; he wanted to be assured that she was safe and on the next flight. Chris raised an inquisitive eyebrow. "Bloody phone lines from the Falklands," Rupert said. "Line went dead. But at least she got there safely. The next stage is the Ascensions and then on home in a couple of days."

"Don't worry, she'll be on her way in no time. I can contact Peters when we get back and find out how it's all going. Relax, she's in good hands," Chris finished, placing a hand on his shoulder squeezing in reassurance. Rupert looked up and smiled.

"No, you're right, better than being on a civvy flight. Come on, we need to get an update. Let's go and see Rafe."

They moved through to Rafe's office and sat down to discuss the latest market intel and the progress on the harbour deal. All the details had been ironed out and completion was to take place within days. Monies paid and the office would run at a serious profit. Two more deals had been put forward for consideration by foreign clients, both of which looked entirely plausible.

"So everyone is happy," Rafe commented, smiling.

"Yes, indeed – everyone except Siobhan. Is she ill?" Rupert asked.

"It is strange, yes, I don't know. She appeared a little fraught and, well…stressed, perhaps?"

"Never mind, we'll no doubt see her later at the apartment," he finished blandly. The meeting finished and Rupert picked up the phone to report back to HBJ's UK head office of. The conversation went well and the day progressed at a pace.

Later that morning Rupert had another embarrassing task to attend to: the return of the Land Cruiser for repairs.

He had made arrangements for the Toyota to be picked up from Rosario and returned to the dealership. The rental had been arranged through HBJ's London office and they needed everything to remain above board. Chris had thought it best for Rupert to visit the dealership and offer them some form of explanation, and Rupert had told the service department that they would need some repairs to the car and a courtesy car whilst it was being repaired. Rupert made up a story about being hijacked in Rosario by a group of armed thugs. The head of the service department expressed sympathy and said he was more than happy to oblige – until he accompanied Rupert outside and looked at the Land Cruiser.

"Madre de dios!" he shouted. "What have you done to this beautiful car?"

Rupert shrugged: "I think the people who hijacked it used it for target practice. One of them must have got in the way of a bullet, judging by the blood." The car was a write-off despite being only a few months old. The manager was angry and palmed Rupert off with a horrible little Toyota Carina Mark 11 as a replacement. The car was gutless, with only 73 bhp, and handled so badly he immediately nicknamed it The Boat. Upon returning to the office he told Chris what had happened and they both laughed as Rupert mimicked the little man who had been so horrified at the state of the Land Cruiser.

"Don't know what he's so worried about. You should see the state of some of the vehicles I have returned," Chris said.

"Well it's hardly James Bond, is it?" Rupert said. "I mean look at the bloody thing. Here we are, international men of mystery going around in a fucking shoebox on wheels." They made jokes about ejector seats and revolving number plates until they'd exhausted the subject.

Alex finally returned at lunchtime with a story about meeting some other agents, networking, discussing sites and deals, and Rupert just smiled benignly and let it wash over him. The was no point in making a fuss: a far bigger issue was about to surface. They hit the phones and the day moved swiftly on in a blur of frenetic activity. News of Rupert and Chris's return with promises of foreign interest in investment had spurred on everyone to try and tap into the money source. They left the office at about 7pm, but they were still not the last to leave; Alex was speaking into his Dictaphone as they left, but quickly picked up the phone and began dialling. Chris and Rupert noticed and exchanged a wry, complicit smile.

They waved a cheery good evening and left for the lift. The day had been good for the pair of them and they had quickly fallen back into their former roles: Rupert as the boss and Chris as the junior taking instructions. Yet, as Rupert had realised on the road, in any action or strategic planning Chris immediately took control and both men expected him to do so: it was a strange, capricious relationship, he mused.

They stopped for a beer on the way home down by the beach. Clinking the two bottles of Quilmes together, they quenched their thirst, and as he came up for air Chris commented; "Well she should be in the Ascension Islands now. Don't worry, she'll be fine," he reassured Rupert.

"I didn't say a word," Rupert said, as if denying that he had any care in the world.

"You didn't have to; you're thinking too loudly," Chris joked. "She'll be a lot safer there than on the Falklands," he mused. "I wonder how they are going to alert the potential invaders that the good guys have arrived in force?"

"I'd imagine we'll find out as soon as we're meant to, especially when they are made aware of the case. On that note, I think we should head back to the apartment so I can check on the satphone."

They finished their beers and strolled the half mile from the beach to their apartment building. They both looked up and saw that there appeared to be no sign of life from Siobhan's room. It was still daylight so it was still too early to need lights, but everything looked quiet.

"No sign of her, then. No great surprise, I guess," Rupert said. "My guess is that she is shacked up safely with Maria and her family, ready for a flit over to Colombia and her friends in FARC."

Chris snorted in response, but made no comment. They headed up the stairs, both men now too suspicious and wary to take the lift just in case. As a final measure of confirmation, they knocked on Siobhan's door, but as they suspected there was no answer. They returned to their apartment and the first thing Chris did was call the hospital in Rosario to check on Sophie. She was still under sedation, but he was told that all her vital signs were strong and they were likely to take her out of intensive care in the next day or so. Following the call he picked up the satphone. Upon receiving a reply he jerked upwards, shouting to Rupert.

"Quick," he said. "Turn on the TV."

Rupert scrambled for the remote and turned the TV to a news channel which, in line with most Latino commercial channels, was appalling; made up of dreadful commercials, over-dramatized events and weather forecasts presented by underdressed bimbos wearing little more than skin-tight clothes and a smile. The channel broke for a newsflash; a formal visit from a UK Foreign Office official to the Malvinas, showing the extra security and troop presence there. Apparently, according to the news, this coincided with extra-curricular Royal Marines Commando training exercises pertinent to other theatres of war not connected to the Middle East. The item mentioned that at least three Commandos (they called them Battalions) of Royal Marines and ancillary equipment, including armour, had been flown in for extensive testing and assessment prior to deployment in the Middle Eastern conflict.

Security, the report said, was on high alert given the readiness for operations in the Middle East, and the reporter hinted at the possibility of a Royal visit to inspect the troops in the near future. There were a couple of interviews with various Argentinian top brass, including the foreign minister and a general, who reacted with varying degrees of shock and anger at this obvious sabre rattling exercise by the British government. It represented, they said, deliberate antagonism towards the Argentine government and their rightful claim to the Malvinas.

"Well, and that answers our question for us. They don't seem very happy do they?" Rupert joked.

"It shows a strengthened position on our part, but they may well still be mad enough to attempt an invasion despite the odds. Three Commandos, that's about 2,400 troops, plus the men already there – our boys and the armoured units. That's a pretty substantial force, but is it enough to dissuade them from attempting an invasion? I hope to God it is," Chris declared. "Listen, I need to go out for a run; clear my head."

"You're keen, especially after a beer. I'm knackered after our first day back," Rupert declared, shaking his head at Chris's dedication, and he was also slightly puzzled: something didn't quite ring true, he thought. Chris left about ten minutes later, padding off into the evening. Rupert continued to watch the news, and was rewarded with a smaller item on the maiden voyage of the SS *Esmeralda*. She was, the report said, on her way to the Falklands as a sign of goodwill, despite the high-handed and antagonistic attitude of the British Government. Her passengers and crew were looking forward to being welcomed on the Malvinas. A short film clip showed some passengers being interviewed and saying how excited they were to be visiting the islands. They were, of course, all couples, Rupert saw, dressed in civvies; big smiles, all grins and high spirits. It was a perfect PR exercise, of course, but it left the possibility of the invasion proceeding. Rupert hoped to God that Claire was safe on the Ascension islands.

Sometime later Chris returned from his run, looking hardly out of breath, despite the dry, evening heat. He had soaked his running singlet but still looked fresh. Beginning his stretching routine, Rupert filled him in on the last news item, which made him pause in his routine.

"Really?" he said, and resumed his exercises. Rupert finished his summary and added his concerns. All Chris did was murmur to no real effect. Then, instead of finishing with a Wing Chun routine or work on the heavy bag, he towelled off and walked past Rupert to the wardrobe. As he passed, Rupert caught a whiff of that odd smell again, the same smell that he noticed before their trip to the Falklands. Before he could comment, Chris opened the secret compartment and withdrew all the equipment, including the guns. He took them to the table, spread out a sheet of newspaper and proceeded to strip and clean them. Finally happy, he reassembled them.

"Shame we didn't get that Browning back off Siobhan: It wouldn't surprise me if the bitch has taken it with her. I'm off to check her apartment now that it's dark." He pulled a set of lock picks out of his bag and set off up the stairs, returning some ten minutes later.

"Yep, all cleaned out, she's gone for good. Not a real surprise though, is it? Now I want you to pack a small bag. The small rucksack you have been running with will do," he said, pointing to the small, black rucksack Rupert had been using to build up his stamina by filling it with full, plastic water bottles. Rupert was puzzled.

"What for, and more importantly, what with?"

"Emergency precaution, probably overreacting, but better ready than not. Passport, money, change of clothes, razor, stuff like that and here," he said, passing the Smith and Wesson pistol. "Keep this on you now or at least put it in that bag. Just in case."

"Now you're starting to worry me. What's going on?" Rupert asked, genuinely concerned. It felt to him as though the game, whatever it was, had just been turned up about five notches.

"It may be nothing, but think about it: they have a military invasion planned; an armed escalation on disputed territory; we're known to be the enemy – or at least their agents. We have no political immunity and we're targets for more than one hostile faction. One of which happens to be the secret service of our host nation. Sleep well!"

"Shit! You certainly know how to reassure a chap."

Chris laughed mirthlessly. "Yeah, welcome to my world. Don't worry, I've been in worse shit than this. We'll be fine, but we just need to be prepared for every eventuality."

Rupert packed his bag, and put it into the wardrobe along with Chris's sack. They retired to bed, ready for whatever the next day may bring.

Chapter Thirty

The following day was an anti-climax for Rupert. From Chris's dire warnings he had expected the world to end. Instead he started his day with a run in the park, a shower and then they went straight to the office to finalise two more deals. One of these was the second phase of the Waterfront development, which another UK fund wanted a slice of. At two hundred and fifty million dollars it was a huge capital investment, and given that the project was still two years from completion and the groundwork had only just begun, it showed a level of positivity and commitment that would forge a sense of optimism and send prices upwards. But the rewards were substantial for savvy investors, showing a healthy twenty-five percent profit on cost, with huge overrun contingencies which if not used could see it return up to thirty percent.

Rupert was delighted with the prospect of completing a project and bringing in record fees, despite his nagging doubts concerning their future in BA. He revelled in the glory of doing heady deals while he could, and it made him realise that above anything else – above the danger, the thrill of combat, the excitement of playing spies with Chris – what really drove him was the thrill of the deal, a kill in a sense he fully understood.

It was a satisfying thought, and it reassured him that when this was all over, what he wanted more than anything else was to see Claire again in more stable circumstances.

He grinned at this epiphany, shaking his head at his own cupidity. His thoughts were interrupted by the telephone.

"Brett."

"Darling, it's me."

"Claire! How are you? Did you get the hell out of Dodge? Where are you?"

"I'm in one of the most beautiful spots on Earth – the Ascensions. It is so lovely. We must come back together."

"So you're safe? I am so relieved. How long are you there for? Was everything OK on the Falklands?" his voice was strained, there was so much he wanted to tell her.

"Yes, but I've never seen a place so busy. Those massive aircraft were constantly flying in and out, and I've never seen so many soldiers and so much equipment: they even had tanks and field guns. Everything was crazy. The..." The line suddenly went dead.

"Hello, Claire? Fuck it!" he exclaimed harshly, his voice carrying through the open door of the glass partitioned office. The others looked up at his outburst. "What is wrong with the bloody phones in this country?" he asked.

The others smiled and shrugged, except Chris, who was obviously thinking rather more sinister thoughts. He came through to Rupert's office, where he was out of earshot of the others.

"Funny how it got cut off when she's about to say more about the Falklands – and I guess, the military build-up. Bear in mind what I said last night. That cruise ship will be there or near there very soon," he finished quietly.

In response, Rupert just raised his eyebrows.

The day seemed to go on forever, or so it seemed to Rupert. The hours crawled by and he realised he probably wasn't going to hear from Claire again that day. He hoped she was in the air somewhere, perhaps in the back of a Hercules, lumbering home across the world to RAF Brize Norton. Later that afternoon the two of them left the office and went back to the apartment, stopping off at the local branch of the hire car company they'd used in Rosario to drop off the Range Rover and fighting through the rush hour traffic in the Carina, which lacked the benefit of air conditioning.

They both changed into running gear and set off for a gentle four mile run to loosen up after a tense day. They came back hot and sweaty but feeling better. Chris flung open the balcony doors to the gentle evening murmur of traffic. They preferred it to the dry air-conditioning and the balmy sea air wafted in, creating a calmer atmosphere. The breeze blowing in from the ocean cooled them down as they sipped cold drinks on the balcony. Going in first, Chris flicked on the TV to the national news channel, keen to see if anything more had emerged about the Falklands. By his calculations, the ships should be there any time soon. He was not to be disappointed.

"Rupert, come and look at this!" he called. Rupert came in off the balcony in time to see a news item announcing that the huge cruise ship that they had seen sail away from Argentina a couple of days ago had been turned away from the Falklands. The official reason given was that the British Commission understood that there was a bad case of influenza aboard the ship and they could not take any chances of an infection taking hold on the islands, where the hospital was small and the resources limited. They ship would need to return to Buenos Aires and remain offshore for a quarantine period of at least two weeks to ensure all cases were cleared. The cruise ship captain denied this, but to no avail, and in the background of the report Chris and Rupert saw large numbers of British soldiers on the harbour side and a large C130 transport plane descending for landing with what looked like a dozen more on the apron to the side of the runway.

Chris and Rupert turned, grinning at each other, clinking their glasses and whooping in excitement. "Gotcha!" Chris said. "Whose divine inspiration was it to come up with that excuse, I wonder?"

"Well, if they can't land, they can't invade. What about the freighters?" Rupert asked.

"They'll probably turn back without any fanfare. It's the troops on the ground in numbers that would have made the difference, and they aren't going to be there now. It also means that when it gets there HMS *Endeavour* will have a legitimate excuse to police the boundaries and keep any unaccountable ships away from the place. Anyway, that's the only deep water port; anywhere else they would have to come in on the small loading boats from way out, and they'd be easily stopped. They'll have troops all over the island watching for any invasion – especially my boys."

"We did it, Chris, we stopped it. Makes it so much more worthwhile knowing we were successful. I am glad Claire is out of it. We just need to get Sophie on the mend and we can all go back to normal. Have you heard anything today?"

"Yeah, I called the hospital," Chris responded rather diffidently. "She's regained consciousness and seems to be on the mend. They'll get her out and we can concentrate on the job in hand. Worry over," he finished. Rupert smiled to himself, wondering how a relationship between a tough SAS soldier and hardened spook would pan out.

They showered, and as the evening darkness closed in they settled to a light meal in front of the news. The programme was interrupted by the ring of the telephone. Chris jumped up to answer it, hoping it would be Sophie.

"Adams?"

"Get out now!" A woman's voice. Valentina. The line went dead. Chris's military training overrode all conscious thought.

There was no dithering. The switch just flicked and Chris's mind went straight into active mode.

"Rupert, get ready to go – immediately. No questions, just grab your sack from the wardrobe. Food, water, we're off." Rupert's face was a picture. One minute they had been celebrating a great success, the next they were preparing for a hasty departure. However, in the short time he had been with Chris, Rupert knew that everything was being done for a good reason, so he buttoned his lip and moved quickly.

Chris flicked shut all the new locks he had fitted to the outer door at the beginning of their stay, glad that he had prepared well, not only with the locks but extra hinges. Next, moving swiftly around the apartment he switched off all the lights bar two small table lamps. He quickly changed into his running shoes, grabbing his own emergency bag and retrieving all the equipment from the bottom of the wardrobe, placing everything in the leather holdall in which it had all arrived.

"Right let's go," Chris ordered.

"Wait, let's make it look a little more realistic."

"What?" Chris demanded. Rupert for once, ignored him, grabbing a pad and a pen and scribbling fast.

Rupert,
See you tomorrow. Off to see Sophie, have a good time.
Chris

He left the note in full view on the main table. He smiled to himself at this flourish and indeed so did Chris. "OK, now let's hustle."

Chris moved quickly towards the balcony, a puzzled Rupert following him, eyeing the coil of nylon rope in his hand. They were in time to see two cars and a dark van jolt to a halt in front of the apartment block. Rupert looked over the edge to the street below two storeys down.

"Shit, how can we escape down there now? They are bound to see us or have a guard at the bottom."

"We're not going down. We're going up." Chris said, pointing towards Siobhan's balcony. Quick as you can, follow me."

"What?"

"No time to argue. When I get up, pass me the rope, I'll pull up the bags up, you follow."

Chris looped the handles of the bags and knotted them securely, then stood on one of the chairs and balanced on the balcony rail, using the wall for support. He repeated his manoeuvre of the previous evening, reaching up and grabbing the upright rails of the balcony above, hoisting himself in a perfect curl, securing a foot hold and then manhandling himself up and over the railings. He made it look easy, like a gym exercise on bars. He quietly motioned for Rupert to sling up the rope, which he did. Chris caught it deftly and hauled up the bags.

"Come on, quickly," he whispered. "Push the balcony doors to. The lock is shot open, so it will wedge closed."

Rupert complied, looked down and then up. *Not in my job description*, he thought. His palms were sweaty with the heat and fear. He proceeded to follow Chris by standing on the chair and then on to the balcony rail. *Shit*, he thought, peering through the darkness to the streets below, *I can't do this.* "Come on, Brett," he muttered to himself.

From beyond the doors he heard the sound of a raised voice shouting; "*La policia, se abren, se abren.*"

He jumped and nearly fell. "Come on," Chris whispered urgently. "You only have a minute. The door won't hold any longer."

They heard two thuds. The police were kicking at the door in the expectation that it would splinter like all normal apartment doors would under heavy assault. Rupert came alive and reached upwards, his hands grasping the metal railings above him. But his palms were sweaty, and as they took his weight his hold began to slip. He watched in horror, gripping with all his might but to no avail.

A hand wrapped itself around his wrist so tightly he nearly shouted at the pressure. He looked up to see Chris's arm thrust through the balcony railings, muscles and sinews writhing like snakes as he took the whole of Rupert's body weight on one arm. The tension showed on his face as the weight bore down against the metal. Chris pulled using his other arm as a fulcrum and slowly, inexorably, he brought Rupert up higher, the muscles in his arm popping and swelling with the effort, allowing Rupert to renew his grip and swing his legs up for support. Finally, the weight was removed as Rupert secured his purchase and at that moment the door below gave way with a screech of splintering wood. Hard footsteps were heard as the intruders' boots thudded across the tiled floor

Above, Chris helped Rupert over the railings, motioning with a finger to his lips for silence and bundling him into Siobhan's apartment, silently closing the double doors to the balcony. "Watch your footsteps," he hissed in Rupert's ear. Rupert nodded in response, and they sat quietly, recovering from the strain of the climb and the stress of nearly being captured. Listening with bated breath to the commotion below, they heard loud voices, crashing furniture and overturning tables. Nothing seemed to be spared. The balcony doors below crashed open and footsteps thudded as one of the intruders looked first down then up. He shouted *"Nada."*

Then one of them found Rupert's note. They heard in Spanish. "One is going to his bitch, the embassy woman, so he will be on the road to Rosario. The other is out and will probably be back later. Close it down. Now, restore order here. We will return tonight. We get him and trap the other one. *Vamanos.*"

Rupert gave the thumbs up to Chris who nodded with a wry smile. "We let them leave, give them about half an hour then we slip down unnoticed – hopefully," Chris whispered.

They heard the vans and cars drive off, and the normal evening sounds returned: music, loud voices, cars honking and noise from the street. They knew nowhere was ever quiet in BA. The noise would help mask their descent

For what seemed like an eternity, the Chris and Rupert waited. Finally Chris signalled Rupert to move. He had wondered whether to put some music on, gambling that they did not know of Siobhan's departure, but decided that it wasn't worth the risk. Chris explained quietly what they would do. The rope was not long enough to reach the ground and give a slip knot to retrieve it but it was long enough to bypass their floor and get to the next balcony below quietly, which they did. The rest was easy and they soon found themselves standing at the side of their building in shadows, complete with their kits and the holdall

"Where to now? The Boat?" Rupert asked, referring to the Toyota Carina.

"No, they'll be watching the underground car park. Don't worry I have another plan, one I think you'll like. We're going for a little walk."

Chris marched off down a side street, and after several twists and turns, they ended up in a slightly less salubrious part of the city, underneath a flyover where there were a number of small workshops, built using the structure above as a framework to house the units. He stopped at a scruffy looking unit with a roller shutter door, bearing the legend *Los motores de Frank*. He undid the padlock on the small pedestrian door that was built into the shutter and stepped inside with Rupert following. As soon as Rupert entered, his nostrils were assailed by a familiar smell: a mixture of engine oil, grease and other garage smells. He saw various cars in the place, along with ramps and tools – in fact everything a garage should have. He snapped his fingers.

"That's it. That's what I could smell on you. So this is where you were."

Chris smiled enigmatically. "I always like to have a back-up plan," he said

Chris was standing in front of a car covered with a light tarp. With a flourish he pulled back the cover to reveal a dull, faded green car with rust spots; it looked generally unkempt but it was the car in every petrol-head's top ten; a Ford Mustang 390 fastback. The car made famous in the film *Bullitt*

"Bloody hell. Steve McQueen eat your heart out!" Rupert exclaimed. "Look at this beauty. Where did you find it?"

"There are hundreds of them down here, all exported from the US, in fact some were even made down here under licence. You can pick them up for buttons."

"Does it go?"

"Yep, this is where I've been most evenings, working on it. I left it looking shabby but worked on the engine, brakes, suspension and so forth. A real wolf in sheep's clothing. I had the side windows blacked out for more privacy, and it's got a 4.2 litre turbo lump in there. Come on, there's no time to waste. We need to get going and I'll answer all your questions once we're moving. Roll up the doors and I'll pull her out."

With that, Chris unlocked the car, threw the bags in the back and started it up. At the turn of the key he was rewarded with a roar as the engine burst into life, dropping to a throaty burble as the revs dropped to a tick over. He eased the car forwards through the narrow gap offered by the raised roller shutter door and onto the quiet side street. Rupert lowered the shutter using the side chains, secured the pedestrian door and climbed into the waiting Mustang. The inside, he noticed, appeared just as shabby as the outside, and it smelled musty, a heady mixture of petrol, oil and old leather.

"Lights are good," he commented as they pulled slowly away trying to attract as little attention as the car would allow.

"Yeah, I upgraded the bulbs and put a direct feed in. Two more main spots on the front too, it'll help with the country roads."

"Talking of which, what the fuck is going on and where exactly are we going?"

"Well first off that was Valentina on the phone warning me, I'm ninety nine percent certain."

"Valentina?"

"Yes, I was rather surprised too. Despite everything, I think in her own strange way she quite liked me and was genuinely upset when we split up. There was something in her eyes, more than just the casual fling sort of look. I don't think she is an out-and-out spy. Yes, she loves her country and maybe it has something to do with her old man being a former general. I don't know, but in any event, I'm glad. We would have been caught with our pants down and no mistake. Sometimes you just get a lucky break, and the way we have been going, I think we deserved one."

"You're right, even with your extra locks on the doors – which initially weren't even shut by the way – we would never have had time to climb up, only down, and that way we would have ended up in a firefight with the bad guys: not good!" Rupert exclaimed.

"Tell me about it."

"So where the hell are we going? The embassy? Kieko's, Paraguay, Uruguay, that's the closest, just across the river?"

"Not the embassy. Remember we're only UK citizens and we could be considered to have broken the law: shooting people and causing death by dangerous driving will do that. No, it would cause a major incident and one that the UK government would ultimately have to concede. We would never get to the airport and I for one do not want to spend any time in an Argie jail, especially being British. Do you?"

Rupert shook his head vehemently and rolled his eyes; "Er, no."

"Right, just as I thought. So no to Kieko's. They're civilians and I wouldn't want to bring a shitstorm down on him. Also – well, he is Argentinian and he may turn all patriotic on us, you never know…" Chris left the statement hanging there. "Paraguay, they'd be expecting that, especially as we have been that way before and it is an obvious escape route. You can bet that the borders will be tight as a duck's arse now – especially Uruguay. Sure it looks easy to just pop across the river, but it's also really easy to seal off in an emergency.

No, we are heading for Argentina's old enemy, Chile. It's a huge, porous border and I have a few friends there waiting for us at an LZ. We can use the satphone to liaise once we get close and find a good spot. We'll head straight out on the 188 then peel off at Junin and take Route 7 all the way to Mendoza. Longer but much safer, and I'm hoping that we will have a few hours start before they realise that they have been fooled. Probably until say, 7am tomorrow, so about eight hours or so if our luck holds."

"Have we got a map in here?" Rupert asked. "Also this beast will guzzle gas, which means a lot of stops, and we might be seen."

"First off, look in my bag on the back seat, there's map in there folded up in the side pocket."

Rupert reached back over the seat whilst Chris drove steadily out of the city, keeping to the speed limits and heading west. Reaching into the back, all he could find was a folded piece of material.

"Is this it? It feels like silk."

Chris smiled. "It is. On all ops – and I class this as one – we are always trained to have an escape route that includes a map of all the areas needed, including details of the specific area of crossing. It's always on silk: virtually indestructible, difficult to burn or tear, won't run, easy to hide, folds up small: it's perfect. Now look at Route 7, follow it to the mountain pass beyond Las Cuevas at Cristo Redentor, and that's the official border crossing. Very mountainous, easy to hide, lots of places to cross illegally. As to fuel, I've got spare jerry cans in the back, which should get us there without stopping. We're all set. We've got our own food and water in bottles, so we are good to go."

Rupert shook his head in amazement. *Some prior planning,* he thought.

"So, how and when did you get this?" he asked, tapping the dashboard.

"Well, I took myself off one evening and scouted around; there are always places like Frank's, usually near bridges in every big city. Money talks. He was amenable, sold me the car for not very much and let me do it up when I could. I spun a yarn about sending it back to the UK as they were rare there and, well here we are. It's all paid for; I'll get it back from Regiment funds.

"Matey, I will happily pay for it myself if it gets us out of here in one piece."

"Our main problem is going to be at the border crossing. I know from experience that they will ask for insurance and ownership papers, although hopefully that will not be a problem."

"Where exactly are we going to cross?" Rupert asked, tentatively dreading the answer and knowing that it would not be straightforward if he knew Chris at all

"High up in the Andes, as I said. There is a famous statue up there marking the lasting friendship between Argentina and Chile: *Cristo Redentor de los Andes,* the statue of Christ the Redeemer. Well that's what it's supposed to represent anyway. In reality they're still not the best of mates, as you know, especially on the polo field.

"Anyway, we'll leave the main R7 just before passport control and head up to this statue. And literally one step is Argentina, the next we'll be in Chile. I've heard of tourists just walking across; the problem occurs with taking cars. I'll have a chopper ready to pick us up on the Chilean side and bang, we're gone. We can land at an airport all legal, let them see our passports and we're off back home care of HM Government. All we have to do is get there safely," this last part was said with a wry grin directed at Rupert.

"Yeah, I know your simple solutions, I won't even start to list the chapter of events that got us to this point…" he tailed off with more than a little emphasis as the car left the outskirts of Buenos Aires and picked up speed as they drove off into the night.

CHAPTER THIRTY-ONE

Boston

The same joyful feeling of relief and escape was not shared at the offices of USE Oil, where Phillips was listening to a tirade from Kelly, who was incandescent with rage. He ranted about the lost opportunity, the incompetence of the Argies, the group he'd sent after Chris and Rupert and any other available target on which he could vent his spleen. He fixated on the money he'd lost, both to the IRA and in terms of the cost of armament for the Argentinians. He was now bent on revenge and wanted someone's head on a pike. Brad and his three colleagues were all dead at the scene of the accident. The fact that he had managed to put down fire and hit one of the opposition before he'd been killed did nothing to assuage of feelings. So he turned his focus to the other potential targets.

"How did they miss them, those two fucking Limey surveyors? I thought they hit them late at night. Where the fuck are they? Why haven't they sealed up the country? I want them found and whacked. Hell, I'll even fly down there myself and do it old style with a baseball bat. Fuck them!" he screamed finally. "And what about the girl?"

When the shouting had finally stopped, Phillips ventured a reply. "She's still in hospital in Rosario, under diplomatic guard. We can't touch her. They think the soldier-surveyor is on his way to her now. It's hard to…"

"No not that one. The other one, the one that flew his god-damn girlfriend in for a holiday or something. She was one of the four in the car watching the base. Where the fuck is she?" He cried. "Find her and wipe her out. See how her goddamn boyfriend feels then, yeah?"

"I think she might have left the country. A special plane was chartered out of BA to the Falklands and she could have been put on any number of the flights that are going from there to Ascension and then England. My guess is she'll be safely back in the UK by now and I don't think she was anything more than Brett's girlfriend. I had MREC check her out. She's a surveyor, works in London, never been abroad for more than a couple of weeks holiday. She's clean."

"Yeah? That was what they said about the other two, and look what happened. The one that took out your team in BA single-handedly is probably Sas." He pronounced it as a word, the way the Northern Irish did. "Right, no excuses; O'Driscoll or one of his mates can earn their money. I want a hit on the girlfriend. I want them to pay. If we can't get at the hard men, we'll make them suffer the same kind of pain I'm feeling right now. Find out who she is, where she is, and sort it. No fuck ups, OK?"

Phillips nodded in acquiescence, but inside he was less than certain about the idea. He wasn't squeamish, he'd done this before, but the thought of taking out an innocent woman just for revenge didn't sit well with him. He also knew it could bring the hounds of hell down on them if they took out soft civilian targets like that. He shrugged, realising that Kelly wouldn't see sense just now. Best just to get onto the Quartermaster in Ireland and put it into place. But he did not like it at all; Kelly was losing it, becoming a loose cannon and there was little if anything more dangerous than a powerful man in a fit of rage. Never make dangerous decisions in haste, that was Phillips' motto.

He placed a call to Northern Ireland via his contact at MREC in Argentina. If anything, they were even more angry than Kelly. They relished the idea of helping and were not at all squeamish about retribution. Phillips shook his head in disgust, but orders were orders and he was pretty angry himself about the whole operation going south.

Two calls later, he had the information he needed about Claire and passed it on to the Quartermaster, who took it in his stride, remaining as noncommittal as he could, given the guarded nature of the conversation. The plans were set in motion and Phillips hung up with a sigh.

London

The telephones at MI6 were ringing off the hook, and Johnston and the team were celebrating. It could have all gone wrong and he could have ended up with a huge amount of egg on his face, he considered. Even Peters had congratulated him on his strategy and for putting his career on the line by authorising the immediate departure of troops to the Falklands. In short, everything had been a success. All that was left was for Brett and Adams to return home safely.

He was annoyed about Siobhan Clifford, but he felt slightly vindicated in his suspicions of her loyalty and at least she wouldn't put anyone else in danger with her traitorous actions. The two men had had a lucky escape there, he mused, but luck was always half the battle in their game. His thoughts turned to Napoleon's philosophy on lucky generals, but the shrill ring of the telephone cut in on his thoughts.

"Johnston." It was Paul Carter, MI5 head of operations in Northern Ireland. After the usual exchange of pleasantries Carter cut to the chase.

"We may – or rather you may – have a problem about to arrive on your doorstep. We've been monitoring operations with the Quartermaster, as you know." He paused for acknowledgement of inter service relations.

"Indeed and it is much appreciated, passing us the intel. I'm grateful," Johnston tugged the appropriate metaphorical forelock. "But why the urgency, is something wrong?"

"Yes, we believe so. You are of course aware that we've been monitoring the calls and transmissions of the Quartermaster and his band of merry men. Well, he had an interesting one from the US earlier, and I believe despite the guarded nature of the call that they are ordering a hit on someone with an address to be supplied. We do know that it is on the UK mainland, probably in London."

"I see. Any more info? Who was the call from in the US?"

"It was a Boston exchange; GCHQ tracked it with the help of our American cousins. Somewhere in central Boston."

Johnston jumped in, cutting Carter short. "Are you sure it was Boston?"

"Positive. Secondly, from the transcript of the conversation I don't think it's a military target. Something a little more circumspect, I feel."

"We are watching one or two at the moment; but the Boston angle gives me cause for concern. Can you fax me a copy of the transcript please?"

"Certainly. It will be with you shortly."

"Thank you Paul, it's much appreciated."

There was the hint of satisfaction from Carter. "Not at all old chap, glad to be of service."

Johnston ruminated, steepling his fingers as he gazed out

over the Thames on another grey day in January. He could not quite believe what his mind was telling him. They were going after Rupert's girlfriend, Claire Sewell. Would they really do that? Just to get their own back? Someone over the puddle has gone rogue, he thought.

The mopping up operation in the Falklands had gone well and only one member of the group was missing: O'Driscoll. Somehow, using native cunning or sixth sense, he had avoided capture and disappeared. There had been two ambushes by the SAS, one of which had ended in a brief firefight, but he was not accounted for in any of these groups. All the others, including two more PIRA members, had been rounded up and arrested. It was anyone's guess whether he was still on the islands. Perhaps he'd escaped on a friendly trawler and was on his way to Columbia or Argentina. It was not only irritating but a dangerous loose end. Even more so with the intelligence Johnston had just received.

He considered his alternatives for a few minutes, then he picked up the telephone, decision made.

Chapter Thirty-Two

Argentina

The first few hours along Route 7 to Junin had gone well,
After eight hours' driving through the night they were
about half way to their destination, and the morning light was
breaking across a surreal landscape of stark contrasts, rolling hills
and spectral trees that stretched their shadows out towards them.

Chris had taken a break from driving four hours previously,
and after dozing in the passenger seat he woke feeling refreshed
and ready to take over his shift. He cranked up the seat of the
Mustang, rubbing his eyes in the dawn light. The sun was rising
over rolling hills behind them, sending arrows of red and gold
through to the far horizon in front.

"Where are we?" He asked

"Just coming up to Vicuna MacKenna," Rupert answered.
"We're about halfway there, according to the map. We'll pull
over to refuel soon. We're below a quarter and I don't trust the
gauge."

The flat landscape came into focus more clearly as the sun rose
higher. Small copses of trees lined the road at sporadic intervals,

and Rupert pulled over by the side of one. The dirt track layby served them well. They refuelled using two jerry cans, and forty litres later, they were on their way again with Chris driving.

"This map is amazing, who would have thought of silk?" Rupert commented.

"Yeah, it works well, and if the Japanese Samurai could make effective armour out of it, why not a humble map?"

"They made armour from silk?"

"They did, yes. They laminated it, stiffened it and hey presto, proof against arrows and even bullets when guns took over from arrows as the weapon of choice. Amazing really, but it works, I've seen tests done."

They continued their conversation on weapons and tactics, passing the journey in companionable conversation, and for the moment, the danger of their predicament faded. They were constantly observant – especially Chris, who felt that either through roadblocks or air support they would be lucky to avoid some form of chase. Too much had been thwarted; too many egos had been crushed and opportunities lost.

They carried on along Route 7, nearing Lujan de Cuyo at the foot of the Andes. They had been travelling for about 11 hours and there was still no sign of anyone following them. Chris's level of worry was growing, although he'd seen no perceptible threat from the Argentinian security forces. Sometimes he though the'd sooner have his enemy in plain sight than imagine they were there.

London

Claire had returned to a wet, cold English January. The grey of the London skies was made worse by the fact that she had just left the balmy warmth of Argentina and the Ascension Islands, arriving from thirty degree heat to that typical British dampness; that marrow-chilling cold that hovers just above freezing point, refusing to turn the rain to snow and at least make the place look pretty. The constant grey skies and drizzle were already making her depressed and she had only been back two days. Instead of moping around the flat, she had gone straight back to work, throwing herself into the next deal. Anything, she thought, rather than sitting there twiddling her thumbs and thinking of Rupert stuck in Argentina, not knowing when he would come home.

Fears for his safety were always at the forefront of her mind. Despite his protestations that all was well and that nothing would happen now that it was all over and they were back in the relative safety of BA, she had seen the news reports on the Falklands, she had heard all the reports that the islands were safe. She was not naive enough to believe that the Argentinians, the Americans, the IRA or whoever was behind it all were just going to roll over and play dead,

Damn it, she thought, *I love the stupid bastard and I want him home with me.*

It was Friday and she left the office unusually late. Normally Friday was a poets day, but she had nothing really to go home to. There might be a few local friends in the Ladbroke Arms – no one too close to be nosy, just some people to share a companionable drink with before heading home to their flat. In fact, she thought, if it was quiet, she'd head home to Gloucestershire for the weekend, walk the dogs and see her parents. The awful weather always seemed more bearable in the country.

She pulled the thick, grey worsted coat tightly around her, belting it at the waist and smiling as she put on the red beret she'd bought in Argentina. She had been so proud of it; it was a sign that she'd just come back from a holiday somewhere warm. The bright colour cheered her up on this dismal day.

Heading for the tube she picked up an Evening Standard, looking for any news from the Falklands and Argentina's response, but all the pages were filled with news of the Middle East and the war in Iraq, which was now a full-blown, bloody conflict.

Entering the tube, she struggled through the crowds of late commuters, all battling to get home at the end of a busy week. It was still pretty crowded so she didn't see that she was being followed. Her tail left the tube with her at Notting Hill, and followed at a distance, seeing her enter Ladbroke Street and walk on towards Wilby Mews.

If Claire had turned and looked, she would have seen a nondescript man with darkish red hair, hunched in a Donkey jacket against the weather – although it was nothing compared to the North Sea gales that hounded his native Belfast. He stooped as he walked, giving a deceptive idea as to his real height. He made no sound in the soft soled, work-style boots he wore. He merged with the passing flow of pedestrian traffic, completely innocuous. As he started to turn in under the archway of the terraced street he stopped, cupping his hands against the flare of a match and was rewarded with the first grey-white wisps of smoke of a newly lit cigarette.

Moving undercover to get himself out of the drizzle, he saw the woman in the red beret hesitate, then enter the Ladbroke Arms. He waited patiently, puffing on his cigarette for five minutes until he was sure that his prey was staying in the pub for at least a drink or two.

Satisfied, the man stubbed out his second cigarette and moved off around the back of the terrace, through the grounds of a nursing home, where he nodded to a colleague waiting in a dark Ford Escort. He counted down the numbers to the address he had been given. It was the work of a moment to vault the fence into the garden at the rear of Claire and Rupert's house.

The grounds were in complete darkness, curtains drawn against the foul evening. While the ground floor flat was protected with concertina bars, the upper windows were less well-secured. The small flat roof onto which the man pulled himself offered access to a sturdy drainpipe. He scaled this, overhanding himself, bracing carefully and quietly against the wall, and within a few seconds he was up onto the broad ledge of the first floor window. The lock on the window proved easy to overcome; a quick slide of a blade and it was released. The window slid up and he was in. The front window of the sitting room overlooking the street afforded a good view of the main entrance of the pub at the end of the road on the corner.

He watched carefully from the side of a partly drawn curtain. After an hour and a number of false starts, the figure in the grey coat and red beret finally appeared in the doorway of the pub. The frosted glass of a typical London boozer partially masked her, until she stepped out into the night, where he could see her more clearly in the dim light reflected from the mellow glow of the pub windows.

Across the street in the house opposite, the upper floor windows were also in darkness, but another set of eyes followed Claire as she left the pub. The watcher put a two-way radio to his ear.

"She's leaving the pub now and heading for her flat. Everything looks quiet, but stay alert. Douglas out."

Chapter Thirty-Three

Argentina

Chris and Rupert were making good time. They were about eleven hours into their journey, and they had just passed San Martin on a back road that was one of the larger settlements in the region of Lujan de Cuyo, the last significant town before the border crossing at Las Cuevas.

"We'll pull in here for some petrol," Chris said. "It's quiet enough and there's still no sign of the opposition. We're only about two hours from the border now, and we'll hide among the rest of the tourists and day traffic hoping to cross."

"Do you think it will be busy? I'm worried about the border guards; they're bound to have been put on alert for us now. Surely every potential border crossing will be aware of our possible escape," Rupert said.

"We'll get close, and if it's crowded, which apparently it can be, we'll take another route or just ditch the car and walk over. Don't worry, I have contingency plans and I've used this border before," Chris replied.

Rupert looked sceptical, but he had learned to trust Chris.

It was a measure of the soldier and the man, he considered, that hardly anything seemed to get to him, that he always stayed calm and reflective in any stressful situation. It was this quality, more than any sign of bravado, that instilled confidence, and Rupert was reassured that nothing bad would ever happen when he was around.

Chris, who by now had nearly two days growth of beard to match his dark hair and was speaking Spanish like a native, was taken as an Argentinian by pretty much everybody. So, no suspicion of foreigners would be aroused, even if a general alarm was raised in the area. They were at the foot of the Andes now, following a winding road that was getting higher and colder with each mile.

Their destination was nearly in sight, and a feeling of quiet confidence was beginning to settle over Rupert. A long switchback just outside Uspallata sent them still higher into the mountains, and they were less than eighteen miles from the border. Traffic was building up and they found themselves in the middle of a convoy of tourists, small lorries and local traffic. They were passed by the occasional large artic coming from the other direction, transporting goods from Chile. The mountain road was not the widest and at times it got a little too close for comfort; especially as Rupert was driving this last leg, so Chris could message his Regiment colleagues over in Chile.

They soon found themselves approaching Las Cuevas, a small town that lay just before the huge seven-kilometre tunnel that was burrowed through the mountainside from Argentina to Chile. The traffic started to slow as they approached passport control.

"From the looks of this, we're about two hours from getting through," Chris commented, having got out of the stationary Mustang to look up at the queue of traffic, shielding his eyes against the harsh sunlight. "But I don't like it. I feel very exposed and they seem to be taking an inordinate amount of time. They're being very thorough, which is unusual for Argies. It doesn't feel right."

Rupert looked around at the smooth, red rock sloping ever more steeply up from the road to the peaks, where huge glaciers and snow still clung to the hills. Rupert suddenly felt hemmed in and claustrophobic. There was nowhere to run; the mighty Andes seemed unwilling to let them leave the country they had thwarted. But to the left he noticed another road – if you could call it that. A dusty red track of gravel and broken tarmac led to a number of restaurants, including a rather inviting *Chocolateria Aconcahuac*, which looked like a mini Swiss chalet stuck on an Argentinian mountainside.

"Where does that go?" Rupert asked, pointing at the road.

"Up to the statue. The Christ the Redeemer monument at the top of the old pass they used before the tunnel was built," Chris replied. He looked at Rupert for a second, then made a decision. "Drive," he said. "I'll contact the guys over the border."

They peeled off down the bumpy road, setting off a plume of dust as they passed the blue and red chalet buildings that reminded Rupert of Legoland or Toytown. The road soon deteriorated into a red, rocky track of sandstone grit as they passed a signpost indicating that this was the way to the *Cristo Redentor* statue. Although they'd left the traffic at the border crossing, they weren't entirely alone. Tourists who wanted to see the statue and the odd adventurous driver were heading up to the top of the high pass into Chile.

"Well, here we go. The last leg," Chris said. "Better this than queuing in line like a stationary target for the next two hours."

"But won't it be the same when we get to the top of wherever we are going? I mean, the border is the border, isn't it?" Rupert queried.

"Don't worry, we'll be fine," Chris answered curtly, and for the first time Rupert detected a slight edge to his voice, betraying the tension that he clearly felt.

After about a mile the road took a series of hairpin turns, with a steep drop to one side, as the gradient grew more severe, cutting through the red rock of the mountains. Then, just as he thought it could not get any worse, the track began as a series of switchbacks every three to four hundred meters. Each sharp bend gave Rupert a stomach churning lurch as it corkscrewed through one hundred and eight degrees. The drop to the valley far below was a vertigo sufferer's nightmare. As the road led them ever upwards, the landscape became starker, and the gullies in the sandstone where the sun couldn't get to were rippled with streaks of dirty snow showing starkly against the red of the rock.

In one of the short straights between the hairpins, Rupert looked in his mirror and to his horror, he saw a decrepit Toyota trying to overtake him, with a yawning chasm opening to their right. The car screamed past, its gears whining, pulling in just in time to take a line before the bend, to the howl of engine revs and squealing brakes.

An hour later they arrived at the apex of the of the track, which levelled out onto a dusty plateau of the same red sandstone. It looked like a landscape from Mars. They parked the car alongside other tourist cars next to the customs house, a red building with a terrace at the front and a flagpole bearing an Argentinean flag which fluttered in the wind. There, at the base of a rock, stood the statute of Christ, mounted on a block of stark white marble, his hand raised, holding the eternal cross. Turning around, Rupert marvelled at the view.

"God, it feels as though we are standing on the top of the world up here: its surreal." He turned through three hundred and sixty degrees, admiring the stunning view. "The air is so clear," he declared.

"Yeah, its impressive. Now let's get the bags and get ready to roll. The chopper should be here soon. We need to work our way towards the border, so let's wander over and admire the statue. Just do the touristy thing and look casual."

Chris nodded at the two border guards, who wore large mirrored sunglasses and guns at their hips, posturing in the afternoon sunlight as they grinned at a couple of young female tourists.

Chris patted the bonnet of the Mustang. "Sorry to leave you, old girl. You've served us well." He smiled.

They turned like typical tourists, heading towards the statue. Rupert produced a small camera, and asked one of the girls to take a photo of Chris and himself posing in front of the edifice. The girl grinned and did so, and he photographed them in return. It was a little bizarre, Rupert thought. They were waiting on a knife edge, their lives in the balance, taking tourist photos.

They wandered casually across to the other side of the statue, the Chilean side, out of sight of the Argentinian customs guards. The guards were looking at the girls again as they walked back to their car. Chris and Rupert watched other tourists cross the border on foot, take photos and then return. A few of the tourists walked as far as the Chilean customs house some two hundred metres away, so they followed suit, gently working their way across no-man's-land towards the castellated structure on the Chilean side. No one raised a protest, there were no cries of anger, nothing.

Then it happened. The walkie-talkie at the waist one of the Argentinian border guards squawked. He broke off from checking the papers of a car trying to pass through the checkpoint. There was a sudden consternation; an urgency born of fear; clearly the word had got through; they had realised that this area, through whatever means, was the likely spot. Maybe Frank the garage owner had spilled the beans and identified the car; maybe it was a lucky guess. Either way, Chris and Rupert knew the game was up. The border guards pulled their guns from their holsters as they looked around for the suspects.

The two officials ordered everyone who was wandering around the monument and had drifted over the border to stop and return to the Argentinian side. They shouted in the direction of Chris and Rupert, demanding in Spanish that they stop and return to Argentina. Chris pretended not to understand, and waved, pointed to the Chilean guardhouse and nodded, walking towards it, feigning a misunderstanding. Chris and Rupert were within feet of the steps of the Chilean guardhouse and comparative safety. But then the Chilean officials also started to shout, asking what they were doing and ordering them to produce papers.

Then the first shots rang out. It would have represented a declaration of hostilities towards Chile, so the Argentinian guards shot their pistols up in the air, the 9mm rounds echoing off the mountains. Both Chris and Rupert instinctively ducked and span around to face the threat. They heard one of the tourist girls shriek with fear. Chris dropped the small rucksack he'd been carrying and dipped into the now open leather holdall which contained, amongst other things, the Diemaco rifle. He knew what he would face in an Argentinian prison.

At that moment, the steady beat of rotor blades sounded in the air and a grey blob appeared, rising up on the air currents from behind the mountains like a giant condor. The red stripes and crosses on the decals identified it as a Red Cross emergency rescue helicopter. Its forward trajectory halted abruptly as it slewed forward, nose up in a fast halt. It dropped quickly, its blue lights flashing from the side of the fuselage, the downdraught causing a whirl of dust and sharp gravel in a hundred metre spread.

The pilot had chosen to come into land over the rough rock and soil, rather than the helipad spot that was directly in front of the Chilean outpost. Everyone ducked instinctively, protecting their eyes to ward off the choking red dust and flying gravel. In the ensuing confusion Chris and Rupert ran towards the Chilean customs house, effectively shielded by the dropping helicopter from the vexed customs officials on the other side.

As the helicopter hovered inches from the ground, a figure gestured from the open door, shouting. "Chris, mate, come on!"

They needed no second beckoning. They ran forward, tossed the bags inside and threw themselves in after them, their feet landing on the running rails. As soon as the contact was made, the howl of the Westland Lynx's turbos split the air as the airframe strained, reeling backward and spinning through a hundred and eighty degrees to head back in the direction from which it had come. As soon as he realised that the escape was not a matter for the Red Cross, one of the Argentinian officials raised his pistol, aiming for the cockpit of the helicopter.

In response, the door gunner on the port side of the aircraft sent a straight line of machinegun fire straight across the front of the two men. Dust spurts sprouted in front of them, as the high velocity 12.7mm rounds struck the rock. The two customs officials cowered in fear. The threat dissipated, the hyper manoeuvrable Lynx rolled over, span away and within a matter of seconds it had disappeared from view; the only evidence it was ever there was the diminishing whoop of its rotors and the dust spalls it left in its wake. It was a perfect manoeuvre, beautifully executed.

The bewildered customs officers on both sides looked on in amazement. The Argentinians believed that they had diced with death to protect the honour of their service and the innocent tourists, especially the two pretty ones, and were convinced that they had narrowly escaped execution at the hands of mercenaries in a helicopter.

Inside the Lynx, Rupert was clinging on as he looked down

into the valley thousands of feet below through the open doors of the helicopter. Chris, who had been in similar situations before, gave Rupert the thumbs up sign and clapped a set of headphones on against the wailing of the wind noise and engines; Chris looked out at the zigzag of road that led down from the top of the pass on the Chilean side.

"Do you know what?" he shouted into the microphone. "I'll miss that car!"

Chapter Thirty-Four

London

The intruder watched the progress of the woman as she headed towards the flat. Moving away from the window, he made for the landing at the top of the internal staircase, screwing a silencer on to his Browning as he stepped into the shadows, just out of sight of anyone ascending the staircase. He heard the jingle of keys as the outer door opened, the woman's tread on the steps and finally the metallic click as the internal lock was turned back. The woman flicked the light switch and ascended the dog-leg staircase.

The MI5 agent in the flat opposite radioed his two colleagues. "All clear so far. She's in. Stay alert; we expect a visit anytime now. If not tonight then soon. The boyfriend will be back in the next two days. We hear he is safe and well. Douglas out."

It had been with some reluctance that Johnston had handed the operation over to MI5 but strictly speaking it was a matter of internal security and outside Six's ambit, as they dealt with foreign security matters. All Douglas knew was that the life of a young woman was on the line as a result of one of MI6's operations. Across the street, he saw the landing light go on, clear evidence of safe entry.

The window of his flat was slightly ajar, the owners safely out of harm's way for the evening. The night was silent and Douglas strained every nerve, listening out for any footsteps or untoward sound. It was then that he heard the two reports. The first was the muffled *phut* of a silenced pistol. There was no mistaking the second shot which came almost simultaneously. It was the sound of a full, unsuppressed 9mm round exploding like a canon in the night. A second silenced report echoed the first as a third shot was fired.

"Go, go, go!" shouted Douglas, running down the stairs of the flat. Another figure ran along the street. "Back carpark, Davies, now!"

A car careered around the corner, entering the nursing home car park at speed and screeching to a halt. One figure stayed with the car, the other ran for the back gardens along the rear of the houses. In the street, agent Douglas and the other MI5 operative barged through the front door of Claire's flat. Douglas ran up the stairs and drove his shoulder against the inner door, which split open as the simple Yale lock broke from its catch. He ran up the stairs, turning as he did so, the Glock pointing ahead of him in a two handed grip, finger waiting on the hair trigger to shoot at the first sight of a target. He backed up the last two steps, but no target came into sight. He heard the rasp of wood on wood as the rear sash window was opened. He started to run up the last two steps and saw the supine figure in front of him, red beret askew, blond hair falling across her face. There was a dark stain of black liquid pooling around her like a shadow in the darkness.

"No," he shouted, kneeling in front of her and putting pressure on the main wound in the centre of her chest in an effort to stem the blood flow. "Stay with me, come on," he demanded. Behind him the other agent came up, his gun raised, pointing at a limping figure. The gunman's hands were raised and an evil grin pulled taut across his sunken features.

"You're too late. I never feckin miss. But the bitch was fast, she got me." O'Driscoll gestured to his leg which was bleeding heavily, soaking his jeans. "Stopped me escapin'. Fuck her, couldn't get out the window." The Belfast accent was strong.

Agent Douglas looked up as the woman breathed her last rasping breath. A few last bubbles of blood frothed at her lips.

"You bastard!" Douglas shouted, lurching up at the gunman and grabbing him by his jacket, his other fist raised. The killer just looked at him, expecting the blow; he'd had far worse on the streets of Belfast and at the hands of the security forces, and he could take a beating.

Douglas hesitated, shaking with rage. He relaxed a little and said "That's too easy. I'll think of you rotting in solitary confinement for the rest of your life."

The gunman laughed in his face. "You really t'ink so? Ye're a feckin eejit. I'll be out in ten years, earlier if there's an amnesty. I'll be laffin' while you're still mournin'." He grinned at Douglas and spat at him, daring him to strike. There was no remorse or contrition, and his voice was filled with hatred and mockery. Douglas saw the lifeless body in front of him and snapped. He swung a wild roundhouse punch, catching the killer on the jaw, but instead of letting him drop, his left hand caught the back of his collar, drawing him in and down to meet the upcoming knee, spreading his nose across his face with a satisfying crunch of cartilage. The other agent tried to intervene.

"Ben, let it go, he's not worth it," he pleaded.

It might have worked, but at that moment O'Driscoll just laughed at him through bloody teeth.

"You haven't got the bloody guts to–"

Douglas grabbed the gunman by the throat and the back of his jacket, dragging him with a strength borne of rage towards the open window from which the gunman had tried to escape. At the last minute, the other agent realised what he was going to do.

"Ben no, don't–"

His remonstration was cut off as Douglas pitched the man headfirst through the open first floor window. O'Driscoll screamed briefly. He didn't somersault, he landed straight on his head on the flat roof he had recently climbed onto. His neck snapped with an audible crack and he was still. Douglas spat down at him, snarling in bloody rage. He turned and faced his colleague.

"I don't care. Tell them what the fuck you want," he snapped.

The colleague nodded. "He fell as he was trying to escape. The leg wound threw him off balance," he replied.

Police sirens were sounding outside, shutting off the mews. Douglas went back to the landing, removed his jacket and covered the head and shoulders of the dead woman, and stood next to her, shaking in grief and shock.

CHAPTER THIRTY-FIVE

Chile

The helicopter landed at Aerea El Bosque in Santiago, the closest major military base in Chile. It was also attached to a civilian airfield nearby. The Chilean authorities had given no formal written authority for the mission, but had cooperated privately and offered help and equipment to the British forces planning the rescue. Chile retained full deniability should there be any fallout from their neighbours.

The Lynx helicopter was wheeled into a hangar, where the decals and red stripes of the Red Cross were quickly removed, along with the rest of the overlay transfers. The helicopter that emerged was in full British army livery. It was refuelled, including its long range tanks, and immediately set off with just the crew to liaise with a British destroyer at sea. It would eventually return to its base in Belize.

The three SAS men, with Rupert in civilian garb, transferred to Santiago International Airport for the flight back to London. The bags of weapons and the satellite phone Chris had been carrying were redirected to the British Embassy in Chile to be returned to Stirling Lines. It was now a fourteen-hour flight back to Heathrow and home.

Safely in the departure lounge, Rupert tried to call home. He looked at his watch. Ten to six. That meant it would be ten to nine in the UK. She would surely be in, he thought. The call went through and rang for a long time before it was answered.

"Claire? Is that–" he was interrupted by his own voice on the answering machine. He cursed. Where the hell was she? he wondered. He called her parents, with no response. Damn it. His mind raced, searching for an answer as he began to worry. Something didn't feel right. As he returned to the others, Chris asked if he had managed to get through, although Rupert's face said it all.

"No, just the answering machine; she's not at her parents either. I'm really worried."

"Rupert, mate, it'll be fine. I'd try with the satphone if I still had it, but it went back to the embassy with everything else. As soon as we get back, call her from the airport, and if there's still nothing, we'll make a detour to see that all is well, OK? Have you tried her mobile?"

"Thanks, Chris, that's much appreciated. Yes, but you know it only works in certain places, It's pretty unreliable at the best of times. The walls of the flat are thick, no signal." As an aside Rupert noticed how the 'old' Chris had emerged. He had been playing a part for the last few weeks, and he was now clearly a soldier again – a subtle difference from his surveying persona.

Boston

There was concern of a different kind in USE Oil's offices. The concern was not for safety, but for the successful end to a life.

"Well?" Kelly demanded as Phillips entered the room. His

face was a mask of insouciance, which Kelly, despite all the years of acquaintanceship was unable to read.

"It was a success, the girl is dead. MI5 and police all over the place. However–"

"I knew there was a 'but' coming," Kelly muttered. "Go on."

"It seems that O'Driscoll was hit; tried to escape and fell from the first floor window, breaking his neck."

"Careless bastard. Clearly they were aware that we might have been seeking revenge on a soft target. Must have used the girl as a decoy. Doesn't really matter, it'll hurt them and teach them not to play games with us. Fuck him, he ain't no use to us anymore anyway. What about the two surveyors, any news on them?"

"Apparently they made it to the border. The Argie customs guys tried to stop them, but they were too slow and they got away." Phillips proceeded to outline what had happened from the information received from MREC

"Chile? Ah fuck 'em, but someone must've helped them get out at such short notice. If they're just surveyors, I'm the president of the United States! Well, they'll be back in UK now with tight security, but one of them will wish they hadn't crossed me when he finds his girlfriend dead." Kelly snorted with a malicious vindictive grin on his face.

He looked up at Phillips. "What the fuck…?" he said.

They were the last words Michael Kelly ever spoke. Phillips fired twice, hitting Kelly in the chest with both shots. He walked over to his twitching body and put a final round through his head. Taking the silencer off his own automatic he picked up Kelly's desk phone and called an unlisted number that rang somewhere in the depths of the Pentagon.

"The Irishman has departed as arranged," he said. "Am I safe?" Philips listened for a minute. Finally he said "Thank you. I have the funds from Argentina still. The transfer to O'Driscoll was bogus, and our friends across the water tell me he has departed too. We'll consider it a payoff, shall we? Details of this entire operation are listed in button-down mode with my lawyer, and will be released to the international press in the event of my untimely death. I'm sure you will agree that it is in both our interests that I remain healthy."

Phillips listened to the response, smiled and hung up. The orange groves in California would be blossoming soon, and a one-way ticket in his new identity was booked from Logan in two hours' time.

London

For Rupert, the flight was interminable, and unlike the other three soldiers who seemed to be able to drop off wherever they were, he failed to sleep on the plane. Fifteen hours later they arrived at Heathrow and Rupert almost ran to the nearest public phone. There was still no answer and the machine cut in after a number of rings. He returned to the others shaking his head.

"Nothing."

Vince, one of Chris's colleagues, was looking serious. "What is it?" Rupert demanded.

Vince was holding an early edition newspaper bearing the headline: *Shoot out in Notting Hill. Two dead including suspected terrorist.*

Rupert's face drained of colour. His hand moved to take the paper, not believing what he was seeing. He saw the address, Wilby Mews, and started to shake. Little in the way of specific information was given, and the victims of the shooting were not named. Special Branch and security forces were believed to have been involved. He looked up at the others, tears filling his eyes. He couldn't believe it; his senses refused to take in what his eyes were telling them

"No…" was all he could manage. All energy evaporated from him

"Rupert, come on," Chris shouted at him, shaking him by the shoulder. "You don't know it's Claire: she's alive until you know otherwise."

Rupert did not respond. Passing through the Arrivals gate he was still in a daze, his legs moving as if in a dream as his world fell apart around him. The soldiers exchanged worried glances behind his back and steered him towards the exit barriers. They were familiar with violent death and knew how to deal with it; but it never got any easier, especially with close relationships.

Chris stayed back, scanning the crowd for threats as Rupert moved on with the other soldiers. The waiting crowds, all expectant, searched for loved ones, and a sea of faces blurred before Rupert's eyes. They passed through the exit gate, and as though sensing something was wrong the throngs of people began to part, seeing the expression on Rupert's face and the fearsome countenance of those around him.

Looking straight ahead, Rupert's eyes finally focussed. There in front of him was a wary looking man he did not know, and beside him a suntanned blonde. Rupert's mouth dropped open. He blinked once, then twice, to determine if he was hallucinating before finally managing to accept what his eyes were seeing.

"Claire?" He ran forward into her arms. "I thought, I mean… the paper said that you were dead, shot…" he was silenced by a kiss and a hug so hard that he could not breathe.

The three soldiers looked on in surprise, while the Special Branch officer grinned slightly and continued to keep a proprietorial eye upon his ward.

Rupert turned as Chris approached. Chris still had the taut skin and healthy glow of someone in peak physical fitness; his lithe frame moved easily across the concourse. He nodded in recognition at the Special Branch operative, who tensed as he walked towards him. "Easy tiger, I'm with the good guys," he said.

Chris turned round, approaching Claire and Rupert. In an effort to defuse the tension, he made a typical mocking comment; "What no hug for me, home from the wars? Why don't I get the girl?"

Claire turned, wiping her eyes, smears of mascara running across her face.

"You do, you idiot, except she's back in Argentina now, and if you let her go you're more stupid than I thought," she retorted, laughing at him, opening her arms and giving him a hug. Pushing apart to arm's length, she smiled gratefully.

"Thank you for bringing him back safely; you're a special man, Chris Adams. Thank you for daring and winning."

He grinned. "Just part of the job ma'am, just part of the job," he quoted, putting on a terrible American accent.

"Joe Friday? *Dragnet*? Really?" Claire responded caustically.

Chris shrugged, laughing it off.

"Chris, I know we'll talk; but please come and see us soon. Bring Sophie with you if they can spare her out there. I owe you a lot, mate, thank you," Rupert shook Chris's hand, did a mock salute with one finger and Chris was gone, disappearing into the crowds using his chameleon-like qualities to become just another face in the crowd.

Rupert turned back to Claire. "I guess that's what you call the strong silent type. And talking of silent, my darling, I know I should have said this sooner." he dropped to one knee on the marbled concourse, "but will you marry me?"

"Oh Rupes, of course I will, now get up for God's sake!" Her eyes lit up with tears of emotion as she pulled Rupert up off the floor. "But on one condition, no more adventures and playing at spies. Please." she said.

He held his hands up in mock surrender. "I promise. I'm so

happy to be back and see you safe, I would agree to anything. But what happened at the flat?"

"Later, let's get to the car first. I want to tell my parents… oh Rupes, we're getting married." Her voice was so loud that Rupert thought that the whole airport would hear her. The Special Branch officer shook his hand, offering his congratulations, and hurried them to a waiting unmarked police car that drove them into the city and took them to the flat, which had now been cleaned and cleared of all evidence of the shooting. As they entered the flat, Rupert felt slightly odd, a feeling that was exacerbated by the fact that the stairs and landing carpets were missing.

"I need a cup of tea," he exclaimed, flopping onto the sofa. Claire returned shortly with two mugs of tea.

"First decent cuppa since the Falklands," he declared and then repeated his question from earlier.

She told him what she knew. She had been directly approached two days ago by someone called Johnston from MI6, who asked her to meet with him. Rupert's eyes narrowed at the mention of the spymaster's name. She had met Johnston, who had introduced her to another man from MI5 who would liaise with her directly from that point on. Claire was told that she would be under constant protective surveillance for the next few days; certainly until Rupert returned. They told her that they had been warned by foreign intelligence that a contract had been put out by person or persons unknown, and they were concerned for her safety. Claire was introduced to a female MI5 agent who looked similar to her and was the same height and age. She would be substituted any time that they felt her life was in danger.

"From then on, for the next few hours, I felt terribly exposed and frightened. Then I thought 'pull yourself together'; there you were risking life and limb in some dreadful banana republic, surely I would be safe here until you got back. Anyway, I had almost forgotten by the last day, not having seen hide nor hair of anyone good or bad.

"Then suddenly everything changed. I went to the Ladbroke Arms for a drink after work and there was the agent. She just identified herself as Claire, I never even knew her real name. Anyway, she approached me in the pub and told me that we were swopping places and I was to go with that Special Branch chap who met you at the airport. She took my coat, beret and we swapped handbags." She hesitated here, almost breaking down.

"That was…that was the last I saw of her. She took my place and she lost her life so I could live. Bloody bastards. Who goes after an innocent woman? What kind of shit does that?"

She cried then as the emotional rollercoaster of the last twenty-four hours made itself felt. Rupert reached over and held her tightly, easing her through the sobs. After a short while, he reached around turning her towards him.

"Come on, we need to get out of here. Pack a bag. I'm taking you home to your parents. You'll feel safer there; they'll look after you and you can relax." He then looked slightly concerned. "You will still marry me, won't you?"

"Of course I will, you idiot. That's the best thing to have come out of all this."

Epilogue

London, February 1991

After a week of recuperation, Claire and Rupert returned to work, where Rupert received a telephone call from Johnston a few days later.

After the usual preamble, Johnston asked if he could buy Rupert lunch at his club. It was, of course, the Special Forces Club, where everything had begun months before.

It started out as a rather awkward meeting, coming to terms with everything that had happened, but as lunch progressed, both men relaxed, especially after the second bottle of claret had been opened. Johnston filled in the few remaining gaps for Rupert concerning the intelligence gained from Northern Ireland by MI5. He confirmed that it had been O'Driscoll who had carried out the execution and then died while trying to evade capture. He had escaped the Falklands somehow and returned at the request of USE Oil to assassinate Claire, as retribution for Rupert and Chris spying for the British Government. It had left a nasty taste in everyone's mouth, he declared, USE Oil's shares had dive-bombed for some reason and its director, Michael Kelly, was believed to have disappeared along with a very large commission payment that had been due to be passed to a European client. One of the big boys, Exxon or Shell, it didn't really matter which, was in negotiation to buy up the company and amalgamate its remaining assets under its own umbrella.

"One agent crippled, certainly never to work again; one badly wounded and an MI5 officer killed: I hope those bloody islands are worth it!" Johnston declared venomously.

"Talking of which, how is Sophie? Claire wanted to get in contact with her, is that possible?"

"It is up to Miss Carswell, but I think she will agree to that. I'll get her to call Claire at her work number. As to her health, yes, she has recovered well. The advantage of youth and the ministrations of Sergeant Adams, who did a good job with the first aid; saved her life, apparently."

"Also, um Claire…" here Rupert hesitated. "She wanted to write to the agent's parents who died; she only knew her as *'Claire'*. Would that be possible? I really don't know what the form is."

"Off the cuff no, we don't normally allow that sort of thing, but I'll think about it and let you know," Johnston finished abruptly; the walls had come down again. "But I would like to say," he started rather awkwardly. "How much we appreciate what you did. For what it's worth, HM government is very grateful. There may be an honour in it for you. A civilian one, of course, but we'll see." Rupert raised his eyebrows in surprise. He continued, "You know it has been interesting, surveyors seem to be able to go anywhere pretty much innocuously."

Rupert's warning antennae started to twitch; he sensed danger coming and realised that the thank you lunch was only part of the reason for the meeting.

Johnston continued unabashed. "Well, it occurs to me that from time to time, we could use intelligence gathering sources off the book, so to speak, and well, you seem to have a knack for it. I wondered if I might call on you again if the need arose?" The hook had been baited and dropped gently into the water, and Johnston waited for Rupert to bite.

"I am flattered," Rupert responded sincerely, "but I am afraid I promised Claire there would be no more James Bond stuff, she only agreed to marry me on that prerequisite."

Johnston the spymaster reappeared; he laughed it off, opening his hands in gentle submission and nodding in acquiescence. But Rupert could see his mind whirring; he knew a time would come when he'd have a use for someone of Rupert's talents. He gently changed the subject.

"Congratulations by the way, on your coming nuptials, I am sure you will be very happy." He raised his wine glass in salute. Lunch meandered on for a few minutes more, until by common consent it was time to go. They parted, hopefully Rupert thought, never to meet again.

Edgeworth, Gloucestershire, June 1991

Rupert and Claire had considered that there was no apparent reason to put the wedding off for any substantial period of time, so they waited just as long as it took for the warmth of the early summer to arrive. Claire had wanted a holiday in Cornwall and that was where they were going for their honeymoon: somewhere safe and familiar, and if the weather was kind it was the best place in the world to have a holiday.

The wedding was a glorious affair, the sun shone and the clouds of past events had been banished by time. Rupert had been as good as his word, once the year-end dividend had been accounted for. He took the full commission for himself on the deals he and Chris had made out in BA and then divided it with Chris upon his return and settlement in January. That way, he explained, it would get round any official attempt from the Regiment or the government to try to claw it back from Chris. For Chris it was a huge sum that would allow him to buy a house; for Rupert, it was all in an agent's life. Chris and Sophie Carswell attended the wedding in their official capacities as usher and maid of honour respectively. They had got together back in the UK and it remained to be seen how things would work out, as Claire had said, "between the Spook and the SAS man". For Claire and Rupert it really had been a deal too far, and Claire was glad she was back safely in the arms of the man she loved, embarking on a new life in the comparatively safe world of surveying.

The End

To start reading Book3 instantly visit:
https://books2read.com/u/m0VD80

Acknowledgements

Again my thanks to my editor Perry Iles for all his splendid work, going above and beyond to make sure everything was factually correct, improving my writing and keeping me on the straight and narrow. My family for their continued love and support.

I had a good deal of help from a large number of people who gave a lot of their time in enabling me to hopefully get it all right and correct. These include: Peter Dove, Herman Faigenbaum, Michael Ford, Will Keohane, Toby Greville, Zahra Lucas, Paul Lees, Alistair McHaffie, Jamie Oarton, Dr. John & Dr. Geraldine O'Sullivan, Dr. Angela Rowntree, Stephen Swain, Dave Taylor and Matt Waller.

Much of the information, particularly military and operations, was well outside my field of expertise and I could not have written the book without the time, effort and knowledge of the following: Alastair, Colin, David, Elizabeth, Gabriel, Marcus, Max, and Stuart. You know who you are.

A MESSAGE FROM SIMON

I know that you have over a million choices of books to read. I can't tell you how much it means to me that you choose time to read one of my books.

I really hope that you enjoyed it and that you found it entertaining. If you did, I would appreciate a few more minutes of your time, if I may humbly ask for you to leave a review for other readers who may be trying to select their next reading material.

If for any reason you weren't satisfied with this book please do let me know by emailing me at simon@simonfairfax.com The satisfaction of my readers and feedback are important to me.

Best wishes,
Simon.

A Deal With The Devil: Deal series book 3

A new challenge, a new market and lives to play for.

Rupert Brett is back and it is 1995, with the property markets raging and the Sub-Prime madness just beginning.

The Irish Sea, a shipment of drugs is intercepted, the IRA lose the cocaine and their most feared enforcer, Tir Brennan, is captured.

Deauville, a wealthy French aristocrat has a terrible accident with far reaching consequences.

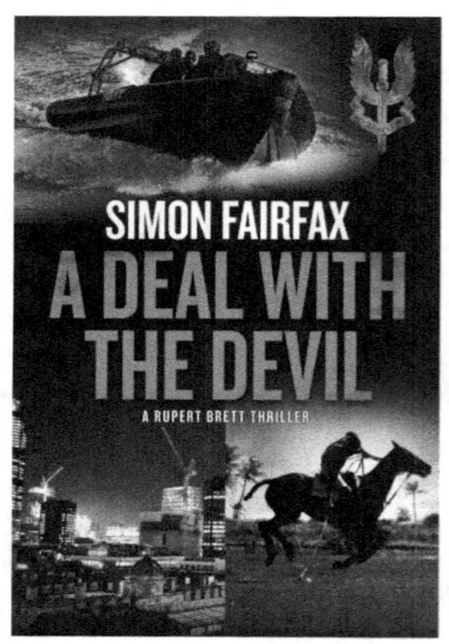

Bogota, the head of the old drug cartels is dead and Ballesteros is now running new routes to the US and beyond.

The events are all linked and somehow drugs are being smuggled with impunity across the globe. With a source originating in Palm Beach, US, Rupert Brett is again asked to go undercover, with SAS Sergeant Chris Adams as protection. They must find out how the drugs are being smuggled into the corporate world of property, polo and high finance. The answers run deeper than either could imagine and a dangerous former nemesis returns, throwing their lives into danger.

To start reading book 3 instantly visit:
https://books2read.com/u/m0VD80

Historical Background

When it came to researching this book, I was of course only too familiar with the property world of the time, the state of the market and factors affecting the world. It was a different world to the one we now live in, especially in terms of technology. Mobile phones were still quite rare – in fact they were virtually non-existent in Argentina. In the depths of the British recession of the late 1980s, American companies did indeed buy out many leading British firms, seeing it as an ideal opportunity to secure a base in the UK and in markets worldwide. For them it was the perfect time to buy into a depressed market and pick up top cash-starved British firms at rock bottom prices. The new firms were then re-branded and new offices were opened internationally in the world's major cities, including Buenos Aires, as described in the book.

We are all too familiar with the First Gulf War and how it came about. The events described in the book are based upon factual research, and the vast majority of British armed forces were deployed into that theatre of operations, especially the shipping. It would have been the perfect time for the Argentinians to mount a second invasion of the Falklands. The more research I did, the more life seemed to imitate art: the British Embassy had indeed only just been reopened after seven years, the Argentinians did treat all British subjects with great suspicion. Many polo players were followed and British embassy staff especially came under very strict surveillance. It is also true that the vast number of Argentinian agents were women, and that they did indeed prefer blondes – hence Operation Marilyn. But the Argentinian government were also desperate for cash injections to bump start their economy, and welcomed foreign investment.

The US was at that time looking for new oil suppliers through new oil corporations. They did, I understand, have talks with many South American countries, including Argentina. One can only speculate on the nature of those discussions. The IRA was in disarray at the time, due to the dirty war being waged by double agents and the drying up of cash from the US following the realisation of what terrorism really meant. There was also a real link between the IRA and FARC, and three IRA members were each jailed for seventeen years in 2007 for training FARC operatives. There were many Irish immigrants in the Falklands and Argentina and you still get polo players called Pablo O'Donnell or Franco O'Sullivan today.

I did have to take a liberty with the affair in Dar Es Salam, which did actually occur, but two years after the events in this book. But I needed it to help prove my story. On the subject of facts, one of 'my sources' recommended a book to me to help with my research: *Blind Man's Bluff*, by Annette Lawrence Drew, Christopher Drew & Sherry Sontag. It is an amazing account of Cold War submarine espionage and a fascinating read.

In Argentina there was a huge property surge at the time in which the book is set, and many British and foreign investors did go around buying land, building their own polo estancias in many areas. The estancia near San Miguel exists and is exactly how I have described it. It is a beautiful oasis of calm and one of the loveliest places in the world. The Open in Palermo is an extraordinary event, and if ever you get the chance, do go and watch it. It is the most amazing display of horsemanship and skill you will ever witness. It is also an incredible atmosphere and an experience that you will almost certainly enjoy even if you know nothing about polo.

Finally – and this is a SPOILER ALERT if you are for some reason reading this ahead of the book – the Chilean border at the Christ the Redeemer statue is as I describe it and people do just wander across. Secondly, as I researched images of cruise ships, I found an article dated 2013 from the *Daily Mail* which described a cruiser being turned away from the Falklands with over 3,500 people on board because of a suspected flu epidemic on board. I wonder...

I hope you enjoyed this story; Rupert will return soon in a new book: *A Deal with the Devil*

Simon Fairfax

Email: info@simonfairfax.com www.simonfairfax.com

About the Author

Simon Fairfax studied at Southampton Solent University and spent thirty-five years as a chartered surveyor. Both at home and during his three-year stint in Italy, he witnessed and was party to many multi-million pound real estate deals within the UK and internationally – deals that inspired the plot of his latest novel, *A Deal Too Far*

As a lover of crime thrillers and mystery, I turned what is seen by others as a dull 9 – 5 job into something that is exciting, as close to real life as possible, with Rupert Brett, my international man of mystery whose day job is that of a Chartered Surveyor.

Rupert is an ordinary man thrown into extraordinary circumstances who uses his wit, guile and training to survive.

Each book is written from my own experiences, as close to the truth as possible, set against world events that really happened. I go out and experience all the weapons, visit the places Rupert travels to, speak to the technical experts and ensure that it as realistic, as possible allowing you to delve deep in to the mystery, losing yourself in it for a few hours.

9 781999 655112